ANNIKA

A Romantic Thriller

By
Alison Blake

ALISON BLAKE

ANNIKA © Copyright 2012 by Alison Blake

Originally published in ebook format by Red Dog Pub
Publishing.

ISBN-13: 978-1475191391

ISBN-10: 1475191308

For Rick and Susanne, family.

ALISON BLAKE

PROLOGUE

Annie Malloy first fell in love with Ray O'Brien when she was five years old. She followed him everywhere. Once, he threatened to drown her like a kitten if she didn't stop following him.

"You drown kittens?" She had been horrified.

"Yeah, you little pest. And I'll drown you, if you don't get away from me." Annie had burst into tears. "Oh, for crying out loud." So he had shared a fuzzy Tootsie Roll he had in his back pocket and patted her awkwardly on the back. "Why you want to follow me around anyway?"

"I don't know," she had gulped between sobs and Tootsie Roll bites.

"Well, don't do it no more." And he had run off with his friends.

* * *

When she was fifteen and he was seventeen, they made love.

Afterwards, they lay on the cool pasture grass that had been their wedding bed.

"Sometimes," said Ray, "looking at you, I can't catch my breath."

"Do you think other people feel like this?" She wondered aloud.

"No," he answered, "no one else has you."

"Then you love me?"

"Yeah, of course. You?"

"I've always loved you, Ray."

He raised himself up on his elbows and looked down at her. Even in the moonlight, he could see her beautiful face. She was covered with sweat, her wild thick dark red hair a tangle. One lock lay across her neck. Slowly, he brushed the hair away from her face. Tears leaked down the side of her face, her lips swollen from his kisses. She had never looked so beautiful to him. "I swear to God, Annie, I'll never let you down. We'll always be together."

Together forever.

CHAPTER ONE

Ten years later, in a mansion on Long Island, Annika Rostand sat at her dressing table in a shell pink, silk camisole and panties, trying to control that same wild thick, dark red hair. Finally, she piled it on top of her head, holding it in place with discrete tortoise shell combs. She carefully examined the effect from all angles. Gerard was very particular about her hair; it must be elegant but sensual.

"A man should want to run his hands through it, but he must know to touch you is a desecration."

Next her make-up. It too, had to be perfect.

"Your mouth is like forbidden fruit, my darling," he had said. She shuddered, remembering.

She pulled on a cream-colored silk blouse with cap sleeves, and then beautifully tailored silk slacks in a slightly darker shade of cream. Quickly, she attached diamond drop earrings and put on the delicate sandals that went with her outfit. Finished.

Surely, she would pass inspection.

Suddenly, a strident voice rang out, making Annika jump nervously. "I'm ringing, answer me. I'm ringing, answer me." At one time, she had thought it funny. First thing tomorrow, she was changing her ringtone to a nice blues melody. Taking a deep breath to calm down she picked up her iPhone. Recognizing the caller ID, she pressed the off button. She wasn't in the mood to listen to Sari's last minute excuses for not showing up. She only wished she could cut and run herself.

Putting the phone down, her hand brushed against a small stack of invitations and sent them tumbling to the floor. She retrieved them quickly.

Mr. & Mrs. Gerard Rostand
Cordially request the pleasure of your company
at their annual garden party
on the 25th day of April, at 2 P.M.
RSVP

Three hundred of these beautifully engraved invitations had been sent out. Two hundred eighty-five people had RSVP'd with a resounding, "Yes!"

Gerard's party would be its usual success and, as usual, she, Mrs. Gerard Rostand, would be its centerpiece.

Mrs. Gerard Rostand, the very beautiful, perfectly packaged Mrs. Gerard Rostand deliberately ripped one of the pristine invitations to bits.

"Annika." She froze. Her husband stood in the doorway. "What are you doing?" His voice was honey soft, gently caressing... dangerous.

"It's just a left over, Gerard." They both stared down at the torn pieces of invitation scattered like white petals over her dressing table and on the floor around her feet.

Gerard Rostand raised his eyes from the torn invitation and studied his wife's face. To her disgust, Annika could feel herself flushing and her hands start to shake. Quickly she knelt and picked up the pieces. His presence looming over her.

"Annika? Annika, look at me when I talk to you."

She raised her head and stared straight into her husband's eyes.

"You're very beautiful, darling."

Nervously, she twisted the rings on her finger until the stones were facing inward. Her hands were still trembling.

"Annika, how many times have I told you not to twist your rings?"

Instantly, she dropped her hands to her sides. Several pieces of paper fell back to the floor. She reached for them.

"Oh for God's sake, leave those for the maid!"

Annika froze in fear. Would he hit her now? Surely not just before the party, but the issue didn't arise. Mrs. Washington, the stern faced, thin as a blade housekeeper, interrupted them.

"Mr. Rostand."

Mrs. Washington never bothered bringing problems to the lady of the house. She knew Annika was unimportant and powerless.

"Yes, Mrs. Washington?"

"They haven't brought it, sir."

Gerard forced himself to take a deep breath. For the servants, he always appeared in control, yet they were still leery of him.

"What are you talking about, Mrs. Washington?"

"The caterers, sir. They haven't brought the brand of Beluga caviar you particularly asked for."

"They haven't?"

"No, sir. And what they did bring, it isn't enough."

"Did you ask them why they disregarded my explicit instructions?"

"They said it's what they always bring, sir. No doubt they were trying to save money." Having delivered her bad news, Mrs. Washington left. Not once had her eyes strayed to Annika.

Does she know what goes on up here?

Of course she did, all the servants did. *S*hame piled on top of Annika's fear.

"They disregarded my explicit instructions? They expect me to offer my guests some inferior garbage?" The pupils of Gerard's eyes were dilated. He was moving his head around like a blind man. Any minute now, he would strike out.

Annika cleared her throat. "I'll go to Mrs. Bagacino's," she offered. She made her voice very matter-of-fact, neutral, nothing to draw his rage.

He still seemed like a blind man. "Mrs. Bagacino's?"

"In the village, Gerard."

"I know where Bagacino's is!" His hands were balled into fists. He moved towards her in a blind rage. He's going to hit me, she thought in despair.

"They'll have the brand you prefer."

That stopped him. "They will?" He shook his head, "No, they won't have enough. It's too late. There's not enough time." He was moving towards her again.

"I'll go."

"You?"

"I'll go now." She slipped around him. "There's plenty of time."

"Stop!"

She froze.

"Let me look at you."

She stood absolutely still as he inspected her. He examined her carefully; her hair style, her make-up, her clothing. She was one of his possessions. Her appearance had to be perfect.

"You look very nice. The casual, tailored look suits you."

"Thank you, Gerard."

"However..." he was staring at her critically. "A bit too much, don't you agree, Annika?" He unfastened the diamond drop earrings she wore. "I can see there's still a lot of work to be done on you, my darling."

He handed her the earrings. She stood rigid. What else would he do? He leaned down and kissed her on her forehead. "Don't worry," he murmured into her ear. "I will make you perfect."

"Thank you, Gerard," she said through stiff lips.

CHAPTER TWO

More than eight hundred miles away, a loud whinny from one of the mares woke Ray.

He groaned and buried his face in his pillow. The mare neighed again and this time was answered by one of her stable mates. Ray rolled over onto his back to stare up at the jagged crack that ran diagonally across the entire ceiling. *Gotta fix that,* he thought for the hundredth time.

He had dreamed about prison again. So it was a relief to find he was in his own bed, in his own room, staring up at his own cracked ceiling, listening to the early morning sounds of TearVale Stud.

"Count your blessings," the Reverend was always advising him. Ray made a conscious effort to do just that. *Blessing number 1...*

His bedroom door was suddenly shoved open and Ray's principal blessing came bursting through the door and bounced up onto his bed. "Daddy, why are you still in bed?"

Seconds later, Ray's principal irritant also bounced onto his bed. Ray groaned.

"What did you say?" asked Patrick.

"I said get this damned dog out of my face."

Rufus, an overly large and incredibly clumsy Golden Retriever who accompanied his son everywhere, was busy trying to wash Ray's face with his large and very sloppy tongue.

Patrick hauled the animal back. "Why are you still in bed?" he repeated.

"I had a late night."

With unerring, if faulty logic, Patrick immediately zeroed in. "Are you gonna to marry Susan?"

Ray sat up abruptly. *Where did the kid get these ideas?*

"I haven't even had my coffee yet."

"I just asked."

Ray ran a rough hand over his face in an attempt to focus. "The Ryson mare delivered last night. A foal. I'll be down in a few minutes, Champ. Now get out of here and let me get dressed."

"Okay." Patrick having accomplished his mission hauled Rufus off the bed. Boy and dog left the room as abruptly as they had entered. Ray could hear them clattering down the stairs. Rufus panting in happy agreement as Patrick outlined the day's schedule to the dog.

With a groan, Ray sank back onto the pillow, but in spite of his aching head, he was smiling. God, he loved that kid. Nothing was ever going to separate him from his son again. Nothing! This time, hard work and DNA were on his side. Of course, a little old fashioned, raw luck wouldn't hurt either.

Only seven more days to go

Ray swung his long muscular legs out of bed. Time to start another day at TearVale Stud.

CHAPTER THREE

Back on Long Island, Annika's convertible, a 1951 vintage cream-colored Jaguar, was parked near a side door of the Rostand mansion. A highflying seagull swooped down to investigate something that glittered temptingly from the dashboard. With a screech of disappointed rage, he veered off sharply as the door of the mansion was flung open. From high above, the seagull watched as Annika's tall graceful figure moved quickly to the car. Getting in, she slammed the car door, but instead of immediately driving away, she clutched the steering wheel with both hands and clenched her teeth to stop them from chattering with fear.

Gradually becoming aware of a sharp pain in her right hand, she took her hand off the steering wheel and opened it. The two diamond drop earrings shimmered mockingly at her. With a sound halfway between a laugh and a sob, Annika flung the one hundred and forty-five thousand-dollar pair of earrings onto the passenger seat. Then, wheels spinning, flinging gravel right and left, she drove off in search of Gerard's perfect caviar. Because if she failed him…if she failed him.

Oh, God.

CHAPTER FOUR

After breakfast, Ray was attempting to lead Fireman, one of TearVale's stallions, out to pasture.

TearVale Stud possessed two stallions, Imperial, who was not a top stud and Fireman, who was. But Fireman was getting on in years. TearVale was very much a struggling enterprise. Any little thing could tip it into financial ruin.

Fireman, sarcastically called Fuzzy, because he was such a mean son-of-a-bitch, was giving Ray a hard time as usual. The horse wanted to get to the pasture as much as Ray wanted to get him there, but the beast fought Ray every step of the way. He tried to bite Ray's hand, and then he shifted his position, trying to get Ray within kicking distance.

Patrick, well acquainted with the horse's grizzly-bear temperament, stayed a respectful distance from the animal and kept a firm hand on Rufus' collar.

Despite the stallion's antics, Ray remained calm. His voice was pleasant and encouraging, but his words, if Fuzzy could have understood English, would have blistered the stallion's ears.

"Ever heard of Alpo, you misbegotten son of a bitch?" Ray asked softly.

Fuzzy lunged at him. Ray was forced to tighten the chain he had wrapped around the horse's nose. Fuzzy decided to behave himself for the next few feet.

They had almost reached the pasture gate when Patrick let out a whoop of delight. "It's Grandpa!" he yelled, as a battered looking black pick-up truck pulled into the yard. The boy was delighted. Ray's mouth tightened.

Fuzzy, taking advantage of the diversion rose up on his hind feet, neighing with rage. Ray yanked him down, just barely avoiding the stallion's iron hard hoofs. Finally, the horse was through the pasture gate. Ray slipped the animal's lead rope and got out of his way. Fuzzy took off as if the devil had set fire to his tail. For a moment, Ray forgot how ornery the animal was, and he forgot that his trouble-making father-in-law was waiting. He forgot everything, but the horse's incredible beauty and grace.

The sound of his son's delighted laughter brought Ray back to reality. Taking a deep breath, he turned to face Hugh Butler, his father-in-law.

The scene that met his eyes should have made him smile, instead his eyes narrowed, his mouth was grim.

Squealing with delight, Patrick was being swung by his arms, around the thick strong body of his grandfather. "More, more," begged the boy.

"Sonny, you're wearing me out," protested the older man, but he obliged the boy with another full circle. Then he grabbed the laughing boy up into his arms and gave him a fierce hug.

"Morning, Hugh," said Ray.

Hugh stopped smiling. He gave the boy in his arms another hug and set him down. "Morning," it was almost a snarl.

Patrick, back on the ground, stopped smiling and looked sadly at the two men. "Don't fight," he said in a small voice.

Both men immediately stopped glaring at each other and switched their attention to the boy. "We're not going to fight, Champ," Ray reassured his son.

"Hell no," agreed, Hugh. "Just a little conversation is all. You go on and run along so your daddy and I can talk."

Patrick looked up at his father.

"Go on, son."

Dragging his heels, the boy and his dog wandered off. Both men watched him for a moment before turning back to each other.

Hugh Butler immediately went on the attack. "I hear you finally hit rock bottom, down to your last dime."

Ray studied the older man through narrowed eyes. "You hear wrong."

"Not likely." It was a sneer.

"Using your position at the bank to delve into my business,

Hugh?"

"Why the hell else you think I bother with the damn bank?"

"Just so you can keep an eye on me?"

"So I can make sure my grandson is okay."

"He's fine."

"He's about to be losing his home."

Ray sighed. What was the use of arguing with the old man? They were on opposite sides of everything. "Your information is wrong, Hugh. My loans are up to date. And besides, your bank is involved in just one part of my operation."

The older man studied Ray carefully then smiled a particularly nasty smile. "You're lying through your teeth, Ray, like always." He looked out around him. "This place is just quicksand waiting to sink."

"Which reminds me," said Ray, "I've got work to do."

"I don't give a shit about you, Ray. But Patrick's not going to be homeless, because you're a murdering, worthless piece of shit."

Ray straightened. "That's it." He'd had enough, more than enough. "You're out of here, old man. You're trespassing on my land."

Hugh was not impressed. "You just got days before the sheriff tosses you out on your ass. You want to save this place or not?"

"It doesn't need saving, Hugh. We're doing fine."

"You give the boy back to Sarah and me and I'll see you get some breathing room."

"Give my son to you?" Ray's voice was mild, but his hands were clenched into fists.

"You got no money, you're gonna lose TearVale and there's no decent woman to mother the boy. You could start over somewhere else. Somewhere they don't know you."

"Get off my land, Hugh."

"People around here don't forget, you know." The two men stood almost toe-to-toe, glaring at each other. "They know what you are."

At that moment, a small green Mercedes SL

convertible rolled into the driveway. Its tan top was down, revealing the flowing blonde hair of the young woman driver. "'Cept maybe her."

The woman waved at the two men. Hugh spat so close to Ray's boots that Ray stepped back in disgust. "You gonna marry her for her money, Ray, then kill her like you did my girl?"

Ray's eyes were narrow slits; his teeth were clenched so tightly, he could barely get his words out. "You're not welcome here, Hugh. Don't come back."

The older man laughed scornfully. "Oh, I'll be back all right. When they kick you outta here, I'll be back for my grandson." Abruptly, he turned on his heel and stalked back to his truck, passing the Mercedes on his way.

Susan was getting out of the car as he passed and Hugh stopped with automatic courtesy to hold out his hand and help her emerge from the small car. "Thanks, Hugh." She smiled up at him.

Hugh just nodded to her grimly and continued on to his truck. Susan went to join Ray, tucking her arm in his. Both watched as Hugh swung his truck around and drove off.

"Your father-in-law is not in the best of humor."

"He never is." Impatiently, Ray shrugged her hand off. He was angry and feeling boxed in, so even the light touch of Susan's hand on his arm was a sort of imprisonment.

She appraised him coolly. "Seems, I've come at the wrong time."

Shit! Now he had insulted her. This day was rapidly going down the toilet.

Susan looked up at his profile. He was so handsome, she thought, but hard like granite and had the stubbornness to go with it. "Maybe, I'd better go," she said.

In turn, Ray studied the woman standing next to him. Susan was a lovely woman, tall and coolly blonde with long elegant bones and a dazzlingly infectious grin. She was wealthy, well established, and for some unknown reason, she seemed to want him. She even liked Patrick. He could do worse. Hell, he had done worse.

If he married Susan, Patrick would have a mother.

Susan's credit rating was probably so high that just living in the same house with her would give his financial status a leg up. Besides that, she was a sexy lady. The only trouble was he didn't want to marry a woman for her credit rating. What he did want probably didn't exist. At least, he had never run into it. Not for real.

"Penny for your thoughts, Ray?"

"I was just thinking how pretty you are."

"Ah" She raised an elegant eyebrow. "The man can flirt."

"The man speaks only the raw truth," he assured her.

"But...?"

"No buts about it. You're very pretty."

"But you're not interested." It was a statement.

That was his cue. "Yes," he was supposed to say, I am most certainly interested. I want to marry you. I want us to live happily ever after. I want our credit ratings to intermingle and soar off into the stratosphere. I want you to run interference for me with my son's grandfather. I want. I want. Instead, he leaned down and planted a gentle kiss on her smooth forehead.

She smiled her sunny smile. "Oh, Ray. We would be so happy together."

He put his arms around her and hugged her to him, resting his chin on the top of her head. *Why not? It's what she wants.*

He opened his mouth to speak, but Patrick came running up to greet Susan. With another hug, Ray released her.

She smiled happily up at him and then turned to greet Patrick.

CHAPTER FIVE

Back on Long Island, Annika had reached Bagacino's. In her small, cluttered store, Mrs. Bagacino managed to carry almost every exotic foodstuff imaginable. If Mrs. Bagacino didn't have it, Mrs. Bagacino would get it. All you had to do was ask...and pay.

Informed of Annika's dilemma, Mrs. Bagacino was not sympathetic. "You should have come to me in the first place, Mrs. Rostand."

"Yes, you're right." Annika was suitably humble.

The woman's small beady eyes watched her avidly. Could she possibly know what went on at the Rostand mansion? Yes, of course she did. She knew everything that went on in East Hampton. The servants talked and Mrs. Bagacino listened. Annika, pretending to examine something in the far corner, turned her face away. She could feel herself flushing with shame. Not for the first time, she cursed her fair skin.

"I may not have the amount you need on such short notice," said Mrs. Bagacino, drawing out the agony.

"Whatever you have."

Shaking her head sadly, she said. "Those caterers. You can't count on them." She leaned closer to Annika as if to impart some dire secret. "I personally could tell you stories about them." She rolled her eyes.

I bet you could. And do you tell stories about me, too?

"You should consult me the next time you need caterers."

"We will," Annika promised, knowing Gerard would do no such thing.

As Mrs. Bagacino hustled off into the back room where all sorts of gastronomical treasures were stored, the dark little store suddenly became even gloomier. Glancing back out the door, Annika could see gray clouds scurrying across the sky. A wind had sprung up and was blowing inland from the sea. It carried the taste of salt and the iodine odor of seaweed. On days like this, Annika loved to walk along the beach, watching the waves pounding the land with fury. But not today, not during Gerard's garden party! Gerard expected perfect weather for his party.

Mrs. Bagacino popped up at her side shaking her head sadly, "I'm afraid you're out of luck, Mrs. Rostand."

"You don't have it?"

Mrs. Bagacino shook her head.

"Not even a little?"

"What good would a little do you? There's not enough for three hundred people. Barely enough for fifty."

Oh, God. What should I do?

Annika's mouth went dry. She could feel sweat gathering under her armpits. Gerard would blame her. It would be all her fault.

"Do you want me to send what I have?"

Annika, sick with fear, nodded yes.

"I'll have Fred drive it around to your house. I suppose you want it immediately?"

"Oh, yes. If you would?"

"No problem. Of course. there'll be a little extra charge."

"Of course." Annika wasn't worried about the expense. Gerard never made a fuss about how much she spent. But there wasn't enough! He would blame her for that. And now the sky was growing more and more gray. It never rained on the day of Gerard's party.

Please don't let it rain!

However, before she even reached the car, the heavens opened up. Torrents of rain crashed down on the crushed shells and sand of the parking lot. Annika dove into the front seat, reached back and struggled to pull the convertible's roof back up in place. She was soaked, her hair a dripping mess. The garden party was going to be a disaster! Her breathing became shallow and frantic; her heart was racing.

She started crying or maybe she was laughing?

Mrs. Bagacino peered out at her from the store doorway. *I must look like a maniac, sitting here, soaked, crying, and laughing.* Almost hysterical, she waved gaily at the peering woman.

What would Gerard do to her? Oh God, what would he do?

With trembling hands, she turned the radio on, searching for a weather report. How long would this damn rain last? Why hadn't the radio warned them ahead of time? Look at it come down!

She started the windshield wipers. The car was parked, but she still had to turn the wipers to fast. Even if it stopped raining in the next five minutes, the lawn would never dry in time. The party would have to be moved indoors. Half the guests wouldn't show. Gerard would be furious.

The radio squawked and hummed as she searched among the stations. "Kentucky Derby!" said a clear, confident voice. She was already moving the dial past that station. A country and western singer was crooning an oldie about "sittin' on a dock watching the world go by."

A final torrent of blinding rain slashed down on the windshield. Then the rain stopped as quickly as it had started and a rainbow came out.

Annika Rostand, tears streaming down her face, stared in wonder at its beauty. The rainbow beckoned to her. "Come away," it seemed to call. "Follow me. Follow me!"

Her hand turned the ignition key and her foot pressed slowly down on the gas pedal. Exiting the parking lot, she turned so the car was facing the rainbow. It called to her with irresistible force. She felt a stir of something so long forgotten she barely recognized it. Hope.

CHAPTER SIX

The mare's name was, Hope. Ray had been expecting her to foal for the last two nights.

Mammals usually have their babies at night; the idea being to hide the newborn infant in the darkness and give it and its mother time to gather their strength to travel when day dawned. That goes for all mammals, from aardvarks to zebras. Nature is not interested in the fact that a mare may be safely ensconced in her foaling stall far from the reach of her natural enemies. Mother Nature wouldn't consider she was doing her duty, if she allowed a baby to be born at the reasonable hour of nine in the morning, or even perhaps at noon. No, midnight to three AM was her preferred hours.

This was the mare's first foal. In the Thoroughbred Registry, she was listed as Hope of Kings. She was a pretty chestnut with one white foot and a loving puppy-dog nature, a valuable creature and a favorite of Ray's. Unfortunately, Hope of Kings was owned by Pete Connors, a miserable penny-pinching SOB, renowned throughout the county for suing at the slightest provocation. He was a man who considered arbitration for sissies and "working things out" for losers. Ray, being hungry for any business that would help build up TearVale had made the mistake of taking on his mare.

She had been at TearVale for a month and for thirty straight days, Connors had called, usually just as Ray was sitting down to dinner, to harass and harangue, give orders and poke his nose into Ray's business. The man was a bully, a braggart and worst of all; he knew nothing about horses, except that he owned valuable ones. As far as Connors was concerned, ownership made him an expert. Ray was ready to strangle him.

In truth, Ray was also worried about the mare. She was overdue, big of belly, and obviously uncomfortable. Getting up and lying down frequently, grunting softly to herself, she was the picture of a mother-in-waiting-too-long. Ray was about to call the vet when she finally started to deliver. Almost immediately, she was in trouble.

Watching her anxiously, Ray saw one tiny hoof poke through from the birth canal. All wrong. It was supposed to be two hoofs and front ones at that. This was obviously a rear hoof. The foal had not turned as it was supposed to. If the labor was allowed to continue, it could mean the death of both mother and baby.

The poor mare was confused and in pain. Turning uneasily, looking to the human who had always before been a source of help, she nickered fearfully.

"It's all right, girl. You're going to be fine." Ray patted her sweaty neck. Carefully, he pushed the extended baby's hoof back up into the birth canal.

"Damn." Of all the horses to get into trouble, it had to be one belonging to that sue-happy bastard, Connors. Ray yanked his cell phone from his belt and punched in the vet's number.

"Yeah, hello," said a very sleepy voice.

"Rachel, this is Ray."

The sleepy voice sharpened. "What is it?" Rachel knew he wouldn't be calling for a minor problem.

"The mare that's overdue is in labor and it's a breach." Ray was sweating, despite the cool night air.

"I'll be right there," the vet's voice promised.

She was as good as her word. Ten minutes later, her truck's headlights splashed up to the foaling shed. The tall slender figure of the vet swung down from the cab. She was already reaching into her bag to pull out a syringe. "Okay, get out of my way." She pushed past Ray, who willingly yielded to her.

Three hours later, the foal lay on clean straw looking around at her new world in big-eyed wonder. The mare nuzzled her infant proudly. Both would live.

"You're a great vet, Rachel."

"Remember that when you get my bill." But, she was smiling with relief. It had been a near thing. Both mother and child had been at serious risk.

After Ray had seen Rachel off, he went back to check on the new little filly. A beauty. The mare was proudly licking her baby. When Ray returned, she seemed to shoot him a look, inviting him to share her pride in her new daughter. As always, Ray's heart swelled with joy when confronted with evidence of mother love.

But damn, that had been close.

Ray leaned weakly against the stall doorframe. A birth gone badly was an acknowledged risk in the breeding business. That's why both owners and breeders carried insurance, but with someone like Connors, a bad delivery would have escalated out of sight. The insurance company, in the manner of their kind, would have grudgingly paid off, and then either astronomically hiked his premiums or flat out deserted him. Connors would have screamed to the high heavens. Not everyone knew what the man was like. Some would believe Ray had been negligent. TearVale was teetering between greatness and flat out disaster. If he lost TearVale, Hugh Butler would do everything in his considerable power to get his hands on Patrick. What kind of insurance could he get against that?

An image of Susan's face rose before him.

CHAPTER SEVEN

"Somewhere over the rainbow." Judy Garland's voice sang over and over in Annika's head. She had been driving for two hours when she realized the rainbow had vanished. She looked frantically around, causing her car to swerve. Horns blared, cars zipped past her, their drivers giving her a one-finger salute, and some yelled unheard, but no doubt, obscene things through their closed windows.

Where was she? Oh, my God, she was crossing the Whitestone Bridge into Manhattan!

I've got to get back.

It was impossible to turn on the bridge. A prisoner of the traffic and her own ambivalence, Annika was conveyed into the city. The irony of being lured back here, only to have hope desert her once again, was not lost on Annika.

***

Ten years ago, her name had been Annie Malloy. She was just sixteen years old. It was her first Greyhound bus ride, her first time out of Florida, her first sight of a big city and for the first time in her life, she was on her own.

God, the eagerness with which she had peered out the smeared and dirty bus window. She remembered using her hand trying to wipe a clear spot, but all she managed to do was smear it more.

I was escaping then, too.

Manhattan had been a giant, frightening, exciting wonderland. Even the dingy and slightly menacing Bus Terminal had been exciting. In all her life, she had never seen so many people in one place. And the people! They were so different from folks back home. Outside a National Geographic Magazine, she had never seen so many different sizes, shapes, and races. And they were wearing such weird clothes. The only thing they all seemed to have in common was their shabbiness and their anxiety at finding themselves in this place. She fit right in.

She had had three hundred dollars in her pocket. A fortune! Clutching her dilapidated suitcase, feeling as if the very air was too thick to breathe, Annie maneuvered herself through the crowded bus terminal. Outside, the sunlight was rapidly fading, cooling the air from the heat of the day. There were crowds everywhere. Across the street was a blinking neon sign spelling out, "Coffee Shop."

Her suitcase bumped against her knees as she joined the crowd crossing the street. In anticipation of the light changing, a taxi edged towards her. The light changed and instantly the taxi surged forward. Annie yelped and leaped for the curb. Next to her, a dark skinned man in a turban yelled something after the taxi in a language Annie did not understand. She did however, understand the hand gesture that accompanied his yell. She blushed and looked away.

Pushing open the Coffee Shop's door, she stepped into relative peace and quiet. It was cool and dim inside. There were no customers in the booths lining the wall, but three people sat on stools at the counter. The counterman was slowly wiping down its already shinning surface.

The other customers looked up at her entrance. The lone woman gave her a quick look, sniffed and went back to staring into her coffee cup. The two men both sat up straighter as they looked her over. One of them, with long hair and huge hands, actually licked his lips while he studied her. Annie started to back out, but just at that moment, another man entered behind her, blocking her way. Confused, embarrassed and hungry, Annie stood to one side, nervously clutching her suitcase. It would have been all right if she could sit in a booth but no one else was. Her suitcase was getting heavier and heavier. She started toward a corner stool.

The counterman, who had been watching her, spoke up. "Overheregirly." He pointed to a stool right in the middle, directly in front of him. Annie didn't understand the words, but the gesture was clear enough.

She banged her knees with her suitcase twice; once when she moved to the seat and again when she tried to push the suitcase out of the aisle, under the counter. She was getting very tired of that suitcase.

"Yawancoffee?" The counterman said to her.

"Say again, please?"

"Yawancoffee?"

"Ah...think so."

A cup of dark brown liquid was deposited in front of her. At the same time, the counterman handed her a large booklet that turned out to be a menu. Annie studied it hungrily. This would be her first meal in New York.

The prices!

The counterman was still standing in front of her, still mechanically wiping the perfectly clean countertop. "Whayawan?"

"Say again?"

"Yagottahearingproblem?"

Annie was feeling desperate. "Huh?"

With elaborate self-control, the counterman carefully enunciated his words. "What... do... you... want?"

"Want?"

"Taeat?"

"Treat? Yes, this coffee sure is. It's just fine." She was lying, the coffee was awful and it cost seventy-five cents! She had obviously wandered into an ultra-expensive eating place.

The counterman, giving her up as a lost cause, shrugged and moved off to the new customer who had sat down two stools away from Annie. While she sipped her coffee and searched through the menu for something that cost less than half a week's worth of groceries, she listened to the conversation around her.

Apparently, the counterman had found someone who understood his dialect. Coffee and a sandwich quickly appeared before the new customer.

Annie's stomach growled fiercely as the man bit into his sandwich. Capitulating to the demands of her sixteen-year-old stomach, Annie ordered the meatloaf plate.

Tomorrow, she would find a real cheap place for breakfast. After all, she would need to be sharp when she went job hunting.

What kind of a job would she find? It would probably be something like working behind a counter like this one. Of course, she reflected, for that she would have to learn the local dialect. She couldn't expect too much at first, but once she was settled in and knew her way around, the sky was the limit.

"Getting any work?" She heard the question, but did not realize it was addressed to her. "Hey, girly!"

She came out of her daydream to find the counterman watching her with an avid look. "Did you say something?"

"No, he didn't. I did," said a voice to her side.

Annie turned to the stranger who was seated two stools away. He had finished his sandwich and was now sipping his coffee.

"Ah didn't catch what you said, sir."

"I like the southern accent." The man grinned at her. "I asked if you were getting much work?"

He was a nice looking man, tall and thin with a funny sort of pointed beard just under his chin. His cheeks were shaved clean and his mustache came down to meet his beard in a frame for his mouth. Annie, who had never seen a Vandyke beard before, couldn't decide if she liked it or not.

"Ah haven't started looking yet," she answered him. "Ah've only just now arrived here."

"Just got off the bus, huh?"

"Yes, sir."

The customer and the counterman exchanged looks.

The customer looked her over carefully. "You definitely have possibilities."

"Thank you."

"Of course, only a real shoot will tell."

"Beg pardon?"

"Here." The man took out his wallet and extracted a small card. He turned it over and wrote something on the back. "This is my card. I'm Tad Hirschfield, by the way."

She took the card in wonder. Nobody she knew had

"cards." "Pleased to meet you, Mr. Hirschfield. Ah'm Annie Malloy."

"Well, Annie Malloy, on the back I've written down the name of one of the most prestigious modeling agencies in America. I do a lot of work with them. You might drop by there. Tell Vic I sent you."

"Tell Vic?"

"Uh-huh."

He finished his coffee, stood up, fished in his pocket and left enough bills on the counter to buy all of her high school class hamburgers for a week. "Bye."

"Bye. And thank you."

He was gone. Annie looked down at the business card and smiled. Tad Hirschfield, Photograher, she read. There was also an address and telephone number.

And everybody says New Yorkers are nasty. This is a wonderful place.

***

That night Annie rented a room at the "Y" which cost ninety-five dollars. *For a single night!* It was a none-too-clean, tiny cubical with cracked tiles on the floor.

Jail cells were probably bigger.

The one window was so high up that Annie couldn't really see out unless she stood on her bed. When she did, she discovered it looked out on an airshaft. All she could see was a brick wall about ten feet away and part of someone else's window. That someone else must also have been standing on her bed, looking out. As soon as they saw each other, Annie started to raise her hand in greeting, but the other woman snarled, "What are you looking at?" Then she spit right at Annie who scrambled off her bed and pulled the blinds all the way down.

Tired as she was, sleep turned out to be just about impossible. There were strange creaking noises and an even stranger slithering sound throughout the night. Two women got into a fight just outside her door. Annie, shivering with fear, was afraid to get up and go down the hall to the bathroom. And even though her cubical was in the back of the building, the loud sounds of New York City traffic continued throughout the night.

I'm not spending another night in this place, she vowed. I wouldn't wish it on Mr. O'Brien.

Quickly, she shook off thoughts of Mr. O'Brien. He belonged to her past. The past was dead, as dead as…no, she would not think about that.

***

The modeling agency Mr. Hirschfield had recommended was on the 25th floor of a skyscraper. The elevator moved so quickly, Annie's stomach threatened to relieve her of her modest breakfast. She grabbed the handrail that encircled the elevator, swallowed bravely and concentrated on not being sick. When the door finally opened, she staggered off, trying not to think about the trip back down.

The agency was still closed when she arrived, so Annie waited. She was leaning on the door when a tall, blonde, handsome woman with a terrifyingly confident air arrived.

"You're too early, go away."

"Ah wanted to be sure not to miss Vic."

"Vic?"

"Yes, ma'am. Doesn't he work here?"

"How do you know about Vic?" Annie held out the precious card to the older woman who gave it a quick look. "Tad gave you this?"

"Yes, ma'am."

"That's not usually his style. He doesn't do the chicken hawk stuff."

"Ah wouldn't know about that, ma'am. Ah just met Mr. Hirschfield last night."

"That's some accent you have, honey." Annie didn't know what reply was called for so she said nothing. The woman looked her over carefully as she unlocked the office door. "Come on in."

Annie followed her into a large, carpeted room with plenty of chairs arranged around the wall facing the reception desk. On the walls themselves, were beautiful pictures of beautiful women.

"I'm Vic," the woman announced.

"You are!"

"Vic for Victoria."

"Oh."

"Do you know Tad's work?" Annie shook her head no.

"That's his and that one. Oh, and over there, that one." Vic was pointing at several pictures scattered around the wall. All the pictures were of different women. They were dressed in everything from a simple skirt and blouse to a fantastic "Star Wars" kind of costume. Annie compared Mr. Hirschfield's photos with others hanging on the wall.

"His are the best, aren't they?"

"The guy's a genius." Vic's tone was very matter-of-fact. Apparently, Tad Hirschfield was an acknowledged master photographer.

"So. You interested?" Vic was suddenly all business.

"In working here? Yes, ah am."

"You don't work here, kid. We act as your agent. We book the jobs, negotiate the contracts, collect the checks, disburse the money, and so forth."

"Oh." She thought about it for a moment. "Wow."

"That is, if we sign you."

"What do ah have to do to get signed?"

"Show me some spec shots."

"All right. Ah will. Uh… What are spec shots?"

"Photographs, honey. Like those on the wall. You pay a photographer to take some shots, bring them to me and if I think you have the stuff, I sign you." She made an expansive gesture. "And you're on your way to fame and fortune."

Annie laughed. Vic made it seem real. So possible.

"Do you think Mr. Hirschfield will take my picture?"

"I don't think you can afford him."

"How much do spec shots cost?"

"Cheapest?"

Annie nodded.

"You could probably get away with four or five hundred.

"Dollars?"

"No, Japanese yen. Of course dollars."

"To be honest, Miss Victoria…"

"Vic."

"Vic, yes ma'am. I don't think I can afford that." Annie searched inside her purse and brought out her wallet. "Would these do as spec shots?" She displayed her high school picture and a snapshot her daddy had taken of her, riding an old mare.

Vic took the proffered snapshots out of politeness, even as she was saying, "Sweetie, I don't think...Hmmmm, not bad." She looked up at the anxious face of Annie. "The horse adds a nice touch." She studied the two photographs again. "You're broke, right?"

Annie thought of her dwindling funds. There was no way she could afford to hire a good photographer and still manage to keep a roof over her head. At this point, she was resigned to spending more nights in the YWCA, but even so..., "Everything's so expensive here."

Vic handed back the wallet photos. "Wait here," she said and vanished into an office beyond the reception area carefully closing the door behind her.

Annie wandered from one photo to another. They were all wonderful, but there was no doubt that Mr. Hirschfield was a brilliant photographer. A harassed looking woman with huge glasses and frizzy hair opened the outer door with her own key. She stared suspiciously at Annie, who immediately felt like a trespasser.

"Ah...Miss...Ah...Vic, told me to wait."

The frizzy-haired woman groped in her pocket, pulled out a packet of tissues, carefully extracted one, looked at it searchingly, then sneezed into it.

"Bless you," said Annie.

The woman looked at her in amazement. "What did you say?"

"Ah said, bless you."

"Oh." The frizzy haired woman looked at Annie as if she were from Mars. "Yeah, well, thanks."

The door to Vic's office opened with a bang and Vic came sailing out. "Morning, Doris."

"Morning, Vic."

"Did you make coffee yet?"

"I just got here," the woman whined.

Vic clapped her hands together briskly. "Coffee, now!" Then she turned to Annie. "Tad's agreed to do your spec shots."

"He has?"

"Get over there now. Play 'gofer' for the day and he'll try to work you in this afternoon. You can pay him back if you get any work."

"That's wonderful!"

"It's also highly unusual. You must have really impressed him."

"All I did was drink coffee."

"That reminds me. Doris," she yelled, "Where's my coffee?"

Doris had disappeared into a back room. There were sounds of water running, then a crash and the definite tinkle of broken glass then, "Oh shit!"

Vic and Annie looked at each other. "That's the third coffee pot she's broken in two months."

"Maybe she doesn't like making coffee," ventured Annie.

"Who cares? Here's the address." She handed Annie a slip of paper and stalked off towards the back room. Annie felt very sorry for Doris.

Vic glanced back over her shoulder, "Take a cab," she ordered and disappeared into the back room.

***

"Take a cab." Easier said than done. Annie stepped out of the cool interior of the building into a steaming madhouse of jostling crowds, dashing, honking cars, buses and trucks and the occasional taxicab shooting through the whole mess with suicidal and homicidal disregard for anyone else.

Annie Malloy, just lately from Teardrop, Florida, stood on the sidewalk with her mouth gaping. People brushed by her, bumped into her, cursed her, muttered at her or completely ignored her.

"Taxi!" A tall woman beautifully dressed in a smart suit, stepped decisively off the curb and held up her arm commandingly. Even so, several unoccupied cabs streamed past her, before one suddenly swung out of the flow of traffic, and with brakes screeching, came to a halt at the woman's side.

Before the cab had come to a complete stop, a man dressed in a business suit was shoving in front of the beautifully dressed woman. As Annie watched in amazement, the woman swung the brief case she was carrying into the man's shoulder, knocking him off balance. "I don't think so, buddy," Annie distinctly heard the woman say, as she opened the cab door and climbed in.

The man, rubbing his shoulder, was already looking around for another cab. Annie watched the imperious looking profile of the woman giving instructions to the cab driver. Neither the beautifully dressed woman nor the man she had knocked aside paid the slightest attention to each other. As far as they were concerned, the incident was closed.

Sweet Jesus, thought Annie, this is one tough town. She decided to take a bus.

CHAPTER EIGHT

Ten years later, looking back, her innocence was almost as incredible as her luck…both good and bad.

Hirschfield's studio had reminded Annie of the barns back home. The studio was big and had a high ceiling. Instead of being dark and infused with the homey smell of horses, it was painted a clean flat white and had huge windows running along the top of the room and on the roof itself. It was filled with all sorts of equipment, lights, tripods, cameras, fabrics and make-up tables. There were cables snaking across the floor and there were people. At least ten people were present. They all seemed very busy and they all talked at once. No one was listening to anyone else.

"*Who* are you?" demanded a short, skinny blond man with, to Annie's ears, a weird way of talking.

"Annie."

"Darling," called the skinny blond man to someone in the crowd, "Orphan Annie is here." He burst into laughter. Everyone else stopped talking and turned to stare. There was a titter of laughter from someone in the group, then a giggle, and then they were all laughing.

Annie's face turned bright red.

"All right, all right." The dark haired photographer she had met the night before pushed through the crowd, clapping his hands to get everyone's attention. "Are we here to work or waste time?" Immediately, the people all got very busy.

Mr. Hirschfield looked her up and down. "You're late, Orphan Annie."

Orphan Annie. That crowd had called her Orphan Annie for over a year until finally it had faded away. Only Tad sometimes still called her Orphan Annie. To everyone else, she was Annika, beautiful, cool, collected Annika, Goddess of High Fashion.

But that morning she was Tad's gofer. "Forget that Mr. Hirschfield stuff," he said. "Call me Tad and move that cable out of the way. No, not that one, the other one!"

Heavy handed, sweating with anxiety, she lugged the surprisingly heavy cable to one side of the room.

"Not there, Orphan Annie. I'm shooting there. Lay it on the other side."

She flushed with embarrassment and lugged it to the other side. Sometime during that morning Annie forgot she was an outsider. She forgot the censorious eyes of the others who seemed to know exactly what they were doing. The work fascinated her; lighting the models so that the shadows fell exactly where you wanted them, arranging the clothes so that no wrinkle showed and no drape of fabric hung awkwardly.

I could learn to do that, she thought. I could be a photographer. I could have a real job, make money, and live a real exciting life here in New York City. She would no longer be just the daughter of the town drunk.

She was standing near Danny, the thin blond man who had first called her Orphan Annie. He was carefully applying blush to the exquisite cheekbone of one of the models. Without realizing, she spoke aloud. "I could do that, couldn't I?"

Danny thought she was speaking about his work. "To be a make-up artist? Darling, it takes years to become any good. One has to have an eye."

"Hey, watch it." The model he was working on jerked away from him. "You almost put out my eye."

"Sorry, love."

"No," Annie said. "I meant, I could do that." She pointed towards Tad who was carefully positioning a model wearing a huge straw hat and something that looked like a Greek toga.

Once again, Danny misunderstood. He took a step back and studied her critically. "Well, you certainly have the coloring. With some make-up and a decent hair-do...yes, you could be a model, perhaps."

Oh yes, a model. In her excitement of discovering a new world, she had forgotten why she was here.

"Hey, Orphan Annie," Tad walked over to her, pulling some bills out of his pocket. "You know the deli on the corner?"

"Deli?"

"Where you from, kid?"

"Florida."

Danny, standing near-by, rolled his eyes. "Bet it's not Miami."

"No, Teardrop."

"Where?"

Once again, the studio was hushed, everyone staring at her.

"Ah'm from Teardrop, Florida."

"Oh, my God." Danny did his rolling eye bit again.

"Are you for real, kid?" asked Tad.

"Yes, sir."

"Okay," Tad smiled. "There's a store on the corner, we call it a deli. Sells sandwiches, fruit, soda, coffee, you know, the usual. You take this paper and pencil and go around here asking everyone what they want for lunch. You write it down. Understand?"

"Can they write in Teardrop?" Danny asked innocently.

Danny's assistant tittered. One of the models laughed out loud.

Annie had a vision of her English teacher's face. Mrs. Ryder would blast this little, little...make-up artist, with some well-chosen Shakespearian quote that would leave him groveling. Unfortunately, Mrs. Ryder wasn't here; only Annie Malloy was, and she was tongue tied.

"Ignore him," Tad advised her.

Yeah, right.

"Here's some money." Tad handed her a fistful of bills. Dutifully, Annie went to each person, taking their order. They wanted some of the weirdest things. The three models, ordered non-fat yogurt and salad, ("with the dressing on the side") and bottles of Perrier. Danny ordered a health-nut sandwich and a café au lait skinny. Danny's assistant,

Randy, said, "Oh, it's so difficult to choose. I'll tell you what, dear." He leaned forward as if passing on a great secret. "I'll have whatever Danny's having. He's so svelte, don't you think."

"Uh-huh," Annie nodded agreement. Whatever "svelte" meant.

Tad ordered a ham and Swiss on rye; "Make sure they give you a pickle," and coffee. Nobody ordered barbecue, coleslaw, or anything normal, not even a real coke.

The store on the corner had the word, Delicatessen written in gold lettering on its window. "Deli, Deli, Deli," Annie practiced saying to herself.

The man who waited on her looked like he was from China.

"Not China, no. I'm from the Bronx, sweetie. But my folks came from Korea."

"Oh."

"Where are you from?"

"Teardrop, Florida."

He didn't bat an eye or crack a grin, just nodded solemnly. "We all have to be from somewhere." It was Annie's turn to grin.

"Yes, sir."

When she returned from the deli carrying the carton of food, the energy level in the studio had dropped dramatically.

There was no heavy metal "gets me in the mood," blaring from the speakers. The models were half dressed, with smocks thrown over their shoulders, their hair in huge curlers with pink netting covering their heads. Just like old Mrs. Hemmings back home, thought Annie. Everyone was sprawled around the room, looking bored and unglamorous. Tad was lazily fiddling with a camera. One of the French doors opening onto a handkerchief size balcony was open. Two of the lighting assistants were crowded together on the balcony, smoking. Only Danny and his assistant, Randy, were still animatedly talking. But even they had lowered their voices.

"Darling, where did you go for that food, back to

Florida?" As soon as Annie put the carton of food down, everyone fell on it. Like starving dogs, thought Annie.

"Don't they eat in Teardrop?" asked Danny.

Tad looked up from his camera, still chewing on his sandwich. "Where's your food," he asked?

"I forgot," she admitted.

"Are you dieting?" asked Randy. "Because if you are, I know this doctor who is marvelous."

"No, I just forgot."

One of the models giggled. "Your face is as red as your hair."

"Where's the change?" asked Tad.

"In the food carton."

"Well, take it and go buy yourself lunch. Buy a big lunch."

Annie hesitated. "Now!" ordered Tad.

The deli didn't carry barbecue, so she settled for the same thing Tad had ordered, a ham and Swiss on rye. The orange soda pop and potato salad were her idea. She was starved.

After lunch, the music blared, the models woodenly followed directions, the lighting guy did his thing and everyone told Annie what to do. She rushed around, bringing make-up to Danny for last minute repairs on the model with the tiger stripes in her hair. She moved the cables at Tad's orders. She helped the models change. She held things, carried things, and fetched things. She had a ball. She was part of the group. She was busy. She was in fabulous New York City and she was sixteen years old. Could life get any better?

The last shot ended at three. The music was switched off. No longer buoyed up by the blaring hot rock, the energy level sank. People, who moments before had been yelling to be heard, now spoke softly. Without the competition of the music, the words no longer conveyed hyped up energy and terrific importance. "Want to catch a movie?" "Let's get a drink." "Gotta meet my mom. We're going shopping for a shower gift." Just ordinary conversation.

The models left first.

Annie helped the lighting guys put away their equipment. Finally, only Tad, Danny and Annie were left.

Suddenly, Annie was afraid; not of Tad and Danny, but of going out there into the city. Afraid of leaving this studio where she had felt part of something. Out there, she was just another piece of flotsam. Tad was eying her dispassionately.

"Vic said you wanted spec shots."

She had forgotten. Imagine that. She nodded, yes.

"What do you think, Danny?"

The thin little man cocked his head to one side and studied her. Then he walked slowly around her, studying her from all angles. "Um-huh, Ahmmmm. Uh-huh." He was examining her like Daddy checking out a new filly for Mr. O'Brien. *No. Don't think of Mr. O'Brien!*

She would not think of Daddy, either. And she was not some damn filly. She was not going to be looked over like a piece of livestock.

Before she could speak up and tell Mr. Danny Svelte, whatever in the world that was, to go to the devil, he nodded decisively. "I think so," he told Tad.

"Me, too."

"I can do the make-up and we have enough props for full figure shots, but oh, that hair." Danny rolled his eyes.

"What's wrong with my hair?" Her hands nervously tried to smooth out the bushy curls.

"The color is gorgeous, Orphan Annie, but the cut! Oh, well, I'll see what I can do."

Taking her hand, he led her firmly off to the corner he used as his workspace.

It was over an hour before Danny pronounced her passable. "My God, don't they shave their armpits in Teardrop?"

"Yes, we do, it's just..."

"You look like you have a red beard under there."

There was a choking sound from where Tad was setting up his camera. "Go easy on her, Danny."

"Well, even in Teardrop, they should know better."

"My momma..."

"Yes?"

"My momma thought vanity was courting the Devil."

Tad looked at her thoughtfully. "Your momma may have been right."

Tad positioned her in front of a completely white background. "Loosen up, Orphan Annie."

"Yes, sir."

Suddenly the music was back on, blaring, rhythmic, engulfing her mind and body.

"All righhht."

Annie giggled.

"Throw you head back. Good girl. Now look at me. No, don't smile. Stare at me, hard. Be cold. Be angry. Come on, girl. You're dynamite. And you're about to explode."

Darn right, Annie thought and threw out her arms, feeling a surge of power.

"That's it, that's it. Now turn, whirl."

She whirled, she laughed, she glared, raised one shoulder and smoldered over it. Grinning like a kid, she did the bump and grind that she and her girlfriends had once practiced, until giggling, they had collapsed in a tumble of girlish embarrassment. Only this time she didn't collapse, she went on and on. She imitated a flamenco dancer she had once seen in a movie. "The hands must move like doves." She did a cheerleading leap. The clinging drapery she wore swirled around her.

Two hours later, Tad called a halt. "Okay, that's it." He turned the music off. Annie was panting and wild-eyed. Without the music to sustain her, without the electronic whirr of the camera, she felt naked and exposed. Oh my goodness, what had she done?

Danny was sitting on a crate, arms folded, watching her. Tad, busy with his equipment, didn't even look at her.

"That's it?"

"Come by tomorrow, I'll have the prints by then."

"Okay." Slowly she returned to her old self, carefully washing off the elaborate make-up, pushing her wild hair out of her eyes, returning to Danny the beautiful fabrics that he had swathed her in. Both men were busy, and no one spoke. She was ready to go.

"Uhm. Thank you."

"You're welcome."

"I'll come by tomorrow then?"

"Right."

Tad didn't even bothered to look up at her. He was carefully putting away his equipment.

"Did I do alright? I mean, do you think the pictures will come out...good?"

"All my pictures come out good, Orphan Annie."

"Oh, I didn't mean...I meant, do you think I'll look good, look like a model?"

He finally turned and faced her. "Only the camera can tell us that, Annie. We'll have to wait until the pictures are developed."

"Thank you. Yes. Tomorrow then."

Tad turned back to his work.

Danny was still staring at her. "Danny, thank you for making me look so glamorous." He nodded to her, but didn't speak.

Feeling an incredible let down, Annie left.

After she was gone, Danny stood up and stretched. "Wow," he said.

Tad grinned. "As you say, wow."

CHAPTER NINE

Outside, New York City was as hot and muggy as Teardrop. The only relief was in the shadows cast by the tall buildings. People moved past Annie with slow gliding movements. Annie joined the graceful flow, drifting with the crowd. Her drift took her past chic restaurants gearing up for the dinner trade, delicious odors filling the air and activating her salivary glands. It took her past cheap corner falafel stores where tempting odors of strange spices in deep fat floated out into the muggy, shadowed air. Everywhere she went; there was a low frequency hum that seeped under her skin, and became part of the rhythm of her body. Annie stood very still, trying to pinpoint the source of this hum as her fellow New Yorkers drifted around her in their underwater ballet. Humm, humm. She vibrated to it, low almost gentle, but at the same time invigorating. It was a combination of the traffic, both human and auto, it was the underground rumble of the subways; it was New York. Annie, the newest New Yorker, resumed her drifting.

Back home in Teardrop it would also be dusk, the tempo would be shifting down from slow, to extra slow. But here in New York, suddenly, as dusk drifted towards darkness, the pace began to quicken, voices were raised, backs straightened, strides became brisker. Annie was caught up in the new dance tempo. Music, hot salsa, blared out of boom boxes carried on the shoulders of young men. Annie found herself looking around with eager eyes, taking longer faster strides. This was New York City. She was starting a new life. It would be much better than her old one. She would be a successful model, or photographer or something that would bring her fame and fortune. Nothing was impossible. Maybe even someday a husband, someone she could count on, someone who…no, never mind. Today was a new beginning. From now on, her life was going to be wonderful.

***

On her third day in New York City, Annie awoke in her cell-like room in the YWCA. The walls were still too close and the ceiling too low. The linoleum on the floor was just as cracked and cold as it had been yesterday, but she scarcely noticed it. Today she would see the pictures Mr. Hirschfield, no, Tad, had taken of her.

According to the big clock on the lobby wall, it was seven o'clock. Was that too early to call on him? Probably. She would have breakfast and wait until nine. That was probably a better time to go calling.

Breakfast was an apple and a warm bagel from the corner deli.

She would have liked a cup of coffee, but they charged $1.00 for one cup! Where did they get the nerve? Still, plenty of people were paying it without a murmur.

She spent the next hour wandering around the streets of the East Twenties, a not very inspiring sight. New York City was the dirtiest place she had ever been. Bums were sleeping in doorways, rats were rustling among garbage cans, and people were walking some of the meanest looking dogs she had ever seen. Even the sidewalks seemed harder than they were back at home.

This was not the New York City Annie had been expecting, the one depicted in the old movies they had watched on Ray's TV. The New York City she had been expecting was penthouses, nightclubs, beautifully dressed woman and high-powered men.

At eight thirty, she decided to start walking to Tad's studio.

The neighborhood around the studio was very different from the East Twenties. The buildings were more interesting. None was over five stories tall. Many had decorative ironwork around their windows, doors and roofs. They were set close to the streets, which were narrow and twisting. The stores had huge windows displaying paintings and sculpture. The clothing store windows showed just one or two elegant and exotic looking pieces, not everything higgledy-piggledy like back home. The people were different, too. They looked, not just busy, but happy, interested in what they were doing and what others were doing. People stopped and greeted each other. Sidewalk cafes were filled with people drinking coffee and eating delicious looking soft crescent shaped rolls that gave out an exquisite buttery smell to the still hungry Annie.

I could be happy here.

At Tad's building, she pushed the buzzer for a long time, but no one answered. She tried talking into the grill of the microphone, but without being activated by someone inside the building, it was dead. Sighing, she wedged her rear-end onto the sill of a bricked up window and prepared to wait. At least the constant activity on the street was entertaining.

About an hour into her vigil, she noticed a bushy-haired man carrying garbage cans out of the alley behind Tad's building and leaving them on the street.

"Excuse me."

The man ignored her.

"Excuse me, sir." He straightened up, rubbed his back, looked her up and down and went back to his work.

"I'm trying to get a hold of Mr... of Tad."

The man, carrying another garbage can, walked around her as if she were an inanimate object. "Sir?"

He ignored her.

"Sir?" She planted herself in front of him. He blinked at her and tried to move around her. Remembering the lesson of the beautiful dressed woman and the taxicab, Annie moved with him so she was still blocking his way.

See, being a New Yorker isn't that hard.

He growled something at her.

"What?"

He growled again. This time Annie caught his words. "No English!"

"You don't speak English?"

Once again, he moved around her.

"What language do you speak?" But of course he didn't understand her. Baffled, Annie followed him into the side entrance of the building and watched him grasp another garbage can and heft it up and carry it out.

Since she was already in the building, she looked around. There was a short flight of stairs leading to a closed door. She pushed it open and found herself in the main hallway. In front of her was the oversized elevator with the wooden doors she had used yesterday. She stepped in, pressed the button for the top floor and it rumbled her up to the studio.

She had expected to have to wait in the hallway for someone to arrive, but to her surprise, Tad was already there.

"What the hell are you doing here at this hour?" He was rumpled and irritable.

"You said my photos would be ready today."

"I said, today. I didn't say the crack of dawn."

"You don't have them?"

"Yeah, as a matter of fact, I do."

"Let me see." She was practically jumping up and down with excitement.

In spite of himself, he had to smile at her. "Do you know how much I usually charge for spec shots?"

"How much?"

"A thousand...minimum."

"Ah don't believe ah'll ever have that kind of money." It was the wail of a disappointed child.

"Annie, how old are you?"

"Eighteen."

"You're lying."

"Sixteen," she admitted.

"Maybe you should go back to Teardrop?"

"Ah'm gonna stay here. Ah'm gonna be a big success and ah'm never going back to Teardrop!"

He studied her sadly. "Never going back to Teardrop," he echoed.

"Can I please see the pictures? Please?"

"They're on the table over there."

She crossed the big bare room, her footsteps clear and

precise on the wooden floor. Tad pushed some buttons and the canvas blinds that covered the huge windows dropped swiftly. Sunlight flooded in. Dust mites, until now invisible in the gloom, danced across the room. Pushed against one wall was a large table holding piles of developed photos.

Annie looked down at the different piles. She recognized the two models that had been here yesterday. She recognized the clothes they wore, and the poses Tad had arranged them in. She saw nothing that looked like her.

Tad had come up behind her. He reached around her and uncovered another pile of photos. Silently, he spread them out on the table.

"Who's that?" He didn't answer. "Is that me?" "That's not me, is it?"

"Ah-huh."

"But they're beautiful."

"Ah-huh."

"I'm beautiful."

"Yes, you are."

Awe struck. "I'm so beautiful." Behind her, she heard him chuckle. "I mean, I'm not funny looking. All skinny and redheaded and bony."

"Well, you are skinny and redheaded, but those bones are highly photogenic."

She turned around abruptly. Tad was still directly behind her. Now they were face to face, inches apart. She lowered her eyes and spoke softly, not wanting to speak directly into his face. "Will these pictures help me get a job?"

He looked down at her. Her lowered eyes allowed him to see the incredible length of her eyelashes. That was one of the fascinating things about her. She was red haired and fair skinned, but her eyes and her lashes were dark. From his height, her eyelashes looked like twin fans spread across her fair skin. He felt a tightening in his throat and a slash of desire heavy in his groin.

Tad, a happily married man with a young daughter, stepped carefully away from her. "Yes," he answered. He cleared his throat. "Those pictures will help you get a job.

Quite a few jobs."

"Could I pay you a little bit at a time?"

"Don't worry about it, Annie. I suspect Vic will pay me for them."

"You think?"

"Put them in your portfolio and take them over to her."

"In my port...?"

"You don't have a portfolio?"

"Ah don't even know what one of those is."

"Ah-huh." Tad turned and looked around his studio. He crossed to another table crowded with all sorts of paraphernalia. He returned to Annie carrying a large, skinny, battered leather briefcase with both a strap and a handle.

"This is a portfolio case." He zipped it open revealing plastic inserts. Some of the inserts held photos of a young and pretty woman in various poses.

"Who's she?"

Tad barely glanced at the photos as he removed them from the case and careless tossed them away. "Her? She didn't make it."

He showed Annie how to insert her pictures, making sure the first one seen was a straight head shot. "Might as well knock 'em dead right off the bat."

Annie ran her hands over the scratched leather of her portfolio. "Needs polishing."

"You can do that before you return it to me."

"Okay."

"Now take these over to Vic."

"And then what?"

"Vic will know what to do."

"Thank you, Tad."

"Ah-huh. Remember, you owe me."

"Yes, sir." She laughed with excitement. "Should I go right now?"

Tad looked at her excited face and her lovely young body. The entire world was in front of her. What would she make of it? "Yes, I think you had definitely better go right now."

"Bye." She was gone. The studio echoed with a vast

silence, now that she was gone.

"Bye," he said to the empty room. After a moment, he picked up the phone and dialed. "Vic? It's Tad. You know that girl you sent to me. You remember the hick with the southern accent. Yeah, the redhead, that's right. I just sent her back to you with some specs. We may have something special here. That's right. The camera is in love with her. She glows."

***

Doris, the receptionist, made her wait half an hour before admitting her to Vic's office, but even so, she was moved through a lot faster than the scores of other pretty young women who were waiting. "It's an open call day," explained Doris. She seemed to think that was explanation enough.

"Oh." Annie nodded knowingly.

"You can go on in now," Doris finally announced.

Annie stood up. She could hear her father's voice encouraging her. "Stand straight, princess. You're a fine looking gal."

Annie took a deep breath, opened the door to Vic's office and stepped in.

The office was a mess. Everywhere Annie looked there were memos taped to the walls, the phone, the computer, even the mirror! Papers and proof sheets were stacked so high they spilled over.

There were piles of fashion books and photos everywhere. Vic was kneeling on the floor, busily examining several them. Annie stood just inside the door. Vic didn't look up.

Nervously, Annie cleared her throat. Vic didn't look up, she just switched a photo from one pile to another.

"Ahhhh?" Nothing. "Hello?" Still nothing. "Good morning?"

"Yeah, right." Vic finally looked up. "Oh, it's you. I thought it was that girl with my coffee."

"No, it's just me."

Vic sat back on her heels and looked up at Annie with amusement. "Just you," she mocked.

Annie blushed.

Vic looked at her in amazement. "I can't remember the last time I saw someone blush. I don't think it's allowed in Manhattan." Vic was enjoying herself.

Annie was not. "I have some pictures here."

"We don't call them pictures, dear."

"Photographs?"

"Shots."

"Okay," Annie nodded. She wanted to learn. "I have some shots here. Specs. Tad said to show them to you."

Vic gestured with her hand. "Open the portfolio here, on the floor."

Annie got down on her knees and attempted to unzip the portfolio. The zipper stuck! Annie could feel sweat breaking out. She jiggled the zipper. She pulled, she pushed, and she yanked.

"Don't break it," warned Vic. "Tad will have your head."

Annie was almost in tears. "It won't open!"

Vic reached across, took the leather case away from Annie and calmly unzipped it.

"How did you...?"

Vic waved for silence. She slowly turned each plastic folder, examining the enclosed shots. Occasionally, she would lean closer to a particular shot, examining it minutely. She even produced a small magnifying glass with which she carefully examined some of the photos. Finally, she leaned back. "Damn," she breathed.

Damn?

"You don't like them?" Annie studied the shots again. To her eyes, they were wonderful. They made her seem strange and exotic, wonderfully cool and hot at the same time.

Was she going to be a failure? She hadn't even had a chance to get started yet. Well, what did Vic know anyway? She was just one person. Annie would take the shots and go to other agencies. She would go to open calls. She would not give up. Nothing was going to stop her, because otherwise, she had nothing.

She became aware that Vic was studying her. Annie sat

up straighter; she raised her head and looked the older woman straight in the face.

"Ever hear of The Scarlet Gate?" asked Vic.

"No."

"You're about to make its acquaintance." She stood up and went to her desk. Pushing a button on her phone, she spoke to her secretary.

"Doris, call Carl at The Gate, tell him I have a rush job. He can bill me double, if he takes her right away. Oh, and Doris? Be sure to tell him he's going to enjoy this one."

"Right away, Ms. Vic," came back Doris's tinny reply. "Oh, Ms. Vic?"

"Yes?"

"Avril and Jetta are here for their appointment."

"Tell them to wait; I'll only be a few minutes." She switched her attention back to Annie.

"Here's what I want you to do." She wrote quickly on a rainbow colored pad and tore off the top sheet. This is the address of The Scarlet Gate. It's on 54th and Fifth, two blocks from here.

Annie gazed blankly down at the paper.

"Don't look so scared, kid, it's only a beauty salon."

"Like a beauty parlor?"

"Yes, a beauty parlor. The most famous one in the world."

Annie grinned. "Okay."

"Ask for Carl and tell him I sent you. As soon as you're finished, come back here. Let's see how you clean up."

***

The Scarlet Gate was actually more a cheerful red than scarlet and it wasn't a gate, just a regular looking wooden door. It was set demurely between two white pillars and looked very old fashioned when contrasted with the ultra-modern New York building it led into. A magnificently uniformed doorman, who intimidated Annie so much she was afraid he wouldn't let her in, guarded the door. She took a deep breath, held her head up high and walked right up to the door. Instead of barring her the way as she expected, the doorman held it open and ushered her in with a slight bow.

Inside, the plush carpet matched the door color. There was a very modern looking desk with a very stuck up looking receptionist behind it.

"Yes?"

" Uhm. Ah'm supposed to see Carl."

"Really?"

"Ms. Vic said Carl."

At the mention of Ms. Vic, the receptionist blinked. "One moment."

She pushed a button on her desk and whispered softly into thin air. "Mr. Carl, a lady is here to see you. She says that Ms. Vic sent her."

Although, Annie heard no reply, the receptionist nodded. To Annie she said, "If you'll just have a seat. It will only be a few minutes."

Annie settled herself into one of the fragile looking, but surprisingly comfortable, chairs that were scattered throughout the room. There were fashion magazines lying on small gilt tables, but Annie was too fascinated with her surroundings to pick one up.

The Scarlet Gate's door opened frequently. The people who entered were always women, and to Annie's eyes, they looked rich and beautiful. The snooty receptionist didn't stand a chance with them. They barely acknowledged her. "I do hope Joseph is ready for me," said one particularly striking looking woman. "I'm rather in a rush."

"Yes, Mrs. Arthur." The receptionist was almost gushing. A white door to the left of the room opened and a pretty young woman in a white smock ushered Mrs. Arthur into the inner sanctum.

Several other customers were dealt with before a young woman in a white smock came for Annie. "You're here to see Mr. Carl?"

"Yes."

"This way, please."

The white door opened into an elevator which deposited them in a long bright corridor hung with carefully lighted pictures in beautiful frames.

It looked like no beauty parlor Annie had ever seen or

imagined. Of course, the only one she had ever seen was Miss Jean Ann Tilly's front room made over into a beauty parlor.

The white smocked attendant pushed open a glass door at the end of the corridor. Annie was ushered into a clean red and gilt changing room and told, "Please remove everything and put this on." "This" was a large white kimono with an elegant red design on the back.

"Take all mah clothes off?"

The white smocked one just smiled and drifted out of the room, presumably to give Annie privacy.

Take my clothes off, just to get my hair done? She shrugged and began to undress. When she was undressed, her clothes carefully folded and placed on the chair back, with her white cotton underwear modestly hidden underneath; she wrapped herself in the luxurious kimono, it felt so smooth and soft. Annie stroked it.

I wonder if it's silk.

Then she waited and waited and waited. How long was she supposed to stand here, wrapped up in this funny looking Japanese thing? A horrible thought crossed her mind. What if they were playing a joke on her? Whoever heard of taking your clothes off in a beauty parlor? She could feel herself blushing with embarrassment. What a dumb hick she was!

Impatiently, she untied the waist sash and pulled the kimono off her shoulders. Just then, the door opened and White Smock was back. Annie clutched the kimono to her chest, knowing she was blushing all over. White Smock seemed not to notice anything unusual. "Shall we go?"

"Uhm, sure." Annie turned her back and hastily pulled the kimono back on, clutching it around her, too discombobulated to re-tie the sash.

Their first stop was a white tiled room with small windows high on the walls letting in rays of sun. In the room was a large tub with a huge faucet.

"A bath?"

"A mud bath."

"Say again?"

"It's wonderful for your skin and peace of mind."

"There's nothing wrong with mah peace of mind, honestly."

White Smock just smiled. Stepping behind Annie, White Smock skillfully divested her of her white kimono. Annie found herself stark naked, standing in a white tiled room, with rays of sun streaming in from on high, being invited to step into a large tub so she could take a bath in mud!

Short of grabbing the kimono out of White Smock's hands, there was only one way to hide her nakedness. Annie climbed into the tub. Surely, they didn't mean real mud.

White Smock fiddled with some controls. A strange gurgling sound was heard. A rush of warm, silky dark brown mud rushed out of the dinner plate sized faucet.

In spite of herself, Annie let out a yelp.

"Are you all right?"

"Ah, yeah."

"Doesn't it feel nice?"

"Yes," Annie said in surprise. "It does."

"Just give yourself up to it," advised White Smock.

All right, I will, thought Annie. Slowly the mud filled the tub. Annie allowed her body to sink into its warmth. When the mud had reached her shoulders, White Smock turned off the faucet.

"Last time I was this deep in mud, was because old Honey pitched me into the creek." White Smock looked blank. "Never mind."

There was a pillow on the back of the tub, Annie rested her head back, closed her eyes and let her mind drift. Suddenly, she felt hands on her face. "Hey!"

"A facial," said White Smock. Annie leaned back against the pillow as practiced fingers massaged a cream onto her face.

"What's your name?"

"Donna," answered White Smock. Then she added, "It's important you don't talk while the face mask hardens."

Hardens? But Annie was too relaxed to worry. She felt Donna's fingers in her hair, massaging her scalp from top to bottom, then warm water and the lather of fragrant shampoo being applied. Maybe, I've died and gone to heaven, she thought.

Annie was rinsed off and blow-dried. Her brows were tweezed *(ouch!)*. Her legs and bikini area were waxed *(double, no triple ouch! Not to mention, embarrassing)*. A make-up expert worked on her face and Mr. Carl himself styled her hair. Last, but not least, Ms. Lisa, "our fashion consultant" arrived from downstairs bearing "the perfect little black dress." Ms. Lisa also came bearing gorgeous silk panties with a matching bra and pantyhose. She also brought shoes with heels, so high and delicate, Annie was afraid she would fall and break her neck.

"How do I look?" Annie whirled around like a fairy princess in front of her magical makeover people.

"You have very large feet," commented Ms. Lisa. It was true, she did. Size ten and a half. The others were already losing interest; they were on to their next challenge.

Annie had been behind The Scarlet Gate for over four hours. When she was finally released, she was starved...again. But she had promised Vic she would return to the agency as soon as she was finished at The Gate.

Annie was ushered into Vic's inner sanctum right away. Vic, busy at her desk did not look up immediately. When she did, her eyes widened, she leaned back and studied Annie from head to toe. "Wow."

Annie giggled. "I feel so different." She studied herself in the mirror over Vic's desk. What she saw reflected was a startlingly beautiful, vividly colorful yet chic young New York woman. "I don't look like the same person. I look like a...a model."

"That's still to be seen." Vic's cool tone brought Annie down to earth.

"What do I do now?" Annie asked.

"Now? Now, you go to a group call." Vic handed Annie a sheet of paper with an address written on it. "You go to this studio, tell them I represent you, and see if they pick you."

"And if they do?"

"If they do, do what they say. As soon as you're

finished with the shoot call me at this number." She handed Annie a business card. Remember; keep records if you want to get paid."

"Yes ma'am. Er, how much will I get paid?"

"We'll start you out at fifty an hour."

"Fifty dollars an hour?"

Vic nodded. "Ah-huh. Always let me know what's happening and how long you've worked. Keep accurate notes; time, place, people involved and so on."

"And what if they don't pick me?"

Vic smiled at her almost kindly. "It's not the end of the world, kid. Chances are you won't be picked today. What you do is call me first thing in the morning and I'll send you out again. Any questions?"

Yes, Annie had questions, like, if I don't get this job, where am I going to sleep tonight? How would she be able to keep up this new look of hers without a place of her own? Annie had a hundred questions, but she just shook her head no.

Clutching the paper with the address on it Annie started to leave.

"Wait a minute."

"Yes?"

"What's your name again?"

"Annie Malloy."

"Well, Annie Malloy, we're going to have to change that."

"Change my name?"

"Let's see." Vic leaned so far back in her chair, Annie was afraid she would tip over. "Annie, Annie," mused Vic. "Annika!"

"Annika? What kind of name is that?"

"Get used to it, honey. That's who you are from this day forth, Annika."

A new name, a new look, a new city and new life. "Annika." Annie repeated. Then more loudly, more positively, "Annika!"

CHAPTER TEN

The address on the piece of paper led Annie to a studio very much like Tad's, except this one was on the ground floor. It was all concrete and bare walls, with a terrible echo that interfered with conversation.   There were at least a dozen other very pretty, slim young women present, all models in hope of a job.

"Wait over there," instructed a bored, gum-chewing young man when Annie presented her slip of paper. His wave was so vague that it gave Annie no clue as to where she was to go. She simply joined the line of other young women.

A bald, very tall, very thin white man was walking down the line of waiting models. He was accompanied by a dark-complexioned, overweight, colorfully dressed black woman only half his height. They would stop in front of each model and discuss her as if she were an inanimate object. Occasionally, they would ask one of the models to turn or strike a particular pose, and then they would walk on down the line to the next model. Annie noticed the other models seemed to take such behavior as natural and to-be-expected.

When they reached Annie, the man and woman were so engrossed in their conversation that, although they stopped in front of her, they barely glanced at her.

"I'm telling you, the budget won't stretch that far," said the woman.

"Every time I suggest something the slightest bit original, you say we haven't enough money."

"Well, we don't."

Still ignoring Annie, the two started on down the line to the next model.

"Hey," said Annie. The man and woman, either didn't hear her or they ignored her.

"Hey!" She said it louder.

The woman looked back at her. "Did you say something?"

"You all didn't even look at me."

The man and woman exchanged amused looks, but obligingly retraced their steps to Annie.

Annie opened her precious portfolio, took out several photos and waved them at the couple. "Ah have these great pictures, shots, I mean."

The man, in order to avoid having his eye put out by the waving photographs, took them from Annie's hand. The woman looked her up and down. "What have you done?" she asked?

"Ah didn't do anything," Annie defended herself. "I just thought that you hadn't really seen me. Those are really good pictures...shots."

The woman smiled. "I meant what work have you done? As a model."

"Oh."

The man, who had been studying Annie's photos, interrupted. "This is Tad Hirschfield's work, isn't it?"

Annie nodded. "Tad took them, yes."

The man showed the pictures to the black woman. "Well, honey, you look good, but I'm afraid you're not the type we're looking for today. Maybe at another shoot." She handed the photos back to Annie. They started to walk away.

"Oh. Well, okay. Thanks," she called to their backs.

Apparently, none of the other models met their requirements, either. When the man called out, "Thank you, ladies," all of the others picked up their portfolios and made for the door.

Annie slowly trailed after them. Where was she going to go? Did she even have enough money for another night at the hated "Y"? She certainly didn't have enough for both a room and dinner. As usual, she was hungry.

"Hey, you," called a voice. One of the models in front of Annie turned around. "No, not you. You!" Now several of the models clustered at the door, turned. "The redhead with the molasses accent."

"She means you," said an elegant blonde, standing next to Annie.

"Me?"

"Yeah, you. Come here."

Clutching her portfolio, Annie dashed back into the huge room.

I'm going to get the job. I'm going to get the job. It was a prayer.

"What's your name?" asked the woman.

"Annie, I mean, Annika." Annie took a deep breath, looked coolly at the woman and repeated, "I am Annika."

Years later, looking back, she realized it was at that moment her life changed. At that moment, she left behind little "Annie" and started down the long strange road that was to become Annika's life.

***

It turned out that Marsha and Rog, the short chubby black woman and the tall, thin white man, were the producers of another ad campaign being shot. They didn't want Annika for the original job, but they decided to use her as a background figure in a men's shot.

Annika spent that afternoon learning that not every photographer could make the work as exciting as Tad. She learned to pose for what seemed like hours. She spent her time staring adoringly up into the face of a male model while everyone around them fussed, scurried, and shouted.

Her feet began to ache and the dress she was pinned into, itched horribly.

You're making fifty dollars an hour, she reminded herself. So stand still and smile!

It was five o'clock when they called it a day. Annie, now Annika, new to the process, hung around, uncertain as to who would pay her. Finally, when it looked like everyone was leaving, she screwed up her courage and approached Marsha. "Excuse me, ma'am."

Marsha grinned at her. "Honey, if you're going to carry around a name like, Annika, you're going to have to cultivate a Russian accent, or at least get rid of the corn pone."

"I vill vork on it," Annika assured her haughtily.

"That's the ticket." Marsha turned to go.

"But..."

"What?"

"I was wondering about my pay?"

"What about it?"

"When do I get it?"

"Honey, that's between you and your agency. Vic's your agent, right?"

"Ah-huh."

"Well, she bills us, we pay her and then she pays you. Usually takes about two weeks."

"Oh."

"Something wrong?"

"No, I just didn't know."

"Vic should have explained it to you." Then Marsha smiled at her. "Nice working with you, Annika. You did a great job."

"I did? Great! I mean, thank you."

Marsha opened the door and let Annie out into another New York City evening.

***

The next morning Annie lay in the narrow bed, staring up at the cracked ceiling, trying to ignore the feeling of the walls closing in on her. Having forgone dinner and having little hope of breakfast, she tried to ignore her growling stomach.

I wonder if I can talk Vic into letting me have some of my money early? Should I tell her how broke I am? But Momma always said, "Never let folks know how needy you are, they'll take advantage."

The last thought made her laugh. What did she have that people could take advantage of? Anyway, there was really no choice. If she couldn't get any advance money from Vic, she would be, not only hungry, but also out on the street. The thought of wandering alone through the mean streets of the city was horrible. She had been here only three days, but she already had seen numerous examples of how cold New York could be to the weak and poor.

Annie, *no, Annika,* carefully arranged her thick red hair and applied the new make-up she had gotten at The Scarlet Gate. Her attempts at the elaborate make-up procedure were not a complete success.

Guess I need practice.

She carefully wiped off her attempt at high fashion and applied some gloss to her lips.

No breakfast today, not even a cup of coffee.

"God, how I would love a cup of coffee."

Don't use the Lord's name in vain.

"Sorry, God."

She walked the twenty blocks to the agency.

***

When Annika walked in, Doris, the hapless secretary with the frizzy hair, immediately started chirping. "She's here, Ms. Vic," she breathlessly announced as soon as Annika walked through the door. "Go right in," she urged Annika. "She wants to see you right away."

"Is something wrong?" Please don't let anything be wrong, Annika prayed silently. I need to work.

Before Doris could answer, Vic flung open her office door. "Where the hell have you been?" she demanded.

Annika froze. Impatiently, Vic reached for Annika's arm and pulled her into her office.

"I couldn't get a hold of you."

"What's the matter?" Annika was quaking inside.

"They want you back immediately."

"Who does?"

"Marsha and her gang. They have a new campaign and they want you for it."

"That's good, isn't it?"

"Oh, for God's sake. Even you can't be that green." She suddenly remembered her grievance. "Do you realize you didn't leave a phone number? How am I supposed to get a hold of you?"

"I don't have a phone."

"Well get one."

"I don't have..."

"You don't have what?"

Oh, well, she really had nothing to lose. "I'm...uh...no money," Annika confessed.

Vic studied her miserable expression, then threw back her head and roared with laughter. "Honey," she told the astonished Annika, "You play your cards right and you're the next super model. And you're worried about being broke."

"But I am."

Vic patted her arm. "Not for long, kid."

That day Annika learned what it meant to be launched. Armed with several hundred dollars in cash and the loan of a business credit card, Annika went to work.

"And this time take a taxi."

The morning was spent developing "a look" for Marsha's account. As far as Annika was concerned "the look" was pretty wild, but it did get people's attention. Her long red hair was gelled and moussed until it literally stood on end. Her make-up was dead white, except for her huge brown eyes, which were accented to the point that she seemed to be all hair and eyes. It wasn't until a few weeks later that Annika learned she was selling a perfume called, "Extreme."

The afternoon was spent in shooting. It wasn't until early evening that Annika found herself alone with Marsha.

"I want to thank you for choosing me for this job."

"I didn't really have a choice," grinned Marsha.

"You didn't?"

"Take a look at these proofs." Marsha cheerfully showed Annika copies of the shots taken the day before. Annika saw nothing outstanding about them. "They're pictures of me." She shrugged.

"But honey, they weren't supposed to be pictures of you. You were supposed to be background."

"Oh."

"Whatever it is, girl, you have it. The camera loves you."

"The camera loves you." In the next ten years, Annika

would hear that a lot.

CHAPTER ELEVEN

Vic had called and left a message. "Your new roommate's name is Sari." There was an address.

This time, after work, when Annika stepped out once again into another New York City night she raised her arm imperiously, and to her delight, a cab screeched to a halt.

My goodness, it really works.

The taxi dropped her off in front of a building that was worlds away from the YWCA. There was a canopy, a doorman and carefully trimmed shrubs in square, neatly painted boxes at the curbside. The doorman opened the cab door for her and the front door.

"Your Sari's new roommate, ain'tcha?"

"Yes."

"She had to go out, but she left the key for you," he said, handing her a door key.

"How did you know I was her new roommate?"

"Somebody as gorgeous as you, gotta be a model, right?"

Annika smiled shyly. "Thank you."

"My pleasure, lady. You want anything; just ask for me. I'm Joe."

"Thank you, Joe." She paused, deepened her voice, gave it a breathy quality and then dramatically, she said, "I am Annika."

***

Annika inserted the key into the apartment door. It opened into a small hallway which in turn, opened into a large living room. The floors were polished hardwood. Four large windows, curtained in thin linen, dominated the far wall. One of the windows was open and a slight breeze softly moved the curtains. The sound of city traffic, never absent, drifted up from the street. There were two sofas, loads of pillows on the floor and a few colorful scatter rugs. There were also clothes, ashtrays filled with cigarette butts and take-out food cartons scattered everywhere. The room could have been beautiful. Instead, it was a mess.

Feeling like an intruder, Annika explored the rest of the apartment. The kitchen, a dark gloomy room lit with a flickering fluorescent ceiling light was surprisingly neat. When she opened the refrigerator, she discovered why. Inside were two bottles of champagne, one jar of mayonnaise and a box of expensive looking chocolates missing its cover. Obviously, the kitchen was seldom used.

There were two bedrooms, both furnished, One was a huge mess; the other, aside from clothing strewn everywhere, was basically clean. As Annika was standing in the bedroom doorway, she heard the front door open.

"Hi, there!" yelled a cheerful female voice.

"Hello?" Annika answered, even though she was not at all sure she was the one being addressed.

A beautiful tall slim young woman swept toward Annika. She was dressed in an expensive looking pants suit with a long trailing, gypsy-like scarf wrapped around her neck. "I'm Sari."

"Annika."

"Annika, huh? Another of Vic's girls."

"I guess."

"Well, so am I. My real name is Carol Ann." Then she giggled and was immediately transformed from a sophisticated New York model into a teen-age girl playing at life in the big city.

Annika felt a burst of happiness and confidence. If Sari could make it, so could she. "Do you have another roommate?" she asked, indicating the two messy rooms.

"Nah. That's just me being a slob. Just toss those things onto my bed in the other room."

"How will you sleep?" The bed in Sari's room was already overflowing with clothes.

Sari winked, "I don't do much sleeping here." Suddenly, she got very busy. "Look, I gotta go. I'm meeting my boyfriend at Dizzy's."

"Dizzy's?"

"The club, you know." Annika just looked blank. "All the really cool people make it. It's the place to be… this month anyway." Sari studied her for a moment. "You wanta come?"

"Won't your boyfriend mind?"

"Nah, the more the better, that's what he always says."

***

Annika's first impression of Dizzy's was that it was hot, noisy, smoky and very crowded. She loved it!

Outside the club, which looked as if only yesterday it had been an abandoned warehouse, was a long line of hopefuls trying to get in. Sari ignored the line and pulled Annika along with her.

"It's really exclusive," She shouted over the noise. "It's very hard to get in here unless you're with somebody or you are somebody."

The people in line did not seem to object to them going to the front. Instead of the expected anger, they were watched with a hungry intensity that Annika found a little scary. Obviously, the people in line thought she and Sari were "somebodies."

The doorman of the club, a bored looking bruiser in a torn wife beater shirt, well over six feet tall, grinned at Sari and waved both of them through the door.

"Georgie knows me."

Georgie wasn't the only person who knew Sari. Everyone in the dark, noisy room seemed to know her. As she dodged through the crowd, dragging Annika with her, people yelled her name, grabbed her in bear hugs, and when all else failed, waved frantically to get her attention.

"Are you famous or something?"

"Not yet. But my boyfriend is."

"Who's your boyfriend?" asked Annika. Sari just shook her head, unable to hear Annika over the noise. "Who's your boyfriend?" Annika yelled again.

"I am," answered a tall, longhaired man in his early 30's. He rose from his seat, gave Sari a hug, "H'ya, baby."

And grinned down at Annika.

He was wearing black jeans that looked as if they were made out of silk, a multi colored, baseball type jacket that sparkled with metallic threads and a skintight pink tee. The get-up was ridiculous and very sexy.

"This is Johnny," said Sari proudly. "Don't you recognize him?" she asked anxiously.

Of course, I don't recognize him, thought Annika. I've never met a man who wears pink tee shirts. "I've just never seen Johnny in person before," she said tactfully.

Both Sari and Johnny relaxed.

"Never been to any of my concerts? Where you been, sweet cakes?"

"I just got to New York."

"Hey, I tour."

"I can't wait to see you perform," she said truthfully. She had never met anyone who naturally assumed a complete stranger would recognize him. There was a power to such an assumption that thrilled her.

Annika's first impression of Dizzy's had been of noise and movement, but as she looked around, she realized there was a strict hierarchy. Johnny's party was among several on a raised dais that was strictly segregated from the local yokels who gazed in wonder at the privileged ones.

"This is where the real talent sits," Sari assured her.

"What about the others?"

"Them? They all want to get up here, but Terry and Booboo," she indicated two extremely rough looking individuals, "keep them in their place. I used to be down there," Sari admitted. "You skipped right over."

"Thank you," said Annika. She meant it.

She was handed a drink of something sweet and colorful. Every time she turned around, it was refilled. She never did empty her glass.

Suddenly, Sari clutched Annika's arm. "There she is," she breathed in awed.

"Who?"

"Magna. You know, Magna."

Annika shook her head.

"She's been named the top model in the world for the last three years running. Can you imagine how much money she makes?"

"More than $50 an hour?" Privately, Annika had difficulty imagining anyone making more than $50 an hour.

"Hundreds."

"You're kidding?"

"She's dating a prince." Both girls watched the slim graceful super model.

I really am in a magical land.

"Everybody comes here, don't they?" said Annika.

"I told you, Dizzy's the place. Look she's going to the ladies room. Come on." Sari grabbed Annika's arm and pulled her to her feet. To her surprise, Annika wobbled and had to stop suddenly and fight down a feeling of nausea. Then she obediently followed Sari.

The Ladies' Room was surprisingly luxurious. There were mirrored walls and pink lights. Deep carpets and couches. Several women were sitting around sharing a joint and staring off into the distance.

"This is just for the people on the dais," Sari told her. "The others have another Ladies' Room."

Magna was standing at the mirror looking dreamily at her reflection. "Any coke?" she asked the room in general.

One of the women languidly raised her hand. As if she's in school, thought Annika. Magna spotted Annika. "Who's this?"

Sari answered for her. "A new girl of Vic's." Magna nodded, immediately losing interest.

Several of the women followed Magna's lead and snorted down some coke. Sari was one of them. "Come on, Annika, my treat."

"I don't know how."

"Just snort it, honey," laughed Magna. "Believe me, it comes naturally." The others all laughed dutifully.

Gingerly, Annika took the short pink straw from Sari, leaned over the lines of powder Sari had laid out for her and sniffed. It went down the wrong way. Annika gasped and choked. She started coughing. One of the women shoved her away.

"Hey, not over the snow."

Annika felt her stomach lurch. She barely made it to the toilet before vomiting up everything in her stomach.

"Never saw that reaction before," commented Magna casually.

Annika sat on the floor hugging the toilet bowl. When she finally lifted her head, the other women seemed far away. Magna, smiling, content with the world, carefully applied lipstick. Sari, with a silly smile on her face, sat on the couch, tapping her foot and nodding her head to some private concert going on in her head.

I don't seem to fit in here, thought Annika, as she flushed the toilet.

***

The next morning Annika woke with a headache, a queasy stomach, and a mouth so dry, she drank two glasses of water as soon as she could stagger to the kitchen.

She was alone in the apartment. There was a vague memory of Sari and her boyfriend, Johnny, urging her to accompany them to "this place that's *really* hot."

"But we have to work tomorrow."

Sari had rolled her eyes.

Now it was tomorrow and all Annika wanted to do was crawl back under her covers and never, ever have another drink of alcohol for the rest of her life. And as for using coke again...she would rather die first. Groaning, she groped her way to the shower.

Annika was lucky. That entire morning was spent on make-up. All she had to do was sit in a chair, try to keep her eyes open and sip endless cups of black coffee that someone kept bringing her. By the time, her hair and make-up were done and she had been pinned, twisted and maneuvered into the high fashion dress that they were all making such a fuss over, Annika was awake and alert. It's hard to keep a sixteen year old down.

CHAPTER TWELVE

Several months later, Annika, now seventeen, was still sharing an apartment with Sari. Over coffee one morning, Sari announced, "We've been invited to the Archers' for the weekend."

"Who are the Archers?" Annika poured herself a second cup of coffee.

"I dunno."

"Then how could they have invited us?"

"Vic says we have to go."

"Oh." Later that afternoon, Annika stopped by the agency to talk to Vic. She had spent the morning under hot lights, shifting herself into practically obscene positions, just so some overweight, octopus-handed dress manufacturer could achieve what he called "ads with class."

"He thinks "class" means plenty of ass," Annika told Vic.

As she climbed ever higher on the modeling ladder, Annika was developing a protective shell of irony. She had appeared on two covers, one of them for Cosmopolitan, a TV spot and several full-page ads in Vogue, along with less exalted work. During that time, she had also fended off so many lust driven dress manufacturers and salesmen that she had been given the name "The Russian Virgin." Vic worried about Annika's "don't touch me" attitude.

"It's important not to piss them off, Annika. Be tactful."

"I am tactful," Annika assured her. "I'm just not for sale -- or rent," she added.

"Okay, okay." Vic threw up her hands in defeat. "Just don't let the pricks know you consider them pricks."

"Sari says we're invited to the Archer's?"

Vic barely looked up from her paperwork. "Yeah. Bring

enough clothes so you can change at least three times a day."

"Who are the Archers?"

"They have an estate in East Hampton." Annika just looked at her blankly. "They're very, very rich, Annika."

"Oh...where's East Hampton?"

Vic only just refrained from rolling her eyes. "On the Island. That's Long Island. And, no, you don't know them. That's the whole point of going, it's time you met people."

"I meet people."

"The right people. Contacts, Annika. Contacts. It's what makes the world go round."

So Annika dutifully packed enough clothes to change at least three times a day for two days. She ended up driving down to East Hampton with just Vic in Vic's limousine. Sari had gone off somewhere with JohnnyO and was unavailable.

"Never make top model," was Vic's brisk summing up of Sari.

Weekending at the Archers was like landing on a planet far, far away.

Their house was immense. There were at least 20 bedrooms and even more bathrooms. The floors were of marble, but mostly hidden under rich oriental carpets. There were fireplaces in almost every room, even in one of the bathrooms and the faucets were gold!

"Just plated," Vic assured her.

The walled grounds were lush and green and manicured to a tee. Each blade of grass stood at attention. Mrs. Archer ("Please call me Eloise.") gave Annika a tour. "The grounds lead directly to our private beach on the Sound."

"The Sound?"

"Long Island Sound."

"Oh."

Also there was a heated indoor swimming pool.

There were stables, but no horses. "Very smelly animals," sniffed her hostess. There were two greenhouses, one for vegetables and one for flowers. "Don't you just hate wilted flowers?" The estate was a veritable castle. "Our weekend place."

Including Mr. and Mrs. Archer, they were a party of

fourteen.

Annika was the only one to come down to breakfast before noon. She wandered like a ghost through the empty rooms, until a maid took pity on her and served her breakfast on a shaded patio overlooking the ocean.

No, not the ocean, The Sound, which looked like an ocean.

When the others did present themselves, they were all dressed in various shades of white. After the fifth guest wafted down the broad staircase in white slacks and a pale, off-white polo shirt, Annika got the message. She excused herself and hurried upstairs to see if she had brought anything, aside from her underwear that was white.

Nope, pastel would have to do.

Despite feeling very much like a visiting off-world alien, Annika enjoyed herself. Mrs. Archer was silly, but kind. Mr. Archer ("Call me Ben.") smoked cigars and smiled benevolently on everyone. Most of the guests were very attractive, some were witty, and everyone was very pleasant to her. Gerard Rostand was especially nice.

He arrived on the second day. He was not staying with the Archers since he had a house of his own "down the beach a bit."

"Is it as big as this place?" She had meant it as a joke, but he answered her seriously.

"The house is about the same size, but the grounds are smaller."

"Only ten acres?"

He laughed. "I'll check the deed." They both sipped their Champagne cocktails. "You're not from around here?"

"Florida."

"Palm Beach?"

"Not far from there." She was telling the truth. In terms of miles, Teardrop was only about fifty miles from Palm Beach. In economic and cultural terms, not to mention ambiance and desirability, it was light years away.

Gerard Rostand was in his late twenties and very handsome. He was tall and well-built with broad shoulders and slim hips. He carried himself proudly. There was an arrogance about him that Annika found attractive. She felt it showed self-confidence based on worldly experience. He had light blue eyes and strawberry red hair. He looks like a movie star, she thought. If we had a child, it would have red hair.

You will not think about babies.

Gerard was very attentive to her, helping her find a shady seat in the garden where they all gathered for aperitifs, handing her a towel when she emerged from the pool, fetching her sweater when it grew cool in the evening. Annika was enchanted. She was in a fairytale castle, complete with a Prince Charming.

You've come a long way from Teardrop, baby, she told herself.

"You're looking very pensive," said Gerard.

"It's like a fairy tale." He raised his eyebrow inquiringly. "All this." She waved her hand, taking in the beautiful mansion, the sound of crashing surf, the fairy lights strung around the garden, the soft sound of classical music coming through the French windows.

"Does that include me?" he asked.

"Oh, yes," she breathed before she had time to think.

Smiling he leaned forward and very gently kissed her on the lips. "Annika, you are exquisite."

Her heart was fluttering. She found it difficult to swallow normally. Heat rushed through her body. It was pure lust. She wanted him to take her in his arms and hold her tightly. She wanted hot, hard, demanding kisses, but he just smiled, gently took her arm and escorted her back to the others. A flush of shame rushed through her body. Obviously, the lust was one sided. Did Gerard know what she was thinking? Thank God, it was dark.

The next day, Annika was back in the city and back to work. Gerard did not call. Weeks went by and there was not a word from him.

After all, what could one expect from a fairytale?

***

Her career was barreling ahead. She was booked far in advance. Not a month went by that her face didn't appear on a prestigious magazine cover. Her hourly rate skyrocketed.

She dated lots of men, many of them her fellow models, most of them gay. She didn't mind. They were usually bright, funny and guaranteed not to hit on her. They provided her with an acceptable escort for publicity outings and she provided them with eye candy that was sure to get their pictures in the papers.

One day, Annika, passing a local newsstand, caught sight of her second Cosmopolitan cover shot. She studied it carefully.

The lady on the cover looked very sleek, very sexy, very much in control of her life and her sexuality. I wonder if Ray will see this cover? Will he recognize Annie Malloy? Of course not! Annie Malloy no longer exists for him. Or for me, she realized.

The money poured in. She developed something of a cult following. Fans actually waited around any location shooting she did and asked for autographs. She was interviewed on television.

"I love working with Monsieur Talon's designs," she assured the TV audience. "He knows how to bring to the fore a woman's most alluring features." Talon's business almost doubled after that broadcast.

Later, viewing the taped show in the privacy of their own living room, Annika and Sari were convulsed at her performance. Sari, a wicked mimic, had Annika rolling on the floor.

"No, more. No, more. Stop it, Sari." But Sari, convulsed by her own humor, was herself, doubled up with laughter. "But Monsieur Talon, has brought to the fore (what the hell is fore?) my most alluring feature, which is really my Marilyn Monroe wiggle."

"I do not wiggle," protested a laughing Annika.

"Sure do, baby."

The phone rang. Still laughing, Annika answered it. "Yes, hello?"

"Annika?" It was Gerard Rostand. Annika recognized his voice instantly.

She took a deep breath. "Hello."

"Will you have dinner with me?"

"When?"

"Tonight."

"Tonight? Yes."

"I'll pick you up at seven. Good-bye."

"Wait. Don't you want my address?"

"I have your address, my exquisite Annika. Until seven."

"He didn't even say his name," Annika told Sari. "He knew I would recognize his voice."

"You should have said no." Make him call again. Make him work for it. Geez, don't you know anything?" Sari was indignant. "Don't let him know you're free on the day he calls."

"Oh, my God. I'm not free, I'm supposed to go to that opening with Jamie. I'll have to cancel." She grabbed up the phone and hurriedly dialed.

"Which one are you cancelling?" Sari asked.

An answering machine obviously answered Annika's call. "Hello, Jamie, it's Annika. I'm sorry, but I won't be able to make it tonight. I'll see you later this week." She hung up cheerfully.

"That was short and sweet," said Sari cynically. "Are you in love with this Gerard guy?"

"In love?" For a moment, Annika was capsized back into a river of memories, memories of being in love...with Ray. She could almost feel the happiness spreading through her body into her very soul.

Fool! Stop thinking about him. Just make sure you don't make the same mistake twice.

"I barely know Gerard," she answered Sari. "But I like him. He's very sophisticated."

"Sophisticated? Oh, well, that'll curl a girl's toes. Where's he taking you to dinner?"

"I don't know. What should I wear?" She tore into her bedroom and yanked open the closet doors, peering into her bulging closet. "I have nothing to wear!"

Annika finally settled on a dark blue-green dress of thick material that showed off her porcelain complexion to perfection. The dress rustled when she moved and a faint exotic fragrance flowed around her. She wore her dark red hair up on a French twist, but softened its severity by pulling free some strands to curl beguilingly around her face.

Gerard arrived promptly at seven. "You look elegant and lovely," he praised her.

"So do you," she blurted. Then blushed. God, she was so gauche.

Gerard ushered her into a limousine and whisked her to a lovely old mansion on upper Fifth Avenue. "Adian's is a private club," he informed her.

"I've never heard of it," said Annika, who by this point in her career thought she had been everywhere and seen everything in New York.

"I'm not surprised."

Annika stiffened. What did he mean by that, she wondered? Did he think she was some sort of hick?

There was a doorman there too, but unlike the one at Dizzy's, this doorman was dressed in black tie and tails. Also there was no screaming music blasting out of the doorway, there were no flashing lights and no jostling crowds trying to get in. Apparently, Adian's was so exclusive almost no one knew about it.

The door opened into a foyer with a high ceiling. A maître d'hôtel stood waiting behind an antique desk. He bowed to Gerard and Annika.

"Welcome, Mr. Rostand. Your private room is ready as you requested."

Gerard barely nodded at him. The maître d' turned and snapped his fingers. Immediately, a minion in an old-fashioned bellboy's uniform appeared and held opened the elaborate bronze doors of an antique looking elevator.

Private room?

For a moment, Annika felt a brush of fear. Don't be silly, she told herself. This is Gerard Rostand you're with. He's a socialite, not some sick pervert.

"There is a balcony," Gerard said, as if to reassure her. "We can see everything."

See everything?

They were shown into a small room surrounded on three sides with dark burgundy curtains. The room was furnished with an elegant little table set for two, a love seat, armchair and a side table holding various bottles of wine and liquor. Aside from the candles on the table, a small crystal chandelier on the high ceiling added only slightly more light to the scene.

"It's like a stage set."

"Ahh, but are we the actors or are we the audience?" He smiled at her, enjoying her confusion. Since coming to New York, Annika had been faced with one new experience after another. She had developed a technique that covered almost all contingencies. It was simple and effective. She simply smiled mysteriously. It always worked. She had discovered no one is beyond self-doubt. Annika's mysterious smile would force the observer to assume she was in the know. It was a way not to lose control of a situation. It had always worked... until now.

"You don't know what I'm talking about, do you?"

Her face was frozen into her mysterious smile mode. Oh, God, now she was going to have to say something.

"I always prefer action to observation." She spoke very slowly and softly, giving her words a depth and importance way beyond her understanding of the situation. Then she turned slowly away from him, letting her frozen face muscles relax. What had she just said? Did it make sense? Was he impressed? Was it what he wanted to hear?

"Really?" He sounded amused. With a dramatic sweep of his arm, Gerard drew back the burgundy curtains that covered one wall. It was not a wall after all. The curtains had concealed the fact they were literally on a balcony overlooking a large crowded room. Directly across from them was a much larger balcony where musicians played. Below them were people dressed in elaborate costumes; some wore masks, some did not. Some were modestly and elaborately clothed, and some were almost naked. Indeed, several people were completely naked.

"Oh, my goodness," Annika exclaimed and almost jumped away from the balcony railing.

Gerard was watching her intently almost eagerly.

What have I gotten myself into?

"A true sophisticate learns to appreciate and respect all social mores."

"Ah huh." Annika gazed down at what was frankly an orgy. "So those people running around buck naked and humping like jack rabbits, just have different social mores, right?"

He threw back his head and laughed.

"I've changed my mind, Gerard."

"Oh?"

"I think I'll just be the audience tonight."

"I agree." He cast a contemptuous glance down at the fornicating masses. "Your fastidiousness is very refreshing."

"Do you bring many women here?"

And do they all immediately take their clothes off for you?

"You are the first lady."

As it turned out, the worst Annika was forced to endure was a wonderful supper of chilled vichyssoise, clams on the half shell, and a tiny, but delicious steak. As the waiter, who wore only the top half of a black tie and tails and was completely naked from the waist down described it, "Salad with a delicate, but superb vinaigrette with just a hint of raspberry. I hope Madame likes it?"

Madame kept her eyes firmly on his forehead and nodded her approval in a world-weary manner.

She didn't know how to behave. Should she get angry and leave? But was she really angry? Wasn't she just a little, well, turned on?

If that was so, shouldn't she gaze with greedy eyes at the antics of those below her? After all, she was safe here on the balcony. Gerard showed no inclination to jump her bones.

But after her first horrified fascination, she had no real desire to indulge even in voyeurism. The people below seemed not only to enjoy copulating where everyone could see them, but they changed partners with the indifference of dogs in heat. It was all kind of disgusting and…boring.

The dinner had been delicious, the wine intoxicating, the bare-assed waiter ridiculous and now she was sleepy and wanted to go home.

Like a perfect gentleman, *(Did perfect gentleman take their dates to orgies?)* Gerard delivered her safely to her doorstep. Annika decided it was now or never to take a stand. "Gerard, are you going to call me again?"

"Do you want me to?"

"Yes."

"Then I will."

"But, Gerard...next time."

"Next time?

"Something a little more...."

"More?"

"Well, something a little less."

He kissed her hand. Annika was beginning to like having her hand kissed. "I admire you, Annika." Her heart swelled with pleasure.

"Good night, Gerard." She turned and floated past Joe, the doorman, and all the way up to her apartment.

Luckily, Sari wasn't home. Annika wasn't all that sure how she was going to describe her first date with the sophisticated, intriguing, Mr. Gerard Rostand.

***

Many dates followed. Gerard took her to the opera, the theater, dance recitals and gallery openings. She learned to dress in stark black, sip champagne, nibble on hors d'oeuvres and nod knowingly as Gerard sneeringly dissected the artwork spread before them. Most of the time, she agreed with him; the stuff was usually awful. However, every once in a while, there was a work that was joyful, full of energy and hope. Work that made Annika smile.

She was earning a lot of money now. At one gallery opening, she bought a painting that especially appealed to her.

"You're not buying that?"

Annika smiled her "mysterious smile," patted him gently on the arm and whispered erotically in his ear, "On my wall, not yours, my sweet Gerard." But he was not appeased.

"I see I still have a lot to teach you."

There were times when Annika got tired of being Gerard's pupil and of the predictability of it all.

"You two are like an old married couple," said Sari.

"What do you mean?"

"Every Friday."

"It's not every Friday, sometimes it's Saturday, too."

"Whoopee!" Sari was admiring her toenails which were painted a fluorescent green. "Frankly, my darling," Sari said, imitating some old time actress, "I think even Jamie would be more fun."

"Jamie's just a friend and he's gay. Anyway Gerard is who I want."

Sari, the mimic, cackled like the evil witch. "Be careful what you wish for, my pretty. You may get it."

"Your little nail is smudged," Annika pointed out.

"Damn." Sari applied herself to repainting the offending nail. "So how is he?'

"Who?"

"Gerard. In bed."

"Oh. Well, we don't…"

"Don't what?"

"What you said. We don't…"

"No sex? Why not?"

Annika blushed and looked away from her. "Well, we're not married…"she began.

Sari rolled her eyes. "Give me a break, Annika."

"I don't know why," Annika admitted. "I just...he just...I don't know."

"Maybe he's gay."

"Gerard? Of course he's not!"

"Then why aren't you two doing the dirty dance?"

"He respects me?"

Sari mimed putting her finger down her throat and gagging. "Bet he's gay," she said cheerfully.

A few days later, Annika had lunch with Easy McGee, a newspaper columnist who had been pursuing her with lighthearted lust for more than a year.

Annika smiled her wonderful smile at him. "How have you been, Easy?"

"Shitty. You on the other hand, have been having a wonderful time."

She raised one delicate eyebrow. "I have?"

As an answer, he unfolded the newspaper he had been carrying and showed her a quarter page shot of Gerard and her, laughing happily together at a party.

The waiter delivered her salad. "My name is Jeffrey. "Are you ready to order, sir?"

"Yeah, Jeffrey, another vodka martini."

Annika was studying the newspaper photo. "They took my bad side."

"You don't have a bad side, Princess."

The waiter gave him an smirk and swished away. "Little faggot," muttered Easy.

"He is not," said Annika.

"Princess, I guarantee, Jeffrey is as sweet as they come."

Bewildered, Annika looked around. "Who's Jeffrey?"

A shrewd look came over Easy's face. He took the newspaper away from her and gave it a quick look. "So Mr. Gerard Rostand is not exactly ripping your panties off."

"That is a disgusting thing to say."

"Is it accurate?"

"Not everyone is like you, Easy."

He wiggled his eyebrows. "Pity, isn't it?"

In spite of herself, she laughed.

"If he's not giving you any, why are you hanging around with the guy?"

Annika attacked her salad.

"Ah, I see. You want to be Mrs. Gerard Rostand."

Annika slammed her fork down. "I like Gerard!"

"Do you? What do you like best about him?"

"That is none of your business."

"Can't even think of one thing you like about the guy?"

Getting angrier by the minute, Annika looked him in the eye. "Easy, I have been rethinking *our* relationship."

He raised his hands in surrender. "I promise, no more

digs about Mr. High Society."

He looked around for the waiter. "Maybe, I'd better eat something to go with my martini lunch."

As they ate, Annika considered Easy's question. What did she want from her relationship with Gerard? "I really like Gerard," she leaned forward over the table to emphasize her words.

"Tell me why?"

"You think it's because he's wealthy and belongs to society. Yes, that is important. Why not? Why shouldn't I want that? Everyone does."

"Not everyone, Princess."

Ignoring him, she plowed on. "It's Gerard himself," she tried to explain. "I find him exciting. And charming."

"Charming?"

"Well, he is."

"Gerard Rostand is about as charming as a snake."

"You're just jealous."

"Maybe I am, but believe me, Princess, Gerard is as bent as they come."

"Bent?"

"He corrupts."

"Now you're just being silly. Gerard is only a man, not the snake in Eden."

"Don't let him corrupt you, Princess."

Later, as they were leaving to go their separate ways, Easy said to her, "Have you noticed you're losing your southern accent?"

She smiled her heart stopping smile at him and spoke in her husky foreign voice. "After all, darling," she said, looking deep into his eyes, "Annika, isn't really a proper name for a southern belle, is it?" Before he could answer, she changed the subject.

"I'm going to Paris next week. Giovanni is having a show there, then next month to Milan and in three months to Spain."

"You are becoming very sophisticated, Annika."

"I am, aren't I?" She was pleased with herself.

He smiled at her. "You're a witch, Annika, a

sophisticated witch," he said lightly, "and you've stolen my heart."

Her smile faded. "I didn't mean to," she said. "Someone stole mine a long time ago. It's an odd feeling, living without a heart." Then she laughed, patted his arm and moved gracefully off.

Easy stared hungrily after her.

CHAPTER THIRTEEN

That year, Gerard followed her to Spain. It was not unusual. He was always showing up unexpectedly. They had been in Paris together and London, even St. Petersburg. Once, he had showed up when she was shooting on location in a small, back-of-beyond village in China.

"You must really like me," she had teased him, "to come so far and put up with Chinese bathrooms."

"Chinese bathrooms are an oxymoron," he snapped. "But yes, my exquisite Annika, I am deeply committed to you."

Committed to me? What a weird way of putting it, she thought.

Now they were in Madrid and she had the afternoon off. Gerard had promised her a surprise. "Where are we going?"

"It's a *surprise*, Annika."

He took her to a stadium. She was ensconced in a comfortable shaded seat and presented with a fruit filled, highly potent drink. Music blared from the loud speakers. Annika let her gaze wander from the colorful, cheerfully noisy crowd to the stadium floor. It was sand covered with wooden barriers placed strategically around the sides of the oval ring. A Bull Ring!

She started to rise. "Gerard, I don't think..."

"Annika, don't be so provincial."

"I'm not!"

"I know you better than you know yourself. I guarantee you'll enjoy it."

"And if I don't?"

"We'll leave."

"Promise."

"I promise you, Annika. But you must sit through the

first fight before you make up your mind."

She sank back into her seat. After all, even if she insisted on leaving right now, the bullfight would continue. There was nothing she could do to stop it.

There was rousing music. The crowd yelled, applauded, and shouted. Then, like something out of an opera, a parade of men dressed in beautifully colored, tight fitting costumes, strutted across the ring waving their hands graciously at the adoring crowd. Women were throwing roses and what looked like pieces of metal.

"Is that money they're throwing?"

Gerard smiled. "Hotel keys."

Suddenly, the music faded. Several young men ran out into the arena and gathered up the thrown objects. Someone had thrown bright red lace panties. The man held it up for all to see. The crowd yelled their approval. Trumpets rang out, then silence.

A huge, ugly, black bull was released into the arena. You could almost smell his rage. He tossed his gigantic head, looking for something, someone to attack. Two men rode into the arena on blindfolded horses. The horses' bodies were protected with heavy padding.

"Why are the horses here?"

"Watch."

"Why are they blindfolded?"

"Watch."

The bull charged. He crossed the sand with blinding speed, head lowered, cruel horns pointing straight ahead, slamming directly into the side of the horse!

Annika shot out of her seat. "Oh, no!"

Gerard grabbed her arm and forced her back into the seat. "Don't make a spectacle of yourself. The horse is fine. Look."

It seemed he was right. The horse, knocked sideways by the power and weight of the bull, quickly straightened himself. His rider, taking careful aim, stabbed a brightly decorated spear into the hump on the back of the bull. Scarlet blood trickled down its ebony shoulder.

A second rider, approaching the bull from the other

side, planted his spear. Confused, the bull turned from the first horse and rider and attacked the second heavily padded, blindfolded horse. This horse also staggered, but righted himself almost immediately, as his rider guided him out of the bull's path. Immediately, the first horse and rider again attacked the bull.

Annika watched in fascinated horror as the bull was attacked again and yet again. The frenzied animal whirled first this way, then that way, trying to fix on where the pain and danger was coming from. There were four gaily-colored spears embedded into the huge animal's hump. Scarlet blood trailed lazily down the bull's sides. Annika sat rigid, biting her knuckles. The crowd was cheering. Next to her, Gerard laughed, sipped his drink and watched avidly.

"Why do they do that?"

"The spears? To weaken the bull." Gerard laughed softly. "Soften him up."

"For what?"

"Him." Gerard indicated the matador, who was just now stepping into the ring.   The crowd went wild, chanting his name. "Carlos, Carlos, Carlos."

"The pride of Spain," said Gerard.

Music, lively and loud burst from the PA system.

The spectacle was straight out of Carmen. The matador paraded around the ring as women shrieked and men yelled. One woman fainted, almost falling into the arena. Annika found herself clapping and smiling along with the rest.

Then the music stopped and Carlos went into action. Stepping contemptuously close to the bull, he waved his red cape in the bull's face. Annika could see the bull's eyes light up. It seemed to be thinking, *at last, here is an enemy I can fight!* The bull pawed the ground, lowered its head and charged. Gracefully, the matador slipped to one side. The bull, blindly following the movement of the cape, completely missed his tormentor. As the bull passed him, Carlos slapped the animal with the side of his sword. The crowd roared its approval.

As the dance between man and animal continued, Annika found herself drawn further and further into this formalized ritual of death. The bull was still bleeding, but there was a horrible beauty about the whole scene spread below her, a graceful inevitability. Then, in a split second, everything changed.

The bull turned suddenly and charged straight at the matador who immediately whipped around his cape as a graceful distraction. But this time, as the matador swiveled his hips to follow the flow of his cape, his foot slipped. The cape was dangerously close to his body. The bull, rushing after the cape, brushed against Carlos sending him crashing down into the sand. A moan of horror escaped from the crowd. Finding that the cape had vanished from his sight, the bull instantly turned, his mighty head swaying back and forth in search of the hated red cape. There it was! It was no longer waving back and forth to torment him. Instead, the cape was wrapped around a figure struggling to his feet. The bull rushed forward.

"No, no," yelled the crowd.

"No!" yelled Annika. "Dear God, no." It was a prayer.

Gerard leaned forward, his hands clenched around the balcony rail.

From the corner of her eyes, Annika could see figures on horseback rushing toward the charging bull. But they would never get there in time.

Carlos, entangled in the red cape, was struggling to his feet. He never made it. The bull, traveling as fast as a freight train, hit him full on. The man's body was tossed in the air like a stick figure.

The crowd screamed. Annika screamed with them. Only Gerard was silent, staring, hands clenched, a strange open-mouthed smile, a frozen rictus, on his face.

The bull, triumphant now, would not be diverted. He rushed to Carlos' sprawled body, lowered his head and gouged the limp figure with his horns. He trampled the poor body under his hooves, his thousand-plus pound body cracking bones.

Finally, rescue arrived. The bull, sated now with his triumph, allowed himself to be diverted away from Carlos. Driven through a hastily opened gate, he trotted off with a snort and swish of his tail. An ambulance was driven out onto the sand and Carlos was tenderly loaded into it and driven away, siren screaming.

Annika was crying.

Gerard rose. "Come on, let's get out of here. There won't be anything worth watching after this."

***

In the limousine, returning to their hotel, Annika sat rigid, staring straight ahead.

Gerard was annoyed with her. "Why are you so upset? I would think you'd be pleased; for once the bull won."

"I don't like bullfighting. I will never go again."

"Okay. Okay." They rode in silence. Then he said, "You look like Dracula's bride."

"What?"

"Your mascara's smeared. Isn't it supposed to be waterproof?"

She ignored this. "Gerard...Please, find out about Carlos. His condition," she begged.

He sighed.

"Please."

"Yes, alright." At the hotel, he steered her towards the elevator. "Clean yourself up and become your usual beautiful self."

"I don't feel like going out tonight."

"Of course, you don't, my darling. We're staying in, in the hotel, that is. I have a surprise for you."

"I don't want any more surprises!"

"You love surprises."

"Not anymore."

"Oh, for God's sake, Annika, no one is going to be gored tonight." She hesitated. "Now, go on." When she still hesitated, he came to her and gently kissed her forehead. "Believe me, darling, this surprise, you will like. I'll call for you in two hours."

***

Alone in her hotel suite, Annika stared out the window down at the street of fashionable hotels and restaurants and at the wealthy, bejeweled people who moved along the sidewalk. They looked so civilized. How could they deliberately torture an innocent animal, and then send someone's son into the ring to be mauled and destroyed?

Someone's son. *My son.* The thought just popped into her head. A terrible longing raced through her body shaking her to her very soul.

I will not think on it. I will not think of Mama. I will not think of Ray or of...that bastard. I will never ever go back to Teardrop again. I can protect myself. It's finished. They're finished. None of them matter to me.

She was strong, triumphant. Then it all melted away and vanished into that great gaping needy black hole inside her.

Turning away from the window, she shivered. She was a girl who shunned her past, adrift in this frightening world. A world where sometimes bulls managed to maul the matador, but still ended up as hamburger.

Abruptly, she stalked into the bathroom. She turned the old-fashioned faucets on full blast, poured a handful of green bath salts under the flowing water and ripped off her clothes, flinging them carelessly onto the floor. With relief, she let the steaming, fragrant water close over her tense body.

Two hours later, Annika was putting the finishing touches on her make-up when there was a knock on her door. Wrapping herself in her charcoal gray silk robe, she opened the door to Gerard. He was wearing a beautiful tailored dark suit.

"You're not dressed," he said.

"I didn't know what to wear. You haven't told me what the surprise is."

"I'll choose for you." Quickly, he went through her closet. "Is this all you brought?"

She was sitting at her dressing table, half turned away from the mirror, looking out the window. He could see her profile in the mirror. "Annika! Is this all you brought with you?"

"I like to travel light."

"You certainly do." He dove back into the closet. "This is perfect." He emerged from her closet, bearing a two-layer, filmy cream-colored slip dress. "Do you have a hat?"

"I don't like to wear hats."

"No, you don't need to. Your hair is like a crown." He reached out and stroked the thick dark red curls cascading around her face and down her shoulders. "Wear it just like that."

"You want me to wear my hair down?"

"Yes. I have a present for you."

She leaned forward as Gerard drew from his jacket pocket a beautifully wrapped gift about the size of a small paperback book.

"Open it," he ordered. Annika made herself move slowly to prolong the moment before the gift was revealed. She loved presents.

Finally, the wrappings were off. A slim, brown velvet covered box was revealed. There was no name on the box, no hint of where it had come from. Annika's long slim fingers caressed it.

Gerard, mesmerized by the sight of her white hand on the dark brown velvet, leaned forward. "Go ahead, open it."

Her perfectly manicured fingernail pushed against the small gold latch. With a click, the lid opened slightly. She pushed against it with one finger and it sighed wide open. Inside were two of the most beautiful diamond drop earrings she had ever seen. "Oh, good Lord," she breathed.

He frowned at her reverting to her southern accent. "Do you like them?"

"There is no woman on the face of this earth who wouldn't love them. Are they really for me?"

"Put them on," he urged. She did. They both studied her reflection in the mirror.

"I should put my hair up."

"No!" Another order. She lowered her hands.

"It's more exciting to catch glimpses of them through your beautiful mane," he said.

She laughed. "Next thing you'll be wanting me to neigh like a horse." They both laughed. "Now will you tell me what the occasion is?" They smiled at each other.

He didn't answer her. Instead, still smiling, he said, "Finish dressing."

Taking the dress with her, she slipped into the bathroom and slid into it. She stepped into a pair of gold-toned high-heeled sandals, applied gloss to her lips and, with a toss of her head, emerged to pirouette in front of Gerard.

His eyes seemed filled with love and admiration.

"Am I the girl of your dreams?" she teased.

"I believe you are."

"What are you going to do about it?" Visions of lovemaking filled her mind.

"Marry you."

"What?" They stared at each other. "What did you say, Gerard?"

"I await your answer."

Mrs. Gerard Rostand? Her mind whirled. I'd be a member of Society. Give garden parties on our Long Island estate.

"I like working as a model." The words were blurted out.

"Then you shall continue working until you get tired of it," he assured her.

He's being so reasonable, so nice. What is wrong with me, she wondered? Why don't I just say, yes! yes! yes!

A vision of the last time she saw Mr. O'Brien flashed into her mind. He had handed her the envelope containing a bus ticket and three hundred dollars. A payoff for her to get out of town. "It's a waste of time giving you this money. You'll just blow it, but that's not my worry. Whores always make out. Now get out of here."

She had taken the money, but something had curled up and whimpered inside her.

I'm one of the top fashion models in the whole world, she thought fiercely. I'm not a whore. I make more money in one year than Mr. O'Brien has in his whole life.

"Annika?" Gerard was watching her anxiously.

Do I want to marry him? Of course I do, anyone would.

She took a deep breath. "Gerard, thank you for asking me to marry you."

"You don't have to thank me, just say, yes."

"Gerard...I'm not in love with you."

He stared at her, turned abruptly and walked to the door, turned and walked back and stood facing her. "My darling, Annika." His voice was controlled, soft and kind. "I have been told that in the best marriages, love grows."

"You still want to marry me?"

"More than ever."

"More than ever?"

"I have always admired your beauty and your courage. Now, I also admire your honesty." He was looking directly into her eyes. "And besides," he smiled gently at her, "I have enough love for both of us."

"Oh, Gerard. You are so sweet to me," she said. "If you are sure, really truly sure, then, yes. I would be so happy and proud to be your wife."

He grabbed her in a bear hug so tight that she protested, "I can't breathe." He loosened his hold on her,

"Are you ready?"

"For what?"

"Marriage."

"You mean here in Madrid?"

"I mean here, in this hotel, tonight."

"But planning a wedding...blood tests...a wedding license."

"All arranged."

"How?"

"Knowing the right people can smooth almost any path."

"No. I mean, how did you know I would say, yes?"

"I love you, Annika."

It suddenly crossed Annika's mind that Gerard didn't even know her real name. "You don't really know anything about me."

"Look at me, darling." He was staring intently into her eyes.

He was so good looking. So glamorous. *Why does he want me?*

"Never doubt my love for you."

He sounds like a character out of a soap opera. She almost giggled. But in spite of herself, Annika felt her heart melting with tenderness for this man who was looking at her with such love.

"We'll be happy together."

"Yes," she answered him. "You're right. We will be happy together." He kissed her then, so passionately, she could feel his desire running through him like a hot iron.

CHAPTER FOURTEEN

They were married in a small room off the main ballroom. A Spanish judge who was a friend of Gerard performed the ceremony. The only guests at the wedding were two of Annika's fellow models. Annika was a little disappointed by the smallness of the affair. Not that she wanted a huge society wedding, but she wouldn't have minded having a few more friends present.

"You may place the ring upon your bride's finger," said the judge.

Oh, my goodness, she thought. We forgot all about the ring.

Nervously, Annika gave Gerard her right hand.

"Wrong hand," hissed the judge.

"What?" Annika was bewildered. Gerard smiled at her. *How blue his eyes are.*

Gently, Gerard raised her left hand. He slipped a slim golden ring onto her finger. *He's thought of everything. I'm going to be so safe with him.*

She smiled up at him. He bent his head and kissed the hand on which he had just placed the wedding ring. I can love this man. I *will* love this man, she promised silently.

"I now pronounce you man and wife. You may kiss the bride."

Gerard enfolded her in his arms, pulling her tight against his chest, as if he wanted to hold her forever. "You are my beautiful darling and I will treasure you forever," he whispered into her ear.

***

Their wedding may have been small and private, but the wedding reception was a whole other story. Scarcely had the kiss ended, before the door to the ballroom was thrown open.

It was a full house.

Annika clutched her new husband's arm and stared, open mouthed, at the tables groaning with food, and the band, which sprang into tuneful action as soon as the door opened, but most of all at the crowds of people present. "Where did they all come from?"

"You didn't think I was going to let our wedding go uncelebrated, did you, my sweet treasure?"

There were Counts and Countesses, a Minister of the Royal Spanish government and even a minor royal Spanish Prince with his Princess, there were Americans, Spaniards, Italians, and South Americans; there was even an envoy from the North Korean embassy. Altogether, there were over three hundred guests. But, aside from Gerard and her two model friends, Annika knew no one.

People kept coming up to her and wishing her well, telling her how beautiful she looked and saying what a lovely couple she and Gerard made.

"Thank you." "Oh, do you think so?" "Yes, I'm very happy." "Thank you."

She and Gerard danced the first dance together, but after that, for the rest of the evening, she saw him only from a distance.

She danced almost every dance. She danced with the Prince, he was very charming, but his breath smelled of onions. She danced with a Texas cattleman who made her laugh, but stepped on her feet. She danced with the North Korean envoy to Spain who told her, in very careful English, that this reception was symbolic of the decadence of western culture.

Whirling around the floor in his arms, for the North Korean envoy was a very good dancer, Annika happily agreed. "Yes, isn't it wonderful?"

Her callousness undoubtedly shocked the envoy, but since he too loved to dance, he decided to ignore her politically incorrect and decadent western comment until the music stopped. As soon as the last note died off, he bowed coldly and marched off. Annika scarcely noticed. She barely had time to catch her breath before another pair of arms danced her away.

It was the Prince again. "You are a most beautiful bride," he told her.

Annika was used to being told she was beautiful, but this time, she felt it was really true. "It's because I'm a bride," she told him. "All brides are beautiful."

The prince considered her words gravely. "What you say is true, but some brides are far-away more beautiful than others."

With a laugh, she stopped dancing and dipped him a curtsy. "Thank you, Your Highness." They resumed dancing. "It's especially exciting to have you here," she said. "It's wonderful that you were able to be free on such short notice."

"It is true, three months is not much notification, but Gerard is a good friend of my family, and" he added with a twinkle, "I very much wanted to meet the most beautiful Annika."

"Three months?"

The prince apparently did not hear her. They continued to dance. She stopped abruptly. "Did you say Gerard invited you and your wife three months ago?"

"Yes. Is something the matter?"

"No." She forced a laugh. "Nothing at all." They resumed dancing. "How lucky we are that you could attend."

She was dumbfounded. She didn't know what to think. Was it an indication of Gerard's deep love for her? Was it shyness on his part? Or was it just damn arrogance?

I should be pleased, she thought. He wanted to marry me three months ago. Then she corrected herself. No! He *planned* to marry me three months ago. He actually invited guests to our wedding before he got around to mentioning it to me.

"Gerard loves you," she assured her reflection in the mirror. She had gone into the ladies' room to freshen up her make-up and regain her composure.

Carolyn, one of her co-models entered in time to hear her declaration.

"He sure does, honey. You are one lucky girl."

"Am I?" Annika watched as the woman carefully outlined her lips with a lip brush.

"All that money. He's good looking. Look at the kind of people that came to your wedding."

"Yes, you're right."

"Damn straight, I'm right. Just catch some prince coming to my wedding." Carolyn looked her up and down. "Why the long face?"

"Carolyn, he planned this wedding three months ago. He invited people."

"So?"

"He only proposed to me this afternoon."

The two women stared at each other and then Carolyn shrugged. "What do you care? You caught yourself a top prize."

Did I, she wondered? Who really caught whom?

CHAPTER FIFTEEN

After the reception, Annika bathed in her favorite peach scented bubble bath, slowly dried her soft limbs and massaged her body with a lotion so expensive that back home it would have fed an entire family for a week. She stood naked in front of the bathroom mirror, which was half fogged from the steam of her bath, and watched her reflection lift its arms and drop the silky nightgown over her head. The hem caught for a moment on her right breast before sliding down her slender body. She looked like a half-dressed goddess, emerging from the fog. Her thick dark red hair, curly from the bath, swirled around her pale face. I want this night to be beautiful. I want our marriage to be beautiful.

"Oh God," she prayed with all her heart, "Please let us have a wonderful life together." She opened the door and stepped into their bedroom. Gerard was waiting for her.

He was sitting on the far side of the romantic, king-sized, four-poster bed with a translucent, peach-colored canopy. "Peach colors are so flattering to the naked skin," he had said earlier.

He was dressed in dark blue silk pajama bottoms, and his chest was bare. How handsome he is, she thought.

He stepped toward her and took her in his arms. They kissed, sweetly, softly, gently. Annika opened her mouth slightly, but Gerard ignored the invitation. "I've wanted to make love to you from the day we first met," he whispered into her ear.

"Have you?"

"Did you doubt it?"

"You're so self-controlled, so respectful. I wasn't sure."

"Let me show you, Mrs. Rostand." He put his hands on

her shoulders and released first the right then the left strap of her nightgown. It fell smoothly down her body onto the floor. Annika let out a gasp of surprise. She had expected to undress herself, but this was exciting.

Am I supposed to undress him? Her hands went to the waistband of his pajama, but he firmly removed them. What happened next was the last thing she expected.

His arm around her waist tightened. Instinctively, she tried to move away, but he just strengthened his hold on her and swung her toward the bed.

"Gerard, wait."

He paid her words no attention. Indeed, he seemed not to even hear her. His face was set in mask-like determination. With one arm around her, he swung her naked body, facedown onto the bed. He followed after, flinging his body down on her.

"What are you doing?"

What he was doing was attaching loops of silken cords around her wrists. The cords were already fixed to the bedposts of the romantic four-poster bed.

Annika found herself lying face down, completely naked, her wrists firmly tied so she couldn't escape, and her husband of a few hours lying on her, his hands moving roughly over her body, his hot rasping breath in her ears. It was his breathing, she found most frightening. It was demented. He was mumbling words she couldn't make out. In just minutes, her dream had turned into a nightmare.

Talk to him, she ordered herself. "Gerard. Gerard!"

The response was more mumbled words, the rasping breathing continued.

"Gerard, you're hurting me." He wasn't, not really, but it wasn't pleasant either.

"I won't hurt you. I won't hurt you."

"Stop it! You are hurting me!" She tried to jerk away from his rough hands. He grabbed her hair and forced her back. Now, he really was hurting her. She carefully forced herself to relax. His grip on her hair also relaxed.

"Why don't you tell me what you want?" she asked. "I'll do it."

"This," it came out a growl. "This is what I want." He was plunging against her now. He entered her from the rear, plunging into her anus. He was sodomizing her! It hurt! Oh God, it hurt. Then, suddenly, it was over.

Thank God.

"Noooo!" It was a long drawn out cry of frustration. "Too soon." He rolled off her. She was left, still tied, still face down, and still uncovered. She turned her head, watching her new husband gasping in great lungs full of air, sweat shinning on his body. She was afraid to say anything, afraid to attract his attention. She turned away from the sight of him. A breeze blew in from the open window. The air had cooled considerably with the fall of night; she shivered.

"You're cold," his voice was soft, concerned. He pulled a light blanket up over her body. His hands were gentle, the perfect husband.

"Gerard, please untie me." She made her voice matter-of-fact, unthreatening, and non-judgmental.

Without a word, he reached over and untied the loops that imprisoned her wrists. Then, as if it were the most natural thing in the world, he wrapped his arms around her rigid body, cuddling her to him, kissed her shoulder and fell asleep. Annika, eyes wide open, stared at the ceiling and listened to her new husband's relaxed breathing. Once, when she was sure he was asleep, she tried to slip out of bed. Gerard made a sleepy baby sound and tightened his imprisoning arms around her. She lay awake for hours before finally falling into an exhausted sleep.

Their marriage went downhill from there.

CHAPTER SIXTEEN

They returned to New York and moved into Gerard's penthouse apartment on Sutton Place. They spent their weekends and much of the summer on their Long Island estate. They entertained often. Annika would look at her guests, chic and sophisticated. Did they live the way she lived? Did their husbands do to them what Gerard did to her?

She grew accustomed to being abused in bed, but soon Gerard expanded his repertoire to an occasional twisted arm or a really hard slap across the buttocks. Then the beatings started. Often, he would use a special scarlet leather belt that he had made just for that purpose. It hurt like hell. It made her scream when it was cutting into the soft skin of her buttocks and moan with pain when the beating was over.

She could hear her mother's voice loud and clear, "You made your bed, missy, now you'll just have to sleep in it. Serves you right."

She still worked occasionally. Gerard got a kick out of having a wife who was one of the world's top models. But sometimes her bruises interfered with an assignment. Then there would be a lot of rolling of eyes and "Oo-la, la!" They assumed the bruises were a result of rough love play. They also assumed Annika was a willing participant. They didn't realize she was in pain and frightened.

She was alone. To whom could she turn to? Gerard was not only powerful, wealthy and perverse, he was also ruthless. No one could stand against him. But mainly it was pride that kept her quiet.

She was drinking more, but it wasn't the liquor that was her worst habit. Annika had rediscovered cocaine.

She and Gerard settled into a horrible routine. Unless Gerard was in one of his sexually sadistic cycles, she was free to work, shop and party. He liked reading her name in the gossip columns.

"The beautiful Mrs. Gerard Rostand was one of the special guests at the opening of tinsel towns' newest nightspot."

There was invariably a picture of Annika, her head held high, laughing with delight at something being whispered into her ear by some man whose face, also invariably, was almost obliterated from the picture.

Gerard collected these clippings. Annika avoided looking at them. She knew how false they were.

Surprisingly, Gerard did not object to her cocaine use.

"I like to see you out of control, my darling." There were just two rules Gerard insisted on. "You must never, ever have an affair with another man, my darling, or I will kill you." He had smiled sweetly at her. His second rule was, "Don't even think of leaving me, Annika. The world is not big enough for you to hide."

Annika had just shrugged and slipped her coke dealer a few more hundred-dollar bills.

Cocaine made her life with Gerard bearable. And truthfully there were times, when he was making her crawl around like an animal while he plunged himself into her, beating her with his scarlet belt, she had felt a certain excitement.

Later, after a particularly humiliating and exciting sex scene, Annika, looking into the mirror, glass in hand, had saluted herself. "Congratulations, bitch," she said to herself. "Keep up the good work." She had then spoiled the hard-boiled effect by bursting into tears.

It was at one of Sari's New Year's Eve parties that Annika finally got a good look at herself. Sari had married Johnny-O, her musician boyfriend.

"It's like a fairy tale, isn't it, Annika?"

"A fairy tale?" Annika was sitting on Sari's bed, watching her former roommate finish dressing.

Sari turned, "The two of us. We were just dumb small town kids, and now you're married to this big society dude, one of the richest guys around. And I'm married to Johnny-

O. He's so famous that they have to sneak us in and out of hotels because of all the fans. A fairy tale, right?"

Annika caught sight of her own reflection in the mirror behind Sari. The reflection winked evilly at her. Annika shook her head in an effort to clear her senses. This time, her reflection stuck her tongue out at her.

"You think I'm using too much coke?" she asked Sari.

Sari, who was none too sober herself, was disappointed. "Don't you think it's like a fairy tale?"

"Of course it is. Who wouldn't envy us?"

Sari smiled happily and went back to applying eyeliner. "Johnny-O is such a great guy," she bubbled happily.

Was she serious, wondered Annika? What do they do in the privacy of their bedroom? Could Sari or any woman love a man who did what Gerard did? Weren't all men alike? She twisted her rings with her thumb.

"What's wrong with me?" She had spoken aloud.

"There's nothing wrong with you, honey," Sari assured her. "You're as beautiful as you ever were."

Annika followed Sari back to the party. Gerard, looking bored, was standing by the bar, a champagne glass in his hand and a sneer on his face. Automatically, Annika turned away from him and bumped into a woman she vaguely recognized.

"Sorry."

"No harm done. Here, let me get you a drink." Annika looked down at her empty hand. She could have sworn she had been carrying a glass. Had she already finished it? A full flute of champagne was thrust into her hand. "What shall we drink to?"

Annika tried to focus on the woman's face. "I don't remember your name."

The woman laughed harshly. "So much for fame. I'm Pia Swift, I anchor on ABC."

"Right. Right." The anchorwoman offered her hand. Somewhat dazedly, Annika shook it. "I'm Annika."

"Sweetheart, I know who you are. And I just want to say, you're even sexier in person than your photos."

"You think I'm sexy?"

"Very!" The blond anchorwoman leaned towards Annika.

There was something wrong here, but Annika was too fuzzy with coke and champagne to figure out what was happening.

"In fact," the anchorwoman moved closer to Annika, who automatically stepped back until stopped by the wall. "In fact," repeated the woman, "I had a very erotic dream about you the other night."

Annika laughed. "You and me?"

The other woman smiled a knowing smile. "Don't knock it, if you haven't tried it. And you haven't tried it, have you?"

Annika shook her head, no.

"Would you like to?" The blonde woman watched her eagerly.

"No."

"Are you sure?"

"No."

"I didn't think you were."

"I meant, no, I don't want to."

The woman handed Annika a gold-rimmed card. Blinking stupidly, Annika made out the name, Pia Swift, followed by a telephone number. "That's my private number."

Annika took the card, staring drunkenly down at it. The anchorwoman leaned forward, kissed Annika on the cheek and whispered in her ear, "I can make you happier than any man ever has." Then she was gone.

Annika's mind played back Swift's words, "happier than any man ever has." She snorted, considering whom she was married to, that wouldn't be hard.

There had only been two men in her life and Ray had only been a boy. They had been children playing at love. "But I was happy."

"What did you say?" Gerard was at her side. Annika showed him Swift's card. "She said she could make me happier than any man ever has."

Gerard threw back his head and laughed. "Now that

would be something to see. We must take her up on it sometime."

"We?"

"Oh, I would insist on...observing." Annika's skin crawled. Before she could reply, a staggering body roughly shoved against her.

Gerard put out his hand and steadied her. They both turned to confront the person who had nearly knocked her down.

It was a woman, excruciatingly thin with a ravaged, over made-up face. The straps of her dress had slipped off her thin shoulders and her dress had fallen around her waist, baring her breasts. The woman was crying and swearing at the same time.

"I said I want another line. Is that so hard for you to understand? Come on, be a buddy," she whined to an exasperated looking man ten years her junior. "Get me some coke!" It was a scream.

The whole room fell silent. The woman, indifferent to the effect she was having, focused on Gerard. "How about you, sweetie? Got any white lady for a pretty lady?" She leered at him with what she thought was an alluring smile.

Gerard, smiling back at the wreck of a woman, reached inside his jacket and brought out what looked like a sliver cigarette case. He carefully opened it. The case was filled with white powder. The woman squealed with pleasure. She produced a small silver spoon hanging from a chain around her neck and filled it with the powder. Precariously balancing on her three inch heels, she held the spoon with great care. With a look of almost sexual pleasure on her face, she brought the filled spoon to her nose and inhaled.

"Primo," she pronounced.

Gerard snapped the case shut. "The best that money can buy," he agreed.

"I didn't know you used cocaine," Annika said.

"My dear, I don't. I carry it for your needs. Isn't that what a good husband should do?"

Is that what a good husband should do?

"For God's sake, Magna, pull up your dress," said the

young escort of the drugged woman.

Magna? "Is that Magna?"

The young man, busy with the drugged woman, nodded.

"But she was a great beauty."

"I'm still a great beauty," screamed the woman. She was defiantly stripping the rest of her dress off. She stood there in nothing but panties and high heels. She was pitifully thin. "What's the matter, you fairy? Don't you like the sight of a real woman? I'm a great model. People pay a fortune to see me." She was crying now, great streaks of mascara rolling down her face.

"Magna, please." The young man gently pulled her dress up. Gerard, with a small smile on his face, was watching intently.

"Gerard, I want to go home." Suddenly the midnight bells began to ring.

People started counting down. "9-8-7-6-5-4-3-2-1!" All around them, people were kissing, yelling and blowing noisemakers. The band was playing "Auld Lang Syne."

"Happy New Year, darling." Gerard bent down and kissed her chastely on the lips, the perfect husband.

Later, at home, Gerard made love to her; one of the few times, he was not brutal or perverse.

Maybe this year will be different. A new beginning for both of us, she thought wistfully. She turned to him. "Happy New Year, darling." She was feeling very tender towards him.

He wrapped his arms around her and chuckled.

"What so funny?"

"The look on your face when that woman was coming on to you."

"I am not that way inclined," she said, trying to make light of it.

"Who knows that better than I? Still," here he laughed out loud, "I can't think of a nicer New Year's gift than letting me watch the two of you."

She sat up in bed and pulled the blankets up to cover her naked breasts. "It will never happen, Gerard."

"Never say never, darling." He laughed again and

turned on his side, facing away from her. He was asleep almost instantly.

When Annika finally fell asleep, she dreamed of Magna. "You think you're different than me," gloated the dream Magna. "But you're not, we're sisters, see?" In the dream, Magna held her arm next to Annika's. To Annika's horror, the two arms merged into one. "We're together until death."

Annika couldn't pull free. "No!" She was screaming. Magna turned her death head to Annika. She was no longer Magna; the face was Gerard's.

"Together 'till death."

Oh God. Annika bowed her head in defeat.

It was afternoon, when she finally awoke on New Year's Day. Gerard was gone. Exhausted from her nightmare, Annika sat on the edge of her bed, staring down at her pale feet. Suddenly the dream came back to her in full force. She jerked her arm up and examined it anxiously. It was still her arm.

The first time she had met Magna was nine years ago.

I wanted to be just like her, she marveled. Oh God, she now prayed, please don't let me be like Magna.

But I already am.

Fighting a crushing headache, she pulled herself out of bed. I need something to get me going. No! I will not become Magna. Just one more time won't hurt. No! No! No!

Frantically, she gathered all the cocaine and pills scattered throughout the apartment and stumbled into the bathroom. She flung up the toilet seat and then hesitated. Do it, do it, she urged herself. But I need them, she argued back.

Do you want to be like Magna?

Oh God, no. She flung the pills and powders into the toilet and flushed them down the drain.

"Happy New Year." She watched as the toilet swirled away the evil potions that had enslaved her for the last few years.

The next thing she did was go for a two-mile walk. She wanted to run, but her wind was gone. To her horror, she couldn't even walk briskly for more than two blocks. It was going to take a lot of work to get back in decent shape. She might not be able to do anything about her marriage to Gerard, but there was a lot she could do about herself.

The image of a stoned, naked, emaciated Magna kept flashing through her mind. That is not going to happen to me, she vowed.

When she returned, winded, to the apartment building she was greeted by Charlie, the doorman. "Happy New Year, Mrs. Rostand." He was beaming happily at her. Charlie was always happy and it wasn't just because of the large tip that Gerard always distributed to the building staff at this time of the year. As usual, Charlie's beaming cheerfulness put Annika in a good mood.

"Charlie, you're just the person to ask."

"Sure, Mrs. Rostand, anything you want to know."

"Is there a good gym in the neighborhood?"

"You're kiddin, right?"

"I've never been more serious in my life. I want to get back into shape."

"Geez, you always look beautiful to me, Mrs. Rostand."

She looked at him sharply, but Charlie's expression revealed nothing more than earnest good will. He was not flirting with her.

"Thanks, Charlie." She smiled at him. "You've made my day." He straightened happily at that. "But you still haven't told me if there's a gym in the neighborhood."

"Eight floors straight up."

"What?"

"The whole eighth floor is a gym. Didn't you know?"

Ruefully, she shook her head. She had been oblivious to so much that was going on around her. Unhappiness will do that to you, she thought. Unhappiness and drugs.

So Annika joined the gym. In keeping with the exclusivity of their building, the gym was huge, well equipped and sparsely used. The trainer ("My name is Richard but everyone calls me, Rick") was so happy to see a new face that he pumped her hand up and down and happily took her on a tour of his underused kingdom.

There was a lap pool. "Sixteen laps equal one mile."

"I can do that."

"A lap means back and forth."

"Oh. So that means..."

Rick nodded sympathetically, "Thirty-two, but hey, with a little steady work, you'll be doing a mile in no time at all."

There were free weights and universal machines. There were stair-masters and treadmills. There were air gliders and ski machines that worked both the upper and lower body. There was even a trapeze to swing on and fake walls for climbing. In short, there was everything necessary to become a walking advertisement for physical health.

"All you need to supply is perseverance," Rick told her earnestly. "You keep showing up and I'll work out a program designed just for you."

"It's a deal." They shook hands on it.

At exactly nine o'clock, the next morning Annika put herself into Rick's hands. By nine-thirty, she was covered in sweat, barely able to catch her breath and begging for mercy.

"We've only started," Rick protested.

"Tomorrow," Annika gasped. "I'll be back tomorrow."

"Well..." Annika got the impression Rick didn't expect to ever see her again. "OK, we'll plan on adding a half hour to tomorrow's session."

All Annika could do was nod in agreement. Too tired to shower and change in the locker room, she pulled a sweatshirt over her sports bra and shorts and staggered to the elevator. The maid let her in.

"Mrs. Rostand, are you all right?"

"Going to lie down for a while." Annika staggered on shaky legs over to her bed. She fell onto it face down.

The next day, a very sore, but determined Annika again presented herself at the gym. Rick was overjoyed. "You came back!"

"I said I would."

"They all say they will." Before she could change her mind, Rick set her to work doing warm-up stretches. He was the most exacting taskmaster Annika had ever had. "No, no, your back has to be straight. That's it. Atta-girl."

Annika felt a small thrill of pride in his praise.

"No, no, raise the arm slowly, slowly. Take it on a count of five."

"I did," she protested.

"You're counting too fast. Make it a count of ten."

She stretched every voluntary muscle in her body. Then he had her do it again. Finally, when she felt as rung out as a wet washcloth, he set her to doing weight lifting exercises on the universal machine. Finally, he called a halt.

"I'm done?" Her tone implied; and I survived?

"With the weight exercises. How are you at running?"

"I can barely stand," she protested. Her heart sank as Rick outlined the exercise he wanted her to go through.

"Uhm, Rick, I'm I still a little sore from yesterday."

Nothing could deter Rick. "Sure you are, Mrs. Rostand. That's how you know it's working."

"You mean I'm going to be stiff and sore every day?"

"Nah. See it's like this." Rick was very serious. The Gym was his Church. He was its priest on a special mission from the God of Physical Fitness, an unappreciated genius. "You don't work the same muscles two days in a row. You give them time to heal."

"Heal?"

"Sort of reflect-like."

"Ah-huh."

After the next agonizing twenty minutes, Annika found herself actually having a good time.

"Two more reps."

"I don't think I can."

"Believe me, you can."

As days lengthened into weeks Annika's sessions at the gym lengthened into two to three hours at a time. She stretched. "Straighten out that leg."

"It is straight."

"Straighter."

"I can't."

"Yes, you can."

He was right. It was amazing what her body could do if she just tried. Then it was his turn to rein her in.

"That's enough reps."

"I can do more."

"I know you can, but you're going into overkill." Reluctantly, she released the weights.

She ran three miles on the treadmill every other day. She swam a mile and a half on the other days. She stretched, she lifted, and she swung from the trapeze, hanging from her knees like a schoolgirl.

Annika stopped thinking of cocaine, of uppers and downers, and afternoon glasses of wine. She even stopped her incessant shopping. After all, if she didn't own it by now, it probably didn't exist.

She felt wonderful. Her modeling work picked up, she started going out to lunch with friends, got talked into serving on the board of the local library. Life was good during the day.

The nights, when Gerard was home, were a different matter. That was the only time she had a drink. That was the only time she felt powerless, without energy.

It was awhile before Gerard noticed any difference in her. He was at home one afternoon when she returned. "Where have you been?"

"The gym."

"The what?"

"I joined the gym."

"What gym?"

It's right in this building. On the eighth floor."

"There's a gym in my building?" He looked around the spacious living room, as if he expected to see barbells and treadmills sprouting up from the walls and floor.

Annika was amused. "You only own the penthouse, Gerard. The gym has been there for years."

"I never knew." He followed her into the bedroom and watched as she stripped off her sweat suit.

"A sweat suit? Rather plebeian for you, isn't it?"

She tried to contain her happiness. It was dangerous to be happy around Gerard, but she was still euphoric from her workout.

"I can't do reps in a ball gown, Gerard," she answered good-naturedly.

"You're looking very healthy."

"I'm trying to get back into shape."

"Why?"

"What do you mean, why?"

He grabbed her arm. "I mean, my precious wife, what are you up to?" Without thinking, she jerked free of him. His eyes widened in surprise. "I see," he said. "Getting strong are we?" With evil delight, he reached for her again, his hands closing around her upper arms like vices.

She cried out in pain. He loved that sound.

"Let me see you get away from me now, superwoman."

"Gerard," she protested. "I'm just taking care of myself. Just keeping in shape." His grip was tightening. "Gerard, you're hurting me."

"Am I?" He smiled. "Do you know why I'm hurting you?"

"What do you mean?" Annika had once tried to talk with Gerard about his sadistic behavior. She wasn't about to repeat that mistake.

"I'm hurting you, because I'm stronger than you are."

"Please, Gerard."

"I'm a man. I don't have to train. I will always be stronger than you."

"I know that." He had forced her down to her knees now.

"I am also smarter than you can even begin to imagine." His face was glowing with pleasure. "I know what you're trying to do."

"I'm just--"

"Don't lie to me again or I'll punish you."

Annika accepted defeat. "Yes, Gerard." Her voice was dull, empty, just the way she felt.

He started to stroke her hair. "Since you are already down there, my dear, would you mind accommodating me?"

"Accommodating you?"

"Fellatio." His voice was hard. "You do it so wonderfully. You might say it's your greatest talent." Now his voice had become almost a purr. She hesitated. "Do it!" Resignedly, she unzipped his fly.

Afterwards, he raised her gently to her feet and kissed her arms where bruises from his grip were already beginning to form.

"You may continue with your efforts at the gym, Annika. Just don't overdo it."

Why bother, she thought?

CHAPTER SEVENTEEN

Nevertheless, she had gotten into the habit, so she did go back. She worked harder than ever. "Hey, take it easy," Rick told her. "You training for the Olympics or something?"

She was standing with her feet flat on the floor, her arms reaching for the bar just slightly out of her reach. She gave a little jump, grabbed it, and then pulled herself up until her legs were hooked over the bar. From there, instead of swinging from the bar, she pulled herself up until she was sitting on it. She felt strong and triumphant, but only momentarily. Gerard's words came back to her loud and clear. "I will always be stronger than you. I am smarter than you."

"What's the matter, Mrs. Rostand? All of a sudden, you look real unhappy. You're doin' good."

She swung down off the bar. "Thanks, Rick. I guess this is just an off day for me." She didn't add, "What's the use?"

***

That night the phone rang.

"It's for you, Mrs. Rostand," the maid announced.

"Thank you, Rose." They had just finished dinner.

"Hello?"

"Annika?"

"Yes?"

"This is Pia."

"Oh, yes?" For the life of her, Annika couldn't remember any Pia.

"We met at Sari and Johnny'O's New Year's Eve party."

"Oh, yes." Annika flushed with embarrassment. It was the woman who had propositioned her.

"Have you been thinking about me?"

"I'm afraid not." Annika tried to make her voice very formal and disinterested. She didn't give a damn what the anchorwoman thought, she just didn't want Gerard to realize who was calling.

"My feelings are hurt." God, the woman was flirting with her.

"I can't help that. I'm going to have to cut this call short. We're going out and my husband is waiting for me."

"Is he?"

"You know how husbands are," Annika babbled inanely. How was she going to get this creature off the line?

"As a matter of fact, I do."

"What?" Annika had lost the thread of the conversation. She was acutely aware of Gerard sitting just feet away. He had lowered his newspaper and was frankly listening to her end of the conversation.

"I said I do know how husbands are. Especially yours."

Annika went cold. "What are you talking about?"

"I have it on good authority that Gerard has no objection to us seeing each other."

"Seeing each other," Annika repeated numbly.

"He wants to watch," said the voice of the blond anchorwoman.

"No!" It was not a denial, but a protest.

"Frankly, it kind of turns me on. How do you feel about it?"

"You have the wrong number," Annika mumbled wildly and slammed the phone down. Behind her, she could hear Gerard laughing.

"How could you?" She was in tears.

"How could I what, my dear?" Why did he always pretend he didn't understand how she felt? Sometimes she thought she was the one who was crazy.

"You contacted that...that woman." Annika could feel her stomach heaving. "You told her to call me."

"Absolutely correct." His tone implied, it was the most reasonable thing in the world for any husband to do.

"I told you, I'll never do that."

"And I told you, never say never." Like a cat stalking his prey, he walked over to where she stood trembling. He kissed her forehead. She knew better then to try to avoid him. "The day will come," he assured her. He stroked her bare arms. "The day will come," he repeated.

From that night on, she began to plan her escape.

CHAPTER EIGHTEEN

She made lists, then carefully tore them into tiny bits of paper, and then burned them.

Her first list was a series of questions.

(1) How---money?

(2) Where to go? Gerard must not be able to find me.

(3) When?

At first glance, money did not seem to be a problem. After all, she was free to spend to her heart's content. But that was credit cards, she seldom had any significant amount of cash.

She earned a great deal of money as a model. But ever since her marriage, Vic's agency had been depositing her checks into a retirement account where it was instantly transformed into stocks and bonds. Under normal circumstances, it was a wise financial decision, but under these circumstances, it meant she couldn't get her hands on her money without Gerard finding out. Gerard's CPA supervised the account. A statement was sent to Gerard on a quarterly basis. Like most rich people, Gerard paid very close attention to his financial statements.

The next statement was due in two and a half months. If she stopped depositing her money in that account, she was going to have to leave before the statement arrived.

Two and a half months. Ten weeks! The enormity of what she was about to do terrified her. She was going to defy Gerard; she was going to take away from him one of his prize possessions...her!

She reached for the phone to call Vic. Her hand was trembling so much that she was unable to dial. She tried to replace the receiver and instead, knocked the phone to the floor. God, she was such a coward!

"Would you like me to pick that up for you, Mrs. Rostand?"

Annika whirled around. Oh, God. What if the maid had overheard her calling Vic?

"Thank you, Rose." The maid's neat figure bent over and retrieved the fallen phone. As she replaced the receiver, it rang in her hands. "Rostand residence." She listened for a moment. "Good morning, Ms. Vic. I'll see if Mrs. Rostand is at home." She looked inquiringly at Annika.

"Yes, I'll take it. Thank you, Rose. That will be all." Annika waited until Rose had left the room and closed the door behind her.

"Vic. What a coincidence I was just about to call you." Her voice sounded strained and high pitched to her own ears, but Vic appeared not to notice anything unusual.

"I don't believe in coincidences, darling," said Vic's clear, cool voice. "A thing is either meant or it's not meant."

Annika smiled. Lately, Vic was always talking about good or bad omens and whether or not a thing was meant to be.

Vic was suddenly all business, "Can you do the Frangi shoot or not?"

"It's here in New York?"

"New York, Jersey, Connecticut. Darling, you'll be home every night to that gorgeous husband of yours."

"Lucky me." Then she told Vic how she wanted her future earnings handled.

If Vic was surprised by Annika's request, she said nothing.

That made one item she could cross off her list. At least when she left, she would have quite a lot of money with her.

"I'd like to work as much as possible in the next few weeks, Vic."

"Will hubby let you?"

"Yes. Probably. If the shoot is close by."

"I'll see what I can do."

"Thanks, Vic. You've been a good friend."

"Darling, don't talk that way."

"What way?"

"As if you have a fatal illness."

"No, Vic, I've never been healthier."

Question number two; where to go? A foreign country? No good. Gerard had contacts everywhere and she would be at a disadvantage in a foreign culture. Back to Florida? Absolutely not! Well, where then? Someplace, neither she nor Gerard had ever been. In her frenzied state, all that came to mind was Iceland.

No, Kansas! It was in the middle of the country. Gerard was always making fun of mid-westerners. She would go to Kansas and get a job, as ...as...doing what? She would never be able to model again. Her photographed face was too famous. What else could she do?

When she first came to New York, she had thought of getting a job as a waitress. Better late than never. "Going to Kansas City," she hummed to herself. Gerard would never find her in the mid-west, working as a waitress in a small out-of-the-way restaurant.

The next few weeks were busy ones. Early every morning, she worked out at the gym and every day she worked as a model.

Officially, it was still winter, but the magazines were already doing layouts for their summer issues. That meant that, despite the freezing cold temperature, if the sun was shining, Annika, dressed in a bathing suit, waded bravely out into the icy waters, and splashed with the happy innocence of a child (or an idiot) while photographers snapped away like crazy. They only stopped if the light changed or if Annika's skin became so blue with cold that it clashed with the bathing suits.

The money kept adding up. Annika had over fifty thousand dollars in her secret savings account when Gerard declared it was time to move to their Long Island estate.

"Already?"

"Mrs. Adams has already sent out the invitations."

She had forgotten all about the garden party, but Mrs. Adams, Gerard's efficient secretary, had not.

They had been married seven years and each year, no matter how successful the party, Gerard managed to find some reason she had "absolutely ruined it." Invariably, it gave him an excuse for some particularly special form of sexual barbarity. Annika was convinced Gerard spent as much time planning what he was going to do to her as he did planning the party, probably more.

At any rate, the move to Long Island was the end of her moneymaking. There was still a month to go before Gerard would receive news of the financial changes she had made. He would understand the implications immediately.

I'll have to leave no later than a week after the garden party, she realized. No I don't. I don't have to go. When he asks me about the money, I can tell him I'm saving up to buy him an absolutely fabulous present. He'll be flattered. He might believe me. He might.

Coward! Coward, she raged at herself.

She was terrified of crossing Gerard. In her heart, she knew there was no way she could escape his network of spies. She would be found and then dragged ignobly back to face the music. And what music it would be! Annika whimpered to herself just thinking about it.

She paced in frantic circles around her room. Go or stay? Go or stay?

It's not so bad here. I'm the fabulous Mrs. Rostand. Do I really want to give up all this to be some two-bit waitress in a dreary, greasy hamburger joint?

Ringing her hands, she continued pacing from one end of her luxurious cage to the other.

TRAPPED. TRAPPED. TRAPPED.

She felt as if her heart would burst with fear.

Face it; she finally admitted to herself, you will never have the courage to leave Gerard.

***

The day before the garden party Annika woke with dread. She moved sluggishly through an abbreviated version of her morning routine. When she appeared in the kitchen in search of coffee, the cook was startled.

"Thought you was goin' jogging, like usual?"

"I didn't feel like it." She moved zombie-like through the rest of the morning. There really wasn't much for her to do. Gerard had issued detailed orders to the staff. They didn't need any input from her.

It was lunchtime before she saw Gerard. "What's the matter with you," he asked sharply?

"Nothing."

"You're not eating anything."

"I'm not very hungry."

"Surely, you're not coming down with something on the eve of my garden party?" His voice was now silky smooth, always a warning sign to Annika.

"I'm fine, Gerard." She sat up straight and tried to swallow some of the excellent mushroom and sherry soup Cook had prepared.

She would have liked to avoid Gerard, but that proved impossible. For some reason, Gerard had decided her advice and opinions were essential to the success of his party. He asked her about the flower arrangements, the seating plan, even color combinations.

"But Gerard, all this has been set for weeks. The caterer knows what to do."

"This is our party, Annika, not the caterer's. It will reflect on us. It should mirror our taste."

"My taste?" She was frankly, startled.

"Of course," he answered smoothly. "After all, you are the lady of the house." He was watching her with bright evil eyes, smiling his cat-playing-with-a-mouse-smile.

He insisted she stay by his side all afternoon. "So we can enjoy each other's company."

It was one of the longest days Annika had ever known. But worse was to come.

She had changed into her nightgown and was standing for a moment on the balcony of their bedroom, looking out at the night sky. He came silently up behind her and in a most business-like manner, pulled the thin nightgown up over her head and threw it back into the room. She was left standing completely naked on the balcony, with the lights of the bedroom blazing behind her.

"Gerard!" she protested. He ignored her and shoved her slim body up against the cold marble balustrade. He kissed her neck and shoulders. There was nothing lover-like about his lovemaking. He was rough and indifferent to her as a person. "Gerard, I'm naked. There are people about."

"Only the servants." He maneuvered her over to the corner of the balustrade and bent her backward. The cold stone cut into her back. With rough hot hands, he pushed her legs apart and entered her. He came almost immediately. "Damn! Damn."

He moved away from her. Annika, her back aching from the pressure of the marble balustrade, was too frightened to move. She hardly dared take a deep breath.

He paced back and forth in front of her. "Do you know what I want?" he asked suddenly.

"What do you want?"

"A boy."

She moved an inch or two away from the railing. "What do you mean?"

"I want to take a young boy and do to him what I do to you."

"Oh, my God."

He turned on her. "What did you say?"

"Nothing." There was silence as Gerard continued pacing.

"Have you ever done this to a boy?" she finally asked.

"No. I don't want some street scum. I fancy a young boy..."

"How young?" she interrupted.

"Eight, ten, eleven."

"A child." It was a cry.

"A boy child. Of good family. He and his mother, both mine." Gerard stopped his pacing and came over to her. He stroked her naked stomach. "Someday, you'll become pregnant. We'll have to think about that."

Her skin went icy wet with cold sweat. Nausea pushed up into the saliva in her mouth. Annika pushed past him and ran into the bathroom, slamming the door behind her. She could hear Gerard laughing, as undoubtedly, he could hear her retching into the toilet.

As she washed her green tinged face, she made her

decision. Maybe I'm not brave enough to run away and make a life for myself. But I am brave enough to kill myself. So Help Me God!

It had come to this; death was a comforting thought.

CHAPTER NINETEEN

But she wasn't dead. Instead, she was in her car, miles from Gerard and his ruined garden party, chasing a long departed rainbow. No, by God, she wasn't dead.

***

At the exact time Annika was speeding through the Holland Tunnel on her way out of Manhattan; Gerard was receiving their guests. The rain had started up again and was pouring down as the first car drove under the wide portico at the side of the house and discharged its passengers.

"My man will park your car. Don't worry about it," Gerard assured each guest as they climbed out of their cars under the cover of the green Chinese tiled roof of the portico. Outwardly, Gerard Rostand was all welcoming charm, but inwardly he was raging. His rage was equally divided against God for daring to rain on his garden party and on Annika for daring to be so late in returning from the damn store.

"Annika? Should be here momentarily. You know women, always something they've forgotten at the last minute."

The party was a disaster. Despite the covered portico, despite the fact that the guests stepped from their cars directly undercover, they still managed to track mud across the three hundred year old Persian rug that was his special pride. His damn guests were nothing but barbarians.

The caterers, who advertised they were "renowned for dealing with any and all contingencies," made a hash of transferring their outdoor serving mode to indoor service.

Swearing to himself, he watched as a ham-handed waiter, probably recruited from a homeless shelter, place a serving spoon, instead of the correct silver serving fork and spatula set next to a plate of champagne pâté.

He would never use the firm again. He intended to inform that idiotic woman who was in charge in no uncertain terms, but not until after the party was over. They were doing a rotten enough job when they were trying their best. Gerard could only imagine how these lower class types would react to being told this was their last job with him.

And where the hell was Annika? Naturally, everyone asked.

As time went on, *would this damn party never end*, he became more and more anxious. Despite his glib comments on the general tardiness of women, it was not like Annika. If there was one thing he had taught her and taught her well, it was that he did not like being kept waiting.

The rain was still pouring down. The music, meant to be a gentle background noise outdoors, was so loud, it was almost impossible to hear oneself think. Finally, he told the musicians to take a break, a long break.

"Could dear Annika have had an accident?"

"Annika is an excellent driver, Monique."

"Then where is she?" He had no answer. "Don't tell me the perfect couple is having a tiff?"

"We never argue."

A raised eyebrow was the only reaction to that.

"Perhaps you had better call...someone."

"Highway patrol," suggested a pipe-smoking idiot.

"She wasn't on the highway. Just ran into town for a last minute...." *What the hell had she been getting?*

"The local police then."

"Yes, perhaps you're right." A small group of people watched with hungry eyes as he reached for the phone. "I'll call from the other room. No sense in interrupting the party." He signaled urgently for the musicians to resume playing, and then moved down the hall to his study.

He was damn well going to find out what had happened to Annika. For her sake, that bitch had better already be in a hospital. If not, he would put her there himself.

***

She was out of Manhattan now. Annika opened up the

Jag and roared across New Jersey. She was halfway to Allentown, before it occurred to her to get off the highway and take the back roads. Gerard would be looking for her. He would report her missing to the police. There was no way he would just shrug and let her go. Gerard was an important person, a rich man and she was a rich man's wife. Streaking down the highway at ninety miles an hour was just asking to be pulled over and returned to him. She slowed and took the next exit. She needed a map.

Pulling into a gas station, using her credit card to pay, she filled the tank and bought a map. The main highways were clearly delineated, but the rest was a squiggle of thin lines. I'm in Pennsylvania now. If I take this to, to.... Damn, you can't even tell where one state ends and another begins. Here it is! I go to West Virginia over the Allegheny Mountains.

I can go anywhere I want, she thought in wonder.

I'm free, I'm free, her heart sang. She roared out of the gas station, heading away from the highway.

By late afternoon, she was well up into the mountains. The next time she stopped for gas, it was at a small wooden general store with an old-fashioned gas pump out front. It was so far off the main roads that she was able to fill her tank before going in to pay.

A heavyset woman, about her own age, was sitting behind the counter reading a fashion magazine and munching on a donut.

"Afternoon," the woman said around a mouthful of donut.

"Good afternoon. That donut looks good."

The woman indicated a mostly empty box, heavily stained with grease, still containing two donuts, the frosted kind with colored speckles on top.

"They were fresh this morning."

"Looks good to me. I'll take both of them." Annika helped herself to a carton of milk.

"Gas, donuts, milk," the woman rang up the purchases. "Anything else?"

"No, that's it." Annika handed over her credit card.

"Nice looking car you have." The woman peered out the window. "What kind is it?"

"Jaguar."

"Geez. Never seen one like that before. It's real pretty."

Annika was suddenly terribly conscious of her credit card in the other woman's hand. My God, what was she thinking? Gerard would be able to trace her by her card.

She almost grabbed it out of the woman's fingers.

"Haven't finished yet," the woman objected pulling away from her.

"Sorry."

"Something wrong with this card?" She peered suspiciously at Annika.

"No, it's fine. I just thought you were done. You can check it if you want to."

"We always do," the cashier assured her.

Shut up, Annika silently ordered herself. You're talking too much. This woman will remember you for a long time.

"You look kind of familiar. I thought that when you walked in."

Annika carefully kept her eyes off the magazine the woman had been reading. She knew the issue. She was featured on several pages wearing Smitty's latest creations.

"I've never been around here before," she assured the woman truthfully.

Taking back the credit card, Annika walked casually out of the store, got into her car and drove off at a careful moderate pace. Her hands were trembling and her breath was coming in great gulps of fear.

"Dumb, dumb, dumb. You are so dumb."

As long as she used her credit cards, she might as well be wearing a chain around her neck with the other end held tightly in Gerard's fist. Out of sight of the general store, Annika pulled off the road. Her elegant, meticulously cared for hands trembled as she opened her purse. Aside from her credit cards, she was carrying only four dollars and fifty-three cents.

All that money she had earned and hidden from Gerard. Was there no way she could get a hold of it? She didn't have her checkbook with her. She didn't even remember the account number.

Note: next time you hide money, memorize the account number!

Damn. Don't panic, she ordered herself. Think this through. You've used your credit card twice already. That means Gerard will be able to track you this far. She looked around her. She was in the middle of Pennsylvania. She could be heading anywhere in the country from here. As long as she didn't stick around, following her this far would really be of no help to Gerard.

Ten miles down the road, Annika came to a small town. At the ATM, she withdrew all the machine would grant her, five hundred dollars. Remembering her arrival in New York, with what she had then considered a fortune of three hundred dollars Annika had to laugh. *At least I made a profit.* The ATM spat out her credit card. After counting the money, she shoved the card into her pocket.

Wanting to get as far away from that particular ATM as possible, she continued driving until way past darkness. Only the welcoming lights of a small motel at last persuaded her to stop for the night. She paid cash.

The motel room was basic in the extreme, a bed, toilet, a shower that dripped all night and a TV. A tired Annika channel surfed aimlessly. The only thing on at this hour was an old movie and the news. There was a short Kentucky Derby segment.

"With the Kentucky Derby only six days away," said the off screen TV announcer, "knowledgeable eyes are focusing on three colts. Mary's Joy is the clear favorite." There was a shot of a beautiful and very nervous looking animal prancing around. "Next on the list is Neutron." Another shot of a horse that, except for its color, could have been the twin of the first horse. "There is also, Dangerous Ground." An equally beautiful, but much calmer looking horse appeared. "Dangerous Ground is considered by many to be a long shot."

Annika clicked off the TV and fell onto the bed. The mattress was both thin and lumpy. She slept like the dead.

CHAPTER TWENTY

Six hundred miles away, Ray was also exhausted. A new foal was being born every night, sometimes two in a night. So far, knock on wood, all had survived. If this kept up, and if he didn't drop from exhaustion, TearVale would be a going concern way ahead of schedule.

Uncharacteristically, the next foal decided to make his entrance in the early evening. Ray and Mike, Ray's lone employee, were the midwives in attendance. It was one of the easy births. The mare lay down, delivered herself of a perfectly formed baby, got up, ate some hay, heard the nickering of her new child, turned an enquiring eye toward the strange sound and immediately fell in love. The attraction was mutual.

Mike and Ray stood quietly to one side watching mother and child. "An easy one," breathed Mike.

"May they all go so well," agreed Ray. It was his daily prayer.

The sound of a car driving up diverted their attention. Mike went to check, while Ray stayed for a few minutes longer to enjoy the sight of the two beautiful animals.

Mike returned with Jack Simmons. Jack Simmons was a small man with a large bank account. He compensated for his small stature by spending big. One of the things he had bought was Dangerous Ground.

He and Ray had an agreement. After the Kentucky Derby, win or lose; Dangerous Ground would be retiring to TearVale to stand at stud. They had made their deal over an abundance of drinks and good fellowship in the bar after a meeting of the local Thoroughbred Club. For Ray it was a godsend.

Acquiring Dangerous Ground was a major coup for

such a new smallholding as TearVale. Ray found himself holding his breath every time he and Jack Simmons got together. Until Dangerous Ground was actually bedded down in his stall in TearVale and was chowing down on the gourmet rations that he well deserved, Ray was on tenterhooks.

All three men stood silently watching the equine mother and child. The mare, after a quick glance at the newcomer, went back to thoroughly licking her baby from its pointed little ears to its tiny tail.

"Beauty," grunted Simmons.

"Yep," agreed Mike.

Always restless, Simmons shifted impatiently from foot to foot. "I want to talk to you," he said to Ray.

"All right. Come in and have a drink." As the two turned towards the house, Ray added over his shoulder to his employee, "Mike, keep checking on those two for the next few hours."

"Yep."

Ray's study was a large, whitewashed room with a scuffed wooden floor, an old and much battered desk on which rested a laptop, a phone, a dictionary and a coffee mug holding several pens.

Around the walls were bookcases holding hundreds of books; history of the horse books, studbooks, equine veterinary books, encyclopedia of the horse books and individual pedigree records for hundreds of horses. There were also two mismatched comfortable looking armchairs and an old couch that had seen better days. The study windows overlooked the stable yard. Ray poured them each a scotch and soda.

"TearVale is looking good."

"Thanks." Ray waited, but now Simmons seemed in no hurry to explain why he was here.

Ray hated waiting for things to develop, much preferring to meet them head on. This was not always the smartest policy, as the prison chaplain had pointed out. How had the Chaplin put it? "You might consider cultivating a mite more patience, Ray. Not everything has to be dealt with immediately. Give things a chance to develop naturally. Give yourself a chance."

With a sigh, Ray reined in his impatience. The chaplain was right. Whatever Simmons had come for today, he would get around to it. No reason to rush things. Still...

"You want to take a look at the stallion barn?" Ray invited. "See the skylights we've put in? Dangerous Ground's going to be treated like a king."

Simmons took a long drink. "That's one of the things I came by to talk about, Ray."

"Skylights?"

"Dangerous Ground."

"Nothing wrong with him is there? He'll be okay for the Derby?"

"This deal that you wanted..."

"You mean this deal we have."

"I may have had a few more drinks than were good for me at the time."

"So?"

Simmons put his glass down. "I've been rethinking things."

Ray's eyes narrowed. "We have a written agreement, Jack. After the KD, win or lose, Dangerous Ground comes here to TearVale and stands stud."

"Now that's not how I remember it."

Ray glared at the other man, made himself take a deep breath and carefully put his own glass down. "We're not relying on memory, Jack," he said softly. "That's why we wrote out a contract...on paper...in ink...witnessed by two completely uninvolved people. As I remember it, you wanted to make sure I didn't 'weasel out of it'. Your words."

Simmons waved a dismissive hand. "Ain't worth the paper, it's writ on."

"Drop the hayseed act, Jack, you went to Harvard."

"Which is why I know the contract's invalid. Truth is Ray; I'm not convinced TearVale is up to handling as big a deal as Dangerous Ground. You don't have the connections."

"We discussed all this, Jack. It's why the contract is so

heavily weighted in your favor."

Simmons got to his feet, all five foot four inches of him. Ray was careful not to stand also. He didn't want to remind Simmons of the differences in their height.

When Simmons spoke, his voice was cold and final. "The bottom line is I've changed my mind, Ray."

"Change it all you want, we still have a contract." Ray deliberately kept his voice mild.

Simmons snorted. "Such as it is. Tell you what, Ray. I'm a fair man. I'll pay you a kill fee for the contract."

Ray had had enough. He stood up, looming over the smaller man. "There are no provisions made for a kill fee in our contract, Simmons. You said there was no need for it. 'I'm a man of my word,' you said. "In fact," Ray deliberately imitated Simmons nasal twang, 'My handshake is honored around the world,' is how I believe you put it."

"I was drunk!"

"Tough!"

"Riverwalk Stud is interested. They have a big name."

Ray, feeling as if he were choking with rage, carefully unclenched his fists. "We discussed all this, Jack. In a big outfit like Riverwalk, Dangerous Ground will just be one of many fine horses. Here he'll be the star."

"They have a name, contacts," muttered Simmons.

"You don't need their name. Dangerous Ground will be the king, the contacts will come." He tried to keep his voice reasonable, steady and sure. Don't beg, he ordered himself. Christ, was it all going to slip through his fingers?

"They made me a tempting offer."

"Fuck their offer. We have a deal. Dangerous Ground comes to TearVale after the KD, win or lose."

"And if he doesn't run in the Derby?"

"What?"

"You heard me."

"Why wouldn't he run in the Derby?"

"His coming to TearVale is contingent on his running in the Derby. If he doesn't run, he doesn't have to come here."

"Jesus Christ!"

"I'm willing to pay you a generous kill fee."

"No!" What good would a kill fee do him? Dangerous Ground was a chance in a lifetime. No way was he going to let this little dickhead weasel out of their deal.

The little dickhead stepped forward, jabbing his finger into Ray's shirtfront. "Then if you want Dangerous Ground to run in the Derby, you come up with the rest of the entry fee."

"That's fifteen thousand dollars!" Ray fought the impulse to grab the little twerp by his throat and shake him.

"It's due in two days. What's the matter, Ray? You're a smart guy, right? A guy who can think on his feet. You can raise a lousy fifteen thousand, can't ya? Simmons stared coldly at Ray. "On the other hand, I'm willing to go as high as thirty thousand for a kill fee."

The bastard!

"Oh, I'll get the fifteen thousand all right," said Ray.

"Well then, we got no problem, do we?" Simmons turned on his polished boots, the ones with the high cowboy heels and the lifts inside, and strode from the room. He reminded Ray of a neighbor's vicious little terrier who was always attacking the huge and good-natured Rufus.

"Which makes me Rufus," he thought with disgust. Rufus who couldn't even learn the elementary command to sit.

Where the hell am I going to get fifteen thousand dollars in two days?

CHAPTER TWENTY-ONE

It rained again during the night but, Annika, wrapped in a warm cocoon of motel blankets, was oblivious to the drumming downpour. When she awoke in the morning, it was to glorious sunshine. She barely stopped for coffee, so eager was she to get on the road again.

She was not the only one on the road that morning.

A pair of hitchhikers had been sticking to the back roads for several months now. By this time, they were very good at what they did; their technique was finely honed. There hadn't been a slip-up in weeks.

They preferred couples or singles. They had learned the hard way not to even try when young children were present. Parents were too protective, too paranoid about strangers. Frankly, with all those scary TV programs it was a wonder anyone was willing to give them a lift.

Grassy picnicking areas just off the back roads were their best hunting grounds. Helpful local communities even supplied picnic tables and benches to lure weary travelers.

All the hitchhikers had to do was sit back and wait for a traveler who fit their preferred profile. They talked like that to each other, using words like "preferred profile" and "optimal timing." It gave their activities an extra fillip of style, as if they were FBI agents on the trail of a serial killer. He especially liked the term "serial killing," but she preferred "selective culling." She was the daughter of a farmer...deceased.

They were a few miles west of a Tyner, a small West Virginia town. It had rained during the night, and they were wet, irritable, and as usual, broke.

Down to their last cigarette, they squabbled listlessly over it until she ended the discussion by cuffing him across his face. He raised his arm to retaliate, thought better of it and started to curse her out, checked out the expression on her face and fell silent. She smiled lovingly at him. "Good boy."

By mid-morning, the sun had come out, the grass was green and inviting, but they were still broke and beginning to get hungry.

"Someone's coming." They both froze.

"They're stopping."

"Come on." The two melted into the wooded area surrounding the picnic site as Annika's cream-colored Jag swung off the country road and pulled to a stop. The hitchhikers leaned forward, their eyes hungry and excited.

Annika was singing. The sun was shining, the countryside was beautiful and she was heading toward some of the most beautiful horse country in the world. She was free. She had decided to go to the Derby. She might even place a bet. Wouldn't that be a kick if she picked the winner of the Kentucky Derby?

I should put the top down, she thought. Let the wind rush through my hair, mess it up, whirl it around, make me look like a witch. The thought made her laugh. Almost everything made her laugh today.

One of the nice things about taking back roads, thought Annika, was that you had to go slow. There was time to look around, time to stop and examine anything interesting. On the highway, everything went past so fast, before you had decided you wanted to stop, you were already past the reason you wanted to stop.

Up ahead, she could see a picnic bench under a large shady tree. She pulled up and just sat in the car, enjoying the peace. She could hear a brook flowing busily over some rocks. In the tree, two birds were having a loud and raucous argument. The air smelled fresh and sweet, the sun was warm on her face. Annika got out of the car and stretched her whole body. She felt like a contented cat.

She reached into the window from the passenger side and pulled out a bottle of water. As she straightened, her eyes locked with a pair of dark brown eyes that were staring at her from across the road.

"Well, hello there, buddy," she said. Leaving her car, she crossed the road to stand a careful foot away from the barbed wire fence that was all that separated her from one of the biggest black bulls she had ever seen.

"You are a beauty," she told him. Actually, he was one of the meanest, ugliest looking characters she had ever met, but even mean, ugly bulls like a little flattery, and who knows, maybe to a lady cow he was beautiful. "I saw a cousin of yours in action in Madrid."

Beast and beauty studied each other. Carefully, she reached out a hand and touched his forehead. He didn't move. She moved her hand further up on his head until it rested on a clutch of black curls between two wicked looking horns. The hair felt slightly oily and very coarse. "You need a good shampoo, buddy." He seemed mesmerized by her boldness. She scratched his curls for him. The bull closed his eyes, enjoying the attention. Suddenly, he snapped his eyes open, snorted and flung his head up. Hastily, Annika removed her hand. The bull glared, then turned and trotted away. "All I said was you needed a shampoo," she called after him. He did not turn back. "Guess I was too personal. Gotta watch that." Grinning, she turned back to her car. Two people were standing next to it. They were watching her carefully.

Annika, the New Yorker, did not take the sudden appearance of strangers casually.

"Who are you?" She clutched the bottle of water, her only weapon.

"Hi, there," said the man. He was around six feet tall and had long, greasy-looking hair, which he had pulled back into a ponytail. There was a teardrop tattooed under his right eye. He also wore a skull & crossbones earring in his left ear. The earring worried Annika. In her experience, people who wore emblems, identifying themselves as dangerous, frequently tried to live up to the image. However, his voice was pleasant and his smile friendly.

"Hello," Annika replied. "Where did you come from? I didn't hear your car."

The female spoke this time. "No car." She was shorter than Annika. Her hair was cut so short it looked as if she had shaved her head and it was just now growing out. She, too, wore a skull & crossbones earring, also a nose ring and a navel ring. Her tee shirt was short enough that it was easily visible. Around her navel, she had a tattoo of a snake with its mouth wide open. The snake's tongue was extended and it was positioned so it looked as if the naval ring actually pierced the snake's tongue.

Both the man and woman were dirty with a griminess that comes from long time, dedicated neglect of basic hygiene.

They stared at her. She stared back. Finally, Annika broke the silence. "Nice tattoo."

They both smiled. Neither said anything.

"Well, nice talking to you." Annika made her voice casual, but dismissive. She wanted them to realize, as far as she was concerned, the conversation was over. She started towards her car. Neither man nor woman moved to get out of her way.

"Mind giving us a lift?" It was the woman who spoke. Despite her appearance, her voice was mid-western friendly.

"Sorry." Annika was conscious of how stuffy she sounded. "I make it a policy never to pick up strangers."

The man smiled. "Sure, we can understand that." He didn't seem at all put out. Annika hesitated; maybe she'd been living in New York for too long? Despite their appearance, they seemed pleasant enough.

The two hitchhikers parted to let her pass. As they moved, she was able to see the portion of her car their bodies had been hiding. Her right rear tire was flat.

She stopped. "It's flat."

The woman. "Yes ma'am, it is."

The man. "Want me to fix it?"

"No. I can do it myself." They smiled unbelieving smiles. Their smiles were getting on her nerves. "Thanks, anyway."

They stood there watching her. "Are you going to watch me?"

"Nowhere else to go," said the man.

"Not until another car comes along," said the woman.

"Maybe they'll give us a ride."

"You didn't even say where you're going." Annika was getting impatient with their weird looks and deadbeat behavior. "I may be going in a completely opposite direction."

"Doesn't matter," said the man.

Deciding to act as if they weren't present, Annika opened the trunk of her car and reached in for the jack and spare tire. She got the jack out all right, but the spare seemed fastened down in some way. She hadn't changed a tire in over eleven years.

Horribly aware of the two hitchhikers watching her, Annika scrabbled ineffectually at the tire. Out of the corner of her eye, she saw the woman approach and bend down to pick up the jack Annika had placed on the grass. She smiled at Annika.

"Why don't you let Eddy-Bob fix the tire?"

The man moved in on the other side of her. He, too, was smiling. Gently he moved against her. Annika froze then moved quickly out of the way. Eddy-Bob was grinning.

He reached into the trunk, did something that freed the spare tire, lifted it out and leaned it against the car. When he held out his hand, the woman placed the tire iron and jack into his hand. Without any further conversation, Eddy-Bob quickly exchanged the spare for the flat tire. Annika had to admire his quickness and skill.

He placed the flat tire and tools back into the trunk of her car, slammed the truck closed and handed Annika the keys to the now locked trunk.

"You oughtta stop at the next town and have that tire repaired, ma'am."

"Yes, I will. Thank you." Oh, what the hell. "What direction are you going?"

"Like I said, it doesn't matter."

"I'm going west. I can give you a ride to the next town if that will be any help."

"That's just fine, ma'am. Thank you."

Well, they were behaving nicely.

The woman, ("Hi, I'm Josie.") sat next to Annika; Eddy-Bob sat in the back directly behind Annika. Whenever she looked up, she could see him watching her in the rearview mirror. He was humming to himself. The humming got on Annika's nerves almost as much as their constant smiling.

They'll be getting out soon, she reminded herself. The next town can't be but a few miles. I can put up with anything for a few miles.

"Nice watch."

"Hum?"

"Sure nice watch you got there." Josie was watching her intently.

"Thank you."

"What kind is it?"

"I don't know, it was a gift."

"Looks like a Rolex to me." Annika shot her a surprised look. The last thing she had expected was this woman to be able to identify a Rolex watch. "Must be nice to know someone who gives out Rolexes as gifts."

Her tone was insinuating. Trying to diffuse her own uneasiness, Annika answered her briskly. "Maybe Eddy-Bob will get you one for your birthday."

The idea seemed to stun the woman. "Eddy-Bob? You got to be kidding!" She burst into laughter. "Hear that Eddy-Bob? You gonna get me a Rolex watch for my birthday?"

"Cunt like you was hatched, not born. Don't have no birthday."

Josie's laugher stopped as though cut off with a switch. She had been sitting half turned so she could look at Annika, and with only a slight turn of her head, face Eddy-Bob. Abruptly, she turned and stared straight ahead. Annika thought she was either offended by what Eddy-Bob had said or frightened, but it was neither.

Speaking through clenched teeth, her lips barely moving, without looking at either Eddy-Bob or Annika she said, "I want someone to give me a Rolex watch for my birthday. You know when my birthday is Eddy-Bob?"

Eddy-Bob said nothing. Josie turned to face him. "You know what day I was hatched, Eddy-Bob?"

Through the rearview mirror, Annika watched Eddy-Bob. He hung his head, refusing to meet Josie's hard look. "Fuck, I didn't mean nothing." It came out a mumble, but both Josie and Annika understood him.

"Well, I did mean it, Eddy-Bob," Josie assured him. "As sure as you got all your arms and legs, I meant it."

Annika saw Eddy-Bob look up at Josie. His face had gone dead pale. He looked terrified.

In spite of her own discomfort with the two of them, Annika was impressed. She had never seen a man afraid of a woman before. It was upsetting. It was also, just a little, thrilling.

"Here's a gas station," said Annika with relief. The station was situated by itself at the crossroads of four country roads. There were two pumps, a work bay and a small store. A mechanic was working on an old station wagon; he didn't even look up as they drove in.

Pulling up to the gas pump, Annika jumped briskly out of the car. She purposely left the car door open as an invitation to her two passengers to leave. She was careful to take her car keys with her.

"Where you going?" asked Josie.

"To pay for the gas."

"Why don't you use a credit card?"

"I prefer not to."

"Wait."

Impatiently, Annika turned to face the girl. "What?" By now, Eddy-Bob had climbed out of the car and was standing next to his partner.

"Eddy-Bob will pay."

Eddy-Bob seemed stunned by this announcement. "Huh?"

"That's not necessary." Annika turned again toward the gas station office.

"Yeah. We'll pay. With our credit card."

Those two had a credit card?

"Go ahead, Eddy-Bob, buy the gas."

With a shrug, Eddy-Bob dug a credit card out of the back pocket of his dirty jeans and shoved it into the appropriate slot in the gas pump. Annika noticed that both Josie and Eddy-Bob watched the monitor tensely as if they suspected their card would be refused. They were probably broke or the card was stolen. After Eddy-Bob punched in a zip code, the instructions to begin pumping appeared. Both Josie and Eddy-Bob relaxed and grinned at one another.

Making up her mind, Annika moved back towards her car, feeling almost as if she had to protect it from these two.

"Thank you, but I don't want you to pay for my gas. The gas costs a great deal more than that short ride I gave you is worth."

"So maybe you should drive us further on down?"

But Annika was determined not to be manipulated by these two again. "I don't think so, Josie." She started rummaging in her purse for money to pay Eddy-Bob for the gas.

"I'm wondering why you don't want to use your credit card."

Annika looked up sharply at the insinuating tone of Josie's voice. "That's my business." Then realizing she had made a mistake, "What do you mean?"

The two women stared at each other. Aside from a fly buzzing lazily overhead, there was stillness. Even the air seemed to hold its breath for a moment. In the distance, as through a thick curtain, Annika heard the clink of tools as the mechanic worked on the old station wagon's engine.

Eddy-Bob finished filling the tank, replaced the hose and carefully replaced the gas tank cover. The feeling of everything being suspended in time faded. Then they were back in everyday West Virginia, on a normal April day, and Annika was damned well going to get rid of these hitchhikers.

She held out the exact amount registering on the gas pump. "Here, Eddy-Bob."

Eddy-Bob smiled and moved around the car so he was on one side of her and Josie on the other. He took the money from her hand. Both of them were now smiling. Both of them were standing too close to her, invading her space.

"Hey, Eddy-Bob," Josie spoke softly, her voice an insinuating singsong. "Why you think the ice-lady here didn't use her credit card?"

The question seemed to confuse Eddy-Bob. "Maybe she don't have one?"

"Oh, she got credit cards all right. Probably dozens of them. Dontcha?"

Annika looked around. Inside the open garage, she could see the mechanic working intently. She took a deep breath, preparing to call out to him. She felt a hard small fist slam into her rib cage. More astonished then hurt, she turned furiously toward Josie.

Josie spoke first. Leaning in to Annika, as if straining against invisible bonds, she hissed, "I bet maybe the police would like to know why you don't use all them credit cards you got in there." She gestured with her dirty tattooed hand at the cream-colored purse Annika clutched.

"Police?" The idea caught Annika by surprise. The last thing she had expected was for Josie to suggest calling the police. Annika certainly did not want anything to do with them. Going to the police was the same as going to Gerard. On the other hand, Josie and Eddy-Bob seemed to be turning into a police-type problem.

As if she could follow Annika's thoughts, Josie smiled with satisfaction. "Put her in the car, Eddy-Bob."

From behind, powerful arms encircled her. A dirty hand was clamped over her mouth and she felt herself being lifted off her feet. Eddy-Bob's odor, a combination of stale sweat and horrible halitosis was disgusting. She started to gag.

Thinking she was trying to bite him, Eddy-Bob rearranged his hand over her mouth so it also covered her nose. She couldn't breathe!

She kicked out frantically. How could this be happening in broad daylight, in a public place? The damn mechanic was only yards away. Why didn't he look up? She kicked out again, this time connecting with Eddy-Bob's shins.

"Bitch." His arm around her chest tightened into a crushing obscene hug. Frantically, she tried to twist her head out of his grasp. She needed air!

He pulled her backwards against his hard dirty body. She could feel his belt buckle cutting into her back. He was rubbing himself against her. He had an erection which was threatening to burst through his clothes. He was banging himself against her. It was like an iron knob trying to rip through her. And she couldn't breathe!

Faintly, she could hear Josie giving orders. "Put her in the car." Eddy-Bob's breath was coming in harsh gasps against her neck. At least that son-of-a-bitch could breathe.

"Not the front seat." Josie's voice was exasperated. "In the back."

Annika was shoved through the door held open by Josie. "Get in back with her." Eddy-Bob's hand slipped off Annika's face and loosened from around her waist. Like a cat, Annika slithered across the back seat and opened the back door on the other side. "Stop her!"

Eddy-Bob grabbed the waistband of Annika's slacks and yanked her back inside the car.

"Help me!"

Eddy-Bob grabbed the back of Annika's head and shoved it down against his leg. Without thinking, Annika bit him, drawing blood.

"Bitch." A hard slamming blow from the side of Eddy-Bob's hand crashed against her head just above her right ear. The blow drove her head against his leg. Her teeth were driven into her tongue. Her mouth filled with blood, she gagged on the greasy material of Eddy-Bob's jeans. For a moment, time stopped, fear evaporated, sounds distanced themselves, and there came an awful nauseous feeling of falling into a dizzying gray whirlpool.

Jessie Fields, the mechanic looked up from his work. Weird looking people taking a long time to fill up a gas tank. Nice car though. Sighing, he put down his screwdriver, wiped his hands and ambled toward the Jaguar.

They had changed drivers. The dirty faced female with the baldhead was in the driver's seat now. "You call me?"

She didn't answer him, just waved and boogied out of there like her tail was on fire. Jessie watched them go. The pony-tailed guy was in the back. He looked back at Jessie through the rear window. His face was expressionless. Jessie didn't see the other one. There had been three people in that car, hadn't there? He looked around vaguely, as if he expected the third person to materialize from behind the gas pump. It was hot. Jessie absently scratched his right arm and wished he had a cold beer. Virtuously, he turned back to the waiting station wagon he was working on.

Annika was so dazed that she only became sharply aware of her situation when she tried to take a deep breath, Instead of clean refreshing air, she breathed in a mouthful of blood soaked torn cloth. She gagged, and then choked.

"The bitch bit me," she heard Eddy-Bob's voice complaining.

"So bite her back."

It was when Josie answered that Annika's head cleared and she was instantly aware of where she was and even worse, remembered what had happened.

Eddy-Bob gave a high-pitched giggle. With a rough hand, he shoved the gagging, choking Annika away from him. "Don't spew on me, bitch."

They were driving through the center of a small town. Annika, on the floor, leaned back against the door and tried to control her breathing.

I've got to get out of here.

Between coughs, she studied Eddy-Bob. He was leaning over the front seat, watching where they were going, paying her no attention.

The door behind her was locked, but maybe she could manage to unlock it without Eddy-Bob noticing. She carefully straightened her back so that she was sitting taller, and therefore, was closer to the lock.

Eddy-Bob continued to ignore her. She raised her left arm and massaged the back of her neck. How far away from the door lock, was she? Would her head hide what her hand was doing. Feeling like a contortionist, she felt along the edge of the window, trying to find the lock. There it was! Suddenly the back of Eddy-Bob's hand slammed against her face, driving the back of her head into the car door. The world rocked. The pain was unbearable.

"What's she doing?"

"Trying to unlock the door. Sneaky bitch."

Josie laughed like a hyena. The laugh went on and on. Annika had never heard anything like it. They were crazy!

Eddy-Bob grabbed her by her hair and threw her onto the floor of the car. He casually rested his heavy feet on her. She was nothing more to them than the carpet on the floor. She knew then, as surely, as if they had sent an engraved announcement, they were going to kill her.

The pain in her back from being cramped into such a weird space, plus the pain in her thigh from Eddy-Bob's boots resting on her merged, until she was one giant ache. Only once did she attempt to sit up to relieve her discomfort. Eddy-Bob immediately aborted that attempt by the simple expediency of driving the sole of his boot into her stomach. She had screamed, choked, gasped, and cried.

"What are you doing to her?"

"Stomping her."

Josie laughed. "She sounds like a stuck pig."

"They always do." Eddy-Bob also laughed.

Annika lay curled on the floor, scarcely aware of anything, but her pain and terror. She had no idea how long they drove. Gradually, she realized they were no longer on a paved road. Opening her eyes in a careful squint, she saw the dimness caused by trees on either side of the car. Despite its magnificent spring system, the Jag was bumping and banging as though on a rutted dirt road. No not even a road, it was a track barely wide enough for the car. They were in the woods, Annika realized. She was in the woods, alone with two maniacs and no one would be looking for her.

Eddy-Bob finally called a halt to their progress. "How far we gonna go? I'm hungry."

"So what? We don't have any food."

"Yeah, but the further we go, the longer it's gonna take to go back and get some food."

"Don't worry about your damn stomach."

"I'm hungry," he whined.

"I gotta find the perfect place for the altar."

"How come all your altars gotta be so far from a MacDonald's?"

"Shut up, Eddy-Bob. Your bad thoughts are interfering with me finding the right place."

He gave a disgusting snort of laughter. "I thought bad thoughts were good for the sacrifice."

"I'm telling you to shut up.!"

Eddy-Bob shut up. They continued driving.

***

"Here we are," announced Josie. She braked the car and turned off the engine. The silence was shocking. Annika, still on the floor, felt as if she had suddenly gone deaf.

Josie must have gotten out, because the car rocked slightly. Sound came back with the slamming of the door. "Whatta you think?" asked Josie's voice.

The rear door behind Annika's head opened and Eddy-Bob climbed out over her. One of his heavy boots carelessly hit her side, the other scrunched down on her arm. She fought against screaming with pain.

"Well?"

"It's okay," answered Eddy-Bob.

"Okay? It's perfect. We can have the altar over here."

"I'm hungry," whined Eddy-Bob.

"We'll eat later." Josie's word seemed to be law. "Get her out here."

"Her" presumably meant Annika. Lying on the floor of her car, Annika nervously twisted her rings. She had to get away from these people. No matter what happened, she would not go as a lamb to slaughter; she would fight. Unfortunately, there was no opportunity. Eddy-Bob reached into the car, grabbed her arm and pulled her out, literally dumping her onto the ground. She landed at his feet on her rear-end.

"Whatcha want me to do with her?" he asked Josie. Annika did not wait to hear the answer. She flung her body to one side and rolled away from the man. Jumping to her feet, she started running.

"Yipeee," yelled Josie. "Let's play, catch the bitch." Which is exactly what they did for the next few minutes.

They ran Annika in circles, letting her think she was getting away, and then cutting off her escape. It became horribly obvious that Josie and Eddy-Bob had played this game before. They were experts at it. Finally, Eddy-Bob tired of the game and, sticking out a foot, tripped the desperate Annika as she was making one last lunge for her freedom.

Eddy-Bob completed the capture by the simple expediency of sitting himself down on Annika's legs as he caught his breath. Josie was not pleased. "Whatcha do that for? She still had plenty of play left in her."

"I'm hungry," Eddy-Bob complained. "I wanna go get some food."

"Oh, okay. Hang her up and we'll see how much money she has."

Eddy-Bob hauled himself to his feet; Annika's legs were so numb she was unable to move. He grabbed her by the scruff of her neck and hustled her over to a nearby tree.

Hang her up!? Were they going to kill her just like that?

However, it seemed "hang her up" had another meaning to the two hitchhikers; a very literal meaning. As Eddy-Bob held her prisoner, Josie quickly tied her wrists together then took another piece of rope and slid it between Annika's two wrists. Eddy-Bob took over at this point. Taking the end of the rope, he looped it over a branch of the tree and pulled it tight.

Annika screamed.

"Shut up, bitch."

Annika hung suspended from the branch, her toes just barely touching the ground.

"Can't you hang her up higher? I don't like her feet touching the ground."

"She's too damn tall," complained Eddy-Bob. "We'd have to chop off her legs or something." When Josie said nothing, and just continued to frown, he reassured her. "Don't worry, bitch ain't goin' nowhere. See." He put out a hand and pushed Annika in the small of her back. Annika swung like a giant wind chime. The pain in her wrists and arms was terrible.

Josie grinned evilly. "Guess you're right." They turned

away from her to go about their business.

Eddy-Bob rummaged through Annika's purse. "Just a little over four hundred dollars. The bitch travels light."

"Credit cards?"

"Yeah, a handful."

"Give them to me." Reluctantly Eddy-Bob handed over the cards to Josie. "What else she got in there?"

"Just the usual shit." Impatiently, Josie grabbed the purse away from the man.

"She got Channel make-up."

"So?"

"So, costs a fortune." Josie opened Annika's compact and powdered her face. "How do I look?"

Eddy-Bob shrugged. Josie took out Annika's lipstick and applied it to her own lips with a lavish hand. "Now?"

"Yeah, ya look great, Josie. Great."

"I told you, all it takes is money. Anyone can look great, they got money."

"Ah-huh. I'm gonna go get us some food." He got in the car and carefully turned it around and took off to find the nearest store. Annika could hear the car's progress for a long time before the sound faded. Josie, studying herself in the compact mirror, barely noticed him going.

"Josie. Josie?" The girl didn't even turn around. "Please let me go." Annika hated the begging tone of her voice, but what could she do? She *was* begging...probably for her life.

Without even glancing Annika's way, Josie put down the compact. She began to gather fallen pine branches, carefully heaping them between two slender trees. She continued adding branches until she had built up a sort of shelf, waist high. Not once during all this time, did she as much as look in Annika's direction.

A great lassitude settled over Annika. What was the use of fighting? Why had she even bothered running from Gerard?

The word victim must be tattooed on my forehead.

Jose had finished building her shelf of branches and was now carefully hanging a heavy crystal pendant over the makeshift altar. Annika roused slightly from her suicidal passivity. "What's that for?"

To her surprise, Josie answered. "To summon the spirits, so they can watch the sacrifice."

"What spirits?"

"The helpers. His helpers. They can't see into this world directly. They can only see reflections. The crystal will reflect your agony."

"My agony?"

"They're very sensitive. They can't bear to watch directly."

"But you can?"

Josie, smiling a sly, happy smile, moved slowly over to stand in front of Annika. "Yes," she agreed, "I can stand to watch directly. I like it."

Anger was returning now and with anger came a sort of strength. "Too bad, you didn't marry Gerard instead of me."

"Who's Gerard?"

"Never mind." The two women, only feet apart watched each other intently. "I can get a hold of a great deal of money, Josie."

"Can you?" Josie still had that crazy, sly smile on her grimy face.

"More money than you can imagine."

"The altar's already built."

"You can build others."

"Oh no," Josie explained earnestly. "Once an altar is built, it must be used. They insist."

"They?"

"The spirits. If it wasn't you, it would have to be Eddy-Bob."

"Or even you," said Annika softly.

"So you see, I can't use your money. Too late." Abruptly, Josie turned away and busied herself with picking wildflowers and carefully decorating the makeshift altar, completely ignoring Annika.

The chill of horror Annika had felt when staring into Josie's mad eyes had thoroughly awakened her. She studied the knots around her wrists. The only thing that prevented her slipping free was her own weight hanging from the tree;

her weight made the knots too tight. Unless she had some way of cutting the knots, they were escape proof.

Or, unless my weight is removed.

She turned her attention to the branch to which her wrists were tied. It didn't look that strong. What would happen if she were to put her full weight on it? If she could break the branch, the tension on the knots would be reduced. She could escape.

Josie wasn't looking at her.

Annika pulled on the branch with all her might. It bent...and bent and bent, but gave no sign of breaking. All that she accomplished was more pain in her arms and shoulders. With a whimper of despair, Annika released the branch. There had to be some way out of here!

Well if the branch won't come to me, maybe I can go to the branch.

Another check of Josie assured Annika that the girl's attention was still taken up with her macabre decorating.

Then, very faintly, Annika heard the sound of a car. Eddy-Bob was on his way back. Josie, caught up in her own violent imagination, seemed not have heard anything.

Once Eddy-Bob returned, she would never be able to escape. It was now or never.

Annika pulled down on the branch until she wanted to scream at the increased pain in her shoulders and wrists. Then, just as she had done so often in the gym, Annika bent her knees and pushed off from the ground. Her fingers wrapped around the branch. It was thicker than the bar in the gym and her hands were numb from their long imprisonment, but her life was riding on this. Already the sound of the car was louder. There would be no second chance.

She pulled herself up onto the branch. It dipped perilously beneath her full weight, but again did not break. Bending her head down to her wrists, Annika tore at the knots with her teeth. Oh God, it wasn't working. The knots were too tight. She ripped at them like a wolf attempting to gnaw its own leg off in order to escape the trap. She felt something give. They were loosening!

Josie had finally heard the sound of the returning car. "Pretty soon, Mrs. Rich-Bitch, you're gonna be meeting His helpers in person.

Finally, her hands were free!

Josie turned around and saw Annika perched on the branch like a giant bird of prey. "Hey!"

Without thinking, Annika sprang from the branch, landing directly on Josie. The hitchhiker was knocked to the ground. Annika sprang up, intending to run for her life. But she found herself held fast. Josie, shocked, had automatically clutched the collar of Annika's blouse. She wouldn't let go. The damn material would not tear.

The two women rolled on the ground at the foot of Josie's altar. Annika, grasping for anything, grabbed up a stray branch that was sticking too far out of the altar. She slammed it down on Josie's face. The branch wasn't thick. It didn't do much damage. It didn't make Josie let go. Annika slammed her again and again. Finally, Josie released one hand in order to cover her face.

Holding the collar of Annika's blouse with one hand changed the direction of the tension applied to the blouse. With a ripping sound the buttons popped off, the blouse was torn from neck to sleeve.

The car was getting closer. Josie began to scream for Eddy-Bob. Annika jerked to her feet. Most of the rest of her silk blouse ripped off her body.

Without another glance at the screaming Josie, Annika ran for her life.

CHAPTER TWENTY-TWO

At first, Annika just ran. She leaped over fallen tree trunks, barged through clumps of bushes, staggered over exposed roots, but she kept going.

I've got to get away. I've got to get away. It was a mantra, playing over and over in her head.

Despite her inappropriate shoes, Annika ran strongly.

Yes! She was going to get away!

Her left foot came down in a narrow space between a rock and an exposed tree root. The heel of her sandal snagged on the root, her ankle twisted and Annika fell, twisting her ankle even more.

The pain caused Annika to give out a sharp yell, which she immediately cut off. She lay on the damp ground, panting for breath. Slowly, she extracted her foot from her trapped shoe. Her foot came free easily enough, but her ankle stabbed with pain.

She lay back and rested for a moment. She could clearly hear her two pursuers. They were coming directly towards her.

Have to keep going.

She pulled herself to her feet and carefully applied weight to her injured ankle.

Oh Lord, it hurts! Stop whining. Get moving.

She tried to retrieve her shoe, but it was too firmly wedged. She was running out of time! One shoe on, one shoe off, was too awkward. Abandoning both shoes, she staggered on.

A few steps brought her to another obstacle.

A deep gully opened up at her feet. It cut directly across her path as far as she could see. In order to cross it, she would have to climb down this side and up the other.

The other side of the gully was just as deeply wooded as her side.

I could climb down and travel along the gully itself, she thought. It would be easier.

"Do you see her?" yelled Josie's voice.

Annika didn't hear Eddy-Bob reply, but Josie's voice had been too damn close.

Traveling down the gully would make it easier for them too. She looked around frantically. The gully was deeper than she was tall and ranged in width from about three feet to ten feet. The far side was several feet lower than where she stood.

Directly across from the narrowest part of the gully was a huge tree, its topmost branches all but hidden under its dense foliage. She could jump the three feet, but the damn tree was in the way. The idea of hiding in the tree crossed Annika's mind, but she immediately abandoned it. The lowest branch was way over her head. She would never be able to reach it.

"Where the hell is that skinny bitch?" Eddy-Bob's voice was so close, she expected his heavy hand to clamp down on her shoulder and drag her back to that sick, horrible, deadly altar.

Annika plunged through thorny bushes until she was at the edge of the gully. Directly opposite her was the huge tree. Flexing her knees, she sprang across the gully. Pain ripped through her ankle. She ignored it.

Because her side of the gully was at least three feet higher than the side the tree was on, Annika was actually only slightly lower than the lowest tree branch. Her body cleared the gully easily, her outstretched hands grabbed the tree branch, and her body slammed into the tree trunk with all the force of her jump.

She could feel the wind whooshing from her lungs.

Don't let go!

She was literally hanging on for dear life.

Finally, the air seeped back into her lungs. The bushes across the gully rustled. *They're coming!* Annika scampered up the tree like a squirrel.

It was a giant tree. Annika kept climbing until she came to a crook where two branches formed a little hollow. She was not the first to find it an attractive refuge; a large old nest with broken shells still visible rested there.

Not wanting falling debris to call attention to her hiding place, she was careful not to disturb anything. She was out of breath and out of strength. She leaned wearily against the rough tree trunk. If they discovered her, there was literally nowhere else to go.

From her perch in the tree, Annika could see out over the countryside. Off somewhere in the distance, to her astonishment, she could hear a tractor throbbing away. They were not that far from civilization. The whole world did not just consist of her and the two hitchhikers.

"Ow!"

Annika looked down onto the top of the heads of Josie and Eddy-Bob. They were just across the gully. Josie had slipped and fallen. "Where the hell is she?"

"We ain't gonna find her." Eddy-Bob hauled Josie to her feet.

"We gotta, you dope. It's her or us. Keep looking. She's around here somewhere. Rich bitch can't outrun us."

"She's not my type," Eddy-Bob complained. "Too skinny."

Annika watched as they climbed down the gully and up the other side. They were directly under her now. Thirty feet above them, Annika held her breath and tried to make her mind go blank. She had the primitive fear; they would be able to read her thoughts.

But they did not look up, as they kept pushing their way through the woods. Annika could follow their progress easily.

"Skinny bitch." It echoed in her mind, even after Eddy-Bob had stamped past.

Skinny, skinny, skinny.

When was the last time someone had called her that? Despite the horror of her present situation, the word had a sweet association. But she couldn't remember...

A drop of water, which had been clinging to a leaf on

the branch above her, fell onto her cheek and rolled down her neck to be caught and absorbed by the tattered remnants of her blouse.

She had been hiding in the woods then too, she remembered, the piney woods around her home down in Florida. She was hiding from Ray.

I was mad at him, she remembered. They had argued about...? She couldn't remember. What she did remember was that Ray had gotten so angry with her that he had tossed the water from a bucket he was carrying in her direction. Drops of water had splattered on her blouse.

What we were arguing about?

All she remembered was she had burst into tears and run off into the woods. Ray had been exasperated. "There you go again," he yelled after her. "Every time you don't like something you take off."

She had run to their special clearing, but instead of waiting for him as usual, she had continued past, come to the creek, crossed it, and crawled under a huge pine tree that had fallen years ago. Its felled trunk and twisted branches were now covered with brambles and moss, making a perfect secret cave. The floor of the cave was covered with moss and dead pine needles, cool and softly comfortable.

She was mad, she was upset, and she was excited. Anything and everything to do with Ray always excited her, always had, ever since she was a little girl. But she wasn't a little girl now. She was fifteen years old, but Ray, who was almost eighteen, thought he could still boss her around.

"Hey, Annie, where are you?"

So he had come looking for her after all. The fifteen-year-old Annie smiled. *Knew you would.*

"Annie, where are you?" She wasn't going to answer him. Served him right. "Annie?" No answer. He was becoming annoyed. "Listen you, skinny little thing."

"Who are you calling skinny?"

"Annie Malloy, where are you?"

"You think I'm so skinny ugly, you just go home without me."

"I will." He turned on his heel and walked away. Annie

crawled out of her cave and watched his retreating back.

"Ray?" He kept walking. She had spoken softly, maybe he hadn't heard her. "Ray?" Finally, he stopped and turned around. "Do you really think I'm a skinny, ugly old thing?"

He was trying to be stern, but had to smile. "Never said you were ugly." She went to him and held out her hand. It disappeared into his large one. Then, she flung her arms around his neck and hugged him tight.

"Ah, naw, don't do that, Annie." Then they were kissing desperately, frantically, clumsily. Shocked by their own passion, they broke apart. A bee buzzed nearby. The hot Florida sun burned down on them. It was Ray who spoke first. "We shouldn't be doing that."

"No." She felt disappointed. "But it was nice."

He grinned down at her. "You are a skinny hussy."

They both laughed. They understood each other. After all, they were best friends.

CHAPTER TWENTY-THREE

Ray was the son of her father's boss. Not that her father, Buddy Malloy, ever worked regularly anywhere, but when he did his favorite job was at the O'Brien's horse farm.

Annie was at the horse farm every chance she got. As the two children grew, they worked with the horses. They became excellent riders. They were familiar with the mechanics of horse breeding and the birth that followed. They learned to recognize when a mare was going into labor. It was that, which brought a sudden halt to Annie spending so much time around the farm.

"My little girl does not need to see anything so disgusting," her mother had cried in horror when informed where her daughter had spent the last few hours. "Buddy Malloy, how could even you sink so low as to allow your own daughter to be exposed to, to, to ...I can't even say it."

Her father, smelling of whisky and unwashed sweat, hung his head and shuffled his boots.

"Well now, I don't know what's so bad about seeing a new foal come into the world."

"No, you wouldn't know."

"But, Mama, it was just beautiful."

"That's enough, Annie."

"Mama, I've seen lots of foalings."

Mama had staggered and clutched her heart. "I'm feeling weak, Buddy." Her father had come forward and awkwardly tried to support his wife, but she pushed him away with surprising strength for someone who was having a weak spell.

"Don't touch me. All you ever think about is s-e-x."

"Mama, I'm fifteen years old! Even if you think I don't know about it, at least you must know I can spell it."

"Don't take that tone with me, young lady."

After that, Annie was forbidden to go out to the O'Brien farm after school.

"Your father doesn't need your help, Annie, but I do."

"What kind of help do you need?"

"You can come down to the church office and help me with the mailings."

Mrs. Malloy was a secretary at the Methodist Church. Annie hated hanging around the church office. She didn't like to see the way her mother acted around Pastor Brook, as if the pastor was God, Himself. It made Annie itch with discomfort, especially when she heard two giggling ladies in the congregation refer to her mother as the "Methodist Nun."

But most of all, Annie missed Ray. He had been a part of her life as long as she could remember, and suddenly they were separated.

"Why are you moping around with that long face, young lady?"

"I miss Ray."

"Who?" Mama's tone should have warned Annie, but she was too miserable to care.

"Ray O'Brien, down by Mr. O'Brien's farm. My best friend."

"Don't be ridiculous. You can't have a boy for a best friend." Mama was so sure of herself. So self-righteous.

"Why not?"

"It's indecent, that's why. People will talk."

"About what?" Annie was bewildered.

Instead of answering, Mrs. Malloy yelled for Annie's father. "Buddy!"

"Right here, sweetheart."

"What's this Annie's saying about the O'Brien boy?"

Annie's father began to fidget nervously. "The O'Brien boy?"

"You heard me."

"Ahhh, Ray. Nice kid. Good with a horse. Going to be a big-time breeder someday."

"Have you no shame, Buddy Malloy? How can you use such words around your young daughter and your own wife?"

"I'm outta here," muttered Annie's father, grabbing up his jacket and departing.

Mrs. Malloy nodded to herself, and then turned abruptly on Annie. "Now, you see what you've done. Driven your father to drink, because of your carryings on with the O'Brien boy."

"What carryings on?"

"You're not to see him ever again."

"We go to the same school."

"Never be alone with him. Mark my words, you'll rue the day."

Annie had no intention of obeying her mother's order. She considered it arbitrary, unfair and just plain silly. But Mrs. Malloy was not a complete fool. She may not have known much about her daughter, but she was well acquainted with the story of the forbidden fruit.

She grabbed Annie by the arm and looked her straight in the eye. "I want you to promise me, Annie Malloy."

"Oh, Mama."

Mrs. Malloy grabbed up her bible, which was always close by.

"Swear on the bible, you will never seek out that boy again." Her thin fingers bit into Annie's arm.

"Mama."

Mrs. Malloy gave Annie's arm a shake. "Swear."

"Okay!"

"Say the words." Mrs. Malloy pressed the worn Bible up against Annie's chest over her heart.

"Okay. Okay. I swear I will never seek out Ray O'Brien again."

Mrs. Malloy relaxed her hold on Annie's arm.

"I'm glad to hear you say that, child. I know you will never break your word. You're not like your father."

"Mama, why do you say things like that?"

"I always speak the truth," sniffed her mother self-righteously. "Now go peel the potatoes. I pride myself on having a hot dinner on the table for your father whenever he comes home from work...whenever he works."

Annie was not above sneaking around her mother's restrictions, but swearing on the Bible was another kettle of fish. That was a promise to God.

Luckily, Ray had made no such promise. After several weeks of no contact between them, Ray sought her out after church services.

"Hey, Annie, wait up."

"Hello, Ray."

"What's the matter with you?"

"Nothing."

"Where you going?"

"I promised to help my mother after the service."

"Is something the matter?"

"No."

"Annie, you're not even looking at me." Annie kept her head down and continued moving slowly away from him. "Okay, don't look at me, I don't care. You're always a pest anyway."

"If I'm such a pest, why don't you just leave me alone?"

"Don't worry, I will. I just thought you might want to know Sweet Lady should be going into labor tonight."

"Already?"

"She's right on time. You're the one who doesn't know what's going on. You haven't seen her in weeks."

"Is she all right?"

"You're so interested, come tonight and see for yourself."

"I can't."

"You mean, you won't." He turned and walked away. Annie stifled the urge to call out to him.

Sweet Lady was especially important to Annie. She was a young mare with impressive breeding. But it was her loving, almost cuddly nature that made her especially dear to Annie. The mare had been bred to a stallion with an equally impressive history. This was her first foal. Mr. O'Brien had been bragging for weeks about how great the foal was going to be. "This foal will put O'Brien's Stud on the map. Bring us up with the big boys."

That night, her father didn't come home for dinner. Mrs. Malloy muttered darkly about drunken louts doing devil's work.

Impatiently, Annie corrected her. "He's not with the devil tonight, Mama. Daddy's down at Mr. O'Brien's. A foal is due tonight. Daddy's better than any vet during foaling," she bragged.

"Annie, I thought I made it plain we do not talk about such things. Anyway, how can your father be better than a vet? A vet is a highly educated man."

"I heard Mr. O'Brien say so."

"Really?" For once Mama looked impressed. Then she sniffed disdainfully, "If your father was really any good, Mr. O'Brien would pay him a better wage."

Annie, her hands hidden under the table, clenched them into tight fists. There was no use arguing with Mama. She turned everything around. You couldn't tell her anything, because you never knew when she would bring out your most private information, twist it and use it against you.

That night Annie lay in bed, staring out at the full moon, unable to sleep. She heard her mama's snores coming from her bedroom. Annie giggled, remembering her mother's reaction to Annie's comment. "Of course, I don't snore, Annie. Ladies do not snore." That took care of that. It amazed Annie how Mama could cause something to not exist just because she didn't approve of it.

I wonder how Sweet Lady's doing? Is her foal a colt or a filly? Why isn't Daddy home yet? Has something gone wrong? I wish I could be there.

Annie tossed and turned. The humid Florida night air combined with the bright moonlight was making it impossible for her to sleep. Finally, tossing aside her sweat-dampened sheet, Annie got out of bed and crossed to the window. She reached for the shade pull, intending to lower it and shut out the moonlight. A lone cricket was sounding off down in the back yard. Before she could pull the shade down, another cricket picked up on its song and added its own two-cent's worth. Then anther joined in. A symphony of crickets convened outside her window.

Annie grinned and whispered to them, "I swear, I will never get to sleep with you fellas making such a racket." The crickets ignored her, the concert continued. Annie leaned on the windowsill. There was a slight breeze now; the night was finally beginning to cool off.

From her mother's room, there was a particularly loud snort, and then the normal buzzing snore took up again. Between the crickets and Mama, Annie knew she would never be able to fall asleep. Without consciously making up her mind to do anything forbidden, Annie began to get dressed.

She pulled on a pair of cut-off jeans, yanked a faded green tee shirt over her head and carrying her old boots, tiptoed down the stairs and out the front door, carefully locking it behind her. The Malloys were probably the only family in the county that locked their front door. Mama always made such a fuss about "there being no real man around to protect us, so naturally we have to lock the doors."

Annie sat down on the porch steps to pull her boots on. The crickets, aware of her presence, were shocked into silence.

"Don't you all stop on account of me," Annie urged them. She giggled with a sense of wonderful freedom. She would pay for her sins tomorrow, but for tonight, she was free.

CHAPTER TWENTY-FOUR

At the O'Brien farm, the barn was lit with soft yellow lights. The foaling box itself had deep sweet bedding for the comfort of the mare and her soon-to-be-born foal. When Annie arrived, she found her father, Ray, Mr. O'Brien, and a man she did not know, present. They were talking softly, their attention all centered on Sweet Lady. Only Mr. O'Brien and the strange man took her arrival for granted. Her father, knowing the ruling his wife had made, smiled at her nervously. He was glad to see his beloved daughter, but dreaded the scene that was sure to take place in the morning. Privately, he decided to make himself scarce for the next few days.

Ray grinned happily at her, squeezed her hand and whispered, "I knew you wouldn't let me down."

Annie tossed her head. "That's all you know. I'm here to make sure Sweet Lady's all right." But she squeezed back on his hand.

Suddenly, Sweet Lady grunted, sighed and lay down on the thick bedding. Annie's father leaned over the mare and rested his hand on her heaving sides. "Here it comes," he announced softly.

They all watched spellbound as Buddy Malloy helped guide a new life into the world. When the foal was fully expelled from her womb, the mare sighed and laid her head back into the thick straw. Then, with a heave, she climbed to her feet and turned to examine the results of all her labor.

Ray and Annie's fathers were carefully tearing away the thin membrane that surrounded the foal. Sweet Lady, responding to age-old instinct, moved to her new baby and, with her teeth, finished the job the two men had begun. Ray and Mr. Malloy moved respectfully back, giving Sweet Lady all the room she needed to exercise her maternal rights.

"It's a colt," announced Ray, his voice shaky with excitement.

Awestruck, the humans watched as the leggy young thing worked valiantly to stand. First, the foal unwound his front legs and pushed mightily. But he had not yet mastered his back legs. He tumbled back into the soft straw.

"Come on, you little beauty," breathed Annie softly.

Sweet Lady gently nudged her baby. With this encouragement, the colt tried again. On his third try, he stood triumphantly on long, shaky legs. The humans applauded. The colt looked around in wonder, gave a squeaky little snort, took a step toward his dam and immediately fell down again.

Half an hour later, the young colt was eagerly nursing on his mother's milk, while Sweet Lady munched contentedly on fresh hay.

Mr. O'Brien slapped Annie's father on the shoulder. Both men were predicting a wonderful future for the new colt. "A champion if I ever saw one," declared Buddy Malloy.

"Couldn't agree more, Malloy," said the stranger.

"This calls for a drink." Mr. O'Brien was feeling expansive.

"I won't say, no." Buddy Malloy turned and winked back at his daughter as he followed Mr. O'Brien and the stranger to the farmhouse.

Left alone, Annie and Ray smiled at each other. "I'm glad you came, Annie."

Annie reached out and stroked the mare's neck. "I couldn't let Sweet Lady go through this without another woman present."

Ray gently took her hand. "Come on, I'll walk you home."

The bright Florida moon lit a magic path across the familiar pasture. Hand in hand, the boy and girl followed it slowly.

They meant to go straight home, they really did. But somewhere along the way, the sound of the shallow creek splashing over rocks, the smell of fresh, night-blooming jasmine, and the wine-soft warmth of the air caressing their skin, befuddled their senses, confused their direction and weakened the need to obey an artificial ruling.

Never letting go of Annie's hand, Ray stopped. When she turned to him, he pulled her close. They stood, body to body, staring into each other's face, searching for... what?

Then he was kissing her, or was it she who was kissing him? They were clumsy kids. They even banged their noses. Annie laughed, but Ray didn't. He had this real intense look on his face. He pushed her away at arm's length, but did not let go of her hand. He just looked at her as if he had never really seen her before. Then his hands were all over her.

"Touch me," she murmured, but he was already touching her, cupping the softness of her breasts, stroking her nipples, pebbled by desire. She could feel the hardness of him.

They made love for the first time in their young lives; each with the person they knew would always be the love of their life.

They made love with all the intensity, all the clumsiness, all the desperation of the young. It hurt. Annie cried out.

"What?" he asked, pulling back.

"Nothing. Go on. Go on! He did. Then he was the one who had cried out. His whole body shuddering, an odd sound, half laugh, half moan escaped from his throat.

Later, naked and sweaty, pine needles and grass stuck to their flesh, they lay on the cool grass that was their wedding bed; a cricket sang nearby.

"Sometimes, said Ray, "lookin' at you, I can't catch my breath."

"Do you think other people feel like this?" she wondered aloud.

"No," he answered. "No one else has you."

"Then you love me?"

"Yeah, of course. You?"

I've always loved you, Ray. He put his arms around her and held her so fiercely she could barely breathe. Finally, they separated. It was Ray who spoke first. "We can't tell anyone."

"Okay." She felt disappointed. "But I'd like to tell everyone."

He grinned, and then became serious. "We can't tell anyone. Not until we get married."

Annie rolled over onto her belly. "We gonna get married, Ray?"

"Don't you want to?"

"Of course, I do," said Annie, refusing to let her mind dwell on her parent's marriage, the only marriage she knew intimately. Did she really want to get married? "I want to be with you always! That's the truth."

"Me, too."

He sat up and crossed his legs Indian style. He was so serious. "We gotta wait until you're sixteen."

"That's more than a year!"

"And I gotta be eighteen."

"Three months."

"We'll still be able to … to do this."

"This?"

"Make love."

Make love. It sounded so grown-up. Annie grinned at Ray. "Let's do it again."

They did, only this time it was quieter, gentler, and more tender. Annie began to cry.

"What's the matter?"

"Oh, Ray, I love you."

"I love you, too. I swear it." He raised himself up on his elbows and looked down at her. "I swear to God, Annie, I'll never let you down. We'll always be together."

Later, they rinsed themselves off with creek water. Annie felt no shyness about her nakedness. Ray loved her; he loved her body. Why should she be ashamed?

Hands clasped, arms swinging like children, he walked her home.

"Who was that man?" she remembered to ask.

"Man?" Ray seemed dazed.

"The stranger?"

"He's not a stranger, that's my Uncle Dave. We're

going horse hunting."

"How do you mean?"

"Him and me, we're going to travel around looking for the perfect stallion to buy. One that we can afford. My dad's serious about building up our farm." He became excited. "That's what you and I are going to have someday, Annie. A stud farm of our own. A good one. I want to breed racehorses."

"Racehorses! Here in Florida?"

"No, in Kentucky. How would you like to live in Kentucky?"

To Annie it sounded as exotic as Timbuktu. "I'd live anywhere with you, Ray." They stopped to kiss again. The first faint light of dawn was showing in the east. "I have to get home," Annie said.

They started off again for her house. "When are you and your uncle going off horse hunting?"

"Tomorrow."

"Tomorrow?"

He laughed at her. "Don't worry, sweet little Annie. I'll be back."

"But then you're going off to college."

"I've been thinking about that. When I get to college, I'll move out of the dorm and get an apartment. You'll come on up and we'll get married. Lots of college students are married."

"How soon after you get there, do you think?"

"I don't know, but it'll be soon."

Later, alone in her bed, Annie relived every breathless moment of their lovemaking and every promise they had made to each other.

Mrs. Ray O'Brien. Mrs. Annie O'Brien. No, she would be grown-up then. She would use her full given name, Brianne. Mrs. Brianne O'Brien. It sounded perfect. As she drifted off to sleep, only one passing thought clouded her happiness, she had given her word not to seek Ray out. But I didn't seek him out, she defended herself. I just wanted to be there for Sweet Lady. Everything else just sort of followed.

Annie felt guilty. But not so guilty she didn't wish Ray

wasn't going on a horse buying trip with his uncle for the whole of next week. After all, they didn't have much time. Ray would be leaving for college in just weeks. She was eager to make love again.

In the morning, Mrs. Malloy seemed to notice nothing different about Annie. It was then that Annie realized her mother never really looked at her. Mrs. Malloy began with her usual list of chores for her daughter. "Now Annie, after you finish the dishes I want you to carry the stack of missionary newsletters over to the church."

"Mama, I'd like to be called Brianne."

"Who?"

"Brianne." Mrs. Malloy looked at her blankly. "Brianne. It's on my birth certificate. You're the one who named me."

"Oh, that. Just some nonsense of your father's."

"Brianne is pretty. I'd like to be called that from now on."

"Annie, don't be silly. I have a lot of work to do for the Reverend. I don't have time for this silliness."

"It's not silliness," Annie protested, as her mother bustled out the door on her way to her job at the church. With a sigh, Annie returned to washing the dishes in the sink. Harry, the female cat, twined herself around Annie's ankles meowing loudly to be petted. "My hands are all wet," Annie apologized to the cat. "Harry, do you like Annie or Brianne better?" But the cat, realizing she was not going to be stroked, refused to give her opinion.

CHAPTER TWENTY-FIVE

All the next week, Annie walked around hugging her secret to herself. She was constantly amazed that no one commented on the obvious change in herself. Couldn't people tell just by looking at her? Couldn't they see she was no longer just an ordinary girl, that she had been transformed into a much-loved woman?

Apparently not.

Annie replayed their lovemaking over and over again in her mind. She longed to do it again. Ray was due back from his horse-buying trip at the end of the week. She could barely wait. It was at dinner on the sixth day of Ray's absence that she learned the bad news.

"Mr. O'Brien's asked me to work over his place next four or five days," Buddy Malloy informed his wife and daughter. "Gonna have to work late." He was careful not to look up as he spooned soup into his mouth.

His wife looked at him sharply. "You're not going to just sneak off somewhere and drink, are you?"

"Told you, I'm working."

"Why, all of a sudden, does Mr. O'Brien have so much work for you?"

"Boy of his had an accident."

"Ray?" By the way her mother and father stared at her, Annie realized she had spoken too loudly. She tried to modulate her voice. "Ray had an accident?"

"That's what I said."

"What sort of an accident?" Her voice was trembling. Her mother stared at her suspiciously, but Annie ignored her.

"Don't know, kitten. Anyway, Mr. O'Brien's going up north to see the boy and I'm to work extra." He snuck a quick look at his wife to see how she was taking the news.

"Means extra money," he reminded her.

Mrs. Malloy just sniffed. Annie shoved back her chair and rushed out, screen door banging behind her. "Where are you going?" Mrs. Malloy called out after her. Annie didn't answer. Ray was hurt, maybe dying.

She reached the O'Brien farm in record time. Gasping for breath, she stopped on the small rise that overlooked the backyard of the farmhouse.

Mr. O'Brien was loading a suitcase into his truck. "Mr. O'Brien," called Annie. He didn't look up. She rushed down to the truck. "Mr. O'Brien?"

The man brushed past her. "I'm busy, Annie, don't have time for you now."

"My daddy said Ray's been hurt?"

Annie had never particularly liked Mr. O'Brien, but today she felt sorry for him. His usual reddish complexion was pale and doughy looking. His voice and hands were both shaky.

"Car accident," he explained shakily. "Some damn fool drunk driver rammed my boy's truck."

"Is he all right?"

Mr. O'Brien stopped and looked fully at her for the first time. "He's in a coma." There were tears in his eyes.

"Oh, my God."

He stepped forward and grabbed both of Annie's hands. "You pray for my boy, Annie Malloy. You pray for him."

"I will, sir."

After Mr. O'Brien had driven off, Annie ran to the church and prayed as she had never prayed in her life.

"Please, God, keep Ray safe, keep my husband safe." She began to cry. "Lord, if he's very hurt, if he's in pain..." for a moment, she couldn't go on. She took a deep breath, she was talking to God, this was no time to mince words. "Please Lord, don't let him suffer. If you have to take him, I understand, but please don't let him be in terrible pain."

She became aware of the Reverend standing at the end of the pew, watching her. When he saw her looking at him, he smiled at her. "Is something wrong, Annie?"

"Ray O'Brien's been hurt." She tried to keep her voice

steady but was unable to stop the quiver when she spoke the word "hurt."

"I'm sorry to hear that."

"He's in a coma," she blurted out. "His daddy asked me to pray for him."

"We'll all pray for him," the preacher assured her. "I'll announce it on Sunday and have your mother put a notice in the church bulletin."

Days went by. Every day, Annie asked her father if he had heard from Mr. O'Brien. There was no word. Annie was desperate. She had almost given up hope when news finally came. Mr. O'Brien phoned Buddy Malloy at home to give him instructions.

The call came during dinner. Annie, listening to her father's monosyllabic replies, was driven almost wild with frustration. All the conversation seemed to be about the farm. What about Ray?

Unable to bear it any longer, Annie broke into her father's conversation. "Daddy, ask how Ray is."

"Don't interrupt your father when he's talking to Mr. O'Brien," ordered her mother.

Annie ignored her. She grabbed his arm. "Daddy!"

"What is it, Princess?"

"How's Ray?"

Obediently, Buddy Malloy relayed his daughter's question.

"My girl, Annie, wants to know how your boy is?" He listened for a while, nodding his head. "Ah-huh, ah-huh." Then, to Annie's frustration, they obviously switched topics. "Yes sir," her daddy said. "You can count on me, Mr. O'Brien."

Across the table, Annie's mother snorted her disbelief.

Her father had barely hung up before Annie was demanding information about Ray.

"Well..." Here Buddy Malloy paused to marshal his thoughts. Annie's heart was in her mouth. "Mr. O'Brien says the boy has a broken leg."

"A broken leg? I thought he was in a coma?"

"Yep. Also a broken leg."

"Daddy, is he still in a coma or not?"

Mrs. Malloy turned suspicious eyes on her daughter. "Now, just why are you so interested in that boy's state of health, young lady?"

Annie ignored her mother. "Daddy?"

"Well," answered Buddy Malloy slowly. "Seems he goes in and out of this coma thing."

"Is he going to be alright?"

"Mr. O'Brien says, doctors say so."

Annie, in her agitation was unable to follow the vagaries of her father's sentence.

"Yes or no?"

Her mother cut in. "Now, Annie, don't speak to your father like that. You show respect."

"The doctor says he expects the boy to be fine."

"Thank you, God," breathed Annie.

"May take a while, though," added Mr. Malloy.

"How long?"

"Nobody rightly knows. Also..."

"Also, what?"

"Well, the boy may have some memory loss."

For the first time, Annie's mother seemed interested. "You mean he's going to be an idiot?"

Annie turned on her. "He is not going to be an idiot!"

"No, a course he's not," her daddy reassured her. "Just some memory loss around the accident is all."

"What hospital is he in?"

"Mr. O'Brien didn't say."

"Then how can I..."

"How can you what, missy?" Her mother was watching her very sharply now.

"Nothing," mumbled Annie.

"Mr. O'Brien's due back in a few days," her daddy said. "You can ask him when he gets back."

Annie had to be satisfied with that.

When Mr. O'Brien returned two days later, Annie, who had been on the lookout for him, was at the O'Brien doorstep just minutes after he arrived.

"Hey, Mr. O'Brien."

"Hey, Annie."

"How's Ray?"

"Doing good."

"He is? That's wonderful. When's he coming home?"

"You sure are anxious about my boy."

"You asked me to pray for him and I did. So did the whole church."

"The prayers worked." Mr. O'Brien left his doorway and walked out across the yard toward the fenced pasture where some very pregnant mares were grazing. Annie tagged along at his side.

"Is Ray coming home soon, Mr. O'Brien?"

"Be awhile yet. Leg's broken."

"But he's not in a coma, no more?"

"Nope." Mr. O'Brien's whole attention was on the mares. "Looks like Pretty Papoose is going to be foaling any day now."

"Yes, sir. So Ray, he's just like he was before, only except for his leg?"

"What do you mean?"

"His memory and everything?"

"First, he didn't remember who he was, then he did, but he didn't remember who I was. But he's got that all straightened out now."

"So his memory is as good as ever?"

"Doc says it will be. Right now, he's got a big chunk of his life missing. But it will come back to him."

"That's good." Annie felt a faint sense of alarm. "What chunk of his life is he missing?"

"Oh, last six months or so. Doc says it will come back."

Mr. O'Brien pulled a cigar out of his shirt pocket and lit it. Annie, who disliked the smell, moved upwind of him.

"But when's he coming home?"

"Hard to say exactly."

"Maybe I could call him," Annie was thinking out loud.

Mr. O'Brien was amused. "That's nice of you, Annie, but your mother's not going to let you make any long distance calls."

Annie had to admit the truth of that.

"Don't worry. I'll tell him you asked about him," Mr. O'Brien reassured her.

Annie, although far from satisfied, could think of nothing else to do but wait.

Three weeks later, Ray had still not returned. Mr. O'Brien was beginning to regard her constant questions with annoyance. Her mother looked at her suspiciously and her daddy was, as usual, determinedly oblivious to any deep emotions of those around him.

Then Annie's period was late. It was late by one week, then by two. She knew what it meant, but could not really believe it. Tall, skinny redheaded Annie Malloy could not possibly be pregnant, could not possibly be someone's mother.

At the town library, she furtively searched through "Our Bodies, Ourselves". She didn't even dream of checking it out. If she tried that, the librarian, Miz Peters, would be on the phone to her mother before Annie was out the library doors.

What am I going to do? She had to talk to Ray. Back she went to the O'Brien farm.

"Mr. O'Brien?"

"Got some news for you, Annie."

"Yes?" Her heart leaped with hope.

"Ray's not coming home."

"He's not? But you said he was much better."

"He is. My brother, Dave is taking him on down to college. He's missed too much school already. Leg in a cast won't stop him from studying."

Annie thought about the implications of Ray entering college. "How's his memory?"

"Seems fine."

"Then he remembers everything? He isn't missing a chunk of his life anymore?"

"He remembers good enough." Mr. O'Brien studied her coolly. "What's this all about, Annie?"

Annie didn't know what to say.

"I can always tell when a mare's caught," he said slowly. "You're carrying aren't you?" Annie flushed with shame.

"I'm not a mare, Mr. O'Brien."

"No, you're not." He continued studying her. The sight of her seemed to enrage him. "You're just a little slut thinks she's gonna land herself a rich husband."

Annie was so astonished, without thinking she blurted out, "Ray's not rich."

"Compared to white trash, he is."

This was terrible. Before her eyes, Mr. O'Brien was turning into a monster. "I need to speak to Ray, Mr. O'Brien."

"I don't think so, missy. My boy's gonna finish college and get himself established before he settles down. And when he does, it won't be with the daughter of the town drunk."

"My daddy is not..." she died off. What could she say? "My daddy is better than a vet when it comes to foaling. You said so yourself."

But Mr. O'Brien had made up his mind. "I'm going to have a little talk with your mama."

"No! Please don't tell her."

Without a word, Mr. O'Brien disappeared into his house, the screen door banging behind him.

Panic. After all, she was only fifteen years old. What would her mother say? What would her mother do? And Daddy, how could she face her father?

I'll run away, she thought. I'll find Ray. I know where his college is. I'll hitchhike.

The screen door swung opened and Mr. O'Brien stepped out. "Girl," he said to Annie, "you come on in and wait. Your mama's on her way over."

Trapped! With her head hanging, not daring to look up at him, Annie edged past Mr. O'Brien, into the house.

"Sit over there," he indicated the worn living room sofa. Annie sat.

***

The talk between her mother and Mr. O'Brien couldn't have gone worse. Mr. O'Brien did most of the talking. Annie's mother kept opening and closing her mouth like a fish.

Why doesn't she stand up for me, thought Annie miserably. How can she let him say those things about me?

"Now, I'm telling you right off, Mrs. Malloy, my boy is not going to marry that girl."

"Yes, I understand, Mr. O'Brien."

Annie, unable to stay quiet any longer, burst out, "But Ray said-"

Mr. O'Brien cut her off. "Why do you think Ray hasn't come home, young lady? He's the one insisted on going straight on to college. Couldn't figure it at the time, but now it makes perfect sense."

"It does?"

"He's staying the hell away from you!"

It was Annie's turn to open and close her mouth like a fish. Could that be true? Had Ray rushed off to college to avoid her?

Mr. O'Brien leaned back and watched the faces of the two women in front of him. "Here's what I'm prepared to do."

What Mr. O'Brien was prepared to do, was send Annie (whom he kept referring to as "her") off to "this home I know of where she can have the kid and nobody'd be the wiser."

Mrs. Malloy's ears pricked up at that. "Nobody would know?"

"Not unless she talked."

"Oh, Annie won't say a word, Mr. O'Brien. Not a word."

"What about the baby," Annie asked in a small voice?

"Don't worry about that."

"But-"

"Be adopted," said Mr. O'Brien shortly. He looked hard at Mrs. Malloy. "We agreed?"

"Yes, Mr. O'Brien. Certainly."

"Where are you sending me?" Annie was suddenly terrified. "My Daddy won't let you send me away."

"You go running to Buddy Malloy, the whole town will know."

"I don't want to go away," whispered Annie.

"Let me tell you something, girl. Buddy Malloy gives me any lip; he'll never work for me again." It was a threat that carried a lot of weight.

Mrs. Malloy and Mr. O'Brien agreed that Annie would leave in two days. Walking home together, Annie burst out, "You don't even know where he's sending me. Didn't get an address or anything!"

For a moment, Mrs. Malloy looked uncertain. "I'm sure it's alright, Annie. He'll know a good place for you and you can write and tell me where you are. No! Better not do that. There'll be talk at the post office."

Annie tried again. "Daddy isn't going to want me to go."

"You listen to me, missy. If you'd done as I told you, you wouldn't be in the family way. Working for Mr. O'Brien is the only thing that keeps your father out of the gutter. Do you want to be the cause of his ruination?"

"No ma'am."

"Then you do as you're told and thank the Lord, Mr. O'Brien is willing to help us in this terrible, terrible disgrace." Mrs. Malloy started to cry.

"Oh, Mama." Annie felt as if she would die of shame.

CHAPTER TWENTY-SIX

Two days later, Annie was driven north to Pensacola by a silent Mr. O'Brien.

"Mr. O'Brien, are you going to tell Ray where I am?"

Mr. O'Brien was silent so long; Annie thought he wasn't going to answer. When he finally did, what he said was so chilling to her that Annie found herself wishing he had never spoken.

"Annie, I'm trying to be kind here."

"Yes, sir."

"My boy knows all about your situation."

"He does?" Annie felt her heart lifting with hope.

"That he does. He thinks this is the right way to handle the problem."

"The problem?"

Mr. O'Brien looked at her coldly. "You're the problem, Annie, you and this illegitimate child you're carrying."

Annie, who admittedly hadn't given much thought to her baby, had at least never thought of it as "illegitimate."

"Is that what Ray said?"

"He doesn't want to see you again, Annie. And he sure as hell isn't interested in any baby."

After that, Annie just sat silently in the car until Mr. O'Brien had delivered her into the hands of Miss Bartlett.

Miss Bartlett, a middle-aged woman, carefully scrutinized the check Mr. O'Brien handed her, then shifted her inspection to Annie, finally sniffing with disapproval.

"You've got your instructions about the baby," Mr. O'Brien reminded the woman.

"I understand perfectly, sir," Miss Bartlett assured him.

"Good-bye, Annie."

"Good-bye, Mr. O'Brien." She watched, as he turned

and walked back to his car. Suddenly, she ran after him. "Mr. O'Brien, please if you could just give me Ray's telephone number, I need to talk to him."

"Now you listen to me, missy. No little whore is going to ruin my boy's life. When you leave here, Miss Bartlett will give you some money. Take it and leave. Don't you come back to Teardrop." With that, he was gone.

***

Overall, life at Miss Bartlett's wasn't that bad. There were three other pregnant girls staying there. Two of them, Angel and Chelsea, were almost twenty. They mostly kept to themselves. The third girl, Gwenny, was only thirteen and obviously terrified. She attached herself to Annie on the first day and in the months that followed

One by one, Miss Bartlett drove the two older girls to the hospital. They were away for a few days, then returned, no longer pregnant and without their babies.

After a few weeks, "once they have their figures back," Miss Bartlett sniffed, the girls departed. Their places were immediately taken by two more frightened girls in the early stages of pregnancy.

"What happened to Angel's baby?" Gwenny asked in a frightened voice.

Miss Bartlett did not reply.

When Chelsea returned without her baby, Gwenny was terrified. "What happened to *your* baby?" she demanded.

"Adopted."

"Where to?"

Chelsea just shrugged.

"I'm keeping my baby," Gwenny declared, her voice ragged with incipient hysteria.

"But you're just a baby yourself."

Indeed, to Annie the very pregnant Gwenny resembled nothing more than a fat baby.

Tears came into Gwenny's eyes. "I don't care, I'm keeping my baby."

"Then why did you come here to Miss Bartlett's?"

Uncertainty crossed Gwenny's round face. "I don't know. Mama said I should."

The thought of keeping her baby had occurred to Annie also. "After all, I don't have to give it up, if I don't want to," she thought.

She experimented with names for the baby, Adam, if it was a boy, and Barbra Allen, if it was a girl. "And I'll make sure people call you by your right name," Annie vowed to the unborn child.

For all her brave thoughts, Annie knew she would not be able to keep the baby. She doubted she would even try. Then something happened to make her determined. Her baby had hiccups.

"What's wrong?" she pleaded with Miss Bartlett.

"Nothing to worry about," said the efficient Miss Bartlett. "Just hiccups."

"Hiccups?"

"They'll stop soon enough."

She was right, after a while they did stop, but not before Annie realized she was carrying a real live human being in her womb. A person who got hiccups! A baby who needed to be cared for and loved.

Her mind was made up. No matter what the difficulties, she was going to keep her baby!

Annie spent the morning practicing. "Miss Bartlett," she said in her most haughty tone of voice, "I've decided to keep my baby."

She had no difficulty at all imaging Miss Bartlett's sniff and her brisk, no-nonsense answer. "I'm afraid that's impossible, Annie," she would say and that would be that.

Annie tried to marshal arguments, but even to her own ears, they sounded impractical and childish. Finally, she decided that no matter what Miss Bartlett's reaction to her announcement, there was really nothing the woman could do about it. *After all, it's my baby.*

Surely, they would want her to sign something at the hospital. "I just won't sign," she assured her bulging stomach. "They can't take you without my agreement and I just won't agree, That's that!"

Surprisingly, Miss Bartlett offered no objections when Annie announced her new intentions.

"Miss Bartlett," Annie's voice was too loud. Miss Bartlett raised an eyebrow. Annie lowered her voice. "I'm going to keep my baby." It came out almost as a whisper.

"What did you say, Annie?"

"I'm going to keep my baby." Too loud again.

Miss Bartlett just nodded. "Whatever you want, Annie." It obviously was a matter of no concern to her.

The baby kicked her approvingly. A warm glow spread through Annie's mind. For the first time in months, she felt at peace.

Two nights later, Annie was awakened by Gwenny. "Annie, something's the matter."

Reluctantly, Annie opened her eyes to discover a distraught Gwenny standing by the bed. The girl was shivering with fear and clutching her belly. Her nightgown was soaking wet. "Annie, I wet myself." A spasm of pain crossed the young girl's face and she clutched her stomach harder and moaned.

"I'll get Miss Bartlett."

"No, don't leave me!" Gwenny clutched at her, causing Annie to hesitate, but when Gwenny gave a scream and fell to her knees, Annie pulled free and ran to find Miss Bartlett.

Miss Bartlett, even aroused from a deep sleep, was her usually efficient self.

"Contractions," she pronounced. "Also," she added with distaste, "your water broke."

"What's happening?" wailed Gwenny.

"The baby's coming."

"No."

"Where's your overnight case?"

Annie ran to Gwenny's room, hauled the small tan case out from the closet, and carried it back. "Here it is."

"I'll get the car."

"No, wait," screamed Gwenny.

Miss Bartlett ignored her. "Help her down the stairs to the front door," she ordered Annie. "I'll bring the car around."

Awkwardly, Annie put her arm around the whimpering wet girl and guided her down the stairs.

Gwenny clutched at Annie's arm. "I've changed my mind."

Annie, who in her rotund condition was having trouble navigating the stairs herself, just nodded comfortingly.

"No, I mean it, Annie. I've changed my mind. I don't want to do this."

"Do what?"

"This."

"Gwenny, you can't change your mind now. You've got to have the baby."

"No, I'm not gonna. I want my mama!"

"Sweetie, you're going to be just fine. I'll come see you at the hospital."

"Come with me now," pleaded Gwenny.

Miss Bartlett put a stop to that nonsense. Efficiently and briskly, she maneuvered Gwenny into the front seat (on which she had prudently laid a rubber sheet) and drove off, ignoring Gwenny's pleas for Annie to come with them.

Annie, watching them drive away, shivered in the night air. Pretty soon it would be her turn and she was just as frightened as Gwenny.

***

Annie was not allowed to visit her friend.

"She'll be back here in two days."

"With the baby?"

"No."

"She wants to keep the baby."

"The baby is dead." Annie's mouth dropped open. "It was stillborn." Miss Bartlett explained.

"But it was moving. Kicking her. I felt it."

"Obviously, it was alive at that point."

"Does Gwenny know?"

"Yes."

Little Gwenny did not return to Miss Bartlett's. "Her mother is taking charge."

"Even before she gets her figure back?" Annie asked with a sudden vicious anger.

"I believe they are not going directly home."

"Of course not."

A week later, it was her turn.

"You are having contractions," Miss Bartlett informed her.

"No," said Annie. She too, had decided she didn't want to do "it."

The efficient Miss Bartlett took out her stopwatch and timed the next three contractions. "Yes," she said. "I'd better call the doctor."

It was amazing how little Annie remembered of the next few hours. The highlights were pain, sweat and bright lights in an echoing tiled room.

"I'm keeping my baby," she reminded the nurse. "I won't sign anything."

"Sure, honey."

She was finally given medication.

"Will it stop the pain?"

"No, but you won't remember it very much, after a while."

"I'd rather you stopped the pain," she begged.

Even though she was the center of all the activity, nobody really seemed to pay much attention to her.

"Don't push."

"It hurts. Owwww"

"Now push. I said push."

"I am."

"Push harder."

"It huuuurts!" There was a gush of relief, but still the contractions came. She heard the wailing of a baby. "What is it?" she asked. "A boy or a girl?"

"Push again."

"Again?" There was a second gush of relief as the afterbirth was expelled and finally the pain stopped. There was a sweet hazy peace.

"What is it?" she asked again.

"This will make you feel better." The nurse was injecting something into the IV line.

"I already feel real good," she said and immediately fell into a deep sleep.

Next, there was bright sunlight shinning directly onto

her closed eyelids. Annie screwed them shut and tried to remain in her blissful drug induced sleep.

"What about the baby," she heard someone ask?

"It died."

"Poor thing," said the first voice.

"Poor thing," agreed the doped Annie. Poor baby, poor mother. Going through all that and then a dead baby."

Annie felt the cool hand of the nurse checking her IV site. "This will make you feel better," said the nurse from far off and Annie dove back, deep into the ocean called sleep.

When she woke, again she was very groggy, but able to open her eyes. She was in a private room. It was nighttime. Lights from the parking lot below flickered like yellow stars. She was very tired.

"Nurse?" Nobody came. Annie fought the desire to fall asleep again. "Nurse?"

A middle-aged black woman in a too tight white pantsuit appeared in her doorway. "Are you the nurse?'

"No, honey. I'm the aide. You want something?"

"Can I see my baby?"

The woman hesitated a moment then said, "I'll get the nurse."

Annie rested her head back on the pillow. This giving birth was an exhausting business.

Instead of the nurse, Miss Bartlett came through the door. Annie was pleased to see a familiar face, even Bartlett's. "Have you seen my baby?"

"It died, Annie."

"What did?"

"Your baby."

Annie was suddenly wide-awake. A deadly chill ran through her body. "That's not true, I heard my baby crying."

"The baby only lived a short time."

"No. I heard my baby crying. It was a strong cry. I heard it."

"I'm sorry, Annie."

"No you're not. You don't, you don't..." Annie broke into tears. "You're not sorry."

"I've come to take you home."

"Home?"

"Back to my place."

"Until my figure comes back," Annie said softly. She lay back in bed. "Miss Bartlett?"

"Yes?"

"Was it a boy or a girl?"

Bartlett hesitated a moment. "A boy."

"Can I see him?"

"Annie, he's dead."

"I want to see him!"

A nurse glided in and did something to her IV. Annie drifted off to sleep.

The next day, Annie returned to Miss Bartlett's. A month later, she left for New York.

In all that time at Miss Bartlett's, she had not once heard from Ray. He didn't even know his son was dead.

***

That was all so long ago.

A breeze blew through the tree in which Annika was hiding, almost like a cradle rocking her. Why, oh God, why, had she brought all that back to mind? It had been over years ago. "Damn. Damn. Damn."

It had grown late; the sun was low. Here in the forest there were deep pockets of impenetrable darkness in the shadows of sunlit trees; a dappled world. There was no sign of the two homicidal maniacs. Was it safe for her to come down?

The wind was really picking up now. Her cradle-like hiding place rocked dangerously. *Down will come cradle, Annika and all.* Far better to get down under her own steam.

It was surprisingly difficult. Going up had been easy, her muscles had been charged with adrenalin and fear had lent her acrobatic abilities she no longer possessed.

She was still afraid, but the immediacy was not as great. Now she had time to notice just how high up she was and how thin the branches really were on her particular tree. She moved slowly, freezing at the slightest creak of the branch under her weight. The last several feet she slid with her belly tight against the rough tree bark until her feet finally touched ground. Still no sign or sound of her two maniacs.

She had planned on heading away from Josie's altar, but once on the ground, she realized her choices were limited. She had either to retrace her steps or take off through the dense forest. As the crow flies, civilization might be only a few miles away, but Annika was not a crow.

Complete darkness could only be an hour away. Already, she could barely make out the way down and out of the gully that had effectively saved her life.

"They won't be able to see any better than I can," she told herself. Gingerly, she placed her weight on her injured foot. Surprisingly, her ankle held. There was a little pain, but not enough to stop her. She started down the gully. Almost immediately, Annika was reminded she was barefoot.

The gully was strewn with rocks. When she wasn't stubbing her toes, she was sinking ankle deep into squashy-marshy forest debris. It was all she could do not to yelp with disgust when she put her foot into a particularly boggy patch.

Finally, she was out of the gully and moving carefully down the barely visible trail. It led to the clearing that contained Josie's altar. Annika nervously twisted her rings as she peered into the clearing. The altar was still there, but there was no sign of her car or the two maniacs. Her car, her purse, her shoes and her watch were gone. The clothes she wore were filthy and so torn they barely covered her. In fact, she noted ruefully, they did not entirely cover her. Even her bra was ripped.

With my luck, I'll be arrested for indecent exposure.

On the other hand, she was alive. She was free of Josie and Eddy-Bob and, most importantly, she was still free of Gerard. She smiled a grim smile; life wasn't so bad, after all.

CHAPTER TWENTY-SEVEN

The road, when she found it, was only slightly kinder to her bare feet than the trail had been. She followed it for about two miles until she came to a darkened farmhouse. Could the people be in bed already?

Her feet hurt, one of them was bleeding, she was cold and now a dog began to bark. It would probably come running out at her and slash her to pieces. In the morning, the farmer and his wife would find her lifeless, torn up, barefoot body. They would shake their heads in annoyance.

"The dog got himself another one, Pa," the farmer's wife would say.

"Yep," Pa would say, chewing on a straw as he patted the dog approvingly.

"What we gonna do with the body, Pa?"

"Put it in the barn with the others, I guess, Ma." They would toss her poor lifeless body into the barn, close the door, and go about their business.

Come to think of it, spending the night in a barn wasn't a bad idea. Keeping a careful eye out for the dog, Annika went in search of shelter. The barking dog found her first. It was a ferocious Dalmatian pup who, after it had almost licked Annika to death, followed her into the barn. The pup was delighted to have company. It insisted on lying so close to Annika, it virtually served as her blanket.

"I'm not sure your owners had this in mind when they bought you," Annika told the pup, who wiggled with delight at the sound of her voice. Annika wrapped her arms around the animal and fell asleep almost immediately.

CHAPTER TWENTY-EIGHT

Annika, comfortably asleep in the barn, was awakened by a voice calling, "Sandy. Yo, Sandy. Come here girl." The Dalmatian pup, yapping happily, immediately deserted Annika and bounded off to her owner and her breakfast. Annika, barely awake and very confused, shivered in the early morning air. *Where was she?*

The answer came almost immediately. "What are you doing in my barn?"

A very tall, very thin, white-haired old man, dressed in overalls, a plaid shirt and thick boots stood in front of her.

Annika sat up carefully. Every muscle in her body ached.

"Good morning," she said politely.

"Good morning. What are you doing in my barn?"

Annika improvised quickly. "I was lost." Well that was true enough. She hadn't a clue as to where she was.

The farmer grunted.

"Your dog was so friendly and I was so tired..." she trailed off. It sounded pretty lame to her, too.

"Why didn't you come to the house and use the phone to call someone?" A reasonable question.

"It was so late..."

Another grunt. Sandy, the Dalmatian, was dancing around them, delighted that her bed partner and her owner had met. Annika, conscious of the farmer's eyes taking in her bare feet and torn clothes, wished she had something other than the strips of her blouse with which to cover herself.

The farmer turned and walked away from her. Annika watched him anxiously. Was he going to call the police? But he went only a few feet to a where a lightweight horse blanket hung neatly from a rod. The farmer pulled it down and handed it to Annika.

"Thank you." She wrapped it around herself, relieved to be no longer practically naked and doubly thankful for the warmth.

"Come with me," he said and stalked out. Annika stumbled to her bruised feet, wrapped the blanket more tightly around her and followed him.

He led her to a warm, cheerful kitchen that smelled of coffee and cooking bacon.

"Lookee what I found." He was talking to a woman in a wheelchair at the stove. She was turning bacon strips in a frying pan. The delicious smells caused Annika to almost double over from hunger.

"Feed me!" demanded her stomach.

Her hosts were Mr. and Mrs. Olmsted. Mrs. Olmsted was friendly, helpful, and the only question she asked was, "What do you want for breakfast, honey?" Mr. Olmsted's conversation consisted mainly of grunts.

When Mrs. Olmsted realized the true state of Annika's wardrobe, she dispatched her husband to Sally's room for a pair of overalls, "to cover the poor thing decently."

"Sally's our girl," confided Mrs. Olmsted as her husband disappeared into the back of the house. "She's maybe some bigger than you, though."

Mr. Olmsted returned with a faded but clean sweatshirt and a pair of overalls. Annika stepped into the bathroom to change. As she tossed her ruined cream-colored silk slacks on the floor, she felt something unbending and unsilk-like in one of the pockets. It was the credit card she had stuffed into her pocket so long ago when she drew out the five hundred dollars at the ATM. As money, it was worse than useless. It would lead Gerard right to her. She stuffed it into a pocket of "our Sally's" overalls. The sweatshirt swam on her and the overalls barely came to her ankles. Width-wise, two of her could have fit in them. But she was truly grateful for the clothing.

After a breakfast of bacon and eggs, biscuits with butter and honey ("we have our own hives") and two cups of coffee, she felt ready to take on the world.

"You want to use our phone?" asked Mr. Olmsted. It was the first complete sentence he had spoken since bringing Annika into the house.

"Ah. No thank you."

He grunted with disapproval. Mr. Olmsted wore a perpetual air of disillusionment. He obviously had his suspicions of Annika. Mrs. Olmsted, maneuvering skillfully around the kitchen in her wheelchair, was far more accepting. Despite her crippled condition, she seemed to find the world a good place.

"You need shoes," she informed Annika.

"I know." Annika nervously turned the rings around her finger.

"What size do you wear?"

"Ten and a half."

Mrs. Olmsted was delighted. "So does our Sally. Good big feet, keep you steady on the Lord's earth."

"Yes ma'am."

Mrs. Olmsted turned to her husband. "Herman, did Sally leave any shoes this young lady could use?"

Herman grumpily went in search.

"You mustn't mind him. He's a worrier."

"What is he worried about?"

"Oh, the usual; money, medical bills, a new wheelchair. We just bought ourselves a new truck. The old one was so bad, no one would take it as a trade-in. So now there are payments. Don't you sometimes wonder what the world would be like if money hadn't been invented?"

Mr. Olmsted returned with a pair of hiking boots in pretty good condition. "Only thing I could find."

"They're fine," said Mrs. Olmsted.

"Sally ain't gonna want to lose these," he protested.

"Our Sally lives off in the city," explained Mrs. Olmsted. "Very smart girl. Does something with computers, doesn't she, Herman?"

Herman grunted.

"I could give you these rings," Annika offered, removing her wedding band and engagement ring with its winking diamonds.

"Your wedding rings?" Mrs. Olmsted was shocked.

"I'm not married anymore."

Mr. Olmsted nodded morosely. His worst fears were justified.

"We can't take them." Mrs. Olmsted was firm.

"They're worth a lot of money." Annika turned to Mr. Olmsted. With one hand she took the boots he carried, with the other, she handed him the rings.

"Herman, we can't," protested Mrs. Olmsted.

Annika and Mr. Olmsted locked eyes. "I'll get you some socks," he offered.

"Thank you."

Annika sat down to put the boots on. Her hand looked naked and free without the rings. The boots fit as if they had been made for her.

She said good-bye to Mrs. Olmsted. Mr. Olmsted followed her outside. "How much these rings worth?" he asked.

The true answer would have horrified him; "More than you probably made in the last five years." Annika looked him in the eye again. "Thousands and thousands," she answered.

He nodded. "You want the truck?"

"What?"

"That there truck." With his chin he indicated a truck so old and dilapidated, it almost belonged in a museum. "It runs. I can give you some gas."

"It's a deal." They smiled at each other.

CHAPTER TWENTY-NINE

He was a heartless bastard.

There is nothing wrong with taking finances into account when choosing a wife.

Standing naked in his steamy bathroom, Ray examined his jaw in the mirror. Should he shave again?

"It's not as if you don't like the woman," he growled to himself. "You've been sleeping with her for the last year."

Except for the last couple of months, a little voice in his head reminded him. *You've been avoiding her.*

Ray glared at his reflection. "I like Susan," he said out loud, daring the guy in the mirror to disagree with him.

The guy in the mirror curled his lip at him. *Big deal!*

Ahh Jesus.

"She wants to marry me," he reminded himself. "She knows my situation and she still wants to marry me."

He decided to shave again.

Later, dressed carefully in oatmeal colored slacks and a pale blue shirt with a blue and tan tie, his shoes polished to a high gloss, carrying the suit jacket over his shoulder, Ray gave himself a final inspection. *You look like a man, now act like one.* Ahh Jesus.

He was going to solve his financial problems once and for all, he was going to insure Patrick's future and he was going to acquire a pretty wife.

He felt sick to his stomach.

They had arranged to meet at Antonio's restaurant. Susan was there ahead of him. She was sitting at a corner table, sipping white wine, looking cool and wholesome. *The All-American girl.* She looked up and smiled at him. *What's not to like about her?*

He kissed her soft cheek and sat down opposite her.

"You look as cool as ice cream and I'm already sweating like a pig."

"You look just fine to me, Ray." She laid her hand on his.

Instead of welcoming the familiar touch, a heaviness settled on his chest. Ray ordered Bourbon and water and took a hasty swallow when it arrived.

"You don't usually drink during the day. Celebrating something?" She looked eager and expectant.

Hell, might as well get this over with. Ray cleared his throat. "I've been thinking about us." He stopped. She waited.

"What about us?" she finally asked.

He couldn't go on. She waited. Finally, she picked up her own drink. Her eyes wondered around the room.

"You're not going to ask me to marry you, are you?" Her voice was calm. Only the tightness of her mouth and her rigid jaw muscles betrayed her emotions.

He felt like a louse. Hell, he was a louse. Lay it on the line, he ordered himself.

"I'm practically broke and so deep in debt that if the slightest thing goes wrong, I'll lose TearVale. Hugh Butler is trying to get custody of my son. The fact that I have no wife to mother him, works against me." He snapped his words out angrily. Abruptly he shut up.

She watched his face carefully. "Is that your idea of a marriage proposal?"

He snorted. His mouth twisting in bitter humor. "You're my friend, Susan. I don't drag my friends into a mess like this.

"It's only temporary," she assured him. He shrugged.

"But after it's over, you won't need to marry me will you?" Her voice was thoughtful.

He started to speak. She held up her hand, stopping him. "Let me get this straight. You don't want to marry me, because you like me too much to take advantage of me. But afterwards, when you're not in trouble and don't need my help you won't marry me because, frankly my dear, you just don't give a damn. You don't love me.

"I'm sorry, Susan."

"So am I." Her voice was a whisper. "You son of a bitch." Her voice was still soft. "Now, I understand why we haven't made love in so long."

"You're a beautiful woman, Susan and you deserve a lot better than a debt-ridden, ex-convict."

She looked at him coolly. "I had forgotten about that."

"Then you're the only one who has."

Susan snapped her purse open and rummaged around in it, searching for nothing, just trying to keep her hands busy. She snapped it shut. Her eyes gleamed with unshed tears. "The truth is, you don't care about me the way I care...cared about you." She stood up.

Ray rose with automatic politeness. What the hell could he say?

"Did you know that Paul Mellon asked me to marry him?" Her voice was pitched higher than her usual tone.

"I know that he's crazy about you."

"Yes, he is. It's a nice feeling to be the one who is loved for a change." She raised her chin defiantly. "I'm very fond of Paul."

Without another word, she turned on her heel and walked out of the restaurant.

Well, you handled that beautifully, asshole.

"Isn't the lady going to eat?" The waiter was standing at the table a salad plate on his tray.

"She lost her appetite," Ray said wearily as he peeled off some bills and handed them to the man.

***

The Hustonville Bank was across the street from the restaurant. Convenient, being able to screw up his personal and professional life in just one small block.

Off to the east, dark clouds hovered, but here in the center of town, the sun was blinding in its noon intensity. Ray slipped on his dark glasses and stared moodily at the bank. Resignedly, he started to cross the street, then stopped.

Damned if he would beg!

His back straightened, his head came up, and his step

became a stride. Nothing was going to stand in his way. If he had to ride Dangerous Ground himself, that horse was going to run in the Derby. The mental image of himself in flashy jockey colors, twice the size and twice the weight of the other jockeys, urging an exhausted Dangerous Ground across the finish line at Churchill Downs flowed like a movie across his mind. He grinned to himself. Failure was definitely *not* an option and he intended to enjoy every damn second of the process.

***

The Hustonville Bank was of white brick. Its floors were highly polished hardwood. Although the air conditioning was more than adequate, antique fans circled lazily overhead adding to the feeling of old money and the stability that implied.

Ray, entering from the sun-blinding street, stopped just inside the door, took off his dark glasses and allowed his eyes to adjust to the interior dimness.

"Morning, Ray."

"Morning, Sally Ann. Elliot in?"

"He's meeting with someone at the moment. Y'all want some coffee?"

Ray shook his head, no. "How long you think he'll be?"

Before the secretary could answer, the door to the office opened and Elliot himself appeared in the doorway. His back was to Ray and he was talking to someone in his office. "If you think it's absolutely necessary...?"

"I do," said a familiar authoritative voice that raised Ray's hackles. Hugh Butler, Ray's father-in-law came striding through the door. He stopped abruptly as he came face to face with Ray. Both men studied each other coldly. Elliot turned to see what was going on. His pale complexion turned an unbecoming shade of blotchy red.

"Oh, Ray, you're here. Good. Good." He was almost wringing his hands. Without moving his body, Ray turned his head and looked thoughtfully at the loan officer.

"Ah, you know Hugh, don't you? Of course, you do, of course you do. Ahhh...."

"Shut up, Eliot, you're babbling," snarled Hugh. Elliot,

closed his mouth with a snap. Without so much as another look at his son-in-law, Hugh Butler pushed past him and exited the bank.

Ray swiveled slowly to watch him leave, and then he turned back to the nervous looking loan officer. "Problems, Elliot?"

"No, not at all." The man gave a nervous high-pitched laugh. "Very forceful man, your father-in-law."

"Quite a coincidence running into Hugh here."

"Well, he is on the bank's board of directors."

"So he is," Ray said thoughtfully.

Elliot ushered Ray into his office and went around to his seat behind the desk. "Now," Elliot rubbed his hands together briskly all the while being careful not to meet Ray's eye. "What can I do for you?"

Ray lowered his lean body into one of the client chairs and crossed his long legs at the ankle.

He started mildly enough. "I need to extend my credit."

"Ahhhh." Elliot mopped his brow with his handkerchief.

Very unbanker-like, thought Ray. Not often you see a loan officer sweating, it was usually the other way around.

"And how much were you needing?" Elliot was still avoiding eye contact.

Ray told him. Elliot's eyes opened wide. "That's a good deal of money."

"TearVale is my collateral."

"Yes, yes, of course." Moisture was beading Elliot's narrow forehead. "However," here Elliot began coughing. Ray waited until Elliot's coughing fit had finally run its course.

"However?"

"Well, we do, that is the bank does... I mean there is already a mortgage."

"I have enough equity in TearVale to cover the additional loan, Elliot."

"But we're a bank, not a real estate office."

Ray was getting impatient. He didn't like jumping through hoops at the best of times and running into Hugh

Butler always put him in a bad temper. Having to bicker with this sweaty loan officer wasn't improving his temper. "TearVale is going to be a multimillion dollar operation, Elliot. You know it and I know it.

"That of course is possible," Elliot conceded, "but..."

"And," continued Ray as if the other man hadn't spoken, "Hugh Butler is only one of the directors of this bank. How do you think the others will feel about you turning down business? Business fully backed by equity in TearVale?"

Elliot visible trembled. Ray stood up. "Draw up the papers, Elliot. I'll be back within an hour to sign them. I have other business to take care of."

Elliot stood up behind his desk and made a last ditch effort. "I'm not sure...I have to confer with..." His voice died off.

"Confer with whomever you all like, Elliot. But have those papers ready when I get back." Ray slapped a genial hand down on Elliot's pudgy shoulder. "See you in an hour." He tried to make it not too obviously a command, but that's what it was and both men knew it.

Elliot nodded. "Yes, in an hour. I'll have Sally Ann..." Again his voice died down uncertainly as he looked around his office apparently hoping his secretary would simply appear out of the blue.

Ray was already out of the office. "Elliot wants you," he said to Sally Ann as he passed her desk.

Outside on the bank's steps, Ray paused, drew in a deep breath and unclenched his fists. Damn Hugh Butler! Would he never get that man out of his hair?

CHAPTER THIRTY

The truck, for which Annika had traded her hundred and fifty thousand dollar rings, was in terrible shape. First of all, it took three tries before it would even start. Once going it became obvious it didn't have one working spring. Every rut, pothole and just plain bump, sent Annika bouncing off the seat against the top. The roof itself was missing any lining it might once have had. The metal was visibly rusted on the inside, but at least it appeared to be whole. Then it started raining.

Okay so the roof wasn't completely without holes, just a few small ones and they were not directly over her head. The window was another thing altogether. The driver's side window neither opened nor closed all the way. Rain was free to bounce through. There was a hole the size of a dessert plate on the floorboards next to the gas pedal. Annika could see the muddy road passing under her feet as she drove. Occasionally, some of the mud splashed up into the cab of the truck. At least the windshield wipers worked, sort of. They moved aside most of the rain, but in exchange left wide streaks on the glass. It was possible, but difficult to see where she was going. Annika slowed even more.

Despite bartering her rings for this wreck of a truck, despite the fact that she was being rained on and splashed with mud, despite the fact that she had lost everything to the hitchhikers, Annika was at peace with herself. She had a full belly and dry clothes. She was alive and still free of Gerard. She grinned. Life was once more an adventure.

CHAPTER THIRTY-ONE

Two hours later, Ray, having signed for the money, then immediately written a check and overnighted it to the Derby committee, was on his way home. It started raining. Hell, it started pouring. Lightning and thunder split the sky. Every pregnant mare at TearVale would probably go into labor tonight, if they weren't already. Visibility was almost zero, and the county road was underwater in dozens of places. It took Ray more than twice the usual time to get home.

The rain was pounding on the roof of his truck. It sounded like hellish jackhammers trying to break through into heaven.

It was a relief when he finally turned into TearVale's lane. He planned on driving right up to the back door and parking his truck under the overhang. Instead, he came to a splashing-sliding halt when he spotted the small, bedraggled figure standing in the middle of the yard. "Patrick?"

"Patrick!" He opened the truck door.

"Daddy." A soaked Patrick came running to him.

"Pat, what are you doing out here in the rain?" Ray grabbed his son and pulled him into the truck. He took off his own jacket and wrapped it around the shivering child.

"Rufus is lost." Patrick's lower lip quivered. "I can't find Rufus."

Ray could barely hear his son over the pounding rain. "What?"

"I can't find Rufus." The boy burst into tears. Ray put his arms around his son and sighed.

"Don't worry, son. That dog is too damn much of a nuisance to disappear for good. He's just out somewhere chasing a rabbit."

CHAPTER THIRTY-TWO

Annika drove through the rain for hours. Eventually, her boots became soaked and her feet grew cold. The partially open window was no longer amusing. She was cold and wet. Lightening flashed in the sky, followed within seconds by thunder cracking so loudly, she was sure the sky was breaking open. She could smell the ozone from the lightning flashes.

The hard dirt road had turned to mud. Even going as slowly as she was, the truck still slid this way and that. She was careful not to clutch the wheel with a death grip nor try to force it out of the slides. So far, she had been lucky. According to a sign she had just passed she was only three miles from a town called Hustonville.

Suddenly, out of the corner of her eye, she saw movement. The truck was swerving toward the movement. Whatever it was, she was going to hit it!

Knowing better, but not knowing what else to do, Annika swung the steering wheel away and applied the brake. Luckily, for her, the brakes were in as bad a shape as the rest of the truck.

Obedient to her command, the truck's nose swung in the direction she turned the wheel. The rest of the truck ignored her. Suddenly, she found herself on a merry-go-round. Her foot slipped off the clutch. Immediately, the truck's engine stalled. However, the truck's body continued to swing on its axis. With the cab staying in more or less the same area, the truck bed swung in a 360-degree turn.

"Oh shit." Despite the profanity, it was a prayer. Don't turn over, don't turn over, she silently begged.

There was an odd bump, and with a squishy sound of a flattened mud pie, the truck came to a standstill. Annika was once again facing in the direction, she had been going and shaking like a leaf. *I need a drink.* The image of an ice-cold vodka martini with two olives sprang to mind.

As suddenly as it had started, the rain stopped. The sun seemed to leap out from behind the now lacy clouds. Warmth seeped into her shivering body. Annika forced herself to relax. "Deep breath," she ordered herself and did so. "Now slowly release. Another deep breath." She could feel the tension leaving her body with every exhalation.

"Okay, now let's see if the engine starts." Before her hand could reach the ignition, there was a sound: soft, babyish, frightened, not even a cry, just a whimper for help.

Oh God, I've hit someone! Pushing the heavy rusted cab door open, she climbed reluctantly down into the mud. There was nothing to see on the driver's side. There was no one in the front, either. It was on the passenger side, in the back, that she found him. At least, he wasn't under the wheels. He lay a few feet from the truck. When he saw her, he made that whimpering sound again and tried to wag his tail. Her victim was a very large, mud-covered dog.

"You poor thing."

The dog whimpered in agreement. He seemed friendly, but even friendly dogs who are hurt will bite. Annika approached him carefully. Apparently, nobody had ever told this particular dog that, when injured, he was supposed to be dangerous. He wagged his poor, sodden tail happily at her approach and tried to sit up. He made it, but not without a cry of pain. There he sat, a big muddy creature, tail wagging, right leg held off the ground, a big goofy grin on his face.

Tentatively, she held her hand out to him. He immediately licked it. The tail wagged even more. He tried to stand, cried out, raised his right front leg and fell over.

Annika looked around helplessly. Aside from the dirt road itself, there wasn't a sign of any human construction. The dog wore no collar. They could wait here for hours before someone else came along.

"What am I going to do with you?"

Wag, wag, pant, pant.

"You're too heavy for me to lift into the truck."

Wag, wag.

"Oh shut up."

Wag, wag, pant, pant.

She couldn't just leave him here on the road.

Inside the bed of the truck, there was an old and very holey canvas drop cloth. It looked bad and smelled worse. Nevertheless, Annika pulled it out, folded it over several times, in an attempt to obtain a reinforced piece of material and brought it over to the dog. He had been watching her anxiously as she walked away from him and over to the truck. The closer she came back to him the faster his tail wagged. When she bent down to put the folded canvas on the ground, his big sloppy tongue immediately began washing her face.

"Enough, boy." But she was laughing. It was surprisingly easy getting the dog to lie on the canvas, wrapping him in it, and dragging it over to the truck. The hard part was getting him into the truck. "Pretend you're a seventy-five pound barbell," she instructed him.

The dog yelped in pain several times. "I'm sorry, boy. I really am. Just be brave now." By the time he was safely ensconced in the truck bed, she was sweating.

Now to see if the damn truck would start. When she turned the key and pressed the gas, it made a grinding sound, then a rumbling sound and finally it kicked over. *Yes!*

Gingerly, she started down the road. Under the hot afternoon sun, the mud was drying fast. As it dried, it left deep ridges and ruts. Annika had to drive even more slowly than when the road had been a track of solid mud.

She looked over her shoulder at the dog in the back of the truck. He was lying patiently, his nose down on the truck bed; he raised his eyes without moving his head to stare back at her. She could make out his tail slowly wagging.

It took over an hour to travel the last three miles.

When they finally hit paved road it was just a narrow two-way blacktop, lazily dissected by a fading white line, but to Annika it was Civilization with a capital C. There was even a sign; "Hustonville," it proudly proclaimed. A large arrow pointed off to the left.

"We're going to Hustonville," Annika informed her passenger.

Wag, wag, pant, pant.

The doddering old truck seemed rejuvenated at the thought of going to town via a paved road. It stopped making that horrible labored dragging sound, restricting itself to a few simple clangs and some gasping-choking sounds from the engine.

When they finally reached it, Hustonville surprised Annika. It was a small country town, but was also a wealthy one. The beautifully restored stores along Main Street reeked of chic and sophistication. The local grocery boasted a sign proclaiming it sold only "natural, organic" foods. No gas stations or fast food joints blotted the manicured pastoral atmosphere of Hustonville's main street. Indeed, Annika was to learn, there were no fast food joints in the entire town, although even the inhabitants of Hustonville were unable to do without gas. A station was hidden around a bend in the road just outside of the town.

All the stores on main street had their awnings extended, providing the pedestrians with shelter from the sun. People moved from one pool of shade to another with the languidness Annika always associated with the South. The only evidence of the pounding rain that had gone on for so long was a freshness in the air and the sparkle of the green lawns.

The town was both quaint and rich looking. To distinguish it from other such places, Hustonville had a distinct horsy ambiance. There were elegant hitching rails outside several of the stores.

Annika's truck stood out like a sore thumb. She saw a parked police car, its driver eying her suspiciously. Acutely conscious of the fact that the truck was unregistered, she was carrying no license and anyway did not want to have to identify herself to anyone, Annika decided to forestall police questioning.

"Excuse me, officer."

The policeman got out of his car and moved slowly toward her. "Ma'am?"

"Can you tell me where there's a vet's office? Ah have a pup back there who may have a broken leg." From years back, she dredged up her soft Florida drawl.

Luckily, the officer was an animal lover. He gave a quick glance into the back of her truck.

"Wag, wag, pant, pant."

Grinning at the injured animal's goofy friendliness, he directed Annika to an animal hospital just out of town. "You can't miss it," he assured her. "Best vet in the county."

"Thank you."

A sign welcomed them to "All Creatures Hospital." As she followed the curved driveway around to the back of the building, she could see a small stable and three corrals. Two of the corrals held horses calmly nibbling on hay. One of them picked up his head to study the truck as it pulled into a parking spot near the door. This was a much more elaborate setup then she had expected. In fact, she wondered if the vets here even treated small animals.

"Well, it says, All Creatures," she reassured the injured dog.

Pant, pant, wag, wag.

He was as friendly as ever, but Annika noticed her injured pal hadn't moved from the spot where she had more or less dropped him.

"Be right back," she told him.

Inside was a dim hallway leading to the front of the building and an empty reception counter.

"Hello?" There was no answer. Annika looked around for some sort of bell or buzzer to ring in order to get someone's attention. Nothing presented itself. It must be later than she realized. But the door had been unlocked.

"Hello?" Louder this time, but still no answer. The reception area was a narrow rectangular room that ran along the entire front of the building. Aside from the front door and the hallway through which she had come, the only other door was behind the reception counter. Feeling like a trespasser, Annika stepped behind the counter and opened the door.

Inside was a brightly lit area. To the left was a lab and

to the right were several closed doors. Annika knocked on the first door. No answer.

She opened it and peered inside. She found a square examination room furnished with a metal-topped counter that held several drawers, doubtless filled with animal medical supplies. A large window was in the back of the room, which looked out onto a cheerful green lawn dotted with large trees. Annika could see white plastic chairs and a picnic table. She closed the door and went on to the next one. Another knock, no answer, a quick look, exactly the same as the first room. Where was everyone? At the third and last door, she knocked again. Again, no answer. She opened it to find this room was as dim as the corridor. A drape had been drawn across the window. Squinting, Annika made out a shape lying on the examination table. It moved. Annika's heart rate skyrocketed. There was a sound, a moan? Annika had taken a step into the room; now she moved back. Her shoulder bumped against the doorjamb. Reflexively her right hand reached out and pushed the light switch. There was a human body on the table!

The body moved. It spoke. "Oh shit."

"Hello?"

The body sat up. "Will you please turn that damn light off?" Annika switched the light off. "Thank you."

"You're welcome."

The body groaned and got off the table. "Oh, my back." The body went to the window and slowly pulled aside the drape. Sunlight flooded the room. "What time is it?"

"I'm not sure."

"I was up all night with a foal that did not want to leave the womb. Little bugger knew what was waiting."

The body was revealed to be a woman in her 40's. Tall, thin, dressed in dark blue corduroy slacks and a rumpled blue denim shirt. Her brown hair was short and curly and shot through with streaks of gray. Her voice was ordinary with only a slight soft southern drawl. She turned and faced Annika. They studied each other. What Annika saw was a no-nonsense woman, with a long horsy looking face unrelieved by make-up, a generous mouth and eyes bright with intelligence.

What the other woman saw was a dirt-encrusted, tired-looking young woman, with a long elegant body, a queenly way of holding her head, beautiful red hair that was at this point, an absolute mess, and big brown eyes weary with fatigue and disillusionment.

"You look as if you need a doctor, not a vet."

"What? Oh no, it's not for me. In the back of my truck, a dog." She stopped. How to explain herself to this woman?

"A dog?" prompted the vet.

"I think his leg is broken."

"Well, let's go see." The vet seemed fully awake now. She led the way outside to the old truck. Wearily, Annika followed her.

Naturally, the dog was delighted to see them. Pant, pant, wag, wag.

"Rufus, is that you?" The dog's tail went into high gear.

"You know him?"

"He belongs at TearVale. How did you get a hold of him?

"We ran into each other. Where did you say he belonged?"

"TearVale. Stud farm about five miles from here." She maneuvered a small gurney next to the truck. "Give me a hand." Between the two of them, they managed to move Rufus from the back of the truck onto the gurney. When they were finished, both women had had their faces thoroughly washed by Rufus' affectionate tongue.

"At least, he doesn't hold a grudge," said Annika as she petted the animal. "You can tell he's in pain."

"Ah-huh. He's a good old boy. By the way, I'm Rachel Lee."

"How do you do? Ahm, I...."

"Any name will do," said the vet good-naturedly. "Hey-You" gets awkward after a while."

"I'm Brianne Malloy."

"Brianne? Nice name."

"Thank you."

"Well, I'd better call Rufus' owner before I start any

treatment." She went away down the hall leaving Brianne and Rufus alone in the treatment room. Wearily, Brianne sat down. Rufus gave her hand a lick.

"How am I going to pay for your treatment, boy? Your owner wouldn't happen to be rich, would he?"

Pant, pant, wag, wag.

CHAPTER THIRTY-THREE

Ray hung up the phone.

That damn dog was always getting into trouble.

Ahh well, Patrick loved the mutt. The kid had been worried sick about his pet. At least when Pat got home from school Rufus would be here waiting for him. As usual, the thought of his son caused Ray's mouth to curl in a smile.

"Must be good news."

Ray turned back to Karen, a neighbor and good friend who owned the nearby Gate Stud.

"The prodigal mutt has been found and as usual it's going to cost me to get him back."

"He's in the pound?'

"At Rachel's with a broken leg."

"Ah, poor baby."

"Yeah well I've got to move it to get into town, pick up *poor baby* and get back in time to meet Brownstein; he's bringing me his new mare."

Karen grinned at him. "Damn, Ray, I'm going to have to keep an eye on you. TearVale is getting too successful. Next thing I know you'll be taking business away from me."

"Gate Stud is too busy right now, Karen."

"True," she agreed. "Want me to pick Rufus up for you? I'm going in to talk to Rachel anyway."

"Yeah? Great. You're a lifesaver, babe."

"That's what they all say."

As Karen started to leave, Ray called out, "By the way, do you know of anyone who needs a job, has an IQ over ten, and isn't afraid of horses?"

"IQ over 10? By the time you get their name someone else will have hired them."

"Well, if you run into anyone like that will you hire

them for me before they can get away? I trust your judgment."

She waved casually. "See what I can do," she said.

***

Back at the vet's Annika, alone with Rufus, tried out her new name. "Brianne," softly she tried it out again. "Brianne," she spoke more clearly. Rufus seemed to approve. "No one," she confided to the dog, "has ever called me Brianne. Brianne," she said again, with more assurance.

"Brianne," said Rachel Lee coming back into the room.

Annika started guiltily. "Yes?"

"I've got approval to go ahead with treatment. Someone will be down to get him in a while."

"How much will it cost?"

"How much do you have?" Rachel seemed amused.

"Ahhh. Nothing at the moment."

"You down here looking for a job?"

Looking for a job? The idea startled her. She was a rich and famous super model. She was married to Gerard Rostand a wealthy member of the jet set. She was Annika.

Forget Annika!

It was the newly christened Brianne who answered. "Yes, I am."

"TearVale might have something. This is their busy time right now. You know anything about horses?"

"I was brought up on a horse farm," said Annika/Brianne, stretching the truth just a bit.

Rachel nodded. She had drawn up a hypodermic. "Give me a hand here."

Annika, no! Brianne, held Rufus' head while Rachel gave him an injection. Within minutes, the dog was sleeping peacefully. The two women worked together in companionable silence. By the time, they heard the sound of a truck driving up, Rufus' leg was set and he was beginning to come around.

A small, dainty looking woman walked into the treatment room.

"Hey, Karen," said Rachel.

"Hey, Rachel. I'm picking up..." then she caught sight

of a groggy looking Rufus. "Dear God, what's he gone and done to himself this time?"

Rachel patted Rufus on the head. "He has a talent."

Pant, pant. Wag, wag.

Karen gave a lady-like snort.

"He's going to be fine," said Rachel. "Needs to keep the cast on for about a month. Should be as good as new."

"Positively accident prone," muttered Karen. "Looks like he had a mud bath." But she seemed glad to see him and petted his muddy head affectionately while expertly dodging his tongue.

"Karen, this is Brianne Malloy," said Rachel. "Brianne, meet Karen Talbot."

"Hello," said Brianne shyly.

Karen wore tailored slacks and a pink and white sweater. Her boots were polished and her make-up was expertly, if too-lavishly, applied. For someone who worked on a farm, her hands were very well cared for. TearVale was obviously a wealthy operation. They would have plenty of staff. Brianne's heart sank. They would never hire some wanderer off the street.

Nervous, Brianne found herself talking almost non-stop. "I'm awfully sorry about your dog. I'm afraid he and my truck had a collision."

"He's not my dog. Belongs to Pat."

"Pat?"

"Patrick. Little boy. Owner's son."

"I broke the leg of a child's pet?"

"Yep."

There didn't seem to be anything to say to that. Not the most opportune time to ask for a job. Luckily, Rachel had no such qualms.

"Brianne says she grew up on a horse farm. She's looking for work."

Karen looked up. "What kind of a horse farm?"

"About twenty horses. They did some breeding, some training. Mostly Morgan's, but there were some thoroughbreds also."

"And what did you do?"

Brianne cleared her throat nervously. She was surprised to find that just speaking about those days caused her pain.

"I mostly helped out my dad. He was a wonder with mares. Also great with the youngsters. I must have helped deliver over a hundred foals. Also," she spoke more rapidly now, not wanting Karen to lose interest in her. "Also, I worked with the youngsters, halter training them, teaching them to load and unload from the vans."

Karen looked at her doubtfully. "I don't know. There's some valuable horseflesh down at the Vale."

"I see." What could she say? Karen didn't know her. She didn't want a stranger messing with the farm's valuable animals. Brianne could well understand her position.

Rachel butted in. "I wish you'd give her a job."

"Why?"

"If she's not working, she can't pay my bill for patching up Rufus."

Karen smiled. "I think the Vale can cover it." She watched Brianne pet the dog.

Pant, pant. Wag, wag.

"He sure does like you."

Brianne smiled. "I imagine Rufus likes just about everyone, doesn't he?"

"No," said Marsha thoughtfully. "Not everyone. How are you at mucking out stalls?"

Brianne looked up with a wry smile. "That's my specialty."

Just like that, she was hired.

CHAPTER THIRTY-FOUR

Ray was unloading sacks of feed when a friendly voice called to him. Ray turned in surprise.

"Reverend. I didn't hear you drive up."

The Reverend John Potter was in his seventies. A tall thin man with a definite stoop to his shoulders, he wore his usual uniform, an ancient, but very neat dark blue suit with white shirt and a red and blue striped tie. His thick white hair was worn in a no-nonsense crew cut. He was the minister at Ray's church and had been a regular visitor when Ray was in prison. In fact, the only visitor.

"How have you been, Ray? I haven't seen you for a while."

Ray grinned. "Church attendance so low you have to make round-up calls on your congregation, Rev?"

Reverend Potter smiled politely at the joke. His voice was mild but insistent. "How are you, Ray?" he repeated.

Ray shifted around in surprise and stared at the man. "I'm fine. Why shouldn't I be?" When Reverend Potter didn't answer immediately, Ray's voice sharpened. "What's up, Reverend? Why the sudden concern?"

"I hear Hugh Butler is on the rampage again."

Ray snorted. "Hugh's always on a rampage." He shrugged. "He blames me for Carol's death." Ray's jaw tightened, his eyes grew bleak. "And he's right, a husband is supposed to protect his wife, even from herself."

The Reverend put his hand on Ray's shoulder. "You should know by now, Ray, the only actions we really have any control over are our own. The only way we can help others is by example and love."

There was moody silence for a few moments, and then Ray turned back to the barn. "Well, I've got work to do.

Care to help stack hundred pound bags of feed, Reverend?"

The old man sighed. "There was a time." His voice was wistful. "Ah well, everything in its season. Come to church next Sunday, Ray. I miss your after-service critiques. Without you there to take me down a peg or two, I fancy myself quite the orator."

"Sunday is the day after the Derby," mused Ray.

"What better way to give thanks?"

Did the Reverend have any idea, just how desperately he needed to be thankful? If things went badly at the Derby, if Dangerous Ground was injured, or ran last, or any one of a hundred things that could go wrong, TearVale would be finished. For a moment, Ray had a picture of himself and Patrick, down at the heels, hobo packs over their shoulders, trudging down a dusty road. The picture in his mind was colored with an old-fashioned sepia tint.

He shook his head impatiently. Nothing like that was going to happen. In fact, if things went badly, what would happen was far worse. Hugh Butler would make good on his threat. He would use Ray's poverty and prison history to get custody of Patrick. And by God, that was never going to happen!

"Ray?"

Ray shook his head angrily. He didn't need anyone's sympathy. Not even from someone as good intentioned as the Reverend.

"I have to get back to work, Rev." He turned to head back to the barn.

"Ray." Impatiently, Ray stopped and turned back to the minister. "Remember, Ray, a man's life may change in an instant. What he makes of that change is his true measurement." Then with a friendly wave of his arm, the Reverend John Potter turned and left. Ray stared after the old man.

"A man's life may change in an instant." No one had to tell him that. He had spent four long years in prison, because of an ill-considered instant. Shaking his head angrily, Ray returned to work.

CHAPTER THIRTY-FIVE

Gerard Rostand was indulging in one of his favorite pastimes, imagining in exquisite detail, exactly what he was going to do to Annika when he had her back under his control.

First, of course, before he so much as touched her, he was going to tell her of all the delights awaiting her. He would strip her naked of course. Then he would ...no, that would come later.

First, he would totally humiliate her. Put her in the doggy position, call in one of the maids to take care of the bed, and while the maid was there, he would pour ice-cold water on Annika's naked ass. Annika would try to move of course, but by merely using his voice, he would force her to resume the doggy position. Then he would take up the rod of passion, a very colorful ivory stick, it was dyed red, a thin flexible rod about three feet long and an inch wide and smooth as glass. He would run it up and down her ass crack, an unspoken promise.

The maid would be frightened of course and try to leave, but he would order her to strip the bed, "so the linens aren't bloodied." Gerard permitted himself to laugh out loud. He could image the maid's face. When she was finished, he would tell her to leave.

She would run out and Annika would be alone with him. No one would interfere, they wouldn't dare. Then he would...there was a knock on the door. Gerard looked down at himself and stoked the discretely expensive fabric tenting over his erection.

"Come in."

The door was opened by a rail thin man with a prominent beer belly. He had greasy looking skin and his teeth had were grayish and looked porous enough to crumble at the first bite into anything not liquid.

Disgusting, thought Gardner.

"You Rostand?" asked the man.

"I," said Gerard, not bothering to stand, "am *Mr.* Rostand and you are ….."

"I'm White."

The moron didn't even realize he was being put in his place.

Gerard watched with distaste as White slouched across the room. The philistine didn't even bother to take note of the priceless antique furniture or admire Gerard's exquisite taste in the arrangement of the room. Without being invited, he slumped into the seat opposite Gerard's.   "You want me to find your Misses, right?"

Swallowing his fury at having to deal with such a cretin, (another sin Annika would pay for) Gerard handed him two carefully printed sheets. "A picture and all the information you'll need."

White studied it carefully. "How much cash?"

"I beg your pardon?"

"How much cash did she have on her?"

"Very little, I'm sure. When she ah…"

"Dumped you."

"She did not…I am concerned about my wife. It is unlike Annika to behave in such a fashion."

"Never done it before?"

Gerard gritted his teeth. "Never."

"You two have a fight?"

"We did not."

"No boyfriends?"

"None."

White's cold eyes watched Gerard with surprising shrewdness.

"And she never ran off before?"

"That is what I said."

"I need the names of her friends."

"I have already covered that area. She is alone. I want you to find her and then you are to contact me."

"You don't want me to bring her back?

"No, that particular pleasure will be mine. Do not inform the police, no matter what the situation is."

White shrugged. "I work for you.

"Exactly. Find her and you will be amply compensated."

For the first time, White looked around at his surroundings. "Oh, I'll be amply compensated whether or not I find this here lady." He was looking at a full-page picture of Annika, dressed and made up as a wife, not a super model. "I already told you my rates."

"When you find her there will be a handsome bonus. The quicker you find her the more handsome."

"Okay." The man nodded and rose from his chair. "Anything else?"

"Nothing. You know your way out."

God, the man was actually malodorous. The stink of sweat and testosterone poured off him. The room would be aired as soon as he was off the premises.

After White was gone and the windows flung open, Gerard's thoughts returned to Annika as his hand returned to his fly.

CHAPTER THIRTY-SIX

Karen and Brianne decided Rufus should ride to TearVale in Brianne's truck. His muddiness and the truck's general dilapidated condition were obviously a match. The three woman easily lifted Rufus into the back.

"See you later, Rachel," said Karen and briskly marched off to her Cherokee.

"Thank you for fixing up, Rufus," Brianne said to the vet.

Rachel shrugged. "My job."

"Yes well, you did a good one. And thank you for getting *me* a job."

"Part of our all-around service," grinned the older woman. They shook hands and Brianne climbed into the cab of the old truck and followed Karen's gleaming Cherokee out of the hospital yard. When she looked back, the vet had already disappeared into the building. Probably going to catch up on her interrupted sleep.

As soon as they left town, white rail fences sprang up on either side of the two-lane road. The fences enclosed mostly empty green pastures. Occasionally, Brianne, *Brianne, Brianne. I must remember my name is, Brianne,* glimpsed beautiful, sleek thoroughbreds peacefully grazing in the lush grass.

Fifteen minutes later, Marsha turned down a narrow private road. They passed under a stone pillared gateway from which hung with a large sign.

TearVale Stud
Home of Great Thoroughbreds.
Birthplace of
DANGEROUS GROUND

217

The private road wound past a white, single story, comfortable looking house, then around some neatly kept stables, and finally came to a stop in front of a long low building that at one time had also been a stable.

The two women lifted the wiggling Rufus down from the truck. The vet had fashioned a walking cast for the animal, so he was able to clump around. Wag, wag, pant, pant, lick, lick.

"Yeah, yeah," said Karen, expertly dodging the dog's tongue. "Go find Pat," she ordered the dog.

First, he finished thoroughly licking Brianne's face, and then he clumped happily off in search of his boy.

A big sleepy looking guy ambled into sight. Karen waved him over. "Mike, this is Brianne."

"Oh, yeah. Hi," the man said, his face brightening when he got a good look at Brianne.

"Hi, Mike."

"Brianne's going to be the new hand."

"Oh, yeah?" He looked real happy about that.

Karen looked amused. "I'll show Brianne The Lodge, then steer her out to the mare's barn and let the boss man know she's here. Think you can get her started?"

Mike didn't answer. He just stood there, staring happily at Brianne. He seemed like a happy sort of guy.

"Mike?"

"Oh, yeah. Sure. Started?"

"She's here to work, Mike."

"Oh, yeah. I can do that." He nodded his shaggy head vigorously.

"Come on, Brianne," said Karen, "I'll show you around."

As Brianne followed Karen, she glanced over her shoulder. Mike was still standing there staring after her, his mouth was open.

"You get a lot of that?" asked Karen.

Brianne blushed. "I'm a good worker," she assured the woman.

Karen just shrugged. "This is The Lodge," she said,

pushing open a door. The Lodge had been converted very nicely into a series of large clean rooms. "This room's empty, you like it, you can have it."

Brianne peered passed Karen. It was about the size of two stalls, the walls were whitewashed, and there was a bed, a chest of drawers and a rocking chair, everything neat, clean and utilitarian. The room had two doors, one opened directly to the outdoors, the second, opened to the corridor where they stood. "Bathroom's down there and there's a kitchen the other side. Food's provided, but you do your own cooking and cleaning up."

"Okay," agreed Brianne.

"You can make sandwiches for lunch. Stuffs in the refrigerator.

"Sounds good." It sounded great: a bed, bath, food, horses, work and a salary.

"Get yourself a sandwich," suggested Karen. "Then head out to the mare's barn. That's it over there." She pointed to a nearby structure.

"Got it."

"I've never hired for TearVale before. Do me proud."

"I will." Brianne stood in the door way and watched Karen drive off, then made for the kitchen. It had been more than seven hours since Mrs. Olmsted's generous breakfast and she was starving.

Later, still munching her second turkey sandwich, Brianne made her way to the mare's barn. Mike met her halfway there and showed her around. There were three sets of stables. One for mares with new foals, one for pregnant mares and mares waiting to be impregnated and one for stallions. The stallion barn was set away from the others.

"Right now, there are only two stallions," Mike told her. "Imperial and Fireman. Imperial's still pretty young, but the boss says he's not top class. Boss'll probably sell him. Fuzzy's top class alright, but he's getting old."

"Fuzzy?"

"That's what we call Fireman."

"Why, Fuzzy?"

Mike scratched the top of his shaggy head in an effort to

stimulate thinking.

"I don't know," he admitted. "He sure ain't warm and fuzzy. He's one mean son of a bitch. Don't never turn your back on him,"

"I'll remember."

"You know how to clean a stall?"

"Of course," Brianne assured him.

"You gotta clean these three down to the clay." He indicated the stalls to be done. "When you've got them completely empty, spread around some of this lime here."

"Okay."

"Use gloves. You have gloves?" Brianne admitted she didn't.

"There's a pair on the wheelbarrow."

"Okay."

"Cause your hands are real pretty."

She looked down at her grubby scratched paws and tried not to smile. "Thank you, Mike. But don't worry about my hands."

"After you've sprinkled the lime, lay down the shavings. Lay it deep. Boss don't want any hock sores."

"Okay."

Mike continued standing there. He seemed reluctant to leave Brianne on her own. Brianne hastily finished the rest of her sandwich, and then pulled the wheel barrow into the first stall. "Do I save the shavings that are still dry and use them again?"

"No, take it all out to the muck heap. We're putting new mares into these stalls. Boss wants everything should be brand new, just for them." Brianne nodded and started shoveling the used shavings and horse droppings into the wheelbarrow. "Don't forget to build up the shavings higher on the sides of the stalls than in the middle."

"I know," Brianne reassured him.

"But make it plenty deep in the middle."

"Okay."

"These stalls were supposed to have been done yesterday, but Jessie came to work drunk. Boss fired him. He don't put up with being drunk. And no smoking in the barns."

Brianne just nodded.

"I'll be in the stallion barn if you need me." He finally left.

Brianne worked on peacefully. She loved the smell of a horse barn.

An hour later, she was still happy. She was also dripping with sweat and had to stop work frequently to blow on her blistering hands. She was strong and healthy, but it had been many years since she had wielded a pitchfork.

"Hello," said a young voice.

"Hello," she replied.

"Are you taking a break?"

"I'm taking a breather."

"Oh." He was thin, about nine or ten, with big gray eyes, tanned skin and dark red hair, darker than hers. There was something familiar about the cast of his eyes. Whomever he reminded her of, the memory was a good one. She smiled at him.

"My name's Brianne."

"I'm Patrick."

"Hi, Patrick."

"Are you the lady who ran over Rufus?"

"Well...yes."

"Thank you for taking him to Rachel." As if conscious of the fact that he was the topic of conversation, a now clean Rufus came clumping into the barn. He crowded so close to Patrick, the boy was almost knocked off his feet.

"Rufus, you dope," said Patrick.

Wag, wag, pant, pant.

Grinning, Brianne, returned to work.

The boy watched her quietly for a while, and then, "Do you like horses?"

"Yep."

"Do you have any horses of your own?"

"Nope."

"We board thirty, but we have five of our own," he said, obviously mimicking someone's business-like tone.

"That's a lot of horses."

"Well..." The boy fell silent, absently stroking his dog's head. "I heard my daddy say it's the bank that really owns them." He looked worried.

For some reason, Annika wanted to reassure him. "That's how a lot of businesses are run. Banks are like a silent partner."

"I don't think our bank is so silent."

Brianne started to laugh, then realized Patrick wasn't being funny. He was really worried.

"I don't think a stud that breeds a horse like Dangerous Ground, has too much to worry about from a bank," she assured him.

Suddenly, he was animated, his voice eager. "That's what Daddy says. He says if Dangerous Ground wins the Kentucky Derby, we're all set."

Wins the Kentucky Derby! If Pat's father was counting on a Derby win to stave off the bank, he must really be in desperate straits. Imagine staking everything on one horse race, especially the Derby. That was the equivalent of planning your financial future based on winning the lottery.

"Pat." It was Mike.

"Hi, Mike. Look how good Rufus is getting around."

Wag, wag, pant, pant.

"Oh, yeah." said Mike as he tried to fend off the affectionate dog. "Your dad's looking for you."

"Where is he?"

"He and Miss Ellis are at the house."

The boy smiled. "Alicia's here?"

"They're waiting on you."

Patrick started off at a gallop. "Bye, Brianne," he called as he disappeared.

"Bye, Patrick."

Mike was looking over the stalls Brianne had cleaned. "Hey, you work good."

"Thanks. Who's Alicia?"

"Huh? Oh, neighbor lady, got her eye on the boss."

"Patrick looked very happy when you mentioned her name."

Mike shrugged. "Kid wants a mother."

"Where's his real mother?"

"Gone."

"Dead?"

Mike shrugged.

There didn't seem to be anything more to say on the subject, so Brianne kept working. But Mike was eager to keep their conversation going. "Alicia's pretty savvy 'bout horses."

"Sounds good."

"She has lots of money, too. So does Karen," Mike added.

Great, thought Brianne, Patrick has a father who is willing to bet the farm on a horse race, and as back up he's got himself a rich girlfriend, two girlfriends. Brianne hadn't even met the man and already she disliked him.

"She's damn pretty looking, too," said Mike wistfully. When Brianne didn't rise to the bait, he said, "Okay then, after you finish here, you should take a break, then come on down to the stallion barn. More mucking out."

"Okay," Brianne agreed. She was dead tired, but she hadn't felt so peaceful in years.

Mike looked around, but could find nothing else to hold him there. He nodded to himself and with obvious reluctance, left the barn and Brianne.

Brianne continued with her work and her thoughts. So Patrick had a daddy who gambled and married rich women and a mother who just ran off and left him. For a moment, Brianne felt a blasting hatred toward that unknown mother.

Whoa! You don't know anything about the woman, she told herself. Anyhow, why are you so concerned about Patrick? She should be worrying about herself, not some chance-met kid who looked very well cared for. But there was something about Patrick...the way his eyebrows slanted, forming sad question marks.

Just like daddy's!

So that's why she was so ready to like him, he had eyebrows like her daddy's. Plus Pat really was a sweet kid. He was probably within a year or two of the age, her own son would have been if he had lived. *Don't think about that!*

She turned with a vengeance to her work.

Brianne was spreading shavings in the last stall, when she heard Patrick's high-pitched excited voice. Looking down the open center aisle of the barn, she saw the boy with a man and woman. Patrick was running ahead of the adults, then running back to them, while Rufus clumped awkwardly after him. Brianne smiled at the antics of the boy and dog. She paid little attention to either the man or woman.

The same could not be said for the woman. "Who's that?" she asked.

"That's Brianne," Patrick answered. "She's cleaning out the stalls for the new mares."

The woman was frowning in her effort to remember something. "She looks like...."

Patrick interrupted. "She's the lady who ran over Rufus."

His father grinned, "And naturally we immediately gave her a job." He patted the clumsy dog affectionately.

"Rufus likes her," explained Patrick.

"In that case, I hope we're paying her enough."

"Aren't you going to interview her yourself?" asked the woman.

"Sure, but I trust Karen."

Just then, there was the sound of a horse trailer turning into the yard. The three turned and went back outside.

***

Fifteen minutes later, Breanne was just finishing carefully piling the shavings around the edges of the last stall. She was wet with sweat. Wood shavings clung to her clothes and hair, making her sneeze. Her back ached and her hands were on fire with blisters. She would have killed for a drink of water.

"Hello there," said a voice behind her. Slowly, Brianne turned around. The woman was standing in the shadows so Brianne had difficulty making her out clearly.

"Hello."

"You look a mess."

Exactly how do you answer a comment like that? Brianne moved to the stall door. The woman stepped back, giving Brianne plenty of room to pass her.

"I'm Alicia Ellis."

The rich neighbor who has her eye on Pat's father. Brianne could see her clearly now, a streaked blond, shorter and slightly rounder than Brianne, but very good-looking. Her clothes were expensive and sensible for barn wear and her hair had been cut by an expert . She looked expensive.

"I thought you might be thirsty." She handed Brianne a bottle of spring water.

"Thanks." Brianne took the bottle and drank deeply. When she finally paused for breath, the bottle was almost empty.

"Patrick tells me your name is, Brianne."

"Ah-huh."

"Do they call you Bree?"

"Sometimes."

"When I saw you from a distance, you looked familiar."

Oh-oh. "I don't believe we've ever met," Brianne said truthfully.

"No," agreed Alicia. "I guess I was mistaken?" She sounded uncertain.

Brianne changed the subject. "Do you work here?"

The idea seemed to amuse the other woman. "I'm a friend of your boss. She was still studying Brianne thoughtfully. "This isn't your usual line of work, is it?"

Oh God, thought Brianne, I'll never be able to escape if I can't even pull this off. "I'm multi-talented," she answered stiffly.

Alicia's eyes flicked over the freshly bedded stall. "Yes, you do good work." It was obvious she was still curious. "Nice meeting you, Bree."

"Thank you for the water."

"No problem." She was gone.

Brianne allowed herself to breathe freely again. Still, she would be moving on again in a few days.

Right after the Derby, I'm out of here.

CHAPTER THIRTY-SEVEN

After dinner, Brianne carried the wooden rocker out of her room and placed it under a nearby tree. She rocked slowly as she sipped a cup of tea. She was tired, but at peace with herself. Gerard belonged to a far-away world. For the time being, she was safe.

It was almost dark when Patrick and Rufus found her. "You want to see Emerald Sister?"

"Who's Emerald Sister?"

"If she comes into season on time, she's going to be Dangerous Ground's first mare. After he wins the Derby," he added.

"Sure, Patrick, I'd like to see her." She got up lazily and followed the boy out to the stables.

"She's our mare," Patrick explained. "So we get to keep the foal. Here she is."

They stopped in front of a stall with the top half of the door open. The mare immediately popped her head out the door and nuzzled Patrick's hand. "Isn't she a beauty?"

Since all Brianne could see of the animal was her neck and head, she had to take Patrick's word. The mare had a kind eye and a beautifully shaped head.

"She's Irish bred, so that's why she's called Emerald Sister."

"Makes sense." Brianne stroked the velvety nose of the friendly mare.

"When Dangerous Ground comes to live here, we're going to make lots of money, Daddy says." He stopped himself and in a more grown up voice, started again. "My *Dad* says people will send us their mares from all over." Then in his excitement, he dropped the more grown-up appellation, "Daddy says Dangerous Ground is going to be the foundation of TearVale."

"After the Derby?"

"Yeah."

"What if he doesn't win the Kentucky Derby?"

Apparently, this was something Patrick had never thought of.

"Of course, he's going to win." His voice grew uncertain. "Daddy says he's a champ." He suddenly grinned, "Like me," he added cockily.

Just then, Mike, in search of Brianne, came into view.

"Mike," Patrick ran towards the man. Emerald Sister snorted at being dismissed so abruptly and pulled her head sharply back into her stall. "Mike, what if Dangerous Ground doesn't win the Kentucky Derby?"

"He's got a pretty good chance. That's a good horse, lotta heart. But, like maybe you should talk to your old man about Dangerous Ground, you know."

Patrick took off to find his father, then stopped and came back to Brianne.

"Don't worry, Brianne," he assured her, "everything's going to be fine."

She smiled down at his earnest face with his two question mark eyebrows. A sweet warmth swept through her heart. How she would love to have a son like Patrick. He turned and ran off to find his father.

CHAPTER THIRTY-EIGHT

Next morning, Brianne met Patrick's father.

She was bathing the new mares that had come in yesterday. One by one, she would bring a mare into the wash area within the barn, attach their halters to the cross ties and, after making sure the water was neither too cold nor too hot, completely wet the mare down. Some of them objected, noisily. One pretty little gray named Grace Kelly, tried her damnedest to kick Brianne.

But Brianne had a soft voice and a soothing manner, so eventually the ticked-off mare quieted down. Taking a large sponge from a bucket filled with a mixture of horse shampoo and water, Brianne soaped her all over, including the mane and tail. Finally, she poured the remaining shampoo-water mix over the horse. Grace Kelly snorted with disgust.

The hardest part was making sure she rinsed away every bit of shampoo. Dried shampoo, Brianne knew, would cause itching, and itching caused scratching and scratching lead to all types of skin problems.

As she worked, she heard a familiar voice in her head. "Rinse them good, girl. Two, three times, if you have to. A little water never hurt a horse. It's the left-in shampoo causes problems."

She smiled as she worked. It was her daddy's voice that she was remembering . Intruding into her memories was another voice, hauntingly familiar yet unknown. It was a real voice, she realized, coming from the office at the end of the barn.

"Now what about that damn well?" asked a strong deep voice. She knew that voice. Where had she heard it before? Whoever it was, he was talking to Mike.

"It's all taken care of, boss."

"I should have done something about it a year ago."

"Ain't nobody been hurt yet, Mr. O'Brien."

Mr. O'Brien! Oh God. Brianne felt her knees give way. She leaned weakly against the soapy mare. Grace Kelly, sensing her strong emotions, moved uneasily. Automatically, Brianne soothed the animal. She must have heard wrong! That was it; she heard it wrong. Mike had a mumbling way of talking. Who knew what name he had really said? It could have been Brown or Bryant or O'Bannon or anything. She had to make sure.

Leaving the still wet horse, Brianne moved down to the office.

Taking a deep breath, straightening her shoulders, she pushed open the door and entered the room.

It was empty, except for a dusty desk with a phone and two mismatched chairs that had seen better days. She looked around her wildly. Was she going crazy?

Then she heard the voice again. They were just outside. She moved to the cobwebbed window. She saw Mike with a man she guessed to be Patrick's father. They were in full sunlight. Mike was facing toward her; all she could see of the other man was his back. Relief flooded through her body. This was a much younger man. He could not be the Mr. O'Brien she remembered from her girlhood.

Their conversation over, Mike went off. The other man turned towards the barn. He seemed to be looking directly through the streaked and dirty window, straight at Brianne.

Since he was standing in bright sunlight staring into the dimness of the office, she knew he could see nothing, but the dark square of glass. Brianne, however, saw him clearly. Ten years had passed. He had grown from boy to man, but there was no mistaking him. Patrick's father was, Ray O'Brien, the boy who had loved her, impregnated her and deserted her!

**

The old cliché is true, time can stand still. Brianne literally stopped breathing.

The wet mare was making her displeasure known by stamping her feet and giving out with an occasional indignant whinny. Brianne awoke from her trance. Oh God, the noise would cause Ray to come to investigate. He would come into the wash area. They would meet. *Never!*

She ran back to the mare, trying to soothe her down.

I've got to get out of here, her mind screamed. I can't see him. I can't! A hot flush of hatred flooded through her entire body. She had to calm herself, her emotions were too strong, she was frightening the mare. A frightened, full-grown horse is no laughing matter.

Take deep breaths. Breathe. Breathe. Slowly. Slower. Slower. Concentrate only on the horse.

Finally, she was calm, she could think again. How, in all the wide world, did he and I manage to end up here? But of course, it was not really all that incredible. Long ago in a sweeter world, they had planned this.

"A horse farm in Kentucky," they had dreamed. "Breed thoroughbreds," he had said.

"Maybe win the Kentucky Derby," she had half-joked, half-wished.

"Why not?"

Why not? For him, the dream had come true, he had TearVale, he had a rich girlfriend. "He even has a son." This last burst out from her. *He even has a son.*

She felt weak with defeat and despair. All these years, she had refused to think about it. Now, she was defenseless against the raw emotions that blazed back as strong as if the horror was just happening.

It was the mare that saved her from running screaming out of the barn, it was the mare that saved her from picking up the nearest deadly object and attacking Ray with it.

Slowly, methodically, Brianne finished wiping the mare down. She led the shinning animal out of the wash area to the cross ties in the sunny drying stall. Absentmindedly, she fed the animal one of the carrots she carried in her back pocket. She patted the mare's strong beautiful neck. She knelt to paint the mare's front hoofs with oil while she considered her options. There was really only one.

I'm getting out of here.

***

Ray O'Brien walked into the mares' barn looking for his new employee. Might as well introduce himself. Patrick was certainly taken with her. Even though he was not yet ten, Ray thought his son was a good judge of character. Thinking of his son always made Ray smile. He was smiling when he found his newest employee carefully oiling the hooves of a freshly washed mare.

The soft rubber matting had masked his footsteps, so she didn't hear his approach. Unnoticed, he was able to observe her for a few moments. She was dressed in ill-fitting and well-worn work clothes. But even in an ungainly squatting position her movements were graceful.

She reminded him of...but he was always being reminded of Annie. Even now, after all these years, he still found his heart beating faster, his instincts on full alert at the thought she might be near. Anything could start him off, a woman's height or some stranger's graceful gesture, even the sight of a crescent shaped scar just behind the right elbow. It was amazing how many women had small crescent shaped scars.

He still vividly remembered how she had gotten it. She had been five. A nuisance. They were scrambling across the rocky streambed when she fell. She had bled like a pig, but she refused to cry. It flashed back into his mind as clear and sharp as if it was yesterday. The emotions that accompanied the memory were also clear and sharp; happiness, tenderness, friendship and exasperation at this little kid who insisted on following him everywhere. He was still thinking of that long ago day when his newest employee stood slowly, stretched her cramped muscles and turned. They were face to face.

For moments, his mind simply failed to acknowledge what his eyes were telling him.

"Hello, Ray." Her voice was cold.

His emotions, confused and intense, slammed into gear; hate, pure and simple. *The bitch!* His lips curled in contempt. "What are you doing here?"

"Washing horses." She gestured to the shinning mare.

He looks exactly the same, she thought, and completely

different. Long ago, she had loved a boy. That boy had proven cruel and uncaring. That boy was now this man standing before her. Her hands shook with rage. To hide their shaking, she shoved them into the pockets of her baggy overalls.

This is my enemy.

I hate him, she yelled silently inside her head. I want to destroy him. I have to get out of here, she thought wildly.

"You've got to get out of here." His voice was cold, hard, and furious.

What right did he have to be angry with her? "Yes," she agreed automatically, "you're right."

"Have you spoken to him?" His jaw was clenched so tightly, he could barely speak.

"To whom?"

"Don't play games with me, Annie."

That got to her. "My name is Brianne," she said coldly. "I have finally become Brianne."

He was confused by her coolness.

"But you'll leave?"

Yes, she would leave. Oh God, yes. She couldn't wait to get away from him. She threw down the brush she had been using to paint the mare's hoofs, brushed her hands together then turned on her heel and walked out. There was nothing keeping her there.

Sitting in the neatly raked parking area, her old truck looked even more pathetic than she remembered. Would it even start? Looking to neither the right nor the left, Brianne climbed in, said a quick prayer to the God of Ancient Trucks, and turned the ignition. Of course, nothing happened.

Ray followed her outside. She's going too willingly, he thought. What damage has she already done?

"Wait a minute." His voice was rough with anger. "What did you say to him?"

She turned her frozen face and looked at him.

"What did you say to the boy?" To his horror, his voice was pleading.

"Patrick?"

"What did you tell him?"

So he does know about our son, she thought bitterly. Was he feeling guilty? No, not Ray. He just didn't want his precious Patrick to know what a monster he had for a father.

"I would never hurt a child."

He laughed bitterly. "No, you've already done that."

"The run-in with Rufus was an accident."

"Rufus?"

"The dog," she was impatient to get away.

"Why did you do it?" The words burst out of him. "How could you do it?"

She had to get away. She couldn't bear having him this close! She tried the ignition again. This time, with a tired cough, the engine caught. As she eased it into gear and steered the truck out of the stable yard, Ray raised his hand in frustration and slammed it hard against the side of the truck. The ancient truck shuddered under the blow.

He wants to kill me…we want to kill each other.

CHAPTER THIRTY-NINE

Once again, she was running away.

Automatically, Brianne turned back toward Hustonville. It was only as she approached the town's sole gas station that she allowed herself to think.

Where was she going? She was worse off now than when she left Gerard. The clothes she was wearing were ridiculous and aside from a credit card, which she could not use, she was broke. Both her manner of dress and her truck would attract police attention. Even if she were able to obtain gas, this old truck would probably not last the day. How far behind was Gerard?

She pulled the truck off to the side of the road and stopped the engine. She couldn't just keep running. *Think.*

Her thoughts were not pretty ones. She had been shocked, even frightened when she first saw Ray. But she was not frightened now. She was enraged. That bastard! That...that destroyer of babies. By now there was no doubt in her mind that if he hadn't abandoned her, their baby would have lived. That this was a flawed argument made no difference to her. He was the cause of her baby's death! He had killed their child. Now, here she was, running away from her baby's murderer.

But what else could she do? Then the answer clicked into place. *You can avenge your dead baby.*

Avenge? How? But she already knew the answer. She had the perfect means of Ray's destruction available to her, Gerard.

What if Gerard were to find her with Ray? It didn't matter what happened to her, what mattered was what he would do to Ray. Unconsciously, Brianne smiled a very cruel smile.

But what if Gerard doesn't find you, asked her inner voice?

I'll just have to make sure he does. I hate that man.

Unbidden into her mind a small, confused voice asked, "Which one?"

Her truck needed gas. She reached into her pocket and brought out the shiny platinum credit card. Time for some shopping, first gas and then clothes.

***

Annika found Hustonville's Boutique Alley with the true homing instinct of a champion shopper. Her boots and overalls initially caused some consternation in the rarefied atmosphere of expensive finery. However, Brianne was a perfect size six, she knew how to wear clothes, she had great and expensive taste, and she had her trail-blazing plastic credit card to pave the way. She was also long past the time when salespeople could intimidate her.

She bought underwear and stockings. She bought a sleeveless blue and cream flowered, slim column of a dress that dropped to flair softly about her hips. She bought a cream and tan summer silk suit. She bought shoes and sandals. She bought nail polish and expensive shampoo. She bought make-up.

More prosaically, she bought jeans that fit and several tee shirts, also sneakers and socks, and a pair of paddock boots. She even bought a very elaborate hat, the kind one would wear to the Kentucky Derby.

Her final stop was an electronics store, where she asked a lot of questions and made her last purchase.

Finally, she found a small Italian restaurant with a leafy patio in the rear. She was the only customer who wanted to sit out on the patio.

"It is maybe too cold today, lady?" suggested the waiter.

"This is fine," she assured him. She ordered Angel hair pasta, a glass of house wine and privacy.

The wine came first. She sat sipping it and staring at the brick wall that surrounded the courtyard. What looked like a grape vine twining over a wood trellis and trees in big pots were there. A bird sang sweetly. In spite of the waiter's worries, the afternoon sun was warm on her shoulders.

Do I do this or not? There must be a someway, I can ruin Ray and still escape Gerard. But no, any way she looked at it, her plan invited disaster for herself. I don't give a damn, she decided. It's payback time for that...that bastard, Ray!

She picked up the mobile cell phone that she had just bought. The salesman had assured her the call could be traced to this general calling area, but not to a particular town.

If she was going to do it, now was the time. Taking a deep breath, she dialed her husband's private number.

Four rings then a pick-up. The voice, so familiar that, for one terrified moment she feared he would reach through the phone and grab her. "This is Gerard, leave your message." Short, to the point, arrogant.

Perfect, she had gotten his answering machine. She spoke three short sentences into the phone.

"This is Annika. I want you to know I'm never coming back to you." She paused and took a deep breath then, making her voice as softly sexy as she could, she added, "I have a new man now." Then she hung up.

It was time to return to TearVale.

***

She was half a mile from the stud farm before it occurred to her that she could not just wander back in and take up where she had left off. Ray would literally throw her off the place.

It was the truck, giving one of its periodic asthmatic wheezes, that gave her the idea. She continued down the road until TearVale's gate was in sight, pulled the truck over to the side of the road and killed the engine. Climbing out, she sorted through the litter in the bed of the truck until she came up with a thin, rusted, but still strong metal rod. She had no idea of its original use, but it was perfect for what she needed.

She lifted the hood of the truck, unscrewed the radiator cap and plunged the metal rod down into the ancient radiator hoping to break through its rusted bottom. Nothing happened. The radiator ignored her efforts. "Hell."

She stepped back and appraised the truck. A blown tire was not as dramatic an obstacle as a punctured radiator, but it would have to do. Taking the metal rod, she plunged it into the thinnest looking spot on the left rear tire. It blew immediately. She would not have been able to travel much further, even if she had wanted to.

She was considering whether to just present herself at the Lodge or wait to be found when the problem was solved for her by the appearance of Mike in the TearVale truck.

"Bree, what you doin' here?"

She ignored the question. "Hi, Mike. Old tire's finally had it."

"I'll fix it for you." He started to get out of the truck.

"No spare," she said hurriedly. Actually, she had no idea if there was a spare or not. "Can you give me a lift back to the Lodge?"

"I'm supposed to pick up something for the boss."

She smiled sweetly at him. "Come on, Mike. It will only take a minute and I have too many packages to walk." She gestured to the truck bed, brimming with her purchases.

Mike blinked slowly. "Yeah, sure, I guess so."

"Thanks." Before he could change his mind, she began transferring the packages to his truck. He got out and helped her.

"What is all this stuff?"

"I needed a few things," she said vaguely.

"Oh."

Five minutes later, Brianne was back at the Lodge. *Now what?*

She decided on the bold approach. After all, it didn't matter what Ray thought, all that mattered was that she be here with Ray, when Gerard found her.

Hours ago, she had been told to take the Bedford mares out to the near pasture after she had bathed the others. Might as well just continue on as if nothing had happened.

Mike had warned her to make sure the gate was closed when she left them there. Since, all horse people were automatically fanatical about insuring gates were securely closed, she had raised an eyebrow in surprise.

Mike had hastened to explain. "See that pasture runs alongside state land. There's a killer gully just on the other side of the fence. We lost a colt there once. Broke his leg. We had to put him down. Boss didn't know whether to cuss or cry.

So he cried over little dead horses, did he? What about babies? What about my baby? The bastard!

***

Brianne, was escorting the second mare to the pasture gate when Rufus, leg cast and all, came charging along, intent on getting Brianne to give him a good belly rub.

To the mare, already skittish at being in a new place, the sight of the panting, wagging, cast wearing, clumsily clumping, large dog bearing down on her was unnerving. With a whinny of horror, she whirled away from Rufus and attempted to lunge past Brianne. For a moment, Brianne feared the frightened animal would head for the dangerous gully that was so near.

The terrified mare kicked her heels out at Rufus and plunged through the hastily open gate, dragging the puny human holding the lead rope along with her.

Rufus stopped short in amazement, shocked that anyone, even a dumb horse, would respond to his friendliness by trying to kick him!

In the meantime, Brianne, after being dragged several feet, finally remembered to drop the lead rope. While this did stop her from being dragged all over the pasture, it also caused her to fall face down into some of Kentucky's finest bluegrass. Her face missed a fresh deposit of horse droppings by all of six inches.

The mare, free of her human encumbrance, galloped happily off, her terror a thing of the past. She dashed in circles, sometimes close to Brianne, sometimes half a pasture away.

The silly mare was in the pasture where she was supposed to be, but Brianne could not just go off and leave her. The lead rope was still attached to the mare's halter. If the animal happened to step on the rope, it would jerk her head down. The horse, thinking her head was caught by some invisible menace, would panic. In her panic, she could cause serious injury to herself. The silly little brute was worth a quarter of a million dollars. Brianne had to remove that rope.

Question: How do you catch a young, healthy horse that is dashing happily and furiously around a large pasture?

Answer: You don't. You let the animal come to you.

Already the mare had slowed and was watching Brianne out of the corner of her eye.

No-way was the puny two-legged human animal going to catch her. She was ready to play.

Brianne reached into the back pocket of her jeans and pulled out a carrot.

The soft snap of a breaking carrot was heard. The mare's ears pricked forward. The luscious, beautiful scent of fresh carrot drifted across to the animal. Forgetting her desire to be forever free, the mare trotted eagerly over to Breanne. She just loved carrots!

Carrying the hard-won lead rope, Brianne latched the pasture gate and turned in exasperation to Rufus. "You dumb mutt!"

Wag, wag, pant, pant.

Rufus threw himself down on his side and waved his unbroken legs in the air, inviting Brianne to rub his tummy. He was convinced humans were invented expressly for that purpose. Brianne obliged.

She talked to him as she rubbed his hairy belly. "Where's your boy, huh, fella? Is Patrick in school?"

"What the hell are you doing here?"

Brianne sat back on her heels and looked up into the angry face of Ray.

She forced herself to continue petting Rufus. "My truck broke down."

"Not my problem."

She stopped petting the dog.

This man killed my baby.

In her mind, Ray had progressed from the man who had

abandoned them, then to the man who was responsible for her baby's death, and now finally to an outright murderer.

"Why are you so anxious for me to leave, Ray?"

His face flushed with rage. "What do you want?"

"What do you think?"

"I don't have any money."

She laughed. "You have more than I do."

"How much do you want?" His teeth were clenched.

Instead of answering directly, she stood up and looked around the pastures. "This is quite a place."

One of the mares, wandering over to the fence to see if there were any carrots in the offering, butted Ray affectionately with her head. Ray patted her absently. Brianne just waited. It didn't matter to her what he said, as long as she was here when Gerard showed up.

"If you think you've landed in clover you're dead wrong." His laugh was an ugly, bitter sound.

Money, money, money, she thought. Just like his father. Give the bitch some money and she won't make trouble. Well not this time.

"TearVale is mortgaged up to its eyeballs," he said.

Ask me if I care.

"Dangerous Ground was bred at TearVale," she pointed out.

"So that's why you're here." He looked off in the direction of the gate. There was a long silence. "He may have been bred here, but he's not mine. He turned back to her, his eyes filled with anger. "You know how it works. Believe me, babe," his tone was bitter and taunting. "You haven't fallen into any honey pot here."

"You're right, she said, I do know how it works. That horse will be worth millions to any farm that gets him for stud."

"Yeah, but I get him only if he runs in the Derby and wins, otherwise the bank just moves in."

She looked at him with contempt. "You bet your home on a Derby win? Jesus, Ray why don't you just buy lottery tickets?"

"Simmons convinced his pal, the judge, our deal was

only meant to go through if Dangerous Ground wins."

"And if he doesn't?"

"TearVale is finished." There was a long brooding silence. "I had to pay the lawyer's fees," he said. "I even had to pay most of the entrance fee for the Derby. Simmons figured if I wanted him to run, I should pay."

"Is that a lot of money?" In spite of herself, Brianne was curious.

"For me, it's a fortune." Oddly enough, Ray was finding it a relief to finally talk about his problems, even to Annie, his enemy. "The only good thing is, if Dangerous Ground wins I own part of him."

"And will he win?"

Ray shrugged. "He can. Will he? We'll know in three days, twelve hours and some odd minutes."

"What will you do if he loses?"

There was a long silence. When he spoke, his voice was firm and decisive. "Start over."

"Then you believe in second acts?"

For the first time he looked at her squarely. "Yes, I do."
There had been no second act for her baby.

She nodded to herself. Gerard would grind Ray into the ground and then piss on him. "You always were a sucker," her voice dripped with contempt.

For a moment, she thought he was going to hit her. His face had gone pale, except for a flush along the top of his sharp cheekbones, his eyes, the eyes she had once thought so beautiful, so loving, now looked at her with hate. He took a step towards her. His hand came up. Involuntarily, she stepped back and turned her face away, waiting for the blow. It never came.

Finally, she looked back at him. He put his hand down. She was embarrassed at having backed away from him. He was studying her intently.

"Used to being slapped around, are you?"
Goddamn him!

She didn't answer. Finally Ray spoke. "I want you to leave quietly and I want you to leave now."

"It's nice to want things." She watched a gray mare in

the next pasture rub her back against a white fence post. "Considering what you told me, our future financial arrangement depends on who wins the Kentucky Derby. So I guess I'll just be staying on at TearVale until the running. In fact, I think I'll attend with you." She smiled at him and batted her eyelashes, "I do hope you've reserved a box?"

"Oh, no you're not." He roughly grabbed her arm. His dark handsome face twisted with rage. "You're leaving now." His large callused hand completely encircled her upper arm. She could feel the burning heat of it. The heat penetrated all the way to her bones, to her very soul. Instinctively, she jerked away and to her surprise, he released her.

Suddenly, Rufus started barking. His tail was going like crazy. He started off in his awkward clumping walk. The school bus was delivering Patrick home.

Ray took a step towards her. His posture was threatening. "Don't you say anything to him."

"Why Ray, you can trust me." She smiled her nastiest smile. "I won't say a word." He was judging her by himself. He was the child-killer. She would never do anything to hurt Patrick.

Patrick came running over to them. "Daddy, Brianne, look what I got." He was proudly waving a paper with a big red "A" on it. "In science." His voice was amazed. "I got an "A" in science, can you believe it?"

"Congratulations, son."

"That's wonderful, Patrick." He looked so proud of himself. Brianne felt a tightness in her chest. Patrick was such a sweet child, so sure of his father's love, so sure of the goodness of his world. *While my child molders in his grave.*

"Go change out of your school clothes, Champ."

"Okay." He ran off happily.

They were alone again. "He's smart, isn't he?" she said. Before Ray could reply, Mike, driving the truck off road, drove up to them.

"Hey Boss." He glanced curiously at the two of them.

"Mike. Anything come up while I was in town?" Ray was all business.

"Yeah. This guy came by. Said he was interested in breeding one of his mares."

"What's odd about that? That's what we do?"

"This fellow didn't know one end of a horse from another.

Brianne froze. Had Gerard found her already? Apparently, he didn't need any helpful phone calls from her.

"So what did he want?" asked Ray.

Mike shrugged. "Couldn't figure him out. He asked more questions about you than he did about the stallions."

"Such as?"

"Where you were from? How long have you been here? Why did you name the place TearVale? Who else lives here?

"And you told him?"

"Told him to ask you."

Ray nodded approvingly. "This guy have a name?"

"Said, Mr. White."

White or Rostand, wondered Brianne? Her mouth was dry with fear.

"Did he leave a number?" asked Ray.

"Nope. Said he'd get back to you."

Ray shrugged. He had more important things to worry about than nosy strangers.

Brianne found herself sick with worry. "What did he look like?" she asked.

If Mike was surprised at being questioned by Brianne, he didn't show it.

"My height, but real thin except he had a pot on him. Too many beers. Kinda greasy skin. Black hair. His teeth were God awful."

"Sounds like a real beauty," grunted Ray.

Brianne breathed a sigh of relief. Obviously, the man was not her elegant Gerard.

Ray was watching her with narrowed eyes. He had noticed her relief. "Were you expecting someone, Bree?"

"No," she assured him with a confident smile. "Poor little ol' me, I'm all alone in the world."

There was an uncomfortable silence broken by Mike. "Ah Bree, you gonna straighten out the feed barn now?"

"I'm on my way."

"Get in. I'll drive you. You want a lift, Boss?"

"No."

On her way to the truck, Brianne passed close to Ray. He grabbed her arm again. She jumped with surprise. She hadn't expected him to touch her in front of Mike.

"You stay away from Patrick," he hissed in her ear.

She stared down in fascination at his hand on her arm. She pulled away, trying to free herself but this time his hand tightened like steel. She looked him coolly in the eye. "Don't worry, Ray, you're safe. I don't hurt children."

Pain etched itself on his face. "How can you of all people, say that?" Dropping her arm, he turned and walked away. Brianne climbed into the truck cab next to Mike. Unobtrusively she rubbed her arm where Ray had held her. It burned from his touch.

CHAPTER FORTY

Much later that night, lying alone in her bed, Brianne played over and over again the terrible equation her life had become. Long after the moon had risen, Brianne wrestled with the trap she had fallen into, a trap of her own making.

If she stayed, Gerard would come. Her freedom would be a thing of the past. The walls of her gilded prison would slam close and this time Gerard would see to it that she never again had a chance to escape. In exchange for her freedom, Gerard would ruin Ray. And he would do it not just once, but whenever Ray picked himself up and started over again, Gerard would make it his business to see Ray fail. She knew Gerard, she knew how he loved to hurt and destroy. Ray didn't stand a chance.

Ray didn't stand a chance.

Wasn't that what she wanted? Of course, it was.

But there was Patrick to consider. In the first flush of her hatred, she had barely been aware of his existence. Now she was forced to consider how her vengeance would affect him.

He would become the son of a failure. The son of a man who, no matter how hard he tried, couldn't win. What would that teach Patrick? To despise his father? To learn that hard work was a waste of time?

Oh God, I can't do that to sweet little Patrick. Funny Patrick. Darling Patrick. She could see his face with his gap toothed smile and his heartbreaking question-mark eyebrows as clearly as if he stood before her.

In getting even with Ray, Patrick would be the one who suffered.

She tossed and turned. What have I done? What can I do to stop it?

You can leave.

When Gerard gets here, they'll tell him you're gone.

"Where?" he'll ask.

"Don't know," they'll shrug. "Stable hands drift on," they'll say.

Gerard would make sure she was really gone. But once he had satisfied himself, he would leave TearVale alone. He would never know about Ray. He would probably hire someone to keep an eye on the place, to let him know if she ever showed up again.

It isn't fair! Damn Ray. He has everything.

"You're right," said the cool voice in her head. "But as long as Ray prospers, so does Patrick. He's a good father."

A good father! That was a laugh. But yes, she was forced to admit that to Patrick, he was a good father.

Sadly, but with a feeling of peace, Brianne made up her mind; she would be leaving TearVale in the morning.

Finally, her eyes closed, sleep was just moments away. Suddenly there was a brisk knock on the outside door. Her eyes shot open. Had Gerard found her already? The knock was repeated. Gerard knock? Not likely. Slowly she got out of bed. The soft folds of her peach colored silk nightgown swirled gently around her suddenly fear chilled body.

As noiselessly, as she could, she crept to the curtained window, but before she could peer out, Ray's voice came through the door. Not loud, but clear and decisive. "Annie, open the door."

Ray? What was he doing here? After their talk out in the pasture, she had thought he would stay as far away from her as possible. For a moment, she considered just ignoring the knock. She didn't need any more complications. Her mind was already made up. She was leaving in the morning. She wanted nothing more to do with Ray O'Brien.

"Annie, open this damn door!"

Without thinking it through, she pulled the door open so abruptly that Ray was caught in the act of raising his hand to knock again.

"My name is not, Annie," she hissed at him. "My name is Brianne."

He blinked at her in surprise. Then, she could have sworn that he grinned. She must have been mistaken. After all, the only illumination was the light from a pale half-moon. Besides, what did he have to grin about?

"What are you wearing?" It was a snarl. No grin there.

"Haven't you ever heard of a nightgown, or do all your women wear jeans to bed?"

As he continued to stare at her, Brianne cast a quick look down at herself. The silky material clung to her long elegant body following every dip and curve. Brianne shrugged. What did he expect? He had gotten her out of bed in the middle of the night.

"I can see right through that thing." Ray's voice was both contemptuous and oddly husky.

Oh, oh. Brianne turned back to her bed, grabbed up the blanket and tossed it around her shoulders, pulling it tightly around her body.

"What do you want, Ray?"

"To talk with you." Without being invited, he entered her small room, forcing her to step back away from the door.

"I don't want to talk to you." Brianne felt a small frisson of fear. Then she straightened her back. She would not be afraid of Ray. All her experience with him had been as protector and mentor. *Except when it really counted,* she reminded herself.

Ray ignored the small sound of protest she made. He closed the door behind him and crossed to the rocking chair, folding his long body into it. Automatically and incongruously, his foot gave a slight push on the floor, causing the chair to rock gently.

"Oh for God's sake," snapped Brianne. As there was no other chair, the blanket still wrapped around her, she sat on the bed, drawing her legs under her. "Okay, talk."

Instead, he asked a question. "Where'd you get that nightgown?" His eyes rested on some of the empty boutique boxes piled carelessly in a corner. "And the other things? I thought you were broke."

She ignored his question. "What do you want, Ray?"

"I want you to leave."

She snorted.

"I have a thousand dollars in cash. You can have it now, tonight, if you leave immediately."

Suddenly, Brianne was enjoying herself. Let him sweat. This was probably the only revenge she would get. She intended to milk it for all it was worth.

"But I like it here, Ray." She made her voice soft and innocent.

To her surprise, Ray lunged out of the chair and grabbed her shoulders. The force of his lunge sent the chair skidding across the floor to bang into the wall.

Instinctively, the two of them froze, waiting to see if the noise had woken Mike, whose room was down the hall.

Brianne looked up at Ray in amazement. His tall figure and wide shoulders loomed over her. The blanket she had wrapped around her, slipped down from her shoulders and onto the bed.

Moonlight illuminated her kneeling figure. Ray drew his breath in sharply. He hated her. She was beautiful, the sexiest thing he had ever seen.

Brianne felt no fear of him. She was well acquainted with what it felt like to be afraid of a man and she felt nothing like that now. His hands on her shoulders loosened.

"Jesus Christ." He dropped his hold on her.

She could still feel the imprint of his hands. It was...was... Brianne could not summon the words to describe how her flesh felt where he had imprisoned it. Her eyes were huge with surprise.

But his gray eyes narrowed as they studied her moonlit face. Abruptly he turned from her. Without a word, he took two long strides to the door, opened it and let himself out. The door closed quietly behind him.

Brianne stared at the closed door through which he had just vanished in amazement. Her thoughts were a jumble.

Oh my God, she thought.

But I hate him, she thought.

First thing in the morning, I'm out of here.

CHAPTER FORTY-ONE

Brianne woke to the sound of Patrick's high-pitched yelling, Ray's cursing and Mike's shouting. Throwing on her clothes, she rushed outside to find a crying Patrick clutching Rufus, (wag, wag, pant, pant) while his father raged at Mike.

"Damn it, Mike I told you to seal up that well. It's a death trap."

Patrick caught sight of Brianne and ran to her, dragging Rufus with him with one hand, as he wiped away his tears with the other grubby hand.

"Brianne, Rufus fell down the well, but I caught him."

Hearing his son say this seemed to enrage Ray even more. "Yes, and if I hadn't come along, you would have been dragged down, too." He spoke through gritted teeth.

"It's bottomless," Pat boasted to Brianne. "It doesn't ever stop, 'cept maybe at China."

"I ordered the cement, Boss," Mike was protesting. "It's coming today."

"Get that well covered, now. Put the cover over it. You can seal it tomorrow, but I want it covered right now."

Mike rushed into the barn.

Brianne walked carefully to the edge of the well. It was a round hole about three feet across. A small wall of cement blocks was stacked around it and some broken wooden boards resting over the top.

"How deep is it?" Brianne asked.

"More than a hundred feet." Ray still looked shaken. "That damn Rufus. Clumsy mutt is always getting into one fix after another." He glared at the animal, who responded to the attention by wagging his tail even more furiously.

"Is it dry?"

"There's a mud bottom. Anything falling in there would

sink immediately. Not that it would matter, the fall alone would have killed him."

Brianne turned pale.

"I dropped a brick in there once," bragged Patrick. "Couldn't even hear it land. You think it really goes all the way to China?"

"I think closing it up is a good idea," she replied.

They watched as Mike came out of the barn pushing what looked like a portable crane attached to a barn cart. In the cart was a thick circular shaped piece of cement, the well cover. Arriving at the well, Mike attached the cover to the crane's sling and using the hydraulic lift picked it up out of the cart, but he was unable to position it correctly. Ray stepped in and manhandled the cover until it was hanging over the bricks surrounding the open well. Both Ray and Mike were sweating.

"Okay, lower it now. Slowly," said Ray as he tried to guide it to its proper position.

But it came down too fast. Fast reaction time saved Ray from losing some fingers. He turned angrily to Mike.

"Are you trying to kill me, man?"

"No, boss. See this here doohickey, it's ahhhh…"

Ray turned away in disgust. In the end the stone managed to cover the well hole, but was slightly too small to overhang the cement blocks. Still it seemed to be secure enough.

"There." Both men were sweating. "First thing tomorrow. And I mean first thing, I want that sealed so tight not even aliens with magic ray guns will be able to get it open. You got me, Mike?"

"Got you, Boss. Don't worry. I'll do it even before breakfast." As if to emphasize his commitment, Mike reached down and grabbed a few loose rocks. He placed the rocks on the well cover. It was a useless gesture, but as a ritual, it seemed to satisfy both the men.

Brianne and Patrick had been standing to one side. Without thinking, Brianne had pulled Patrick close. Despite the fact that he was almost ten, he did not resist, but leaned comfortably against her. She crossed her arms around him.

When Ray turned from the well and saw Brianne and his son together, he caught his breath in horror

Catching Ray's glaring eye, Brianne reluctantly released the child.

"Come on, Pat. Let's get some breakfast." His voice was rough.

Obediently, the boy joined his father.

"Are you angry with me? He asked his father.

"No. Just don't go near that, that...well again."

They walked back to the main house together. "How heavy is the well cover, Daddy?"

"A lot heavier than you are." Then Ray himself changed the subject. "Do you like Brianne?"

"Sure. I want pancakes for breakfast."

"I guess I can manage that."

Patrick had stopped at the kitchen door. He looked very thoughtful. "Do you think Brianne will marry me when I grow up?"

Ray sighed. "Just what I need, a Greek tragedy."

"What?"

"Never mind. Let's get you breakfast."

Just two more days until the running of the Kentucky Derby.

CHAPTER FORTY-TWO

At Ray's order, Mike had put a new tire on her old truck. Brianne fully intended to leave TearVale that morning. But, as usual, the everyday minutia of living intervened in the best laid plans.

She was sitting in the kitchen, studying her map, trying to decide in which direction to head, when Mike found her.

"Hey Brianne, come on. We're shipping five mares to Karen's stud."

"I've never driven a large horse van, Mike."

"Nah, I'm driving, but I need someone for the horses in case there's a problem."

"Are we coming right back?"

"Just there and back," he assured her.

That shouldn't take too long, thought Brianne. She could leave right after they got back. By tonight, she'd be two states away.

"I'll be right there," she said folding up the map.

When she got to the van there was an unpleasant surprise. Ray was there.

"Where's Mike?" she asked.

"I'm driving," he answered. It was almost a snarl. "I need to see Karen."

What she ought to do, thought Brianne, was just turn around and walk away. Instead, she shrugged, what did it matter to her? Besides, Ray obviously hated having her near him. Any little thing she could do to make the bastard uncomfortable pleased her.

Ray was also measuring her, and finally he too shrugged. "Here's the list of mares we're taking. You go get them, I'll do the loading."

Loading five horses was like loading a bus full of unruly

kindergarteners. One of them had to pee and would only do it in her own stall, one of them refused to enter the trailer until Ray bribed her with a green lifesaver, not red, not purple, only green. Two others got panicky at leaving well-known stable-mates behind, and one of them wanted the spot another mare was occupying.

It was almost an hour later when Brianne was finally able to climb into the passenger seat next to Ray.

"God, what prima donnas."

"What did you expect? The cheapest of them is worth well over a hundred thousand."

"Are you saying they know their price tag?"

"They have a pretty good idea."

It was a short ride to Karen's place and a mostly silent one. But this time it was simply quiet. Working together with the horses had temporarily broken through their mutual dislike. For the time being, they were just two people doing a job.

At Karen's there were extra hands to help with the unloading. It went quickly. Ray went off with Karen, leaving Brianne with nothing to do but wait for him. Bored, she wandered around, looking the place over.

It was a well-run stud, larger than TearVale. Everything was neat, clean, and expensive. The paint was fresh, the stable yards neatly swept, the horses beautiful and well kept. Everything that money could buy and expertise could accomplish, was in evidence.

When Ray reappeared, Brianne was stroking the nose of a mare while her colt, hiding behind his dam, watched the human with big-eyed wonder.

Ray walked over to her. "You still love horses."

"Like father, like daughter," she answered lightly.

"I was sorry when your daddy died."

"Yes." She cleared her throat. "Me, too."

"But you weren't sorry enough to come to the funeral?"

Brianne's mouth twisted cynically. "Momma let me know he was dead two days after he was buried."

Ray frowned. He didn't know if he believed her or not.

"Were you there?" she asked.

"Yes. So was most of the county. He was a good horseman."

Brianne smiled. "Yes, he was."

When it was time to go. Karen waved them off. "She seems okay," Brianne said grudgingly.

"Karen? Yeah, she's a great person."

"Does she like Patrick?"

"Patrick? Sure."

"Well that's important, don't you think?"

"Important that Karen like Patrick?"

"If you're going to marry her."

"Marry, Karen! Jesus, where'd you get that idea?"

Brianne shrugged. "Mike said she was rich."

"And you assume any rich woman is automatically on my list of possible brides?"

"Isn't she?"

Ray grinned. "Karen and her girlfriend Jane have been living together for the last ten years. They have a very successful..." here he grouped for a suitable word.

"Relationship?" suggested Brianne.

"Relationship," he agreed.

"Oh." They rode in silence for a while.

"Did you ever marry?" he asked.

She stiffened, and then grudgingly answered. "Yes...it didn't work."

"Sorry." More silence then he asked. "What did you do in New York?"

She took her time answering. "New York is over. Finished for me. I'm starting..." She hesitated. "Starting anew."

"Starting anew," he laughed bitterly. "You do that a lot, don't you?"

"I'm not the one who changed, Ray."

"What's that supposed to mean?"

"Why bother fighting now? It's pointless."

He grunted. Agreement? Disagreement? She didn't care. She wouldn't tell him she was leaving today. She would just go. Let him worry about her intentions. Why should she relieve his mind? And that reminded her, she would no longer be able to use Gerard's credit card.

"I need some money," she said. "How much do you have on you?"

"Right now, you mean?" He was astonished.

"Right now. This minute."

With a curse, he swung the truck onto the shoulder of the road and braked to a stop. He threw open the driver's door and jumped out. Brianne watched him striding back and forth at the roadside. She knew what it meant. This striding back and forth like a caged lion. He was in pain, he was hurt and frustrated. She knew him so well.

No, you don't, she reminded herself! She had never known him. It had all been a beautiful illusion.

Slowly, she climbed out of the truck. He pulled his wallet out of his pocket and pulled some bills from it. "Here," he snarled. "Forty, sixty, sixty-five, seventy, seventy three dollars."

"I'll take it." She held her hand out.

He threw the money at her.

The bills drifted around her and lay scattered at her feet. She just stood there, looking down at them. "Oh, for God's sake." Ray was embarrassed. He picked up the bills and handed them to her. "Here."

"Thank you."

Instead of getting back into the truck, Ray walked over to the white rail fence separating the bluegrass pasture from the road. She stayed where she was.

"This is TearVale, you know."

"What did you say?"

Still leaning on the fence, he turned to her. "This is the beginning of TearVale."

"Everything you always dreamed of."

He snorted. "I forgot to incorporate mortgages into my dreams."

"Yes," she said, "that's the problems with dreams, we forget what they cost." She joined him at the fence.

Without any warning, he turned and pulled her close against his big hard body. Brianne looked up at his tense face. "What are you doing?" She asked stupidly.

For an answer, he pulled her even closer. His eyes burned with sudden passion. He lowered his head to kiss her. His kiss was hard and brutal, grinding against her lips. She gasped and immediately his tongue invaded her mouth. Hot and demanding, he stroked her tongue and the roof of her mouth. He tasted of toothpaste, coffee, and man. Brianne felt her knees weaken. Her hands were pressed against his chest, but she was too stunned to push away from him.

His tongue gentled, his lips were no longer bruising hers. Instead they rubbed her mouth sensually, his tongue, now a seductive suitor.

As his arms pulled her even closer, her hands dropped to her side. Her breasts were crushed against his chest, her belly and pelvis hard against his. One of his hands moved gently down her spine. She shuddered with unexpected passion. His hand moved lower, cupping her buttocks. She could feel him hard against her belly. Now he was rocking his engorged maleness against her. One of his legs pushed between her thighs.

Dazed by the unexpected response of her body to his, amazed that her body still could respond without terror to a man's embrace, Brianne made no protest.

He continued stroking her body, rubbing himself against her aching womanhood. One of his hands cupped her breast, stroking lightly, causing her nipples to harden and pout.

I can't let this go on, she thought.

He must have felt her stiffen with rejection. Before she could protest and demand to be released, he did. Deliberately, he moved his body away from hers. She blinked up at him. His hands dropped from her arms. For a moment, she staggered, and then found her balance. Confused, she looked up at Ray. He was regarding her with unconcealed disgust.

"For seventy-three dollars," he mused. "Dad was right."

Brianne made herself move further away from him.

"Was he?" Her voice was cold as ice. She had her own memories of Ray's father. "Don't touch me again," she warned through gritted teeth.

Ray just snorted. "Not unless I have another seventy-three bucks, huh?"

"You bastard." *God, he's as bad as Gerard.*

"Don't bother putting on an act, Annie. Dad told me everything."

"My name is Brianne and your damn father told me everything, too."

Ray hesitated, *I've hated this woman for years*, he reminded himself. Then why had he kissed her? *God, she felt so good.* His body was aching with want. *She's a lying bitch.* Still he heard himself asking. "What did he tell you?"

She hesitated. What was the point of rehashing those terrible conversations with Mr. O'Brien? She had already made up her mind to go. "It was a long time ago, Ray. Let it go." She turned back to the parked truck.

"Wait." Tiredly she stopped. His voice was horse with pain. "My dad told me how you went away. Didn't tell anyone until he was born. Nobody knew where you were."

Her eyes focused on his mouth, the mouth that was saying all these incredible things. The mouth that had just kissed her and awakened something sweet and painful within the very core of her.

"I wrote to your mother," he continued. "I called. She said...she said," here his voice faltered. "She said you didn't want to see me. Wouldn't even talk to me. She said she asked you and you said no."

Her mother, the Methodist nun, a liar and a hypocrite. *Could she possibly have thought she was helping me?* No, as usual her mother was helping herself, hanging on desperately to her vision of herself as the perfect wife, the perfect mother. *Anyway, it no longer mattered.*

"Your father knew where I was," she turned back to the truck.

"No, he didn't! He told me he didn't know."

Even now, Mr. O'Brien was reaching out to control them. *I will not allow his lies to continue. I will not allow that bastard to win.* She turned to Ray.

"Do you want to know what your father told me?" she asked. "He told me you didn't want to have anything to do with me. WITH US!" She screamed the last words.

"How could you believe that?"

"How could you believe I would just go away?" It felt good to defend herself.

Ray looked punch drunk. "Dad said you sold him the baby."

"What baby?"

"You sold him for a bus ticket to New York and three hundred dollars. You just up and disappeared."

"What are you talking about? My baby died."

"Died?"

"I never saw him. They told me my baby died." Her voice softened. "I thought I heard him crying, but they said he only lived a few minutes. It was a healthy cry. I know it was!"

This was too painful. She didn't want these memories, they were better buried along with her baby. In her head, she heard that cry, over and over again. Ray was talking. What was he saying?

"He did a paternity test. He said I couldn't trust you. Had to be sure he was mine," said Ray.

"What?" She stared at him in horror. "Are you talking about Patrick?"

He nodded.

Patrick, Patrick. The name pounded into her skull almost blinding her with pain.

"But you were married?"

"We didn't have any children, just Patrick."

"Patrick? Oh, God. Oh, God." It was as if a giant fist slammed into her belly, knocking all the wind out of her body. Her knees gave way. She crumpled to the ground, crying like a baby.

Ray was kneeling next to her. Carefully, he put a hand on her heaving back. She was moaning now, rocking back and forth and moaning wordlessly. He pulled her up to her knees. "Brianne, Brianne." She was saying something now. He couldn't make it out. "What did you say?"

"All these years. All these years. How could he do that? He killed my baby."

"Brianne, he's alive."

"But he was dead to me," she wailed. He put his arms around her. Suddenly, she turned on him and begin hitting him with her fists, trying to kill him, trying to make him hurt as she had hurt. He rocked back and grabbed her flailing fists with one of his hands.

"Whoa, whoa, darling. Whoa, baby." Keeping her fists safely imprisoned her pulled her frantic body close to his. She rocked against him in rage and pain. Then she was crying.

There was nothing elegant, nothing sweetly and fetchingly feminine about these tears, they racked her body. She coughed and cried and gasped, unable to breathe through her pain. Slowly he rocked her in his arms. Talking softly to her.

"I'm sorry. My God, I'm sorry." Talking nonsense, just holding her and being there. Kneeling at the side of the road, they rocked back and forth, back and forth.

CHAPTER FORTY-THREE

Much later, Ray drove her back to TearVale. When they pulled up at The Lodge, he got out and helped her down from the truck. Her knees were still unsteady. She looked like a woman in deadly shock. She scared the hell out of him. He held the door open for her.

She just stared straight ahead. Did she even see him? Could she hear him?

"We'll talk later," he said. She didn't react; just stood there, frozen, swaying weakly, saying nothing. He gently led her to her room. If Brianne had been asked to describe what she felt at that moment, her answer would be, "Tired. Exhausted. Numb." As soon as the door closed behind her, she fell onto her bed and was asleep in minutes.

She awoke in the afternoon, confused and disoriented. Had she dreamed it? No, it was no dream. She sat up tiredly. Her body seemed to weigh hundreds and hundreds of pounds. What time was it? Almost three thirty. The school bus would be dropping Patrick off any minute. She had to see him. Just one more time, she promised herself. *Just once, I want to see him and know he is my son.*

And then you have to leave, said the cool voice in her head.

"And then I have to leave," she echoed dully.

Because Gerard was coming.

***

She stationed herself at the near paddock gate so she could watch her son walk up the driveway. It wasn't just the eyebrows he'd inherited from his grandfather. Patrick had the same infectious grin. The red hair he had from her, but it was darker than hers was. His eyes were gray like Ray's. He walked like Ray, so straight and proud.

"Thank you, God," she found herself praying. "Thank you for this precious gift."

As soon as he saw her, Patrick with Rufus trailing, came charging up to her.

"Guess what, Brianne?"

"Hello, Patrick."

"Yeah, Hello. Guess what?'

"What?"

"I didn't fail my spelling test."

She laughed. Ridiculously, her heart swelled with pride. She wanted to reach out and ruffle his hair. She wanted to grab him in a bear hug and never let him go. She wanted to be his mother.

Then he and his dog were charging off to find his father.

It was time for her to go.

***

The one thing she had forgotten to buy on her shopping spree was luggage. Brianne was packing her things into two large plastic bags when there was a knock on her door. "Come in."

The door opened and Rufus came clumping in. "Don't tell me you can knock on doors now?" she said to the dog.

He gave her a doggy grin. Wag, wag, pant, pant.

Patrick pushed the door wider and entered. Her heart caught in her throat. She had not planned on seeing him again. "Hello, honey," she said to him.

"Bree, Daddy had to go into town but he said, can you meet him tonight after dinner?"

I'll be gone by tonight.

"He says he's got something real important to talk about."

"I don't know if I can, Patrick. I should be leaving."

"No," said the boy. "Please don't go."

"You want me to stay?" She glowed with happiness.

"You gotta stay for the Kentucky Derby," he insisted. "It's just two more days."

"I'd forgotten about that."

"How can you forget about the Derby?" He was

amazed. "Bree, I think you should talk to Daddy tonight."

"Why?"

"So's he can tell you to stay."

"Ahhh."

Having delivered his message, the boy turned to go then turned back. "Yes," he said.

"Yes, what?"

"Yes, I do want you to stay." Then he was gone.

Brianne looked down at her packing. Why, oh why, did life always get more complicated, never less? What should she do? Was it safe to stay just a little longer?

In the end, she stayed. After all, what difference could just a few more hours make?

***

That evening, Brianne took a long hot shower. She towel dried her thick hair and combed it neatly away from her face, letting it hang down her back in rippled waves.

Taking a cup of tea with her, she went outside and sat quietly in the rocker, waiting.

Ray came down the drive from the main house, walking quietly, hands in his pockets, deep in thought. The sound of the rocker caused him to look up. Brianne was mostly in the shadow. It was hard to see her clearly. The lights from The Lodge sent a small glow out into the night. As she rocked back and forth, her head and shoulders went in and out of the light. Annie was so beautiful, more so than ever. No, not Annie, he reminded himself. She was Brianne now.

"Hello, Bree."

"Hello, Ray." Her voice was low and lovely and sad, it sent slivers of desire through his body and pain through his heart.

"We have a lot to talk about." Then he said nothing more. There was just a strained silence. He cleared his throat. She studied him.

He's really quite beautiful, she thought. Not the beauty of the male models she was so used to. His was a beauty of roughness and strength. His face was all flat planes and hard angles. Even his hair with its crisp curls faming his face, looked strong and course. The boy she had known had matured well. Deep inside her, she felt a soft tug of longing. *I'd like to run my fingers through that hair.* And then; *whoa girl! This is Ray. Never again!* Her love for Ray was long dead and it was going to stay that way. It had to.

Ray was studying her just as intently.

She made her voice brisk. "What did you want, Ray?"

"Your forgiveness." His voice was rough and abrupt. He was obviously not a man who apologized easily and probably not often.

"It was a long time ago. It wasn't your fault."

"Yes, it was. I knew you. I should have believed in you."

"Yes," she agreed. "I should have believed in you, too."

He snorted. "You were a child. A child having a child. You must have been terrified."

Even though he couldn't really see her in the dark Bree nodded her head. Yes, she remembered. She had been terrified. Oh God, it was all so awful!

There was another silence. Ray seemed to brace himself as if for a blow. "Will you tell Pat?" He asked.

"No"

"No?"

"What's the point? No matter what's happened between us, Patrick has to be protected."

Ray took a deep breath. He was a man reprieved. There was another long silence. Neither knew what to say next. Brianne rose from her chair. He put out a hand to stop her from leaving him just yet. "Let's go for a walk."

"All right."

In silence, they followed the path to the far pasture. Leaning on the fence, watching the moonlight play on the slow ripples of the stream that cut through the pasture, they were finally at ease with one another.

"When did you marry," she asked him?

"While I was in college. She..." he hesitated. "Carol said she was pregnant."

Bree snorted.

"She lost the baby. I'm not even sure it was mine."

"What, no paternity test?"

Ray looked out over the moonlit pasture. "She was as

different from you as day from night." He sighed deeply. "I brought Patrick to live with us. I thought he needed a mother."

Beside him, he heard Bree make a soft pained sound.

"I chose badly. Carol was a druggie. The only reason she married me was to get away from her parents and school. For all I know, drugs may have been why she lost the baby."

"Did you get a divorce?"

"No." His voice was strained with pain. "She died. OD'd." He went on as if once started he couldn't stop with his tale. "I was working at a stud not too far from here. Patrick was what? Two...three. She went off with some...people. Even took Pat with her. They...her friends, dropped her off at the local emergency room and took off."

"Patrick?"

"They dropped him off, too. Hugh, her father came to tell me." Ray stared off across the field, his voice flat, emotionless like a man reciting a not very interesting story that had no connection to him.

"I was at work. He drove up, half-crazy. Yelling, cursing, and crying. He blamed me. Said I was supposed to look after her. Screamed at me, "What kind of a man are you to let something like this happen to your wife?""

"Where was Patrick?"

Ray looked down as if surprised to find her there. "He was with Carol's mother. They, Hugh and Sarah, love Patrick."

"That's good."

"Maybe, maybe not."

"And since then?"

"Since then?"

"Everything's been all right?"

To her surprise, Ray laughed. "Not exactly." She waited. He turned to her, watching her through narrowed eyes. "I killed a man," he said.

Her mouth fell open. "You killed a man?" She couldn't keep the horror out of her voice.

He turned away roughly. "Never mind."

"No. Who did you kill? Why?"

"It was manslaughter. After Carol died. I was drinking."

"You loved her," she said, surprised at the pain the thought caused her.

"God, no. That's what was wrong. I felt nothing. I felt relief...and guilt. She was my wife. I should have taken better care of her."

"Most of us can barely manage to take care of ourselves, let alone someone else."

He nodded. "That's what Reverend Potter said. "He says we each have to save ourselves. All we can offer another is love. But I couldn't even give her that."

His pain is not mine, Brianne told herself. She would not touch him; she would not wrap her arms around him and hold him. She would not!

Instead, she wrapped her arms around herself and shivered.

"Let's go back." His voice was flat and weary.

"In a moment." Her thoughts were running all over the place, the cold was the least of her problems. "Manslaughter. What does that mean?"

Ray sighed. "I was in a bar. Drunk. It was the night after her funeral. This bastard was boasting about supplying drugs to all the lonely local housewives. He boasted they gave him whatever he wanted, as well as money. Someone tried to shut him up. Told him I was present. The bastard got right in my face. Right in my face," Ray repeated as if even now he could still see the laughing, taunting face inches from his own.

"I hit him. I had to hit something." Ray's teeth were clenched in memory, his strong body tense. "Me and my goddamned temper." Forcing himself to breathe deeply, he tried to drive away the remembered rage. Carefully, he loosened his tense shoulders. "The bastard went down. Hit his head on something. Two days later, he was dead, and I was in jail."

"You went to jail?"

He turned to her, his eyes calm. "I spent almost four years in prison, Brianne. I got out three years ago."

Brianne peered up into his face then she looked around

her. "You've accomplished a lot in three years," she said.

"Nothing's accomplished yet," he corrected her. "All you see here is potential."

"Where was Patrick while you were in...away?"

"Carol's parents took care of him while I was in prison." He said the word "prison" calmly, refusing to sugarcoat his life.

"They must be nice people to take care of a child that's not blood kin to them."

Ray thought briefly of his continuing struggles with Hugh. "They love Patrick," he admitted. He turned to her and looked at her lovely profile. "Do you have any children?" he asked.

"Patrick!"

"I'm being clumsy. I meant, any other children?"

Remembering Gerard, Brianne shuddered. "No." Her voice closed off the subject.

He saw her pain. "Brianne, I'm so sorry."

"It's over now."

Not for me, it isn't, he thought, studying the beautiful woman that little Annie Malloy had become. She shivered again. Automatically, he took off his jacket and draped it around her shoulders.

For just a moment, she could feel the warmth of his fingers on her shoulders through her thin tee shirt.

"Thank you."

"You're welcome."

He turned away, his hands gripping the fence rail.

It was so beautiful here, she thought. It was on a night like this they had made love. The memory was vivid, unfaded by time.

Next to her, Ray loosened his hands from the rail and turned to her. "Would you mind?" he asked.

"Mind?"

"I want to touch you."

She stared up at him, mesmerized as he slowly stretched out his hand and touched the hair that was blowing gently around her lovely face. Then he bent his head, his lips just inches from hers. Abruptly, she pulled back.

"No. It's too late."

"I don't believe that," he protested.

"Believe it, Ray," she said gently. "It's far, far too late."

Blindly, she turned away.

"Annie," he said. "I mean, Brianne."

"What?"

"I loved you then."

She replied as if he had asked her a question. "Yes," she said. "Isn't it strange after all that's happened, I still remember how much I loved you, too?"

There was so much pain. She had to get away from her memories, from him. "Good-bye." Oh God, she was crying. Blinded by the tears, the darkness, and the strangeness of her surroundings, she missed the path and staggered as her foot caught on something. His hands grabbed her, holding her steady.

"No. Let me go!"

"I will if you'll stop staggering around like a drunk." His voice was a growl.

She whirled angrily and shrugged away from his grip, panting heavily from undefined fear and unwanted desire. Her hair whirled wildly. In the thin wash of moonlight her face was as white as paper.

He stood, hands on his hips, his eyes fastened onto hers, his face unreadable.

"If you've finished talking I'm going in now." Her voice was cold and clipped.

"Oh, I've finished talking all right."

"Good." She turned away and immediately felt his hands on her shoulders. "No, don't." It was a plea.

"Yes." He turned her to face him. She stared up into his face, barely visible in the night. He was too big, too broad, too tested by time. This was not her Ray, not the boy she had loved. This man was a stranger.

The stranger bent his head and brushed his mouth against hers.

"No, I don't want to," she cried.

I have to get away from him. I have to get away from him. The sentence ran hot like a racehorse around and around in her mind. He wasn't holding her now. He had released his hold on her shoulders as soon as she cried out. She shuddered as her traitorous body leaned into his strong body.

"I don't want to," she protested.

His arms came around her hard and tight, crushing her breasts into his chest. He was kissing her again. No soft brush of his lips this time. His mouth was hard and hot, his tongue flicked against her lips, obediently she opened her mouth to him. He was inside her. The tip of his tongue brushing softly against the top of her mouth, leaving her burned and shaken wherever it touched. In all her life, she had never responded to anyone as she was responding to Ray. His arms pulled her tighter against him, their two bodies melding into one.

She sighed and her arms came up to wrap around his neck. She made a small mewling sound.

"Jesus," he muttered into her mouth. It was a prayer. It was a curse. His hands moved down from her waist, stroking the curve of her buttocks. They cupped her cheeks and pulled her against him. Through his jeans, she could feel the heat of his body and the hardness of his erection. Instinctively, she rubbed herself against it. He growled deep in his throat and lowered his head to kiss the side of her neck before moving on to her ear. His tongue flicked gently along its edges. Her insides quivered with desire. She shuddered and moved her melting body even closer to his hardness.

"Bree?" His voice was hoarse with desire.

Brianne felt as if she was looking down at herself from a long distance, completely disassociated from what her body was doing.

"I can't do this," she heard her voice say. Then, "Let me go."

Watching herself as from a far distance, Brianne saw herself step back, out of Ray's arms. He was letting her go. She wanted to cry out, 'No. Keep me with you.'

"We can talk tomorrow," Ray said.

But of course, they would never talk tomorrow. Tomorrow, she would be far from here. At the thought of that she froze. Never again would she see Ray. Never again would she have a chance to hold him and touch him, to satisfy this incredible hunger for him.

"Wait," she said, moving back to him. How did she go about this? What could she say to this well-remembered, newly met stranger? Reaching out a hand, she rested it on his chest and looked up into his gray eyes. As she watched, they darkened with desire.

In the end, no words were necessary. In the end, he encircled her in his arms, and then he kissed her breasts through the thinness of her T-shirt. She moaned and gasped in shocked surprise, but instinctively pressed herself against him.

His tongue flicked across her aroused nipples. He stepped back and pulled the T-shirt from her slim body. Moonlight turned her pale body into alabaster. Her breasts, small and beautifully rounded took his breath away.

His hands cupped both breasts, his thumbs stroking the nipples. "Ahhh." She arched her back at the incredible feel of his hands on her.

"Do you like that?" His voice was a husky growl.

"Mmmmm" All she could do was moan.

"Tell me," he demanded.

"Yes. Oh, yes." She tugged at his shirt, her fingers clumsy, wanting to feel his bare chest against her nipples.

Impatiently, he stepped away from her and yanked the shirt off over his head.

His body was darker than hers with a faint ridge of dark hair bisecting his hard-muscled belly. His upper chest was smooth, silk on steel. He pulled her tight against him. Her nipples rubbed deliciously against him. He growled somewhere deep in his throat. He kissed her shoulders, the inside of her arms and then back to her breasts.

Brianne, shocked at the strength of her passion, clung to him, letting him do whatever he wanted.

Finally, still keeping his hands tight around her arms, he pushed her slightly away from him.

"If you want me to stop, say so now." His voice was rough and husky with passion. Her senses dazed, Brianne could barely hear him. She didn't answer. "Brianne, you have to tell me."

"What?" Why was he talking? She wanted to melt back against his body. She wanted his mouth on her breast and here he was *talking*.

"Tell me what you want."

"I want...love me. Make love to me." She was whispering almost frantically now. "I want you inside me." She moved against him, rubbing her body against him like a cat, terrified of being left alone and empty.

He put his hands on her buttocks and pulled her tight against him, pressing her against the hard bulge in his jeans. He rocked himself against her until she thought she would explode with desire.

"Do you want this?" His chest was damp with sweat.

"Yes."

"What?"

"Yes."

"What do you want me to do, Bree. Tell me."

"Put it inside me."

His hands came between them, stroking the "V" between her legs. Even through the rough cloth of her jeans, fiery passion seared her.

"Please," she moaned.

He was undressing her now. Exposing her to the moonlight. Turning her whole body into alabaster beauty. Gently, he laid her down on his jacket. Never taking his eyes off her panting body, he kicked off his boots, pulled down his jeans and quickly stepped out of his underwear. His penis jutted out imperiously. The sight of it drove her wild. She could feel the eager wetness between her legs. Her mouth was dry and feverish. As he stood panting above her, she rolled to her knees and reached out her hand. Softly she stroked his rigid maleness. Ray groaned.

He caught her hand, knelt next to her then pulled her down onto the ground with him.

From the waist up, she lay on his jacket, but from the waist down she lay on the cool bluegrass of Kentucky. She could feel the separate blades of grass stroking her behind.

She wiggled seductively.

He was panting, short hard breaths. "Sorry, darling."

"Sorry?"

"I can't wait anymore."

His heavy legs parted her thighs; he cupped her buttocks with his strong, callused hands, and then tilted her towards him. His penis, hard as steel, probed at her softness.

She was slippery with desire for him and burning up. Oh God! She was so hot that her very insides were melting. Then, he was inside her. Hard, so strong, and blessedly cool against her feverish flesh.

She was conscious of nothing, but the point where their two bodies joined. He moved slowly in and slowly out.

"No, don't leave me." It was exquisite torture.

He exhaled loudly, almost laughing then he slammed into her.

"Ahh, Bree, you feel so good." Again and again, he slammed deeper and deeper into her body bringing blessed relief while at the same time igniting new desire in her with every stroke.

She felt his balls stroking her buttocks. They too, were blessedly cool against her fevered skin.

"Harder," she pleaded, arching up to meet him. Sweat poured off his body onto her.

Suddenly, he was kissing her breasts again, as his body continued to smoothly pump itself into her. Supporting himself on one elbow, his slid his right arm down between their bodies. He was touching her between her legs even as he continued to pump out his lust. His long fingers found her swollen clitoris and stroked it. Once...twice,...She couldn't stand it. Her mind and body exploded!

From somewhere far away, she heard him groan out her name, a shudder shook his body, a half laugh, half sob, then he was lying full length on her, still inside her.

Brianne blinked slowly back to reality. The last time she had felt so satisfied, so completely possessed was more than ten years ago...with the same man.

Afterwards, they walked slowly back to The Lodge, their bodies separated by inches. He kissed her gently.

"Come and have breakfast with Patrick and me in the morning."

It felt so good being held by him, to feel his warm breath on her forehead. What difference could a few more hours make? Just once, she would have breakfast with Ray and their son.

"All right."

I'll leave right afterwards, she promised herself.

As the door closed behind her, Ray O'Brien took a long shuddering breath. Was this a miracle or a disaster?

CHAPTER FORTY-FOUR

The next morning was the first time she had been in the main house. Her impression was of woodwork that needed dusting and lots of big windows and bright sunlight, a pleasant and homey place. The breakfast nook overlooked the back pastures which seemed to go on forever, interrupted now and then by polite white fencing.

During breakfast, Ray quizzed Patrick on his vocabulary list. Brianne sipped her tea, looked out over TearVale's acres and felt faint stirrings of happiness.

Patrick finally grabbed up his schoolbooks, yelled, "Bye, Daddy," and ran out of the room. A moment later, he rushed back in. "Bye, Bree."

"Good-bye, Patrick." She pulled him close to her and gave him a quick hug. "Have a good day at school." Then he was gone, racing for the school bus. "Does he do well at school?" she asked.

"Usually. He's pretty good at math."

"I have a son who's good at math?" Brianne turned that over in her mind. She grinned. "He didn't get his math talent from me."

Ray studied her gravely. "Brianne, are you running away from something?"

"Only the last ten years," she answered lightly.

He ignored her facetious tone. "Because if you are, if you need legal help? I know a good attorney."

"I'm not running from the law, Ray, if that's what you think."

"Then let me rephrase my question," he said. "Not what are you running away from, but who?"

She sat back in her chair. Once again, her eyes sought the restful rolling acres of TearVale. "Don't worry about it,

Ray."

"That's not an answer, Brianne."

She smiled gently at him. "I never thought you and I would ever make love again."

The diversion worked. He looked at her sharply, his eyes suddenly intent, filled with a sensual gleam. "We could do it again."

She laughed. "Now?"

"Now."

Suddenly, her mouth was dry. She ran her tongue over her lower lip.

"Now," he repeated.

"Don't you have work to do?" she asked.

"Nothing that can't wait." As he started to reach for her, his cell phone rang. He glanced at the caller ID, grimaced and sent Brianne an apologetic look.

Brianne laughed a very shaky laugh.

"Hello?" Ray said into the phone. Brianne could make out a male voice speaking rapidly. Ray listened, occasionally making an encouraging grunt. Then, "All right. No, I haven't forgotten. Ah-huh. Yeah. Okay." He hung up and turned back to Brianne but just then, there was a sharp knock on the door.

Mike stuck his head in. "Jameson is here about Imperial." Catching sight of Brianne he added, "Hey Bree."

"Hey Mike."

"Ahhh you gonna bathe them new mares today?"

Automatically, Brianne stood up. Ray caught her hand. "Tell Jameson I'll be there in a minute. Bree will be along soon."

"Okay." Mike took himself off.

"It's just as well," Brianne said gently.

"No it's not," Ray muttered. "Wait a minute, Bree."

"Yes?"

"That was Jack Simmons on the phone." She looked at him blankly. "Dangerous Ground's owner."

"Oh right. The little twerp?"

"Yeah, well. Anyway, the little twerp is having a party tonight. It's a pre-Derby party," he explained. "There are dozens of them this time of the year. Simmons is throwing this one and it would be politic to show up."

"I thought you two had quarreled?"

Ray shrugged. "At the Derby level, the horse world is a very small place. Jack and I will have to work together. I consider this party a rehearsal in civilized behavior." He hesitated then said, "Will you come with me, Bree?"

"What about Patrick?"

"He'll be fine. Mike will be here."

She hesitated. Common sense told her time was running out. Gerard could turn up any minute now. It was too dangerous. Just thinking about what he would do to her...

"All right," she said.

CHAPTER FORTY-FIVE

That afternoon, Rachel, the vet, showed up. She seemed pleased to see Brianne.

"So you're still here. Good. I like my recommendations to work out."

Brianne smiled back.

"It's certainly worked out fine for me."

Rachel had come to check out the pregnancy status of two mares that had been serviced by Fireman. "See if they've caught or not. We may have to send Fireman in for a second try."

Brianne brought the first mare out of her stall, put her in the cross ties and stood at her head, soothing her, as Rachel did her examination. Running the portable sonogram over the mare's belly, Rachel kept her eyes on the monitor she had set up on a feed barrel.

"Good," said Rachel with a smile. "This one's caught."

Brianne returned the now officially pregnant mare to her stall and brought out the second one.

After running the sonogram over the second mare's belly, Rachel frowned. Apparently, she didn't like what she was seeing. Using a well-lubricated, very long glove, Rachel carefully inserted her hand and arm up to the elbow, into the mare's vagina. The mare moved with what Brianne considered understandable restlessness.

"Easy girl," Brianne soothed her. "At least, you don't have to put your feet in stirrups."

"Uh oh."

"What?" asked Brianne.

"Twins," grunted the vet.

"Oh." Brianne knew what that meant. Horses were not properly built to deliver twins. It almost always resulted in the mother suffering, sometimes dying during delivery. And of course, one or both of the twins could die with her.

With the tips of her gloved fingers, Rachel carefully felt the two round objects that were the twin embryos. "I hate to do this," she said to Brianne. "I always wonder if I've removed the wrong one. Ah well." With a sigh, she carefully pinched one of the embryos until it had lost its roundness. Now the mare was pregnant with only one foal. Rachel withdrew her arm.

The mare snorted with annoyance. Brianne fed her a carrot and returned her to her stall just as the school bus dropped Patrick off. Brianne watched as Patrick came rushing over.

"Don't let's mention this to Patrick," said Brianne.

Rachel nodded.

"Hi, Bree. Hi, Doc."

"Hello Pat," answered the vet, as she repacked her equipment into her van. "How's that accident prone dog of yours?"

"He's not prone," protested Patrick. "He's just curious."

" Ahh that explains it." She patted the panting dog who, had been waiting at the bus stop and now accompanied his boy. "Tell Ray I'll be back in two weeks to check on things," she said as she climbed into her van.

Patrick and Brianne stood together, watching Rachel drive off. Then he turned to her. "Are they pregnant?"

"What?"

"Pregnant?"

"Pregnant? Oh, the mares. Yes they are."

"Good old Fireman, he never misses. I hope Dangerous Ground is as good."

Brianne smiled down at the boy's enthusiasm. "So do I."

"Daddy says you're coming to the Derby with us.

I am? "Is that okay with you?" she asked.

"It's great. We'll be just like a family." Then, as if realizing he had said too much, he yelled for Rufus to follow him, and galloped off. Watching him, Brianne felt as if her heart was melting with love.

***

That night, after scrubbing herself free of her stall mucking-out odors, Brianne dressed in her cream and blue dress (totally inappropriate for the evening), put on her make-up, natural, *not* Annika-exotic, brushed her hair into a semblance of restraint, and went to the party with Ray.

The Simmons' home was a large mansion, bluegrass fashion, which meant it had a definite ambiance of The Old South; very unlike The Hamptons on Long Island, which went in for what Brianne called "Sea Air and Salt Water Taffy" architecture.

They were greeted by a small blond woman who shrieked with delight, yelled "Ray," and threw her arms around him.

Ray grinned down at her and returned the woman's hug. "No one can say you hold a grudge, Liz."

"Nonsense, darling. Everybody sues everybody these days. TearVale is much the best home for the beast. I've told Jack that time and again."

"And again and again and again," agreed a balding, well-built man, who was only slightly taller than his wife. "Hello, Ray. Glad you could make it."

The two men shook hands, and then Ray introduced Brianne. "Bree, Jack and Elizabeth Simmons, our hosts."

Brianne held out her hand, but Elizabeth ignored it and gave her a hug instead. "Call me, Liz, darling," she said. "So much quicker."

"Brianne is an old friend," Ray was trying to explain.

"Well, Ray darling, one can see that, can't one?"

Liz's husband shook Brianne's hand. "Welcome to our home, Ms...?"

"We'll just call you, Bree. Is that all right?" cut in his wife.

"That's fine." Brianne decided she liked Liz Simmons.

The party was an elaborate one. There was an elegant buffet with small tables scattered around the ballroom. There was a live band and people were dancing.

She danced with her host. His head barely cleared her shoulder, but he danced beautifully. She danced with Tom,

Dick and Harry. Finally, she danced with Ray.

"It's about time," he said, pulling her into his arms. "I had to fight two dragons, a corps of knights-in-arms and pay off three guys ahead of me. You're the bell of the ball, Bree."

"I love to dance," she said laughing. Her body fitted snugly against his. Man-woman, hard-soft, curves and angles all where they should be. The dance was a waltz, dreamy and satisfying.

Ray held her close, loving the way she fit into his arms, as if she was made just for him.

We fit together so perfectly, thought Brianne. I've been designed just for Ray.

Suddenly the band switched tempo. A quick wildness invaded the music, assaulted the blood coursing through Brianne's veins.

It's only a dance, she told herself. But it's a dance with Ray. Brianne was aroused. Her skin flushed, the pupils of her eyes dilated with desire; desire for Ray, here, now, right this minute. Ray was also aroused.

The dance ended. When the music started up again. Ray and Brianne stood very still, taking in big lungfuls of air, their eyes locked in desire. Around them couples drifted past.

Someone bumped into Ray, another couple whirled close enough for Breanne to feel the soft scrape of the woman's silk dress against her arms. Slowly, Ray opened his arms; she walked into his embrace. They moved, not really dancing, too entranced by their own desires to pay any attention to the music.

***

Later, Brianne sat in a small room that had been set aside for the ladies. She was alone, staring blindly into a mirror, as she attempted to repair her make-up.

"Wow, honey. That was some mating dance you two were doing." Liz Simmons bounded happily into the room. "Now tell me everything. How long have you two known each other?" Brianne just smiled. "That long!" Are you two getting married?" Liz was nothing if not direct.

"Married?" The question caught Brianne off guard. She would never be able to marry Ray. She was already married to Gerard.

"Sweetie, say something," implored Liz.

"Do you think Ray is looking for a wife?" Brianne countered.

"Good questions," Liz looked thoughtful. "Up until now, it looked as if Susan was on the fast track to being Mrs. O'Brien. But after tonight, I don't know."

"Who is Susan?"

Liz slapped her hand to her mouth. "Oops." She looked at Brianne out of the corner of her eyes. "Susan Bender. Everyone thought it was a sure thing... until tonight."

Brianne swallowed down the jealousy that shot through her body. "Have they known each other long?" She was trying to sound causal.

Liz patted Brianne's arm. "He's never looked at her the way he's been looking at you tonight."

When Brianne returned to the main room, the music was still playing, and people were still dancing. There was still laughter amid the delicate clink of glasses and silverware, but for Brianne, the whole evening had slightly shifted. Once more, reality had come trippingly along and smacked her over the head.

Of course, Ray had a girlfriend. Had she really expected him to be waiting breathlessly for her to return to him after all these years? She looked around. There he was glass in hand, talking to a tall slim woman who bore more than a passing resemblance to herself.

When she joined them, Ray made the introductions. "Bree, I'd like you to meet, Susan. Susan, this is Bree." The two women smiled insincere smiles and said how pleased they were to meet each other.

Ray, becoming aware of a certain tension in the air, man-like, ran for it. "Bree, you don't have a drink."

"I don't really want one."

He paid no attention. "I'll be right back." He was gone.

Bree and Susan eyed each other. Susan started digging immediately. "Will you be visiting here in Kentucky for long?"

"I'm undecided."

"Ahh. Do you like horses?"

"Passionately."

Something, was it approval, flickered in Susan's eyes. "Do you ride?"

"Like a Comanche," Brianne bragged. At least, I did ten years ago, she added silently to herself.

Susan was outright grinning now. "I have some fine hunters," she told Brianne. "You make Ray bring you on over, you hear?"

"Thank you, I'd like that." Oh well, so what if Susan was good looking, owned horses, and practically lived next door to Ray, Brianne found herself liking her.

Susan took a sip of her drink. Brianne got a good look at her hands. "Is that an engagement ring?" Her heart sank.

Susan held it up so Brianne could admire it. "He proposed yesterday. We're going to have a big old engagement party next week. You tell Ray to bring you."

"Tell Ray to bring me?"

"Why sure, honey."

"Isn't that taking Southern hospitality a bit too far?"

"Bree." Ray had returned. "Here's your drink."

She took it from him and immediately gulped down half of it.

***

They were in the car on their way home when Susan's words came back to her. "He proposed yesterday."

Yesterday? When? Over the phone? Did one propose marriage over a phone? She studied Ray's profile. "Did you propose over the phone," she asked him?

"Hmm?"

"Did you propose to Susan over the phone?"

Ray looked startled. "Propose what?"

"Marriage."

"Marriage! Where did you get an idea like that?"

"From her engagement ring."

It was difficult to see his face in the dim light of the car but his voice was definitely amused. "And why would you think she got that engagement ring from me?"

"Liz said you and Susan were serious."

"Liz!" His voice was a mixture of exasperation, amusement and admiration. "I knew she'd zap me somehow. That open arms welcome was too good to be true."

Brianne wasn't interested in Liz. "So you and Susan...?"

"First you think I have my eyes on Karen and now Susan. Why do you keep trying to marry me off, Bree?"

Feeling suddenly much more lighthearted, Brianne answered with a laugh. "I guess I just hate to see perfectly good husband material going to waste."

"So you think of me as perfectly good husband material, do you?" Brianne said nothing. They pulled up in front of TearVale's main house. "Will you come in for a drink?" Ray invited.

She hesitated. He sat perfectly still, not looking at her, refusing to exert any pressure.

"All right," she answered slowly.

Ray led the way into the living room and switched on the light. The first sight that met their eyes was Patrick, asleep on the couch. He was clutching a large book and had obviously fallen asleep while reading.

Brianne stopped in the living room doorway. Her son looked like an angel. His hair fell in bangs across his forehead, his lips were slightly parted and little puffs of breath were the only sign he was still attached to this earth.

Ray carefully took the book out of Patrick's sleeping hands. Silently, he handed it to Brianne. It was a book on thoroughbred horse breeding. Brianne smiled. "There must be a gene for being horse crazy."

"He comes by it legitimately," said Ray. "From both of us." Gently, he picked up their sleeping child. Patrick mumbled something, but never opened his eyes. Brianne followed Ray as he carried the boy up the stairs into his room.

While Ray held Patrick, Brianne pulled back the bed covers. The boy never woke when he was placed in his bed and the covers pulled up around him. Brianne sat on the edge of his bed staring at the sleeping child. Slowly, she leaned forward and kissed his cheek. Patrick made a small satisfied sound and burrowed deeper under his covers.

Ray was careful to leave the bedroom door open a crack. As they went back down the stairs, he took Brianne's hand in his. At the bottom of the stairs, he turned and gently kissed the mother of his child. Softness and desire radiated through her body. Ray pulled her closer and she came to him eagerly. Her mouth hot on his.

His tongue gently probed her lips. She opened them and sighed with pleasure when he kissed her deeply with his tongue and lips. Losing all sense of time and place, she clung to him. It was Ray who broke away. "Let's get married."

"Married?" What was he talking about? She wanted him to continue kissing her. She wanted to feel his hard strong body against her melting softness. The last thing she wanted was a conversation.

"Married," he insisted.

"Now?"

"Well, not tonight. Tomorrow."

"Tomorrow?" She was trying to think. "But tomorrow is The Derby."

"Afterwards." He was laughing down at her. "I have a friend, Reverend Potter, he'll marry us."

"Don't we need...?"

"Need what?"

"I don't know...a license or something?"

"I'll take care of all that. I'll call him right now."

"Ray it's after one in the morning." She was waking up from her daze of desire. She could never marry Ray. She was already married and Gerard would never let her go.

"Right. I'll call him in the morning. He'll be at the race. We can do it right afterwards."

"Ray, no."

"No?"

"I have to think about this."

He immediately stepped back. "Not such good husband material after all?"

"I just have to think about it." She saw his face close up. "Ray," she touched his face softly with her fingertips, "it's not you, it's me."

"We've always been meant for each other," he said.

"Finding you, finding Patrick. Everything. I just have to think."

"Of course, you do." His voice was very formal.

"After the Derby," she said. "We'll talk about it after the Derby."

"After the Derby." Very gently, he took her hand and raised it to his lips. She could feel the warmth of his breath on her hand. "Will you stay with me tonight?"

"I want--I need to think."

"I see. I'll walk you back to The Lodge."

She tried to distance herself, but he caught her hand and held it firmly. They held hands all the way back.

There was a light on in Mike's room. Otherwise, The Lodge was dark.

This time, when Ray pulled her close to him, there was no soft exploratory kiss. The kiss was bruising, deep and hungry, pure passion. They were both gasping for breath when they parted.

Brianne, fighting not to give into the passion that was turning her body into a lust driven machine, pulled away. If she made love to him now, she would never be able to leave, and leave she must. Tonight.

"Tomorrow," she promised as she fled into the safety of The Lodge. Her last word to him, a lie.

Inside, everything was dim and quiet. Somewhere she could hear a radio, softly playing Country and Western music. Brianne was shaken by the strength of her desire for Ray.

Lust, it's just lust, she told herself. Liar! You've never felt this way about anyone else. But it's just lust, she argued. Right, she sneered. You've come all this way, turned yourself into a pretzel, just for lust.

I didn't know he was here!

You didn't know, but deep inside yourself this is what you wanted. Be honest. No. Yes! I don't know. And that was the honest truth. She didn't know. Could she trust him? Could she trust her own instincts? She didn't even know what her instincts were telling her.

"What a mess," she moaned.

She ran the shower long and hot, then abruptly turned off the hot water and stood under the freezing downpour, teeth chattering. It's not working, she thought with a laugh. I thought cold showers were supposed to be a cure. I still want him. Oh God, do I want him.

As she dried her cold tingling skin, she could hear the radio very clearly and began humming along with the music. She was still humming when the music stopped and the news came on.

"Two carjackers have been arrested," she heard the announcer say. "Josie Billingsly and Eddy-Bob Hutchinson were taken into custody this afternoon after a high speed chase that led the police through three counties."

Good! They got those maniacs. I hope they throw the key away.

The country and western music started up again.

***

What time was it? She glanced at her bare left wrist. Ah yes, the maniacal hitchhikers had stolen her watch. She had forgotten to buy a replacement. Anyway, she knew what time it was. Time to go. She looked around the room she had occupied for so short a period. Everything she owned was packed into two plastic bags. Only the ill-fitting overalls still hung in the closet.

To leave Ray now with no explanation was unthinkable. All she could risk was a note. Composing the note was difficult. She made several tries. At first, she got no further than the salutation. "My Darling Ray," she wrote and immediately crumpled it up. "My Dearest Ray"? That too found its way into the wastebasket. "Dear Ray"? No, it sounded like a business letter. "Darling"? No! Finally, she settled on just plain Ray.

> *Ray,*
> *I have to leave. This is best for all of us.*
> *If someone comes looking for me, just tell*
> *him I have moved on. **DO NOT** say there is*
> *any connection between us.*

I cannot see you again.
Thank you for telling me the truth
about Patrick. Take good care of him. Take
good care of yourself.
Brianne

The note said nothing about her feelings or her regrets. Why dwell on what could not be? She folded the note neatly, wrote Ray's name on the outside, and placed it prominently on top of the chest of drawers where it would be easily seen. Suddenly cold, she pulled on Ray's jacket. She would take his jacket with her.

She picked up her plastic bags full of clothes, turned off the lights and closed the door quietly behind her.

Good-bye, TearVale.

CHAPTER FORTY-SIX

Outside, clouds had appeared and blotted out the stars. The moon was just a pale fuzzy disk. It was so dark she had to feel her way around The Lodge, over to where her truck was parked. She placed the plastic bags in the bed of the truck, covering them with the same ratty tarpaulin she had used to carry Rufus.

Leaning against the truck, she looked up at the dark sky. The wind had picked up, sending the clouds scurrying across the face of the pale moon, sometimes revealing, sometimes concealing. She shivered again. Why was she hesitating? It was time to go. Taking a deep breath, she straightened her shoulders and reached for the door handle. Was that a footstep behind her? She froze. Silence. She was imagining things. No, there it was again.

Something grabbed at her!

Before she could do more than gasp, something slammed hard against her body, pressing her into the truck.

A whispery, frightening voice, right next to her ear said, "No, no, my little wife, there will be no screaming. For tonight, I prefer you to be quiet."

"Gerard." It came out as a moan.

"Shhhh. I said you must be quiet. Did you really think you could get away from me, Annika my darling?

"I wasn't trying to get away from you, Gerard," she whispered. "I just wanted some time, that's all." She hated listening to her own words, her pleading tone.

He laughed softly and hissed in her ear. "I'll give you all the time in the world, my dear. Both of you will have all the time in the world."

"Both of us?"

"As for that new man of yours--"

"No," she broke in quickly. "There is no other man. I just said that to get you angry."

"And you succeeded." He turned her around. Now her back was to the truck. His body crowded hers. She could feel his erection hard against her belly. His breath was in her face. Fear and revulsion battled side by side within her.

"I'm going to be sick!" She gagged and choked. With a curse, he jumped back. Without thinking, Brianne pushed at his moving figure. He was off balance and staggered away from her. She ran.

Why am I even bothering to run? She knew there would be no escape, but she kept running.

She ran into the first open door that was just vaguely visible in the darkness, into the stallions' barn. Imperial was quiet, but Fuzzy whinnied with anger at being awakened so abruptly by one of the humans he despised.

"Shut up, Fuzzy," Brianne begged him in a whisper. The three other stalls in the barn were clean and empty, awaiting prosperity. The stallions' stalls here were much bigger than the mares', each had its own skylight. Consequently, the stallions' barn was usually fairly light. Tonight, however, with the lowering clouds, it was pitch black. Unlike the mares' barn, these stalls did not open into outside corrals so the animals could go in or out as they pleased. This barn was a locked trap.

She turned to run back out, but Gerard was already in the doorway. The only other way out was at the other end of the barn. There was a large door meant for the horses. It was closed. To open it was a noisy affair. Her position would be obvious to Gerard. She was trapped.

She heard him laugh.

"Ah, Annika, Annika." It was almost a hiss. "Ran into a dead end again, have you?"

If he would just move away from the door perhaps, she could sneak around him and slip out. But what good would that do? She couldn't start up the truck without him hearing it. It would take only seconds for him to catch her.

"Would you like to know my plans for you, Annika?" His voice, still very low, was almost pleasant, civilized. "I thought I would take you and the boy--."

"The boy?" It came out loud and clear.

He actually chuckled. "Of course, my bride. We couldn't leave here without your son, could we?"

"What are you talking about? I don't have a...child."

"Surely, you remember how much I dislike being lied to, Annika? I'm going to have to punish you for that, among other things," he added.

"What are you talking about?" There was an edge of hysteria to her voice.

He still spoke softly, quietly, gently, the monster in hiding, waiting to pounce. "I've done my research on you, darling. I should have done it before. Think of all the fun the three of us could have been having?"

"Gerard," she walked out into the central aisle where he could see her. "I'll go back with you. Let's just go."

"After we get the boy."

"No."

He went on as if she had not spoken. "I thought we'd enroll him in Bishop's, my old school. As a day student," he added. "We'd want him home at night, wouldn't we?"

"Ray will never let you take him." She knew that with a certainty.

"The law will be on our side. He stole him from you. You were never married to him. Slut," he added casually. "My lawyers are the best in the world. Your boyfriend hasn't a prayer."

"Gerard, let's just go." She moved towards him. "I beg you."

"Of course you do, my little wife."

They were both still whispering.

As she drew near, he grabbed her and threw her against the stable wall. Fuzzy snorted angrily at the slamming noise. Brianne could hear the stallion moving back and forth.

Suddenly, the horse kicked out with his hind legs against the back wall of his stall. He did no damage, but the sound made both Brianne and Gerard jump.

Recovering, Gerard laughed out loud at the stallion's rage. He forced himself between Brianne's legs. She could feel the roughness of the wall pressing into her shoulder blades.

I can't bear this, she thought. I would rather be dead then go back with him.

Gerard's mouth was on hers, forcing her lips open. She bit him, hard. Blood poured from his mouth. "Bitch." He slammed his open palm against the side of her head. She was knocked onto the ground into the shadows.

On her hands and knees, she scrambled away from the cursing Gerard. Her shoulder hit the wall. Something, a rake; no a pitchfork tumbled over. It's handle giving her a glancing blow on her head. She grabbed hold of it automatically.

The door of Fuzzy's stall shuddered as the big horse slammed into it. Quickly, with shaking hands, she unlatched the door to the stall, grabbed up the pitchfork, slipped in and closed it behind her. Fuzzy was outraged. A human was invading his space.

"Oh, shut up," she whispered to the indignant horse and waved the pitchfork at him. With a horse's excellent night vision, he knew exactly what she was waving at him. Fuzzy was familiar with pitchforks. He had been persuaded to restrain his killer attacks with the threat of a pitchfork before. With luck, Gerard would never think of looking for her in the stall of this angry animal.

The stallion kept his distance, but moved back and forth with even greater agitation. Suddenly the stall door was pulled open. Too late, she tried to hold it closed. It was ripped from her fingers. Gerard, a dark shadow stood in the doorway.

"Annika, Annika, not very bright, are you?"

Fuzzy had had enough. With a squeal of rage, he charged directly at the human who was threatening him in his own doorway. Gerard had no time to dodge. The horse's body slammed into him. Gerard went flying. Brianne could hear a loud crack as his head hit the stall wall. She didn't wait to investigate, but followed the stallion out into the main aisle of the barn.

There Fuzzy, instead of exalting in his freedom, was

growing even more agitated. He wanted to get back to his stall. He wanted to go to bed. He wanted all the damn humans to leave him alone!

"Take it easy, Fuzzy," she crooned to him as she worked her way around him. She had to get out of here!

Fuzzy himself solved the problem by deciding that no damn human was going to keep him out of his own home. He moved away from her soothing hands and tried to reenter his stall. As he did so, Gerard, staggering, appeared in the stall doorway. The horse bellowed in rage. Gerard, having learned his lesson, flung himself out of the stall to one side. Fuzzy plunged past him, striking out with a left back leg as he went. Brianne heard Gerard groan as Fuzzy's hoof hit its mark.

"Gerard?" she said uncertainly?

"Bitch," he groaned.

Apparently, he was not seriously damaged. She turned, still carrying the pitchfork and fled.

Outside, it was only slightly less than pitch black. Hand outstretched, she headed for the truck. Where was it? Nothing seemed familiar. Abruptly, her foot hit sharply against something unyielding. She dropped the pitchfork. Where was it? Her searching hands found nothing. She felt lower, still nothing. Lower. Her hands encountered a rough, cool, rock-like texture that was unnaturally flat. Then she felt rocks of various sizes lying about. Her right hand closed around one that just fit her hand. With her other hand she patted the flat surface. It was the cover over the dry well! Was it only yesterday morning Ray had had it installed? She shuddered when she realized the cover had probably saved her life. The way she was stumbling around in the dark, without it she would have surely plunged down to the muddy bottom. But how did she get so turned around? The abandoned well was in a dead-end ell, with only a narrow opening between the stallion barn, and a feed shed. That was the only way out. She had to move before Gerard arrived.

As if thinking about him had called him forth, Brianne heard a shuffling sound and a husky whisper. "Annika? Annika?"

She froze. Don't move, she told herself. If you don't move, he won't be able to find you. It's dark. If you can't see him, than he can't see you.

Some imp of Satan, must have been in charge of the weather that night. No sooner had the thought of the darkness soothed her fears, than the winds shifted. Clouds drifted and moonlight broke through to illuminate her clearly.

She could see him, too. He was moving in a jerky fashion, dragging one leg, his arms were clutching at his side. "Annika, help me."

Brianne froze. Is he really hurt? A run-in with an angry stallion was a serious business. I could get away from him now, she thought. Run around him. Get to my truck. Escape. Disappear.

"Annika."

Was that a sob? Oh God, why couldn't she just run? Slowly she stood up. "Here I am, Gerard." He staggered toward her, almost falling. Instinctively, she reached for him. His arm went around her shoulders. His full weight leaned on her. There was blood falling from a cut on his forehead. "We need to get you to a hospital," she said.

The arm around her shoulders tightened. She staggered under his full weight. His head was drooping down near her shoulder. "You stupid, bitch." He was laughing. "I'm going to fuck you *and your son*." She tried to pull away but his arm was like iron. "And then I'm going to teach him to fuck you." He laughed again. "Your son, a true mother-fucker."

"No," she said, clearly and calmly, and swung her right hand up at his gloating face. His face splashed!

With a curse, Gerard swung her away from him. She stumbled back and landed on the well cover. Her sudden weight caused it to shift.

Oh my God. Brianne scrambled to get off the shifting cover.

"Bitch." Gerard was coming at her, blood streaming from his nose and a long cut on his cheek. Brianne turned on her knees, trying to get off the cover in the other direction. To her horror, there was a grating noise and the cover slanted downward. Some of the piled up cement blocks circling the well fell away, removing even that scant support.

The heavy cover smashed into her shoulder as it slanted down throwing her off balance. She was falling! Desperately, she flung her hands out, scribbling at the piled up cement blocks, but only succeeded in causing them to come tumbling down. A few fell into the well. One banged hard into her hip. There was nothing to catch her. She was falling. She screamed.

Suddenly, her wrist was caught in an iron grip. Her shoulder muscles screamed in protest, but she had stopped falling.

She scrambled for a foothold, found one and tried to pull herself to safety.

"Ah, no Annika, my dear. I don't think so." Deliberately, Gerard swung her away from the edge of the well. She hung, dangling from his grip.

She squeezed her eyes shut. "Gerard."

"Beg me."

She sobbed.

"Beg me," he repeated.

"Gerard, please."

"Gerard, please," he mimicked. "I like the sound of that. Have you missed me, Annika?"

"Please pull me up."

"Why should I?"

"If I fall, I'll die."

"And this is important to me, why?"

"God damn you."

"No-no." Deliberately, he lowered her.

"No! Please!"

He chuckled. "My arm is getting tired, Annika. Give me a reason to pull you up." When she remained silent, he shook her arm violently, causing her body to swing within the well.

Panic stricken, Annika moaned. "Anything," she promised. "Anything."

Still laughing to himself, Gerard pulled her out of the well and dumped her on solid ground. Breathing rapidly, she lay where he had tossed her. "Get up, Annika."

Wearily, she climbed to her feet. Her body ached in numerous places. She knew the pain would be worse tomorrow.

"Kiss me, Annika." She shuddered. This seemed to amuse him. "When we get home," he promised, "I'm going to buy some new toys for us."

Toys?"

"So I can fully enjoy you...and my new stepson."

"Gerard."

"Imagine the sort of toys I mean, Annika."

I should have died, thought Brianne. If only I wasn't such a coward.

"Come on." He turned his back on her and walked off. She stood swaying tiredly, watching his broad arrogant back wishing she had a knife to plunge into him.

Realizing she wasn't following him, Gerard stopped and looked back. He snapped his fingers impatiently, calling her as if she was a dog.

Tiredly she started after him. Gerard waited until he was sure of her obedience before he stared walking again.

Brianne concentrated on putting one foot in front of the other. They had been walking awhile before it occurred to her to wonder where they were going.

"Damn." She almost bumped into Gerard as he stopped short. "Where the hell are we?" asked Gerard.

Brianne didn't even look around. It didn't matter to her.

"Where's that truck of yours?"

"Truck?"

"Jesus, have you lost what little brains you had? Where's your damn truck?"

"Why do you need my truck?"

"Because I had the cab drop me off down the road from this chicken farm."

"It's not a chicken..." Before she could finish, Gerard whirled on her and slapped her across the face. Hard.

"Where's your truck?" He was gritting his teeth.

Brianne looked around her. They were in the middle of the near pasture. Off to her right was the stable yard where the dilapidated truck was parked. Off to her left was the beginning of the state land.

"Answer me, Annika." But before she could answer he reached out both hands, grabbed her breasts through her thin T-shirt, located her nipples and twisted, hard.

Brianne screamed. Without thinking her hands came up, fingers curled into claws. She raked her nails across Gerard's smiling face.

He jumped back, pushing her away. She lost her footing and fell to her knees, clutching her aching breasts.

Gerard was calling her every filthy name he could think of and his repertoire was impressive. She saw him fumbling with his belt buckle, and then heard the swishing sound as he pulled his belt free.

"I'm going to beat you to death," he promised.

On her knees, Brianne looked up as the belt came swirling through the air. She ducked at the last moment so instead of hitting her in the face it came down on her bowed shoulders. It felt like a burning brand!

Oh God. She jumped to her feet and ran. Gerard came after her, running lightly in her wake. She could hear him laughing.

Without warning, she collided with the rail fence that surrounded the pasture. She literally bounced off it. Her body slammed into Gerard. His feet slipped out from under him and he fell, cursing, onto his back. Impacting with Gerard caused Brianne to be thrown forward, back towards the fence. Her head cracked into the fence post. The pain vibrated throughout her entire body.

Seemingly, in slow motion, her body crumpled to the ground. She was aware of the cool grass soothing her battered head. Everything else was whirling around her. Instinctively, she crawled under the fence, away from Gerard.

Clouds passed in front of the moon again. Once again, the night was pitch-black. Crawling under the fence was a mistake. Brianne could feel her hips and legs start to slide into the rock-strewn ravine below. She hadn't realized she was that close to it. She could picture her body, broken and battered on the rocks below her. Death at least was a sure escape from Gerard.

Her body did not agree. Her arm shot out and grabbed the fence post, stopping her slide down into the ravine. Anyway, she thought, with my luck I won't die, just break my leg.

"Annika."

Oh God, why didn't he just go away? She lay very still. It was so dark she could see nothing, but she could hear the swish of the grass as he came towards her. As soon as the wind brushed away the clouds, he would be able to see her clearly. But just now she was hidden from him.

"Annika!"

He was coming closer. He was at the fence.

"Annika?" For the first time he sounded uncertain. She could hear him climbing the fence. He was right over her. Any minute now, he would find her.

Brianne ducked her face into her arms, hoping to hide its paleness from him.

"You bitch. When I get a hold of you I'll beat the shit out of you."

Brianne clenched her teeth and tried not to shake with fear.

"But I won't beat that boy of yours. Oh no. You needn't worry about that. Do you know what I'm going to do to him, bitch? I'm going to shove my dick all the way up his ass. He's big enough for that, don't you think? What about it, Annika? Can he take my full length? The way his mother can."

The clouds drifted away from the moon. "There you are!"

Instead of reaching for her with his hands, he kicked her lightly with his foot. "Get up, bitch."

Brianne let go of the fence post, rolled over and grabbed his ankle. Throwing the entire weight of her body into it, she pulled with all of her might.

"What...?" Then, as he felt his body leave solid ground and fly through the air, he screamed. A short, high-pitched scream.

Brianne barely heard him. She too was flying through

the air. She hung on to his ankle with grim determination, too stunned at her own action to scream. There was a sudden jarring impact. Gerard's scream was cut off as with a knife. Then...blackness.

CHAPTER FORTY-SEVEN

She probably wasn't out very long. It was a sound that roused her, an odd gurgling moan. Whoever was making that sound had to be suffering. The sound came again. It was coming from her! She raised her head and immediately wished she hadn't. The pain! It was as if someone was rhythmically using dagger points as drumsticks against her skull.

She moaned again. The sound seemed to echo around her. Moan, moan, moan...An echo? What the devil?

This time she was very careful when she raised her head. It still hurt like hell. Everything was so dark.

Try opening your eyes. She did. It was still dark, but more a grayish darkness. Where was she?

She was lying on her stomach, lying on something vaguely soft and squashy. Oh my God! She was lying on someone.

Brianne rolled off and promptly passed out again. This time when she came to, she remembered.

They had gone over the lip of the ravine. They must have fallen twenty feet. She had landed on Gerard! She had to get away from him before he woke up.

Carefully, she tried out the various parts of her body. Legs moved, arms and hands moved. She sat up gingerly. Aside from her pounding head, everything else seemed in working order.

As she tried to get up, she inadvertently touched Gerard's leg. Hastily she snatched her hand back. He didn't move.

She was on her knees now. Gerard continued to lie very still. "Gerard?"

The clouds had disappeared. Now the moon was

shining brightly. She could see everything clearly, including the very peculiar angle of his neck.

Slowly she sat back on her knees. "Gerard?"

She placed both hands lightly on his chest. There was absolutely no movement. His eyes were wide open. "Gerard?"

She moved her hands toward his eyes. No blink reflex. He was dead.

She fought down a scream, forcing herself to breathe in and out. Then the sadness hit.

"Oh, Gerard. I'm so sorry."

She spoke the truth. She was sorry for his wasted life and their wasted marriage. She was sorry for Ray, who would be dragged into this mess, but most of all, she was sorry for Patrick, who would no longer be shielded from the story of his birth.

Tiredly she sat down and reached for Gerard's hand. There was a rustling sound off to the side. Aching head or no, Brianne decided to forgo the pleasure of sitting next to a dead body out here in the woods. Who knew what sort of wild animals were out there, ready to keep them company?

The climb up the gully wasn't difficult, but as she got to the very top, part of the gully wall fell away beneath her. Brianne grabbed for the fence post and held on for dear life. When it seemed as though the rest of the wall wasn't going to cave in, she finally pried her hands free of the post and stood up. Looking down, she could see that some of the gully wall had fallen on Gerard's body, but he could still be easily seen. There would be no difficulty in finding him.

No use running anymore, she thought tiredly. Daylight will reveal it all. With aching mind and body, she trudged back to The Lodge.

CHAPTER FORTY-EIGHT

Back at The Lodge, Brianne stripped off all her clothes. She turned the shower on as hot as she could stand it and washed herself not once, not twice but three times, scrubbing every inch of her body. Aside from her aching head, she had numerous scrapes and aches, but nothing seemed permanently damaged. She found some powdery aspirin tablets in the medicine cabinet and swallowed three of them. Back in her room, she tore up the now useless note she had left for Ray. Today was going to be a horrible day.

After she dressed, she made herself a cup of tea and then went out to face the music. She would wake Ray up, she decided, outline the events of last night and have him call the police. But as usual, things did not go according to plan.

First, Ray was already up and out, second, he had already discovered the uncovered well, and third, he was furious. When she came upon him, he was bellowing for Mike.

"Don't come near here, Bree," he said as soon as he saw her. "The damn well cover slid into the well and half the cement blocks have gone with it."

Mike came running, so did Patrick and Rufus. She grabbed at Patrick and hugged him to her. He hugged her back, released her and tried to peer down the well. His father, who was talking on his cell phone, hauled him back with one hand and handed him to Brianne. "You stay with your...with her," he ordered his son.

Mike peered down into the open well. "Damnedest thing," said Mike. "Coulda sworn it was covered tight."

"Well, it wasn't but it will be this time," said Ray. "As for you." Brianne thought he was talking to her, then realized it was to his son, who was leaning against her. "You are not to come into this area without me. Do you understand?"

Both Patrick and Brianne nodded. Ray smiled to see the two faces, nodding seriously.

Brianne peered into the open well. There was really nothing to see. Fifteen to twenty feet down, the well shaft became so dark no specifics could be made out. She knelt down. This dark hold had almost been her grave.

"Down the rabbit hole," she murmured.

"Bree?"

She blinked and raised her head to find Ray standing just a few feet away. "Yes."

"Move away, the trucks from the quarry are here."

Two trucks pulled in next to the well opening. A steel chute was pulled from one of the trucks and positioned over the well. With a roar that caused Brianne to clap her hands over her ears, tons of rocks were released from the back of first one truck, then the other. By the time both trucks were empty, the well was filled almost to the top.

As the quarry trucks pulled away, they were immediately replaced by a rotating cement truck. As Brianne watched, the heavy liquid cement poured down between the rocks until it gradually flowed to the very top of the well.

"Next week, after the cement has completely dried, we'll spread topsoil and plant flowers," said Ray.

"Flowers?"

"When Dangerous Ground comes here, there'll be plenty of visitors, potential clients, photographers. I want TearVale looking its best. Don't you?" He was watching her intently.

"Yes," she answered.

"Besides," he added, "flowers make people feel happy."

***

"Ray, I have to talk to you."

"And I want to talk to you, beautiful, but right now we've got to hustle if we want to be out of here by noon."

"Noon?"

"The Derby, sweetheart." Ray was kneeling beside a

chestnut mare, checking on a hot spot on one of her legs. He smiled up at the blue-jeaned, tee-shirted, Brianne. "We'll be leaving in an hour," he reminded her.

She had forgotten all about the Derby. She looked around; Mike and Patrick were pitching in to get the inevitable chores associated with horses, done as quickly as possible. Rufus was running in circles, tail wagging, grinning his doggy grin. This was probably not the time to tell Ray that a dead body was lying just beyond his property line. Why spoil the Derby? There would be plenty of time afterwards for bad news.

"I'll be ready," she said.

***

Exactly one hour later, Ray and Patrick appeared at The Lodge to collect Brianne. She was now dressed in her cream and tan silk suit. She wore the elegant cream-colored, floppy-brimmed hat she had bought on her shopping spree. Was that only two days ago? Her make-up was carefully applied and perfect for natural light. Her hair curled softly around her face. In the back, a tortoise shell clip at the nape of her neck neatly confined it. Her appearance was as removed from the elaborate extremes of Annika as she could make it. She wanted Patrick and Ray to be proud to be seen with her. By the expression on their faces, she had succeeded.

And she was proud of the way they looked. Both Patrick and Ray were wearing suits and ties. They were brushed, and shined and so handsome that Brianne felt of lump of happiness in her throat. These are my men, she thought. At least for today. She would not think about tomorrow.

Patrick was shy when she told him how handsome he looked. He hung his head and sneaked a quick look at her from under his brows. "What's the matter, Patrick?"

"Nothing."

"Are you sure?"

"You look different."

"You don't like the way I look?"

He muttered something. "What did you say, honey?"

"You look funny."

"Funny?" Brianne's heart sank. She had thought he liked her appearance. She wanted him to be proud of her. "How do I look funny?"

"You know."

"No, truly I don't. Tell me."

"You look like a regular lady."

"Believe me, son," said Ray. "There is nothing regular looking about Brianne. She's beautiful."

"That's what I meant," muttered the embarrassed boy.

Brianne bent down and kissed him. "If I look beautiful and you look handsome, then we're the perfect couple."

Pat wiggled with delight.

"Where do I fit into this?" Ray complained.

Brianne straightened his tie. "You fit in perfectly," she assured him. Her happiness was all the more intense with the sure knowledge it would be short lived.

CHAPTER FORTY-NINE

What should have been a half hour ride took well over an hour. The last five miles to Churchill Downs, home of the Kentucky Derby, were a madhouse. Half the world seemed to be converging on the famous racetrack.

Patrick was beside himself with excitement. "Can we go see Dangerous Ground, Daddy? Can I have a drink of champagne with the grown-ups? What time does the Derby run?"

"Slow down, Champ," said Ray as he maneuvered the car into a reserved parking slot.

Patrick was out of the car first. "Let's go to the stables and see Dangerous Ground," he pleaded.

Ray got out more slowly. "Time for a little lesson in manners, Champ."

"Manners?" Patrick stared at his father.

"This is a social occasion," explained Ray, "not work. There's a lady in the car. What do you do?" Patrick looked at him blankly. "You open the car door for her," explained his father.

Brianne, sitting in lonely splendor, listened with amusement.

"But Brianne knows how to open her door," protested Patrick.

"That's not the point."

"What is the point?"

"Courtesy. Making a good impression."

Patrick was not convinced. "Brianne already likes me," he pointed out.

"It also makes the lady feel special. It shows you care about her comfort."

"Oh." Patrick digested this. "Okay." He marched over

to the car and opened the door for Brianne.

"Thank you, Patrick." Brianne got out of the car.

"You're welcome." He closed the door behind her. "I really do think you're special, you know."

"You're very special to me, too."

Patrick, the social amenities accomplished, whirled to his father. "Now can we go see Dangerous Ground?"

"Now we go to the Simmons' box and greet our hosts," Ray said firmly.

Patrick, nothing if not flexible, switched goals without a blink. "Can I have champagne with the grown-ups?"

Ray looked uncertain. Brianne, who didn't like champagne herself and doubted Patrick would either, answered the boy. "You can have two sips," she promised. "One before the race and one after when Dangerous Ground wins."

"All right!"

***

The Simmons' box was brimming with people. There were friends, other horse owners, Dangerous Ground's trainer and various acquaintances of the Simmons. People kept stopping by to wish them luck.

Brianne had a flute of champagne pressed into her hand as soon as she stepped over the threshold.

"Do you not look a perfect picture?" squealed Liz Simmons in greeting. "Honey, how I envy you your coloring."

"But you look wonderful, Liz," Brianne responded on cue. "What a perfect suit."

"This old thing? It's Armani."

In truth, Brianne thought the bubbly Liz Simmons too short and too round for the Armani look, but there was no doubt the older woman looked good. She glowed with excitement.

There's nothing like excitement to bring out all the glow a person has, thought Brianne. Well, excitement and love, she corrected herself.

As she thought of love, Brianne found herself looking at Ray. At exactly the same time, he raised his eyes to hers. He reached for her hand and gave it a gentle squeeze. A wash of happiness flashed through her body. Then she remembered Gerard.

***

Lunch was served, but Brianne only nibbled at her food. In less than an hour, the Derby would be run. If Dangerous Ground managed to win, TearVale would be a success instead of just another struggling stud farm. The fate of Patrick's home hung on this race. Excitement was building from every corner.

Patrick was not the only well-dressed child present. There was another boy his age. "My son, Tony," Dangerous Ground's trainer introduced the solemn little boy. There was also a slightly younger girl, Tatiana, who seemed to know more than anyone present about the antecedents of the Derby horses. Everyone, adults and children alike, unabashedly consulted with her.

Brianne had finally managed to switch her champagne for a gin and tonic. She had given up on lunch and was listening to Ray argue with Simmons about the relative merits of two brood mares, when Liz grabbed her arm.

"Come on, Brianne, honey. Let's visit the little girls' room."

Good naturedly, Brianne got to her feet.

"Liz, honey," yelled her husband after her, "don't you fall in there."

"Oh, you stop that talk, Jack Simmons."

"I mean it, honey. We all got to be down in the paddock in about fifteen minutes."

"As if I would miss that. Come on, Brianne," Liz grabbed her arm again and propelled her along. "That man," Liz fussed. "I cannot cure him of his bathroom humor."

"Ah well, if that's his only fault."

Liz shot Brianne a shrewd look. "That's not his only fault by a long shot. But all in all, the man's not so bad." Liz Simmons smiled to herself. Brianne figured they were a happy couple, satisfied with their life together. She felt envious.

She also felt anxious. She was braced for a third degree

from Liz, but it turned out all the older woman really wanted was company on her trip to the ladies' room. Liz Simmons was a woman who needed an entourage.

The ladies room for owners, trainers and their wives was an elaborate affair. Aside from the usual stalls, there was a "dressing room" with comfortable make-up tables, good lighting, tissues and a "girl" of fifty-odd years who could produce your shade of lipstick, and pantyhose without runs, or a quick pick-me-up for those ladies who didn't like to drink in front of their menfolk.

"That means she supplies booze for the women whose husbands monitor their drinks," Liz translated for the bemused Brianne.

Finally, there was the "lounge," an airy pink and green room filled with comfortable chairs and tables, on which rested stacks of betting slips and handy souvenir pens.

Brianne raised an inquiring eyebrow.

"Some of my ladies like to bet different than their menfolk tell them to," explained the "girl."

"A runner will place the bet for you," explained Liz. "That way a husband has no idea just how much his wife is betting."

There was a large television in the lounge. Closed circuit TVs were all over the racecourse. The people who ran things were determined to make it possible for the public to be able to view the races and bet from anywhere in the track, even the toilet.

This TV, however, was not exclusively closed circuit. Brianne, emerging from the "dressing room," froze when she saw herself in living color on the 52-inch screen.

It was herself as Annika. Annika at her most exotic, her most fantastic, beautiful, ghostly, eerie. Brianne felt dizzy with disassociation. Here she stood and there she was. The blood roared in her ears. She was deaf and blind to her surroundings. Gradually, she came out of her fog.

A voice close to her was speaking. "I know that woman." Instinctively, Brianne turned her head away. She tugged the brim of her hat down even further to shield her face.

Another voice, etched with admiration. "Lou-Anne, you do?"

"I had lunch with her in New York."

Brianne shot a quick glance at Lou-Anne. As far as she knew, she had never seen the woman in her life.

"Does she really look like that, all white and ghostly? In real life, I mean?"

"Absolutely," Lou-Anne assured her listeners. "She told me that all her life she's tried to fit in, but her looks set her apart. I felt kinda sorry for her," Lou-Anne concluded.

"But was she nice," asked another woman?

Breanne didn't get to hear whether or not Lou-Anne had approved of her. The TV was now showing a video of Gerard. It was one taken after an art auction. Brianne remembered it well. Gerard had just spent over five million dollars on a 14th Century depiction of a particularly gruesome and detailed Crucifixion. Just looking at it had made Brianne shudder. Gerard had hung it across from their bed in their Long Island estate, another reason for avoiding his bed whenever possible.

Seeing Gerard was a shock. It was as though he had come back from the dead. Her throat was so dry she could barely speak.

"What's going on?"

The TV answered her almost immediately. The picture of a smugly smiling Gerard was replaced by a shot of Josie and Eddy-Bob. A gushing female voice announced that they were being charged with the murder of the socially prominent Gerard Rostands.

Brianne let out a shocked "What?" Then looked around nervously, but no one was paying her any attention. The TV screen mesmerized everyone.

On the screen, Josie and Eddy-Bob, pranced and postured for the cameras, managing to look both dangerous and childish. Brianne couldn't begin to imagine how she had ever let them get into her car. What had she been thinking?

Next, there was a shot of Annika's car. "Is this where the Rostands met their tragic end?" asked a lugubrious and anonymous voice.

A perky blond young woman suddenly replaced the sight of Annika's car being towed off to the police evidence yard. "I'll be following this story," she assured her audience. "There will be updates as they happen." She was then replaced by a kitchen wax commercial.

In the lounge, women began exchanging information.

"They found some incredibly expensive diamond earrings," said one woman.

"Did they belong to her?" asked another.

"Yes, they were Annika's," she was assured. "They also found her Lady Rolex. And, guess what."

"What?"

"That horrible looking girl was wearing the watch and one of the earrings. The man was wearing the other earring!"

"No!"

There was a snort of laughter.

So ends Annika. Just another tabloid story. Well, that's how she lived, that's how she should die.

It was at that moment, Brianne realized how completely she had separated herself from her former life. She was actually thinking of Annika as a different person.

But, she reminded herself, the hitchhikers hadn't killed Annika and they didn't kill Gerard. As the implications of what she was thinking sank in, she shuddered. I don't owe them anything, she said to herself. They would have killed me if I hadn't escaped. God knows they wanted to.

You don't know that, she told herself coldly.

They would have, she insisted.

The fact is, they didn't. Annika is dead, but they didn't kill her, you did.

If I tell the police, everything will come out, including Gerard's death.

They didn't kill Gerard and neither did you.

No, I just left him to rot in the gully. If I go to the police, everything will come out. Patrick will know everything and Ray...

What about Ray?

He has a record for killing someone. They'll think he's involved. He could go to jail. He could lose Patrick. *It isn't fair.*

Stop it, she ordered herself! You can't let people, even those terrible people, be charged with a murder they didn't commit.

Yes, I can.

No! You have to tell the sheriff that Josie and Eddy-Bob didn't kill anyone.

And of course, they'll believe some anonymous voice over a phone?

I'll have to go in there--face to face. I can't.

Yes, you can.

I'll have to show them where Gerard is. They'll come to TearVale. Everything will come out. Patrick will end up as a story in PEOPLE Magazine. *No!*

This moral wrestling match was wearing Brianne out. Finally, she admitted defeat.

I'll say the truth about me, she decided. I'll tell how they stole my car and how I escaped.

And when they ask about Gerard?

I'll say...I'll say...I'll tell them to truth about him, too. But I won't mention TearVale or Patrick. Ray will never come into it.

Will they believe me or will they search further?

I'll make them believe me!

Then what? It's finished, you know. You can't stay here.

This time it really would be good-bye to Ray, and to Patrick. No matter what, I can never let the police connect me to Ray. I almost had it all, she thought wistfully.

"Brianne, honey, come on." It was Liz, grabbing at her arm. "We have to get down to the paddock. Isn't this exciting?" Brianne allowed herself to be hustled out of the ladies room, over to the escalator and down to the paddock.

CHAPTER FIFTY

Jack Simmons was a generous man today. He had invited his guests to join him and his wife in the sacrosanct paddock for the ritual of "the mounting of the jockeys." All eyes, not to mention TV cameras, were on the privileged few. Brianne, tugging her big brimmed hat down lower on her face, could have done without the honor. Patrick was wide-eyed with delight.

"Brianne, look, there's Dangerous Ground. Isn't he great?"

Brianne, following his pointing finger, examined the haughty looking colt with great interest. The fortunes of TearVale rose or fell upon this animal. He was a gorgeous creature, beautifully muscled, proud and eager looking. So were all the other well-bred thoroughbreds stalking around the paddock. But the Kentucky Derby was not a beauty contest. Only speed counted here.

"He's going to win, isn't he, Brianne?" Patrick almost begged for reassurance.

"I hope so," she answered him.

"He'll do his best, Pat," said Ray. "That's what we ask of champions, that they do their best."

"He will," Patrick breathed. "You can tell he's a champ."

Brianne was introduced to Dangerous Ground's jockey, Chris Colon, a short, skinny, tough looking man with a big grin.

"Don't you worry, Mr. Simmons," the jockey assured Dangerous Ground's owner. "Me and your colt, we win this damn race."

"From your mouth to God's ears," prayed Liz.

It was time for the jockeys to mount. The trainers threw

them up on the horses like so many bits of colorful fluff, so lightly did they mount.

"Good luck," everyone shouted. "Good luck." The horses stalked and pranced their way out of the paddock on to the track.

"Has everyone bet?" asked Liz nervously. "It's bad luck if you don't bet."

"I haven't," said Brianne.

"You have to, you have to." Liz was almost frantic.

"I'll do it now," Brianne assured her. "I'll meet you in the box," she told Ray.

He smiled down at her. "Don't miss the race."

"I won't." She looked longingly into his face.

"Is something wrong?"

She shook her head, no.

"Come on, Daddy, Come on." Patrick pulled at his hand. "We're going to miss the race."

Ray, ignoring his son, leaned down to Brianne and whispered in her ear. "I love you."

She felt the warmth of his breath and the sensuous tickle of soft hair moving against her ear. "Yes," she answered. "I love you, too. I love both of you--desperately."

Ray grinned. "Desperately huh? I'll talk to Reverend Potter right after the race. This is going to be a great day."

He looks so happy, thought Brianne. Abruptly, she turned and left him, heading for the betting window.

She bet everything she had, seventy-three dollars, on Dangerous Ground to win. The odds were 6 to 1. Assuming he won, Brianne stood to collect $438 plus the original $73, all in all, $511. She carelessly stuffed the tickets into her purse. Should she leave now? In the excitement of the race, they might not even notice she was gone. No. Ray would notice. It would ruin his concentration. This race was too important to him. Afterwards, in all the excitement was the time to slip away. *And if Dangerous Ground doesn't win?* The odds were 6 to 1 against him.

No matter what happened, she would still have to leave.

Knowing it was the last time she would be with Ray and Patrick, she returned to the box.

The horses were just entering the starting gate. For once, even Liz was silent. Patrick, his eyes huge and his face white with anxiety, clutched her hand. Ray put his arm around her and gave her a quick hug before returning his attention to the starting gate. Everyone who owned a pair, had their binoculars trained on the track. The race was a mile and a quarter. There were eight horses. Dangerous Ground was in the fourth position. Brianne crossed her fingers and closed her eyes.

"They're off!" screamed the loudspeaker.

Brianne's eyes shot open. Patrick squeezed her hand harder.

"Please, please, please," she heard him whisper.

There was a collective groan from those with binoculars.

"What?" screeched Liz. "What is it?"

The loudspeaker answered her. "Dangerous Ground has gotten off to a poor start. He's late out of the gate." Having delivered this bad news, the announcer concentrated on the other horses. "As expected, Truly Trustworthy is setting the pace, with Exemplar a close second."

"Where's Dangerous Ground?" asked Patrick. No one answered him. Brianne glanced at Ray, but he, along with Jack and Liz Simmons, was rigidly glued to his binoculars.

"The favorite, Mary's Joy, is now making his move. Truly Trustworthy seems to be running out of steam. Neutron is behind him. With half the race still to go, it's Mary's Joy with Truly Trustworthy and Neutron neck and neck. Exemplar is dropping back fast."

"But where's Dangerous Ground?" Patrick's voice was very low.

"I don't know, honey." Brianne answered him. They were still holding hands.

"Dancing Solo is a good length behind Exemplar. The rest of the field is closely bunched, with Dangerous Ground moving up into seventh place."

"Seventh place!" Patrick was horrified. So was Brianne.

"Mary's Joy is holding onto his lead. Neutron now edging past Truly Trustworthy into second place. Exemplar, tiring rapidly is dropping back to sixth place as Grand Slam overtakes him."

There was a sudden note of interest in the announcer's voice. "And Dangerous Ground continues to move up. The colt keeps coming. He's now in sixth place.

"Yes," said Ray. It sounded like a prayer.

"With a quarter of a mile still to go, it's Mary's Joy in the lead with Neutron pushing hard. Dancing Solo is third. Truly Trustworthy is falling back, and here comes, Dangerous Ground!"

It was impossible to ignore the excitement in the announcer's voice as he chronicled Dangerous Ground's forward charge.

Brianne could see the horses clearly now, even without binoculars. She saw the tiring Truly Trustworthy trying valiantly to keep up. But she also saw how he was drifting out to the far side, a sure sign of a tired horse. Unfortunately, Truly Trustworthy was drifting just as Dangerous Ground was trying to pass him on the outside. Once again, a collective groan went up from the crowd. "What's happening?" Patrick tugged at Brianne's hand.

"Truly Trustworthy bumped into Dangerous Ground," she told the boy.

Dangerous Ground, thrown off balance, had slowed enough for Grand Slam to gain on him. The sound of Grand Slam moving up on him seemed to galvanize the colt. Dangerous Ground put his head down, lengthened his body and took off as if the hounds of hell were on his heels.

Dangerous Ground's power clearly astonished everyone, including his jockey, who shouted with excitement and hung on for dear life.

Brianne stared open mouthed as Dangerous Ground passed Dancing Solo, as if the other horse were standing still.

Now the announcer's voice was really excited. "It's Mary's Joy, followed by Neutron and Dangerous Ground, neck and neck!" He was practically screaming into the microphone. Everyone else seemed to be screaming at the same time.

"It's Mary's Joy followed by Dangerous Ground. It's Mary's Joy and Dangerous Ground. They're neck and neck. Here comes the finish line. It's still Mary's Joy and Dangerous Ground. They're at the finish line. It's neck and neck!"

The crowd was screaming. Patrick was yelling. Ray and Jack were pounding each other on the backs. Liz, for once was quiet. A quick look at her, revealed her white-faced and gasping with excitement. Brianne caught her eye. The two women smiled. "Oh my," said Liz.

"Amen," answered Brianne.

"Photo finish," the crowd was yelling. Photo finish flashed the sign in the middle of the field.

Ray stopped pounding Jack on the back and came over to Brianne. He held her hand.

"Daddy?" asked Patrick.

"We wait and see, son." Everyone in the box was very quiet. It was only minutes, but it seemed an eternity before the photo finish sign flickered.

"What's it say?"

A great roar went up. First place...Dangerous Ground. Second place...Mary's Joy. Third place...but Brianne could no longer read. Bellowing with delight, Ray had grabbed her, and lifted her high over his head, then brought her down for a solid satisfying kiss.

"Did we win?"

"We sure did, son. We sure did!"

They all streamed down to the winner's circle. Dangerous Ground, proudly prancing his victory dance, was hung with the traditional blanket of roses.

Lights flashed, pictures were snapped, Liz squealed with delight, Jack Simmons reached out and pulled Ray right into the middle of the winner's circle with him. More pictures and backslapping. Grins and flutes of champagne.

**

Champagne corks were popping. Glasses were raised in toasts. Patrick was given a sip and predictably preferred ginger ale. All was right with the world and all was perfect for TearVale.

Patrick was laughing with delight. Brianne leaned over and lightly brushed her lips against her son's forehead. He barely noticed in his excitement. Time for her to leave.

It would be ages before they realized she was gone, she assured herself. This evening she would call and leave an ambiguous message. It would stop Ray from worrying, but it would not stop his pain and anger.

There was really no choice. If she cleared the hitchhikers and stayed, there would be chaos. Patrick's world would be ripped open, all secrets exposed. She had to do it this way.

CHAPTER FIFTY-ONE

It was remarkably easy to disappear into the crowd. Brianne made her way quickly to a side gate. She would go the sheriff's office and then leave town. Leave the state.

A line of taxis waited just outside the racecourse. All the drivers were standing around a small portable TV where reruns of the Derby were being played for the third time. The drivers were groaning and yelling for their favorites as if, even now, they still believed they could influence the results.

A few of the men looked up as Brianne approached. "Taxi, ma'am?"

"Yes, please."

The driver of the first car in line ostentatiously tore up his losing tickets before escorting her to his cab.

"Where you going, ma'am?"

"The sheriff's office."

He gave her a long look, but said nothing, merely turned the ignition on and started driving. Brianne kept her face turned away from his eyes in the rearview mirror. The last thing she wanted was a conversation.

The driver, recognizing an uncommunicative passenger when he saw one, shrugged to himself and switched on the car radio to keep him company.

The news was on. Naturally, the Kentucky Derby was the first story. "Number 4, Dangerous Ground, pulled off an extraordinary feat today. This is a race that will be remembered as one of the great ones."

"Yeah, yeah," muttered the driver. "Number 4, so what do I have? Number three, that's what I have."

Brianne resolutely shut her mind to both the driver and the news announcer, which is why she heard only the tail end of the newscast. "At least twelve murders. The body count mounts as new grave sites are uncovered."

"What!"

The driver, taking her outburst as permission to enter into a conversation, was only too willing to do so. "Yeah, ain't that something, ma'am?"

"Turn that up, please." Obligingly the he turned the radio's volume higher.

"...identified as Josie Billingsly and Eddy-Bob Hutchinson. Can you tell us anything else about this case, Sheriff?"

"Well," drawled a new voice, presumably the sheriff. "At this time the suspects are busy putting the blame on each other. According to the gal, it was Hutchinson who made her take part in all them killings. She says, he held her a virtual prisoner and she had to do what he said or he'd kill her."

"And what does the man say?"

"Darndest thing, Eddy-Bob's saying the same thing about the Billingsly gal. Says she's a stone killer and that she scares the bejeebies out of him."

"Stop the cab, please."

"Huh?"

"Pull over. I want to hear this."

"I gotta keep the meter running."

"Just pull over."

He did so. They both sat, listening to the radio going on and on about burned and mutilated bodies in hidden graves. When the news was over, they continued sitting there. Brianne was in shock. Music came on. Finally, the driver cleared his throat. "Ma'am?'

"Yes?"

"You still want to go on over to the Sheriff's office?"

"Have they actually led the police to bodies or is it all talk?" she asked him.

"Oh, they been finding bodies everywhere them killers say. Even that guy from back East, that millionaire guy."

They've found Gerard's body already!

"They haven't found the wife yet. But they got bodies all right. Two of them are children."

"They killed children?"

"Two of them. Said they sacrificed them to the Spirit Helpers of Satan." The driver snorted. "Lot of bullshit. Pardon my language, ma'am. But I don't hold with this, no death penalty stuff."

"They've been charged with killing these people?"

"Yep. They confessed, too. But not to killing the society folks. Claim they didn't do them. But they got their car and they got the lady's jewels and they got the man's body. Doesn't matter though."

"It doesn't?"

"Nah, law ain't charging them with killing the society people. The law's just charging them with the dead bodies they got that they confessed to.

Of course now they're clamming up. Lawyer must have got to them. Too late though," he said with satisfaction. "The law's got 'em. Too bad they done away with hanging," he said morosely and spit out the window.

I'm free, she thought. Totally, absolutely, completely free!

"So, where you want to go?" asked the taxi driver.

"Take me back to the racetrack, please. Oh and here." She leaned over the back of the seat and handed the driver all of her un-cashed winning tickets. "This should cover the fare."

He examined them carefully. "Yes, ma'am!"

***

The celebration was still going on. Brianne tried to slip into the box unobtrusively, but Ray spotted her immediately. "I was just about to send the troops out looking for you."

She smiled up at him. This is Ray, she thought, I've loved him all my life. I will love him until the day I die.

"I love you," she said.

Patrick came up and leaned shyly against her. She hugged him gently, naturally. "I love you, too," she told the boy. He smiled up at her.

"I think it's time I met your Reverend Potter," she said to Ray.

"Way past time," he agreed. He bent his head and gently kissed the woman he loved.

Annie had grown up. Annika was gone. Brianne had finally come home.

EPILOGUE

Happiness, mused Brianne, is so much simpler than misery. When you're happy you're eager to get up in the morning. When you're happy, you kiss and touch and laugh a great deal; even food tastes better.

It was six months after the Kentucky Derby. Dangerous Ground (unofficially known as Sweetie, no sarcasm intended) had taken to his new duties with gusto. It would be at least three more years before they would know if he had passed on his blazing speed. In the meantime, he was happily eating, galloping around the pasture and scoring with the ladies.

Brianne was in TearVale's living room watching the news. "Eddy-Bob, one of the Hitchhiker Killers" said the mellow voiced announcer "has been found guilty of first degree murder and was sentenced to death today."

There was a shot of a cleaned up Eddy-Bob sitting at the defense table, looking stunned. As the camera lingered on him, tears flowed down his face. Brianne remembered how she had pleaded for her life and felt no pity for him at all.

A warm hand landed on her shoulder, she looked up with a smile for her new husband.

"I wonder when Josie will go on trial," she said.

"Probably never," he answered. "She was declared mentally unfit."

"So what happens to her?"

He shrugged. "Spend the rest of her life in an insane asylum."

"At least they weren't charged with Gerard's death."

"Or yours."

She had told him everything. God, it felt good not to

have any secrets or secret fears. They had decided when he was old enough, to tell Patrick everything. That was their new family motto: No secrets.

THE END

If you enjoyed ANNIKA and would like to be notified of new books and special deals on books, please go to this URL and sign up for notifications.

http://eepurl.com/NFWyr

or go to my webpage at

www.alisonblakewriter.com

Made in the USA
San Bernardino, CA
29 September 2017